Shameless

Walking After Midnight

Maggy's Child

One Summer

Nobody's Angel

This Side of Heaven

Dark of the Moon

Shameless

KAREN ROBARDS

**Doubleday Large Print
Home Library Edition**

Gallery Books

New York London Toronto Sydney

Rights Department, 1230 Avenue of the Americas,
New York, NY 10020.

GALLERY BOOKS and colophon are registered
trademarks of Simon & Schuster, Inc.

Manufactured in the United States of America

ISBN 978-1-61664-282-2

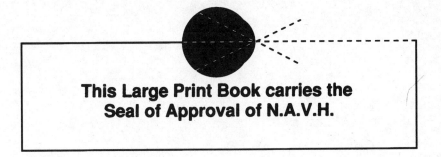

**This Large Print Book carries the
Seal of Approval of N.A.V.H.**

This book is, as always, dedicated to my husband, Doug, and my three sons, Peter, Chris, and Jack, with lots and lots of love. It is also meant as a thank-you to those of my readers who enjoyed Scandalous *and* Irresistible, *and have been waiting for Beth's story. Enjoy.*

April 1817

Chapter One

IT WAS, LADY ELIZABETH BANNING thought ruefully as she looked up into the reddening face of her latest fiancé, all the fault of her damnable temper. Again.

"Are you telling me that you're *jilting* me?" William demanded incredulously. The Earl of Rosen was of average height, with a slightly stocky build that Beth suspected would, in middle age, run sadly to fat. But just now, at age twenty-six, his square jaw, regular features, speaking blue eyes, and thick fair hair worn à la Brutus were enough to ensure that he was held to be a very handsome man by those of the fairer sex—and which of them were not?—interested in such things. Of course, that assessment was undoubtedly helped along by the fact that he was also possessed of an income of something in the nature of twenty thousand pounds a year.

Which she was, regrettably, in the process of whistling down the wind.

"I am not jilting you. I am telling you that I feel we should not suit."

Standing in front of one of the pair of tall windows, thickly curtained in claret velvet, that adorned the far wall of the small, book-lined library of Richmond House—the palatial London home of her brother-in-law the Duke of Richmond—with William less than an arm's length away, Beth was conscious of a draft curling around her shoulders. They were left bare by the fashionable décolletage of her slim, high-waisted frock of gleaming gold silk, its color chosen with care to set off her fiery curls. Really, the room seemed surprisingly cold despite the fact that a fire crackled in the hearth in deference to the crisp temperatures of the early April night. Instead of shivering, though, she folded her arms over her chest, lifted her chin, squared her shoulders, and held

William's increasingly incensed gaze without flinching. Conversations of this sort were never easy, as she had learned from way too much experience. Still, it had to be done, and she had already put it off too long.

"You cannot be serious. My *mother* is here." William was practically quivering with outrage. His mother, Lady Rosen, was one of the ton's highest sticklers, and over the course of the last two Seasons had made no secret of her opinion that Beth was *fast*. Beth had little doubt that William's announcement that he meant to marry her had brought floods of tears and recriminations down upon his head.

"I am really very sorry." Beth looked up at him remorsefully. The idea that he had stood up to his formidable mother for her made her feel even guiltier. She *was* sorry. Their engagement, which at the moment was known only to their immediate families, was of a little more than a week's duration, and she had regretted it within hours of accepting his offer. She should have told him so immediately, of course. But he was *such* an eligible *parti,* while she, at twenty-one and embarked on her third Season, was no longer in the first blush of youth and well past the age at which most of her contemporaries married. Having brought William up to scratch—mostly, she admitted to herself, to spite his acid-tongued sister—she had thought, hoped, wished that if she tried very hard this time, things might be different.

They were not. She had tried her best, and still her stubborn heart refused to cooperate. She liked William well enough. She did not, however, love him, and she knew now she never would.

She could not marry him.

Had she not, three weeks ago, overheard Lady Dreyer, William's high-in-the-instep older sister, insisting to Princess Lieven, the most top-lofty of the Almack's patronesses, that no matter how much he dangled after her William would never be so foolish as to make Lady Elizabeth Banning, with her shocking reputation and scandal-plagued bloodline, an offer, she would never have accepted him in the first place.

But she had overheard, and the die was cast. The remark had both hurt and infuriated her, and when William, with, admittedly, some considerable encouragement on her part, did indeed come up to scratch, she had accepted him on the spot. Suspecting even then that she would live to regret it, she had added the proviso that they tell no one outside their immediate families until her brother-in-law the Duke, who stood in place of her guardian since both her parents were dead, should come up from the country, from whence he had arrived, most unexpectedly, earlier that evening. Still, whispers of an engagement had run like wildfire around the ton, so much so that Beth had actually found herself in the absurd position of seriously considering marrying the man simply to keep the gossips from saying she was playing fast and loose with yet another gentleman's affections.

Fortunately, she was not yet as foolish as that.

"I spoke to your brother-in-law not an hour since." William was breathing hard and his hands had closed into fists at his sides. "I told him then that I hoped to be able to announce the engagement at midnight tonight, and he made no objection."

"Which is why I am telling you now," Beth said. Her older sister Claire, Duchess

of Richmond, had told her of William's conversation with her husband, which was
why Beth was giving William his congé in
the middle of Claire's ball. The timing was
less than ideal, Beth knew, and she blamed
herself for delaying until circumstances
forced her hand. William was angry, as he
had every right to be. She, on the other
hand, would remain cool and composed.
With that laudable objective in mind, her
tone was eminently reasonable, and she
laid a placating hand on his forearm as she
spoke. The sleeve of his bottle green satin
coat, which he wore with a pale yellow waistcoat and white inexpressibles, felt smooth
beneath her fingers, but the tension of the
limb beneath spoke to how very far from
being placated he actually was. *"Before* the
announcement is made. That way, neither
of us need suffer the slightest degree of
embarrassment."

"Embarrassment . . ." William's eyes
bulged and his face went from puce to
purple. "My God, they are already betting
on it in the clubs. At White's, the odds are
five to one against me getting you to the
altar and ten to one against you actually

going through with the ceremony and be-coming my wife."

"How dreadful." Beth was genuinely shocked. Her lips pursed, and she shook her head in disbelief as her hand dropped away from his arm. "Gentlemen will truly bet on anything."

William sucked in air. "Is that all you can say?"

"I'm sorry," she offered again. Muffled by distance, the lilting strains of the first notes of the quadrille reached her ears. They had exited in the midst of a country dance, which had clearly run its course. She had pounced on William as soon as she had spotted him in the ballroom, but as he was more than passing fond of his own voice, it had taken her some time to detach him from the group he'd been edifying with a detailed account of his role in some long-past hunt. Now, with the quadrille striking up, Mr. Hayden, to whom she rather thought she'd promised the next dance, would be searching for her. Time to end this. "But when you have had time to reflect a little, I'm sure you will agree with me that it's for the best. Truly, we should not suit."

"But . . ."

Prolonging this served no purpose. She started to turn away, adding with finality, "Pray excuse me. I must return to the ballroom now."

"Wait." He caught her arm above the elbow, his fingers gripping just a little too hard for comfort. She turned back to him with raised brows. "It's too late to draw back. I've sent the announcement to the papers. It is to run in tomorrow's edition."

"Oh, no." Beth thought of the torrent of gossip that would sweep over her—over her family, over William and his family—in the wake of her publicly crying off from yet another engagement, and she winced inwardly. There was already so much notoriety attached to the Banning family name that this would be in the nature of heaping coals upon an already smoldering fire. The resulting blaze would be intense. Her eyes went to the clock on the mantel. It was a few minutes past eleven p.m. Almost certainly, the presses would already be printing. There was little chance of withdrawing the announcement now. "You should not have done so."

"You mean, I should have remembered that you have jilted two previous fiancés and expected you would do the same to me?"

She didn't like the tone of that, but she had to admit that, from William's point of view, she probably deserved it.

In any case, there was no undoing what was done. She gave him a small, wry smile. "Well, at least you may take comfort in the fact that no one will attach the least blame to *you*."

"You're right about that." From his expression, it was apparent the fact did not please him. "But the scandal will besmirch us all."

Catching her other arm, William jerked her toward him. Taken by surprise, Beth found herself coming up tight against his chest. The top of her head reached the bridge of his nose, which meant that they were almost eye to eye for a pregnant moment as their gazes collided. Supremely conscious that she was in the wrong— and also that a good portion of the ton was present at her sister's party and would thus be able to hear any loud altercation

that occurred inside the library—she confined her reaction to firming her lips and
narrowing her eyes at him warningly.

"William—" she began.

He rushed on, cutting her off, his fingers
tightening around her arms until they dug
painfully into her soft flesh, clearly undeterred by the fact that she was now rigid
against him and her eyes were starting to
shoot off sparks.

"But of course, this is nothing new to
you, is it? I am but one in a long line, after
all! You left Amperman practically on the
steps of the church, and you threw Kirkby
over less than a week before the wedding.
I should have been warned. Indeed, I *was*
warned! Everyone I hold dear advised
me against making you an offer. She's
shameless, a hardened flirt, they said.
There's bad blood in that family. Look at
the father, wed four times, a drunkard and
a dreadful loose screw. Look at the sisters,
both the subjects of sordid scandals.
Shocking reputations, the pair of them,
and the third girl's no better, I was told
more times than I can count. But more
fool I, I chose to disregard those who I now
perceive to have had my best interests at

heart, even my own mother. And this, *this* is my reward!"

By the time he finished, he was breathing hard. The ambiversions he had cast on her sisters' characters caused Beth's slim black brows to snap together in an ominous line over her delicate nose. Her delft blue eyes took on a decidedly militant sparkle, and a flush—that curse of all redheads—heated her porcelain skin. Still, mindful of the gathered company that would dearly love to add yet another page to her family's already overflowing book of sins, she kept her composure, albeit with an effort.

"If this is how you see fit to behave, I am very glad I decided we should not suit." Her tone was icy, and she disdained to struggle, although she had little doubt that she would have bruises on the morrow from where his fingers were digging into her arms. "Unhand me, if you please. I repeat, our engagement is at an end, and I wish to return to the company."

"Unhand you?" William's mouth took on an ugly twist, and a hard gleam appeared in his eyes. He shook his head at her. "Oh, no. You'll not play fast and loose with *me*.

I've not the smallest desire to become the laughingstock of White's, or the subject of my friends' pity, or the world's jests. You gave your word, and now you *will* marry me."

"Now there you're out: I won't." There was a decided snap to her voice as her patience frayed. Beth attempted to pull her arms free without success, her determination to be cool and collected almost lost in a hot rush of temper, which she just managed to keep from getting the better of her by remembering the proximity of a potential audience. "Let me go at once."

"No." With a quick move that caught her by surprise, William snagged a hand in the neckline of her gown and yanked. The delicate silk tore like paper. Gasping, looking down at herself in disbelief, Beth realized that the top of her dress had been all but ripped away. Only the fluttering gold ribbons tied beneath her breasts kept the ruined garment from dropping to her feet. Except for the flimsy barrier of her near-transparent chemise, she was now naked almost to the waist. The firm white curves of her generous bosom swelled indecently above the filmy muslin undergarment that revealed almost as much as it concealed.

"What the *blazes* do you think you're doing?" Her eyes flew to his even as her hand clapped over her décolletage in an attempt to shield as much of her flesh as possible from his view. For the moment at least, the shock of it was enough to practically immobilize her. "You must be mad."

"Aren't you going to scream? Half the ton will no doubt come barreling to your rescue if you do." He gave her a sneering smile. As Beth attempted to jerk her arm free, his fingers tightened until they were digging into her in a grip that no amount of tugging could break. If she hadn't been so angry—and so increasingly alarmed—she would have winced at the pain of it. "I, of course, will explain that I was simply overcome with lust for my affianced wife, and you—you will have a choice of marrying me at once, or being utterly, completely ruined."

Beth instantly envisioned the scenario he described and was appalled. Smirking, he grabbed the shoulder of her chemise and yanked. The flimsy cloth ripped with a sharp tearing sound. Only her hand pressed to her breasts kept the garment from disintegrating completely, and prevented her from being utterly exposed.

"You *pig*. Let me go!" Maddened, Beth kicked him, but from his reaction, or, rather, the lack of it, it was clear the contact hurt her toes in their soft slippers more than it did his rock-solid shin. Hampered by her inability to use either hand, she nevertheless fought furiously to tear herself free. "I'll never marry you. Never, do you hear? No matter what."

Despite her rising fury, Beth was careful to keep her voice down lest someone in the milling company that filled the house to overflowing should overhear. To her horror, she realized that he was right in his estimation: if anyone found them like this, the scandal would be insupportable. If they didn't wed immediately, the doors of polite society would be closed to her forever. She would be well and truly ruined. The prospect was terrifying. Though she might flirt with being outrageous, and enjoy fulfilling the expectations of those who called her scandalous just to prove that their gossip meant nothing to her, she had no stomach for finding herself a true pariah.

And the resulting firestorm of scandal would scorch her family, too.

"Oh, I think you will." William smiled that sneering smile at her again even as her eyes shot pure poison at him. Then, grabbing her other arm in such a way that she lost her protective grip on her tattered chemise, which immediately fell so that her breasts were now completely bared, he took a good, long look—and shoved her roughly away from him.

"Oh!" Taken by surprise, Beth staggered backward. The small, sharp cry escaped her lips before she could clamp them together, but she managed to swallow the rest of it even as the edge of the Egyptian-style settee caught the back of her knees. She lost her balance, sitting down hard upon the slippery silk seat.

"You'll pay for this, you . . ." There were no words bad enough to do her feelings justice. She'd started to bounce back up, quivering with fury, both fists at the ready, and never mind that she was now in truth indecent, when he threw himself on top of her, forcing her down into the settee. He lay on top of her, his weight pinning her down, his hands imprisoning her wrists, licking and kissing the delicate cord at the side of her neck.

Beth shuddered with revulsion. She heaved beneath him, jerking her head to one side, craning her neck to escape his disgusting onslaught, all to no avail.

"Get off me! You disgust me, you *cretin*." The fact that she hissed rather than screamed the words at him in no way detracted from their venom. "How dare you attack me like this? How dare you?"

"You'll wed me, one way or another."

"Pray disabuse yourself of that notion! I never will!"

His lips, open and wet, found her averted mouth then, and to her disgust he thrust his thick, wet tongue inside, so far that it felt like it was going all the way down her throat. Gagging, cringing with distaste, suppressing a scream only with the greatest of effort, Beth tore her mouth free, bucking and writhing like a mad thing in a frenzied effort to extricate herself. Her efforts paid off: dislodged, he fell heavily to the floor. Unfortunately, he took her with him, then flipped her onto her back and flung himself atop her again even as she tried to scramble away. The impact knocked the air from her lungs. He trapped her with his weight, grabbing her fists and forcing them above her head, where he pinned them to the thick Turkish carpet. The hard round buttons on his coat and waistcoat dug into her tender breasts as he ground his lower body suggestively against hers.

Dear God, I hate this, she thought, revolted. And she knew that this, this imposition of his flesh on hers, was at least part of the reason why she could not stomach the idea of marriage. To give a man the right to use her so at will . . .

She could not do it.

"Get off me! Get off, do you hear?"

Panting, struggling for all she was worth, she merely succeeded in shifting them both sideways. Breathing hard, still firmly atop her, he forced his knee between hers. He was, Beth was sickened to realize, glancing down between them to ogle her breasts.

"You'll sing quite another tune when you are my wife." His voice was thick. He licked his lips. His eyes still fixed to her bosom, he lowered his head . . .

"Get off."

He meant to put his mouth on her breasts.

"No."

Galvanized by revulsion, heart thumping wildly, fighting to get away with every ounce of strength she possessed, Beth managed to jerk an arm free at last. His attention thankfully diverted, he grabbed for it, but she was too fast: fist clenched, she punched him in the temple so hard her knuckles stung.

"Ahh." He reared up with a curse, face contorting viciously, and grabbed for her hands—both were free now—as she pounded him about the head and shoulders.

"Think you there will be no reckoning for this, you want-wit? I'll see you dead over it."

"Wed, rather," he panted.

"Never."

Shaking with fury and fear, heaving in a futile attempt to throw him off, she went for his eyes with her nails. There was now no doubt in her mind that, if she didn't stop him by screaming for assistance or some other means, he meant rape.

Even as her nails gouged his skin he

slapped her, the blow heavy and shocking. The force of it caused her head to snap to one side and briefly disordered her senses.

"Strumpet. Jezebel. Jade. I'll school you to mind your manners with me. When you are my wife . . ."

Stunned, Beth lost the sense of his words as she found herself staring blindly into the fire. It twinkled merrily at her, oblivious to her distress, and she realized that she was now lying within arm's reach of the fireplace. Then he caught her chin, wrenched her face around, and ground his mouth into hers again.

No. No.

At the renewed assault of that sluglike tongue, Beth went cold with horror. She felt a wave of nausea.

The fireplace tools.

The image of them as she had just seen them standing beside the hearth snapped into sudden sharp focus in her mind.

They were close. Within reach.

No sooner did she realize that than she reached out for them, her groping fingers finding and identifying the ornate silver stand, the small broom, the poker. His mouth left hers—*I'm going to be sick,* she thought—only to find her throat again; he caught her tangled skirt and dragged it up, over her knees, despite her struggles.

Her fingers closed desperately around the poker's smooth iron shaft. An instant later the heavy metal bar arced through the air as she slammed it down smartly against the back of his head.

To her alarm, William merely stiffened, shaking his head a little, his eyes widening as his head came up just enough so that he could stare down at her in disbelief. Terrified that she had not done the thing properly, she hit him again with all her might. The resultant *thunk* made her think of a melon splitting.

He made a little sound like a kitten mewling.

Heart pounding like a runaway horse, she watched with a kind of dreadful fascination as his eyes rolled back in his head and his mouth went horribly slack. Then he collapsed on top of her without another sound, pure dead weight.

Thank God, was her first thought. Her second was, *Oh, no, have I killed him?*

Shaking, heart thudding, breath rasping

in her throat as she struggled to suck air into her lungs, Beth lay beneath his motionless body for a moment in near shock as visions of her own lifeless body swinging from the gallows at Tyburn flooded her mind. Then she realized that she could feel his chest moving, hear the faint wheeze of his breathing, and felt a quick upsurge of relief.

Not dead, then.

With that reassuring thought, she recovered some of her wits, and realized she had to move at once lest William regain consciousness, or—and she couldn't decide which was worse—someone should come in and discover them. Gritting her teeth, willing her poor trembling body to move, she tried to wriggle out from beneath him without success. Unfortunately, there was no budging him. He was simply too heavy.

I'm trapped. What now?

From the distant ballroom, she heard the last flourishing notes of the quadrille, and panic seized her. At any moment someone could open the library door and find them like this.

The specter of ruin flashed hideously in her mind's eye. But even ruin, she decided

in that instant, was better by far than being
wed to this man.

But neither was obviously preferable.

Beth never knew from whence she summoned the strength to shove him off, but
she found it. Wedging both hands beneath
his shoulder, she heaved, then heaved
again—and it was enough. William rolled
limply onto his back, his outflung hand catching and parting the sumptuous velvet curtains that they had been standing in front
of earlier, when she had first told him that
the engagement was off.

She had just rolled onto her hands and
knees in preparation for jumping to her feet
when something caught her eye. Impossibly, a boot was planted there between the
curtains. A man's large black riding boot,
scarred and creased from wear, and liberally flecked with mud.

For the space of a couple of heartbeats,
her gaze stuck there, riveted.

The boot was attached to a leg, Beth
saw as her gaze rose along it inexorably.
A long, muscular leg encased in snug
black trousers. The leg was attached to
lean masculine hips . . .

It was then, with a jolt of pure shock,

that the truth registered: there was a man standing in the window embrasure. Until that moment he had been concealed behind the curtains. A tall, broad-shouldered, darkly handsome stranger clad all in black save for the merest hint of white that was his shirt, silhouetted against the grayer black of the moonlit night beyond. His lean face was absolutely expressionless. His crow black hair was tied back in a queue. Without the muffling effect of the heavy curtains, cold air rushed in across the small balcony that overlooked the garden. Remembering the earlier draft on her shoulders, Beth felt certain that the tall French window had been open all along.

He had climbed in through the window . . . *Why?*

Having shot to his face, her eyes now locked with his. They were as black and hard as pieces of jet. Cold, pitiless eyes that stared narrowly back at her, their expression so menacing that her breath caught.

In that frozen instant she realized, too, that he held a pistol in one hand.

Beth's eyes widened. Her heart skipped a beat. Her mouth went dry.

Said pistol was now aimed directly at her.

Chapter Two

To FIND HIMSELF DISCOVERED by a big-eyed chit was, to say the least, inconvenient, Neil Severin reflected grimly. And never mind that she was young, beautiful, and half naked, flashing as delectable a pair of round, creamy, strawberry-tipped breasts at him as he had seen in quite a while. He quickly closed his mind to the pretty display, blocking it out with practiced ease, just as he blocked out all other potential distractions as and when they occurred. His mission was simple: gain access to the house, locate and assassinate his target, then vanish into the night. Invisibility was his stock in trade. No one ever saw him come; no one ever saw him go.

Until now.

"Who the devil are you?" she demanded in a voice that, not surprisingly, shook noticeably.

At that, his gaze met hers. Her challenging expression and strong language surprised him a little. As a sheltered young lady of quality, which he was almost certain she was, she should by rights have been in the throes of hysterics about now, in the aftermath of what she had just endured. Certainly she should have been frightened of *him*. A stranger to her, and standing concealed behind a curtain, no less, he was a muscular three inches over six feet tall, wide of shoulder and chest, dark as a Spaniard, unkempt from two hard, near-sleepless days and nights in the saddle, with an air about him that had been described as everything from forbidding (at his best) to downright cruel—and he was aiming a pistol at her. Not that it seemed to intimidate her to any observable degree.

As she spoke, her brows snapped together into a frown, and she sank back into a kneeling position from which she continued to observe him keenly. Her eyes moved over his face in a way that told him she wasn't likely to forget a single feature any time soon. With one hand she grabbed at the shimmering gold and cream remnants of her bodice and undergarment and pressed what she could gather up to the truly dazzling curves of her bosom in a less than successful attempt at reclaiming her modesty. In her other hand she clutched something—the poker with which she had dispatched her attacker, he saw as he squinted at it with reluctant interest. With the tiniest flicker of stirring curiosity, he wondered if she was possibly entertaining the thought of using it as a weapon against him. After all, as the evidence of the unconscious man sprawled on his back on the carpet beside her illustrated, it had served just such a purpose, admirably, only moments before, which might have infused her with several degrees more confidence than was good for her. Oddly enough, considering the circumstances, her slightly husky voice was low, as if she didn't care to be overheard. It occurred to him then that she hadn't screamed, not at her discovery of him, which had to have been disconcerting to say the least, and not during her recent contretemps with the man she had felled.

Not once.

His interest thoroughly piqued, he wondered why, and regarded her with heightened attention.

"I *said,* who are you?" she demanded. Her voice was still unnaturally low, but steady. Her frown had deepened into a full-blown scowl.

Neil studied her with the quizzical gaze he might have turned on a strange insect under a microscope. Far from being afraid of him, she now looked almost belligerent, glaring at him through narrowed eyes, her brows meeting over her dainty nose, her grip tight on the poker as if she would spring up and attempt to clout him over the head with it if his answer didn't suit. Unexpectedly, the idea of being attacked by this redheaded slip of a girl tickled his funny bone.

Amusement had become sufficiently rare in his life that he noticed and savored the sensation. And was determined to prolong it, if only for a moment or two.

"A better question, I think, would be, *what have you done?*" His voice, as always, was deep and gravelly, if slightly rusty-sounding from disuse. His tone was impressively awful. His eyes flicked meaningfully from the poker to the man sprawled beside her. Immediately she looked stricken, glancing down at the insensate man with guilt and worry written all over her face. "Robbery? Attempted murder? The authorities are quite harsh with either, in my experience. I would say you're looking at Newgate at the very least."

"I—I . . ." she stammered as her gaze slid over her victim, but then she took a deep breath and lifted her eyes to meet his, her mouth firming.

"It was no such thing," she said, with a haughty lift of her chin. Despite the circumstances—and the enticing jiggle of her barely covered bosom—she could have been a duchess surveying a chimney sweep. "And you haven't answered my question."

"Haven't I?" He stepped out from behind the curtain and moved toward her. *If a thing must be done, 'twas best done quickly,* to quote—or more likely misquote—Shakespeare. His education had been so brief, and abandoned so long ago, that he could never be sure.

In any case, it was the sentiment, not the words, that mattered.

The lady was young, lovely, amusing, and clearly high-couraged, but very much in his way. Moreover, she had seen him, not just a glimpse but well enough to identify him if it ever came to that. The prudent thing to do was to kill her, not with a shot— that would bring the house down about his ears; he had only drawn his pistol in the first place because he had been startled to find an altercation taking place inside the room he had chosen for his entry—but quickly and silently.

Just walk toward her, snap her neck, and be done, he told himself. It would be the work of a few seconds merely. He could deliver another blow with the poker to the hapless gent on the floor—a killing blow, this time—and leave the two of them to be discovered later. Probably each would be blamed for the murder of the other.

Certainly no one would suspect him. He could simply disappear into the night and wait for his quarry to surface at another location at a different hour.

"No, you haven't. And you might as well put that pistol away. I assure you it doesn't frighten me in the least."

He didn't reply, having almost reached her and not wanting to prolong the contact any more than necessary. It really was a shame, but . . .

Something in either his actions or expression must have alarmed her despite the care he was taking not to frighten her into any precipitate action, because she shot to her feet as he drew close. Holding the poker threateningly aloft in one hand, she attempted to stare him down, a difficult task when he was nearly a foot taller and far larger than she was. Plus, the shreds of her bodice shifted with her every movement even as she tried to hold them in place, and her focus was clearly somewhat distracted by the exposure of her bosom.

Despite his best intentions, Neil could not stop his eyes from dropping to take in the view as a rosy bud of a nipple peeked out at him. She must have followed his gaze and glanced down at herself at just about the same time, because she made a small, sharp sound and clamped both arms over her chest. That had the desired result of hiding what she wished to hide, but then the alabaster upper slopes of her bosom swelled temptingly above her tightly folded arms, creating an effect that was almost equally luscious. Neil was conscious of a slight stirring of his body in response, and frowned. When he was working, he rarely got distracted. Her heightened color and defensive look as her eyes shot up to meet his gaze told him that she was aware of the direction his thoughts had taken, and felt at a distinct disadvantage. Her death grip on the poker didn't abate, but it had, of necessity, shifted. The implement's hard black shaft now angled absurdly up past her shoulder, and any credibility it had ever had as a weapon was lost.

"And why is that, pray?" he asked. To his own annoyance, he stopped walking a couple of feet short of his goal to engage her in more ill-advised conversation.

Her eyes never left his face.

"If you were to shoot me, any number of people would come bursting through that door before the sound faded. And you would find yourself taken in a trice."

Neil felt another of those unexpected quivers of amusement. It was her bravado in the face of impossible circumstances, he thought, that was doing it. She was really quite out of the ordinary, and he surveyed her from head to toe with some regret. Killing her was not what he would choose to do could he see any real alternative. It was a waste, and he hated waste. She was the merest chit, and a raving beauty to boot. Her dishevelment, in his opinion, only enhanced her attraction. Besides possessing a truly magnificent bosom, she was temptingly shaped, slender yet curvaceous where a woman needed to be, of no more than medium height yet erect enough to appear taller. Her skin was a flawless, rose-flushed porcelain, and there was enough of it on display to make him certain that she was that way all over. Her face was not the perfect oval of a classic beauty. Instead, it was square-jawed and high-cheekboned, with a stubborn chin, a full-lipped, willful mouth, and deep blue eyes set off by thick black lashes and silky black brows that were, still, meeting above her elegantly carved nose in a ferocious frown. Her presumably once-elegant coiffure was wrecked, and her hair cascaded over her creamy bare shoulders in a profusion of tumbled waves that were the glorious red of Titian. Her expression, though, in no way mirrored one of that artist's limpid beauties; the fire in the lady's eyes as they collided with his blazed even hotter than her hair.

Out of the ordinary, indeed.

"I must certainly put away my pistol, then," he said, and obligingly tucked his pistol away in his greatcoat pocket, then felt another flicker of amusement at her reaction. She gave a great sigh of relief— the soft white swell of her bosom heaved enticingly above her constricting arms as she did so—and most of the wariness left her face. With his pistol out of sight, it was clear she no longer considered him much of a threat. He had only to choose his moment now, and the thing was done. It would be over before she even knew what was happening. He was skilled enough that she would feel no pain.

A comforting thought, he concluded wryly.

She watched him still, her expression severe. "If you are a burglar, I must warn you that you are quite out in your timing:

the house is full of people. There is a ball in progress just at this moment, you know. And perhaps this would be a good time to mention, too, that I have only to scream, and a hundred people will instantly come rushing to my aid."

"Why don't you, then?" he asked, genuinely curious. He almost wished she would scream. He would be upon her before the sound left her throat, of course, silencing her quickly and forever, his hand pushed by necessity, which would make this easier. It had been many years since he'd felt any hesitation at all about killing anyone, but he was conscious of having to deliberately keep reminding himself that in the name of self-preservation he had to kill her.

When his target died, as his target inevitably would, this too-beguiling chit would remember him. It would be trusting too much to luck to assume she would not then associate him with the event.

Get on with it, then.

His footsteps were entirely silent on the deep pile of the Oriental carpet as he closed the distance between them. Years of necessity had made it second nature for him to move without making a sound.

"Oh. Well," she said. "As to that . . ."

She paused.

With interest, he watched the quick darkening of her eyes as self-consciousness suffused them. He was so close now that she had to tilt her head back to meet his gaze, leaving her slender, pale neck more vulnerable than she had any notion of. She was clearly, foolishly unafraid of him.

"I have no . . ." she started up again.

The man on the floor stirred and groaned. The lady jumped as if someone had grabbed her by the ankle, almost losing her grip on both the poker and her bodice in the process.

She took a couple of skittering steps back and looked down at her victim with wide-eyed dismay. The man on the floor lay once again motionless, eyes closed, jaw slack. Drool spilled from the corner of his mouth. A smear of blood was now visible through his fair hair. It was the only real indication that he was not simply asleep on the rug.

"Do you think he'll die?" she asked

anxiously. Neil looked into the big blue eyes that had lifted to meet his again and felt grim. She was very young, very sweet—and very much in his way.

"Probably not. It's difficult to be certain, of course. Do you wish him to?" He took another step toward her, until he was close enough to once again smell the faint, lavender-tinged scent of her. Like the rest of her, it was unmistakably—and titillatingly—feminine. Up close, her skin had the soft, pearlescent gleam of ivory satin. He was certain it would be smooth to the touch—and warm.

It had been a while—a long while—since he'd been this close to this kind of woman. Young ladies of quality were thin on the ground in the places he regularly habituated.

"No, of course not. At least . . ."

She broke off, hesitating, glancing back at the man on the ground. Neil reached out and took the poker from her—she made no protest, seeming more glad than not to be relieved of its unwieldiness—then realized he was, in effect, hesitating, too. The poker posed not the slightest degree of hindrance to what he needed to do, and he knew it.

"Who is he?" Even as he laid the poker on the carpet, Neil recognized that in asking the question he was simply trying to delay the inevitable for a little longer. A glance upon entering the room had told him that the man on the floor was not his target. Therefore, he had no interest whatsoever in who he was. And yet he asked.

"Lord Rosen. He is—was—my fiancé."

"Ah."

The loathing in her voice was unmistakable. Having listened to the determined fight she had put up to defend her honor, Neil gave her full marks for emerging the victor in the encounter. Given her size and style, and the size and style of her assailant, he would have expected the outcome to be very different.

Not, he told himself, that he cared one way or the other.

He cared about doing his job, and that was all. That being the case, he needed to do what was necessary to repair this farcical situation, and be gone.

"Did you end your other two engagements with the same amount of, ah, ferocity?" he inquired, and had the felicity of watching her eyes darken still more with self-consciousness and her cheeks turn even rosier.

"You were listening!" she accused. Then, primming up her mouth, she added, "I've no intention of telling you anything at all until you tell me who you are—and why you came in through the window."

Her tone was haughty, her gaze direct.

To his own amazement, Neil found himself teetering on the brink of being charmed.

"Perhaps I am a guest, and merely stepped behind the curtains and opened a window to blow a cloud without being disturbed. Unaware, of course, that you would soon be enacting your little drama in the very room I had chosen for my respite."

With skepticism evident in the quick twist of her lips and lift of her eyebrows, she looked him up and down.

"Believe me, I am not such a flat as to fall for that."

Her voice dripped scorn. He'd seen many a magistrate on the bench who did not look half so stern.

Again to his surprise, Neil found himself reacting with enjoyment.

Enough, he thought with grim resolve,

and reached for her. At the same moment hurried footsteps and a girlish giggle could be heard just outside the door.

His newest target caught her breath.

"There shouldn't be anyone in here," a man said. A young man, from the sound of him. His words were muffled, but still clearly audible through the door.

"Oh, no," she breathed, and cast a panicked glance up at him. *"Shhh.* We must hide. Hurry."

Grabbing his hand, literally snatching it out of the air scant inches away from sliding around her neck, she dragged him after her as she rushed toward the window he had recently abandoned. Surprising him with her strength—and her ability to remember to keep an arm clamped over her breasts under what were clearly harrowing conditions—she shoved him into the embrasure and then crowded in behind him. With a single gliding step she positioned herself in front of him, standing with her back pressed to his front as she twitched the curtains closed, thus cutting off his view of the room.

Bemused, Neil found himself staring at lush folds of ruby velvet. How the hell had he allowed himself to be dragooned into a potential disaster like this? If they were discovered, there would be just that many more witnesses to be dispatched—or, alternatively, he might find himself looking at his own end, a notion that filled him with disgust at his own stupidity in allowing such a thing to happen.

Glancing down, he saw a mass of tumbled red curls and found his answer. Below that bright crown, the tip of her nose was just visible. Below that, creamy cleavage swelled temptingly. She was breathing fast, and he could feel the slight expansion of her rib cage as she drew in air. The scent of lavender teased his nostrils. Though he had no recollection of how they came to be there, his hands curled around her upper arms. Her skin was as warm, and as silky smooth, as he had imagined.

Damn it to hell and back anyway, you are not such a fool as this, he told himself. Then he realized that, clearly, he was.

His mouth turned down sharply at the corners. His hands tightened on her arms. She glanced up at him inquiringly, her big blue eyes and uptilted face disarmingly devoid of fear.

She had no idea of who or what he was, or the danger she was in.

Beyond the curtains, there was a faint sound: the door opening. Distant music. Laughter. His attention, and hers, shifted, fixing on what was happening beyond the curtains.

"Mama will miss me," a girlish voice said, over the unmistakable sounds of two sets of footsteps entering the room. Neil felt his companion stiffening. She stood rigid against him now, and if she was breathing at all he couldn't tell.

There was a faint click as the door closed again.

"A kiss. You promised me a kiss," the young man beseeched. He and his companion were clearly inside the room now.

"Lud, I did no such thing."

"You did."

A coquettish giggle was followed by the kind of silence that spoke of a kiss taken or given. Neil tried to ignore the soft warmth of her, the unmistakably feminine fragrance, the tantalizing view, and failed abysmally.

Fool . . .

The door opened again. The sounds of music and laughter spilled into the room.

"Rory, whatever are you doing?" another girl scolded, low-voiced. "Mama's looking for you!"

"Oh, bother!" The first girl sounded more annoyed than alarmed. "I must fly to the ladies' retiring room, I suppose, and claim to have been there all along. Sonja, you won't tell?"

"I should," the other girl said.

"'Twas nothing—no harm . . ." the gentleman stammered.

"Our mama won't think so, I promise you that." The second girl's voice was grim as she spoke over the quick shuffle of retreating footsteps. "She—"

The sound of the closing door cut her off. Nothing besides the faint, distant strains of ballroom music could now be heard beyond the curtains. Neil only realized that his hands were sliding sensuously down his companion's arms when she gave a big sigh of relief and slipped free of his hold. But instead of running for her life, as he now almost wished she would do, she leaned forward slightly to peep out through the crack in the curtains. He could feel the firm roundness of her backside pressing solidly against the saddle-hardened muscles of his thighs.

His body's instinctive response was inconvenient, perhaps, but not unexpected. It had been a long time since he had been with a woman. Longer still since the woman had been a lady. And this one was young and beautiful and really quite delectable.

A pity . . .

"They're gone." The relief in her voice was palpable. "Thank goodness they didn't see him."

By *him,* she was clearly referring to her fallen suitor.

Ignoring the reflexive tightening of his groin, Neil glanced at her neck and flexed his fingers. Dispatching her would take no more than seconds . . .

Before he could make a move, she stepped with blithe ignorance through the curtains, putting herself temporarily out of his reach. Neil silently cursed himself and followed. The perfect opportunity had been at hand and he had let it pass. That only made things more difficult for the both of them.

"This can't go on," she said, echoing his thoughts with uncanny precision. She had her back to him still, both arms clamped protectively over her swelling chest, staring down at the unconscious Lord Rosen as if deep in thought. She chewed her lower lip in some agitation. It was obvious that the hideous crocodile-carved settee had been her savior: it stood squarely between the man she had felled and the door, blocking the view of anyone who entered—at least until he walked farther into the room. "I have to *do* something."

Indeed.

"It appears to me that the problem is, you already did." His tone was dry as he stepped right up behind her again, resolved to get the job done and be gone before there were any more complications.

She glanced over her shoulder at him, frowning, her silky dark brows once again almost meeting over her small nose. Her spine stiffened; her shoulders squared. Then she turned to face him.

"I'll make a bargain with you," she said.

Chapter Three

To Neil's surprise, the image that flashed into his mind in that instant was Old Hook Nose surveying the field before sending his weary troops forth to engage the numerically superior enemy at Waterloo. It was an unwelcome flashback—he had never been an admirer of Wellington's, and especially not on that day—but there it was.

As he had learned to his frequent displeasure over the years, there was no doing anything about stray memories. They popped up as and when they willed.

"What kind of bargain?" He knew he was a fool to ask. His fingers were already curving at his sides in anticipation of what had to be done. Her neck was slender, soft—a quick, hard snap and it would be over.

Get it done.

Her eyes held his. They had, he was bemused to discover, changed in a matter of seconds from deep, feminine blue to gunmetal gray.

"If you'll help me, I won't tell anyone about you."

Her chin had the jut and her spine the ramrod stiffness of a soldier's—no, a general's. Wellington again.

Neil's flexing hands stilled.

"Help you what?" The humor of seeing his former commanding officer in this silky-skinned Venus hit him then, and, most unexpectedly, his lips twitched. If she'd feared him at all, that fear was clearly long gone. She was regarding him with a martial light in her eyes that told him that to her mind, she was the one in charge. Clearly, the lady saw him as nothing more than the solution to her problem, with no idea whatsoever that her life hung by a thread. He'd dispatched so many souls over the years that killing was second nature to him now.

As far as he was concerned, his victims had no humanity. They were just jobs to be completed as efficiently as possible. But this redheaded charmer had made herself vividly alive to him, and he was having to work to summon forth the emotionless killer he generally was.

"I have to get *him*"—glancing down, she prodded the slack-mouthed Lord Rosen with a disdainful, golden-shoed toe—"and myself out of here without anyone seeing us. If I don't, if anyone discovers us like this, I will either be forced to wed him—which I won't do—or be hideously, horribly ruined." Her eyes met his. "You came in through the window. I thought perhaps you could help me lower him out of it, then lower me down as well. From there, I could get up to my bedchamber by the back staircase without anyone seeing me, I think. I could say that I gave William his congé, and he left, and I then went upstairs. And—and perhaps you could convey Lord Rosen home, or at least somewhere other than *here*?"

Her tone was hopeful. So were her eyes. His mouth tightened with impatience at himself even as his gaze slid reluctantly over her. Granted, she was beautiful and vulnerable and, yes, even somewhat ridiculously endearing with her resolute expression and glorious hair and arms folded tightly over her bountiful bare bosom—but she was also a danger to him. There was no getting around that. When the time came, she could bring ruination down upon him with just a few words.

Something of his inner battle must have shown in his face, because her eyes widened at him as she added hastily, "I have money, you needn't worry. I'll pay you for helping me. Pay you *well*."

Neil suddenly made up his mind. It was stupid of him and he knew it was stupid of him, the kind of soft-headed error that could end up costing him dearly if, later, anything went wrong, but he realized in that instant that he was going to take a chance: he wasn't going to kill her after all. She was lovely, charming, very young, and totally undeserving of death, an innocent who tonight had simply had the misfortune to find herself in the wrong place at the wrong time. And he wasn't, he was surprised to realize, quite as devoid of human decency as he had long supposed.

To kill this girl simply because she'd had

the misfortune to stumble across him was something that he simply did not want to do.

It seemed that the Angel of Death, as they called him in certain circles, had a heart after all.

Or if not a heart, then something. A shred of conscience remaining to him, maybe. Or at least a predator's lack of interest in killing something that was not its natural prey.

He would take her bargain. As the decision crystallized, he felt the tense muscles of his neck and shoulders relax.

"Very well." He hesitated, then pointed a monitory forefinger at her to underline the point. "But you must keep your end of it, mind."

"You'll help me? Oh, thank you!" Relief and gratitude blazed from her eyes, which were once again that beguiling delft blue. "You needn't worry, I shan't tell on you." Then she made a quick, wry face at him. "Though if you are a burglar it is probably very wrong of me. If you would just engage to find some *other* residence—" Rosen groaned and she broke off, glancing down at her erstwhile suitor nervously. "Um—never mind. Can we hurry this along?

Much longer and someone's bound to discover us."

Rosen was stirring in earnest now. The lady's expression as she looked down at him turned truly alarmed. It appeared that he was, indeed, on the verge of regaining his senses at any moment.

Grimacing at his own folly, Neil moved with quick grace, leaning over the now groaning-in-earnest Rosen. By means of a quick, brutally efficient right to the jaw, he instantly restored him to total unconsciousness.

"Oh, well done," the lady said with unmistakable admiration, and despite his own annoyance at himself and the situation, Neil almost smiled. The reaction felt strange, foreign even, and he realized that it had been a very long time indeed since he had relaxed enough to enjoy a situation the way he was starting to enjoy the fix he was in.

"Thank you," he said. Then, by the simple expedient of hooking a hand in the collar of Rosen's too-elaborate coat, he dragged him over to the window while his new partner in skullduggery followed anxiously along behind.

"Shall I help . . . ?" she began as the

curtains billowed around them. She broke off as Neil flipped Rosen over onto his stomach, then reached down and grasped the seat of his breeches. A heave, and Rosen's bulk was up and over the iron railing that edged the small stone ledge (it was too narrow to be properly termed a balcony) outside the window.

The man was heavy and limp as a sack of stones. For a moment, as his fingers tightened in it, Neil feared that the cloth he was grasping would not be up to the task. But the superfine breeches held. For an instant longer he dangled Rosen by them and the slippery satin collar of his coat, carefully positioning him, and then—not without some satisfaction—he let go.

Fortunate for you we're just one story up, Neil thought as Rosen crashed into the welcoming arms of a stately privet. The prickly branches swallowed him up, all but hiding him from view. Only the faintest gleam of white from Rosen's breeches pinpointed him in the bush.

There was a distant click as the door to the library opened. The sound was unmistakable. Behind him, the lady jumped like a scalded cat.

Neil whipped around instinctively just as she stumbled into him with all the force of a recoiling cannon. The resulting collision almost sent them both over the rail. Had he not had the sharply honed reflexes of a man who was constantly one unhappy surprise away from his own end, he would not have been sure-footed enough to stave off disaster.

"Easy."

He grabbed her shoulders, steadying them both, but she wasn't even paying attention. Her back was to him, and her gaze was fixed fearfully on the crimson velvet wall of the once-again-closed curtains. She was rigid as buckram now. Beyond the curtains, someone was speaking.

"I thought you said my son was in here." The voice sounded like it belonged to an older woman. It was cold, imperious.

"I am sorry, Lady Rosen. Lord Rosen must have left without my seeing him." The other speaker was male, and clearly a servant.

"Was Lady Elizabeth with him?"

"I really couldn't say, ma'am."

"Hmmph." Cloth rustled and heels tapped sharply on the parquet floor as Lady Rosen marched out. Softer footsteps marked the servant's exit. With a gentle *whoosh* and a barely audible *click,* the door once again closed.

"I take it that you are Lady Elizabeth?" Neil murmured inquiringly into the closer of her ears. Her shoulders were slim and supple beneath his hands. They felt good beneath his palms, warm and rounded. Her skin was pale enough to glow faintly in the light of the barely there sliver of moon that was, at that moment, peeping out from behind a gathering tower of silver-limned black clouds.

The smell of rain was in the air. So, closer at hand, was the tantalizingly faint scent of lavender.

Although he faced a night spent moving around in the open, Neil knew which he found more disturbing.

She nodded, then glanced at him over her shoulder. The brisk breeze caught her hair, sending a strand of it fluttering against his mouth. It, too, had the texture of silk. "That was William's mother."

"So I gathered."

"She's looking for him. And me. Oh, I *must* get out of here."

She pulled free of his hands and whisked around to face him.

"Can you lower me down?" she asked urgently, moving to the rail and looking over. The view encompassed the narrow, lushly landscaped side yard, which was screened from the street by an iron fence and a tall hedge, and the high brick wall of the mansion next door. As he happened to know from his earlier reconnaissance of the area, it was presently empty, its owner having apparently chosen to remain in the country this Season. Its windows were dark and shuttered, and its shelter provided the strip of ground beneath with almost total privacy.

"I have a better idea." His hands dropped to his sides, although he was ready to swear he could still feel the heat of her skin on his palms. "I'll get down myself, and then you jump and I'll catch you."

She cast a hunted glance over her shoulder. "Fine. Just hurry."

Vaulting the rail required little effort. Neil dropped lithely to the ground, managing to avoid, with the ease of long practice, both the bush that had cushioned Rosen and the gravel of the walk leading toward the back of the house. He landed on the balls of his feet on soft grass, found his balance, then turned and looked up to find that the intrepid Lady Elizabeth, gleaming ball gown and all, was already clambering over the rail.

"Bother," she muttered as her skirt got caught.

Neil finally succumbed to that lurking, unaccustomed smile as he was treated to a view of slim, shapely calves sheathed in the finest white silk stockings, blue garters tied around flashing pale thighs, and the sweet curves of a round little derriere that was enticing enough to make his loins ache. Then, as she jerked at it and muttered another imprecation, the skirt came free and quickly dropped to cover most of what had interested him. Although her ankles—delicate, fine-boned ankles—and the lower part of those delectable calves were still on display, courtesy of his vantage point beneath her.

It was only when he glanced farther up, toward her face, that he realized the best had been yet to come. The exigencies of holding on to the rail apparently required the use of both her hands. Which meant that the beautiful full globes of her breasts were totally bared. Bathed in moonlight, they were perfect opalescent teardrops that rose and fell enticingly with her every breath.

He was, after all, human. And male. His body stirred sharply and painfully. He swallowed, and stared.

"Close your eyes," she hissed, scowling down at him. She was on the wrong side of the railing, clinging like a cat in the precise place where he had gone over, the one place where it was easiest to avoid both bush and gravel, her toes balanced precariously on the tiny sliver of stone on the outside of the iron bars.

"Drop. I'll catch you." Recovering his focus with an effort, Neil became aware that he was still smiling a little even as he positioned himself beneath her.

"I *said,* close your eyes."

"If I close my eyes, I might miss." His tone was reasonable. He held up his arms for her, prepared to spend the next few minutes persuading her that she could safely drop into them.

Apparently, she harbored no such doubts.

"Cawker," she said severely, and dropped, plummeting like a small golden bird shot out of the sky. She fell into his arms in a rustle of silk and a swirl of red curls, surprisingly heavy for so small a package. His arms closed around her automatically even as he took a step back for balance. For a moment she simply lay there, cradled like a babe in his arms, blinking at him and looking slightly stunned while she recovered her presence of mind and he once again inhaled lavender and treated himself to the view.

Her breasts were soft round globes still jiggling with the aftermath of her landing. Her skin was creamy perfection. In the moonlight, the circles around her nipples were simply dark, and the nipples themselves darker still. His response was instinctive, atavistic. His body hardened to granite; his breath caught; his pulse speeded up.

It took every ounce of self-control he possessed not to lower his mouth to taste one of those small, jutting buds.

Fortunately, he possessed a great deal of self-control.

"You may put me down now." She recovered faster than he did, once more snapping her arms closed over those delectable breasts, glaring at him with well-founded suspicion written all over her face.

"You're welcome." There was irony in his tone as he set her on her feet, knowing that it was folly to do anything else, however tempting the possibilities might be. She'd roused him to lust, but there were plenty of other women available to slake it if he chose. In any case, big-eyed innocents such as she had never been his style.

"Oh—thank you," she said belatedly as she swept her bright hair back from her face with a quick toss of her head. "I really am very grateful for your help." Her arms remained tightly clamped over her bosom; a worried frown marred her brow as she glanced toward the shadowy garden at the back of the house. "If you will come around tomorrow—no, wait, you can't very well call on me under the circumstances, can you? Very well, then. I always walk in Green Park around ten in the morning. If you'll meet me there at, say, the Folly at ten minutes past, I'll have your money for you."

She was practically bouncing on her toes, glancing nervously around, clearly eager to be gone. Neil felt a small pang of regret as he realized that this amusing flicker of warmth that had so unexpectedly appeared in his otherwise cold and disciplined existence was getting ready to go out, and succumbed to temptation for the first time in years.

"I prefer to collect my payment immediately."

Without waiting for her response, he caught her chin between his thumb and forefinger. Even as her eyes widened, he bent his head and touched his mouth to hers. Her lips were warm and soft, slightly moist and parted with surprise. The kiss was a nothing, a mere sampling of the charms he regretted not being able to thoroughly explore, but she jerked her head back and jumped away from him as if burned.

"You *cad*." Her voice quivered with outrage. Her eyes shot sparks at him. "How dare you?"

"Payment in full." He bowed slightly, already regretting what he had done. "Now, if you'll provide me with your erstwhile beau's direction . . ."

Her face was easy to read, even by moonlight. It was clear that indignation at him was struggling with the pragmatic need to get the situation quickly resolved. Pragmatism won out.

"He lives at 29 Beecham Street." With that, and another searing glare meant to wither him, she was gone, darting away toward the dark garden at the back of the house. Neil watched her until the shadows swallowed up even the golden gleam of her gown, and then, deliberately shrugging off a ridiculous sensation of loss, he turned his attention back to Rosen.

He must have hit him harder than he'd thought, because the man was still out. Neil fished him out of the prickly privet—not without difficulty, because he had an aversion to staining his linen, which due to the circumstances was in perilously short supply—and rolled him onto the ground. Then, in the interests of both providing a cover story to explain Rosen's battered state and maintaining his own solvency, he swiftly went through the man's pockets. The pocket watch and snuffbox were of no interest to him, although he took them anyway to make it appear that Rosen had been robbed, but the thick wad of the ready Rosen was sporting was enough to keep him in relative comfort for a number of days. As he pocketed the notes with pleasure, Rosen's eyes flickered and he murmured something incomprehensible through slack lips.

Not without some satisfaction, Neil hit him again.

And that's for pretty Lady Elizabeth, he thought.

After that, it was short work to hoist the man to his feet, support him so that he looked drunk, with an arm draped limply around Neil's shoulder and Neil's hand hooked in the waistband of his breeches, and drag him away from the house. By putting himself to so much trouble he was, he reckoned, even more of a fool than he'd already proved himself to be by allowing the winsome Lady Elizabeth to live. An unwritten rule of his existence was that he never helped anyone but himself, but somehow or another she'd tapped into a vein of chivalry that he'd thought had bled out long since, and here he was: cleaning up a mess that was none of his making.

His mouth twisted ruefully at the thought even as he tightened his grip on Rosen, who, deadweight, was heavy as a man-sized chunk of lead.

The easiest thing to do would be to simply kill the man and have done.

Even as the thought slid through his mind, it was followed by another.

The lady would undoubtedly object.

Neil realized that it was the first time in a long, long while that he had considered someone else's needs besides his own. And it was definitely the first time in his memory that the other person's well-being actually won out. If he killed Rosen, Lady Elizabeth would very likely consider herself a close cousin of the murderous Lady Macbeth—ah, his Shakespeare was coming back to him in spades tonight—with blood on her hands. If he abandoned him, which was equally tempting, the inquiry when Rosen was found might well embroil Lady Elizabeth. And for whatever obscure reason, he was resolved to do his possible to get her safely out of the fix in which he had found her.

Damn the chit anyway.

At thirty-one well-hardened years of age, he was far too old and far too experienced to be swayed by a damsel in distress, big blue eyes, soft, kissable lips, and a truly memorable pair of breasts.

Yet here he was, clearly not as impervious as he had thought.

Which was something he undoubtedly needed to rectify if he wished to live out his natural life span.

By passing through the back gardens of adjacent houses before emerging with his burden at the corner of Grosvenor Square and Brook Street, Neil was able to avoid the line of carriages with their nosy drivers and restive horses waiting in front of the elegant mansion where the ball was being held. He paused in the shadows, waiting unseen while a tired kitchen maid unexpectedly hurried out a close-at-hand door, obviously bent on some errand. A party of noisy toffs complete with top hats and canes piled into a carriage farther along, and he took good care they didn't notice him either. Otherwise, the area was deserted. Oblongs of light from the windows of the houses he skirted were the only other obstacles he encountered, and he avoided those. Rosen was breathing hard, reeked of cologne or some foul hair pomade, and drooled besides. Neil gave a grimace of disgust as he half carried, half dragged the man away from the sanctified air of one of London's toniest blocks into the narrow backstreets and alleys with which the area was honeycombed. There, gaslights smoldered smokily on distant corners, lending an eerie yellow glow to the fog that was beginning to roll in to clog the streets, but everywhere else the gutters and streets were so dark as to make it impossible to discern the identity of anyone. Only a few women were out at that hour. The decent ones hurried along, their heads bowed and concealed by the hoods of their cloaks, the others loitering in hopes of picking up a protector for the night. The men were a mixed bag, gentlemen, drunken and otherwise, mingling with a more sinister sort. Despite the hour, traffic as he neared Piccadilly was heavy. A bath chair carrying an overweight man in an advanced state of inebriation, evidenced by the fact that he was singing immoral ditties at the top of his lungs, trotted past. Crested carriages trundled noisily over the cobblestones on their way to or from the Opera House, or perhaps a private party or a gentleman's club. Finally Neil judged that he had gone far enough, spotted a cab, and hailed it.

Bundling Rosen inside, he gave the man's address, reluctantly handed over a pony for the fare, and stepped back.

The carriage took off with a jerk, and his unwanted problem was thus removed from his life. He was once again free to get on with the business that had brought him hotfoot to London.

He only hoped things worked out as well for Lady Elizabeth.

Perhaps, one day, he thought as he faded back into the shadows of the alley from which he had emerged, sparing her would count for something when the ledger of his sins was being tallied. But then again, against so much sin, probably not.

With that, he dismissed her from his mind.

Only to find that his brief inattention to his surroundings had already cost him dear.

"Top o' the evenin', Angel," Fitz Clapham said as he emerged from a recessed doorway, his hoarse cockney voice making him instantly identifiable despite the darkness, or the curly-brimmed hat that was pulled low over his face and the muffler he'd wound around the collar of his coat for further concealment of his features. Clapham was a good deal shorter than Neil and a good deal older, but strong and muscular as a Brahma bull and deadly as a thrown knife. In the small, insular world of assassins for hire, he was known as one of the best. "Keep your 'ands where I can see 'em, now. Tsk, tsk. Did you really think you'd seen the last of me?"

Considering that the last time he'd seen Clapham the man had been gutshot and lying in a pool of his own blood as hired bodyguards converged on him in the courtyard of a French château, Neil thought he could be pardoned for assuming exactly that.

"What do you want?" he asked, although he knew. On the very edge of his peripheral vision, he watched as the other denizens of the alley, the ones who were there for purposes of their own and wanted no part of this, slunk away like cats in the night. He was already calculating the time it would take to reach for his pistol, which still resided in the pocket of his greatcoat. His conclusion was, too much. If his hand made so much as a move in that direction, he'd be dead before he touched it.

"Ah." Clapham smiled and pushed his

coat aside so that Neil could see the gleaming barrel of his pistol, which, as Neil had
known it would be, was aimed at his heart.
"You made me look bad, you know. I didn't
appreciate that."

That would have been two years previously, when they had both, with neither
knowing of the other's assignment to the
same job until they'd spotted each other
on the premises, been dispatched to remove the former head of French intelligence from the world of the living. Clapham
had failed, felled by an alert bodyguard's
fusillade of bullets. Neil had succeeded.

As he always succeeded. Not one failed
mission in more than a decade's worth of
state-sanctioned murders.

In some small way, he was proud of
that.

"It wasn't my intention," Neil said.

Clapham nodded. "Still." Then, to someone behind Neil, he added, "Check 'im for
weapons. 'E'll 'ave a pistol, for sure, and 'e
carries a toothpick in 'is boot."

Clearly, Neil realized, Clapham had
seen him make use of the slender, silver-
handled knife he always kept concealed in
his right boot to dispatch the sentry who

had, as he had thought at the time, done for Clapham. Even as he had the thought, Neil became aware of two more figures behind him, slowly closing in on him from either side. Although they, too, were cloaked in fog and shadows, Neil didn't have to see their features to know who they were. Unlike himself, who always worked alone, Clapham frequently employed two associates, Moss Parks and Toby Richards, especially when the assignment promised to be more difficult or dangerous than usual. Unlike Clapham, they were stupid. But they were equally deadly.

And he harbored no illusions: tonight the trio's mission was to kill him.

Unfortunately for them, Neil was not yet ready to die.

At the same moment that Clapham aimed his pistol and Parks and Richards, pistols at the ready, converged on him, Neil threw himself at Clapham's knees in a low, fast dive.

"Blimey!" Clapham bellowed, trying without success to leap clear and shoot at the same time. The bullet passed close enough to Neil's right ear so that he felt the wind of its passing, smacking into the cobblestones, then ricocheting with a whine. Neil made contact before Clapham could snap off another shot, the full force of his flying body slamming into Clapham's legs, causing his gun to catapult out of his grip. Clapham went sailing over Neil's back, tumbling forward, providing for the next crucial seconds just enough cover to protect him from Parks's and Richards's guns, which spat fire into the darkness. Screams echoed off the walls around them. The few remaining onlookers scattered.

"Don't shoot!" Clapham yelled, covering his head as he hit the cobblestones.

"Get 'im!"

"Over there!"

A large body—Richards—tackled Neil as he scrambled to his feet, almost bringing him down again. Chaos reigned as Clapham's henchmen temporarily abandoned the idea of shooting him in favor of hand-to-hand combat. In the foggy darkness it was impossible to be certain of exactly what was happening, or who was who. Amidst the thuds and grunts of bodies hitting the cobblestones and blows being landed, shapeless figures of bystanders flitted through the fog like wraiths to watch

from a safe distance while the three princi-
pals in the attack fell on Neil in a blur of
lightning-fast movement. Neil blinked in
pain as a fist landed a glancing blow that
ripped the corner of his mouth. The silver
gleam of a knife plunging at him through
the darkness gave him just enough warning to dodge it. A man—Parks?—screamed
in pain, Clapham cursed, and the sound of
an upstairs window being thrown open
was followed by a woman shrieking, "Timmy,
go fetch the watch!"

The foul stench of the sewage-filled gut-
ter almost under his feet filled Neil's nostrils as he sucked in air, courtesy of a fist the
size of an anvil slamming into his midsec-
tion. Wheezing, he returned the favor with
a punch that sent that particular assailant
flying.

As soon as he realized that he was
grappling only with Clapham now, another
pistol spat, the bullet glancing off the wall
nearest Neil's head.

"Bloody fool, don't be shootin' toward
me!" Clapham yelled, his meaty arms trying
to latch onto Neil even as Neil managed to
tear himself free. Clapham was quick despite his bulk, and snagged a fist in Neil's

coat as he turned to run, jerking him to a halt. Neil whirled, slammed his fist into the man's thick belly, and yanked his coat free. Then he bolted into the darkness, darting toward the mouth of another of the small alleys that honeycombed the area.

"'E's gettin' away!"

Snapping off a quick shot behind him as he ran down the first of the rabbit warren of streets he knew like the back of his hand and that he hoped would be his salvation now, Neil tried to come up with a plan. *Run* was the best he could do for the moment, he decided as his immediate vicinity was peppered by answering gunfire and he ducked down another alley.

So that's what he did, with his would-be assassins in determined pursuit.

Despite his years of loyal service to Crown and country, those who decided such things were determined to see him dead.

Chapter Four

BETH FOUND THAT she was shivering a little as she stole up the back stairs and flitted as silently as possible along the long corridor that led to her bedchamber. The shivering, she thought, was not due to cold, but rather to the shock of William's attack, and had set in only now that she deemed herself really, truly safe. Even after she had dealt with William, the thought of exposure had terrified her. Had it not been for the fortuitous presence of that impossibly handsome housebreaker . . .

Her lips burned as she thought of him. He had, of course, been frightening at first, but at the moment when he'd appeared she'd had far too much disaster on her plate already to worry about any danger she might have been in from him, and in the end he had proved to be a God-send. Without his help, she would never have been able to get herself and William out of the library with no one the wiser. She'd even begun to trust him a little—until he'd proven himself to be as untrustworthy as most men with his unwanted kiss. Still, she hoped, no, prayed, he had kept to his part of the bargain. Her knowledge of him was of the slightest, but still he had struck her as a man who kept his word, so she rather thought he would. If asked, she meant to say only that she had given William his congé and then he had left the premises (which had the virtue of being absolutely true). If an accident had befallen him after that—say, he'd fallen and hit his head— well, she was very sorry for it, of course, but it had nothing to do with her.

With any luck, that story might just see her through.

As luck—bad luck—would have it, Twindle was in Beth's bedchamber as Beth slipped inside the door and quietly closed it behind her. The light from the fire in the hearth and the flickering candles in the sconces on the wall revealed her clearly just as soon as Beth turned around. Tall and spare, clad in austere black bombazine, with a narrow, deeply lined face and silver hair brushed up into a severe bun, Twindle had been first nursemaid, then governess, and finally, as they grew up, companion to her and Claire, and the elderly woman was fiercely devoted to the pair of them, and their eldest sister, Gabby, too. But she was also straitlaced and rather lacking in humor, and completely rigid in her notions of what was and was not proper behavior for an unmarried young lady. Beth was quite certain that if the complete tale of her evening's misadventures should ever come to Twindle's ears, Twindle's scandalized lecturing would continue nonstop until the day one of them died.

"Miss Beth! Miss Claire sent me up to—" Twindle's voice broke off and she frowned as she took in her erstwhile charge's dishabille. "Child! Have you had some kind of accident?"

"'Twas a—most unfortunate thing," Beth began, groping desperately for a version of events that would not completely horrify Twindle. Since the room was only dimly lit and her arms were once again folded over her chest, hiding the worst of the damage to her gown, she was pretty sure that Twindle was reacting to her tumbledown hair and general air of disorder only. If Twindle had seen her torn gown, her old nursemaid would have dissolved into a paroxysm of questions and exclamations on the spot.

"What was?" Twindle's frown deepened.

Before Beth could decide on how much she could safely say, the door opened behind her, nearly hitting her in the backside. Beth shot an alarmed look over her shoulder even as she had to scoot forward to get out of the way. Of course, she thought wryly, just when she truly needed a few moments of privacy to recover her composure and change her clothes, her room *would* suddenly become a magnet for the household.

"*There* you are," Claire said in relieved accents as she entered and closed the door behind her. Her sapphire blue ball gown rustled as she moved. The sapphire and diamond necklace and earbobs with which she was bedecked glittered in the candlelight. Raven-haired, slender to the point of fragility, and still impossibly beautiful at the ripe age of nearly twenty-five, Claire was the sister she had squabbled with, loved as an equal, and done her best to look out for for as long as she could remember, while Gabby, ten years Beth's elder, had mothered them both. Aside from Gabby's health, which was never robust, Beth rarely worried about her: Gabby had enough quiet fortitude to look out for herself, and was happily married and the mother of a brood of three hopeful children besides. Although Claire was now Duchess of Richmond, rich and respected and married to a man who adored her and whom she truly loved, she still brought forth her protective instincts. Beth had always, always known that she, although not her sister's equal in beauty or, regrettably, sweetness of disposition, was a far tougher character than Claire would ever be.

"Shouldn't you be down in the ballroom?" Beth asked her sister with some exasperation, knowing that the gig was up even as Claire's eyes fixed on her and began to widen. There now would be no explaining this away without revealing some version of the truth. Claire's eyes were too sharp— and so was her knowledge of her sister.

"What in the world happened to you?" As Claire looked Beth over, her lips parted in horror. Behind her, Beth could sense Twindle looking her up and down, too. Beth grimaced and gave it up: dissembling in front of these two who knew her so well just wasn't going to be possible.

She would, at least, honor her bargain to the dishonorable housebreaker and keep his presence secret. The rest, she knew, was going to be dragged out of her one way or another, so she might as well get it over with.

"Oh, all right. If you must have it, I gave William his congé." Her voice was flat. As she spoke, she turned and headed across the large bedchamber with its soft green walls, cream-flocked curtains and bed-clothes, and elegant mahogany furniture toward her much smaller dressing room. The first order of business was to get out of her ruined gown before anyone else came bursting in. "He didn't take it well."

"Never say you've jilted another one?" Twindle, sounding aghast, fell into step behind her. "For heaven's sake, Miss Beth, you must—"

"*Lord Rosen* did this?" Claire broke in. Her voice pitched high with surprise and shock, as she, too, joined the procession. Although skeptical of Beth's intention to actually wed the man, she had not been displeased with Beth's acceptance of William, feeling that he offered her headstrong little sister a reliable ballast on which to build her life.

Clearly, Beth thought, Claire was no judge of character. But then, neither had she been.

They had reached the dressing room now; Twindle was only a few steps behind her, while Claire, whom she could see perfectly well through the tall pier glass at the far end of the room, stood just inside the doorway.

Stopping in front of the mirror, Beth met Claire's eyes through the glass. With her back to the room, her hair spilling over her shoulders and her arms folded over her chest, most of the damage to her gown was yet concealed from them. But with both of them watching her like pigeons after crumbs, there would be no hiding the extent of the disaster.

Beth sighed.

"Yes, William did indeed. Could one of you unfasten my gown, please? I don't want to ring for Patterson."

Patterson was her maid and loyal, but Beth wasn't ready to trust her with this. Servants' gossip was notorious for reaching the ears of the ton. And if she was to come out of this with her reputation, such as it remained to her, intact, no word of what had happened in the library must get out.

"You look like you've been dragged through a hedge backward." Indignation colored Claire's voice as she met Beth's gaze through the glass. "I heard that you and Lord Rosen repaired to the library, alone. Then . . ."

Both Claire and Twindle had stepped forward to unfasten her gown, but it was Claire who reached her first, and she was actually touching the tiny hooks and eyes at the back of Beth's gown as her voice trailed off. Through the mirror, Beth watched her sister's eyes widen again as she realized the state the garment was in.

"Your gown is ripped. Ruined, in fact." Claire's fingers ran disbelievingly over the frayed edges of the delicate material, and she took in the destruction visible at the back of the gown by sight and touch before meeting Beth's eyes through the mirror again. "Did Rosen *attack* you?"

Horror was writ large in Claire's face and voice, and Beth was reminded of the nightmare of a previous marriage Claire had endured before wedding Hugh. Her sister had gone paper white, with a strained look around her eyes and mouth that made Beth's stomach tighten. Claire had never fully shared the details of her years-long ordeal, but knowing her sister as she did, Beth felt certain that violence had played a large part in it.

"William didn't actually harm me," she hastened to say. "At least, he didn't—oh, in the end, all it really amounts to is a torn dress. Could you undo the waist, please? I can slip right out of the rest."

There was no point in trying to conceal the ruination of her bodice any longer; Claire was clearly beginning to realize the extent of the damage for herself, and Twindle, bug-eyed, was crowding in right behind her. Giving it up, Beth unlocked her arms from across her chest and pulled her tangle of hair to the front so that the few fastenings on her gown that were still intact were more readily accessible.

"Dear Lord," Claire breathed, her gaze sliding over the tatters of Beth's gown through the mirror. "The *scum*."

"Sit down, Miss Claire." Twindle took charge, pushing the small slipper chair beside the mirror toward Claire as every last bit of color leached from Claire's face. "And you, Miss Beth, hold still." Nudging Claire aside, Twindle started undoing the hooks at the back of Beth's gown herself while Claire obediently sat, her face now white as chalk. That Twindle was almost as horrified as Claire was evident from what she didn't say: in anything less than the direst of straits, Twindle inevitably scolded until the victim was tempted to clap her hands over her ears and repent in sheer self-defense.

But Twindle went to work on the fastenings without another word.

"Tell me the whole," Claire ordered from her perch on the chair. A glance in the mirror told Beth that her sister's eyes burned, and her expression was grim. Another glance showed that Twindle's mouth was a thin, straight line.

Beth sighed. For these two, under the circumstances, nothing would serve but the truth. Or, at least, most of the truth.

"After I told William that I feared we would not suit, he said that I *would* marry him, whether I wished to or not. He ripped my dress, then threw me down and tried to ravish me, on the theory that if he ruined me I would have no choice but to become his wife."

"The *bastard*," Claire breathed. Beth's eyes widened at that. Over the course of a lifetime spent together, she could count on the fingers of one hand the number of times she had heard Claire swear.

Twindle snorted derisively. "Clearly he doesn't know you, Miss Beth. The devil himself couldn't make you do what you don't wish to do, and never could."

"He should be *beaten*," Claire said. "Or brought up before a magistrate. Or at the very least be banned from decent society. When I tell Hugh . . ."

"No, you mustn't." Beth rounded urgently on her sister just as Twindle finished unhooking the last of the hooks and eyes that had, until then, held the ruins of her gown together. The gown sagged forward and she shrugged it down toward her feet with an accustomed wriggle. "Don't you see, you mustn't tell Hugh. You mustn't tell anyone. Either of you."

"He *attacked* you." Claire spoke through clenched teeth. "He cannot be allowed to just—"

"If word of this gets out I'll be ruined," Beth said. "You know as well as I do that my credit isn't good enough to survive the kind of scandal this will bring down upon us."

"We can't just let him get away with—"

"He won't be getting away with it." Beth interrupted Claire fiercely even as she stepped out of the puddle of gold silk that was the ruined dress and kicked it aside. "He will have lost. I won't marry him, and I won't be ruined, either. We must just pretend that I simply gave him his congé and he accepted it like the gentleman he decidedly isn't."

Their eyes met. A new emotion— fear?—darkened Claire's.

"He did not . . . ?" Claire trailed off

delicately, but her eyes held Beth's and her meaning was impossible to mistake: had the attack succeeded to the point where she had been sexually violated? Beth shook her head even as Twindle finished untying the tapes of her petticoat and looked up to catch the answer.

"I told you, the only thing he truly harmed was my gown." As the petticoat dropped around her ankles, Beth stepped out of that garment, too. "Though not for want of effort, mind."

"Thank goodness," Claire said.

"Hold *still,* Miss Beth." Twindle was now working on the strings of Beth's stays. Under her breath Twindle added starkly, "Boiling in oil is too good."

That clearly was meant to apply to William.

"So how did you get away?" Claire asked.

"I hit him over the head with a poker." There was a wealth of satisfaction in Beth's voice. The stays dropped away, and she stripped off the shredded chemise with a feeling of relief. The ruined clothes were far too vivid a reminder of how terrifyingly close she had come to a hideous fate.

"Here, Miss Beth." Twindle handed Beth

her pale blue wrapper, and she shrugged into it.

"You hit him . . ." Claire's voice seemed to fail. Tying the wrapper's belt around her waist, Beth turned to face her sister. Claire's eyes were dark and she was white as hair powder. Then her expression brightened, and a smile curved her mouth as color flooded back into her cheeks. "Good for you, Bethie. I hope you hit him *hard*."

Beth grinned. "I did."

"Never say you killed the man, Miss Beth?" It was clear from Twindle's reproving tone that she considered it a real possibility, and was concerned more about the breach of ladylike behavior aspect of it than the prospect of William's death.

"No." Beth shook her head. "I only hit him hard enough to knock him unconscious. I thought at first I might have killed him, but, as it turned out, I didn't."

There was the faintest note of regret to that.

"What a shame." Claire echoed her sentiments exactly. Then her brow knit with concern. "So am I to understand that Lord Rosen is still lying unconscious in my house somewhere?"

Here was the tricky part.

"Not at all." Although her response was airy in tone, Beth's mind was racing. Lying was not something she did well, and lying to Claire, who knew her so well, was especially difficult even at the best of times, which this was not. Despite the brave front she was putting on, she was still a little shivery, still a little shaky, still not quite herself in the aftermath of all that had happened. The solution, then, was not to lie. Well, at least, not exactly. "He left. By now, I would imagine, he is back at home bemoaning his cracked head."

There. Every word she had uttered was true.

"'Tis a sad crush downstairs." Claire's frown deepened and she looked at Beth with growing worry. "He is certain to have been seen on his way out, even if he didn't speak to anyone. Was it possible to tell . . . ?"

"His head was bleeding." Beth's tone was cheerful as she found herself on solid conversational ground once more. In the interests of making it more difficult for Claire to read any wayward quirks of expression, she reached for the brush on her nearby dressing table and then turned toward the mirror again, presenting her sister with her back as she began to tease the knots from her hair. "But only a little. Nothing that one would immediately notice."

"We're up to our teeth in it for sure," Twindle put in with gloomy conviction, taking the brush out of Beth's hand with a *tcch* of disgust and applying it to her tumbled hair with considerably more vigor than Beth had used. "With Lord Rosen's fair coloring, a bleeding pate is not likely to have escaped attention."

"I feel quite certain he wasn't seen." Beth winced as Twindle found a particularly stubborn tangle and, grasping the hair just above the knot on the provably incorrect theory that doing so would mitigate the pain, determinedly brushed it out.

"How can you be so sure?" Claire was staring hard at Beth as if she was beginning to suspect that there was more to the tale than she was being told. "He may even have gone straight to his mother, in which case we are in the suds. She's looking for him right at this very moment, you know. And for you, too, because he left the ballroom in your company. She was alarmed enough to seek me out to tell me that neither of you was anywhere to be found, which is what brought me up here in search of you in the first place. If Lord Rosen spoke to her before departing, she will now know the whole. And believe me, that stiff-rumped old busybody will have no compunction at all in blackening your name to anyone within hearing distance."

"But Claire, don't you see, by blackening my name, she blackens her son's, and by extension her own as well." Beth took the brush from Twindle, whose vigor at smoothing tangles was making her eyes water, and proceeded to go about the task of restoring her hair to its normal order herself. Besides, even through the mirror, Claire's probing gaze was making her uncomfortable, and watching the brush's progress gave her an excuse not to look at her sister. "She won't do that."

"She's an old witch," Claire said. "I put nothing past her."

A peek at her sister showed Beth that Claire was frowning again.

"Believe me, she'll consider William well rid of me."

"Yes." Even as she acknowledged the

truth of that, Claire continued to frown. Her tone turned thoughtful. "Still, someone needs to tell Lady Rosen that the engagement is broken, and her son is gone, before she sets the household on its ear." Claire caught Beth's eyes through the mirror, and her frown deepened as Beth smiled wickedly at her. Claire held her gaze for a moment, then sighed. "You think that somebody would be me, I suppose."

"You *are* the Duchess of Richmond," Beth responded in what was obvious agreement. "Quite a grand personage, Claire. You must just overawe her with one of your icy stares."

Claire snorted. "Yes, and I must just become the next Queen of England, too."

"She'll likely fall on your neck in thanksgiving," Beth continued encouragingly. "She feels William can do far better than me."

"She'll be as unpleasant as she can hold together, and you know it." Claire pulled a face. "And as for her son doing better, well, she's out there: he never will."

"'Tis we who are well rid of him," Twindle said, taking the brush from Beth and once again applying it with a ferocity that made Beth wince. "Any man who would use you so before marriage would be a monster after it."

Beth shuddered inwardly as the truth of that went home. She was still conscious of a lingering warmth in her cheek where William had struck her. Had she been foolish enough to actually wed him . . .

"Exactly," Claire said. "I admit to being sadly deceived about Lord Rosen's character, and I am only thankful that we found out the truth in time. Now you must just have a bath and go to bed, and leave it to me to deal with Lady Rosen."

Claire's usually tranquil expression was a study in resolve, and Beth had no doubt that Lady Rosen would be vanquished in the most diplomatic way possible, since Claire, unlike herself, was capable of being tactful even while laboring under the most extreme emotions. But for Claire, who disliked confrontation above all things, to be so willing to go to William's mother as the bearer of bad tidings, was a testament to sisterly love, and Beth knew it. She smiled at Claire through the mirror.

"Thank you," she said, then added with a twinkle in her eyes, "Clarabelle."

From earliest childhood Beth had called her sister that—a cow name, as Claire termed it—to tease her, and from earliest childhood Claire had hated the nickname with a passion. Once upon a time, it had been an open invitation to fisticuffs. But the grown-up Claire merely narrowed her eyes at her little sister warningly.

"Careful," she said. "Or I—"

A brisk knock on the bedroom door interrupted. Beth, Claire, and Twindle jumped and exchanged alarmed glances. Even as Twindle moved with uncharacteristic speed to deal with whoever was there, the sound of the door opening reached them.

Chapter Five

"BETH?" A VOICE CALLED.

Aunt Augusta. Grimacing, Beth exchanged looks of alarm with Claire. Not that she wasn't extremely fond of her aunt, because she was. When the three Banning sisters had first come to London, short on money and reputation and knowing no one in Polite Society, their deceased father's widowed, childless sister, Augusta, Lady Salcombe, had agreed to take them under her wing. Now that Gabby and Claire were happily married to wealthy, prominent men and Beth was living with Claire in town, they no longer needed her help. But as the daughters of a father whose shocking behavior and multiple marriages—Gabby, Claire, and Beth each had a different mother—had nearly put them beyond the social pale from the beginning, the three of them were still sometimes looked at askance by society's highest sticklers.

Which is where Aunt Augusta's sterling reputation came in. She moved in the highest circles, was known and respected by all, and was bosom bows with Lady Jersey and several of the other patronesses of Almack's besides. Without her to stand beside them through the various scandals they had tumbled into on their own accord, many of London's best drawing rooms would have been closed to them by now, Beth knew.

"What, pray, are you doing up here?" Aunt Augusta demanded as, with Twindle just visible behind her, she appeared in the dressing room doorway. At nearly six feet tall, with a broad-shouldered, mannish build, she made the small dressing room seem suddenly far too crowded. Her mauve silk gown, fashioned in the tight-bodiced, full-skirted style that had been all the crack perhaps a generation before, added to the impression she gave of taking up far more than her fair share of space. Although she was upward of sixty now, with iron gray hair wound round her head in a coronet of braids, her skin was smooth and unwrinkled, pale as fine china, and, as she would be the first to confess, constituted her one claim to beauty. But her square jaw, thin lips, and piercing gaze gave her an intimidating aspect that, the sisters had come to realize, was largely misleading. Beneath her stern exterior and tart manner, Aunt Augusta had the kindest of hearts.

Now she paused with one hand on the doorjamb, her gaze sweeping past Claire to fix with disapprobation on Beth.

"There is a rumor flying around the ballroom that you, miss, fearing that Lady Rosen will oppose a marriage to her son, have fled to Scotland with Lord Rosen."

"There is talk of an elopement?" Claire asked with horror, while Beth had to smile. It was so far from the truth as to be almost ludicrous. Not that Aunt Augusta, who had known about and approved of her acceptance of William's suit, was likely to find the situation in the least amusing once she learned the whole of it.

"As you can see, Aunt Augusta, it's no such thing," she said virtuously. "I am right here."

Aunt Augusta frowned at her. "I see nothing to smile about. Your reputation won't bear a great deal more gossip, my girl. I should keep that in mind, were I you."

Beth did her best to swallow the smile. Poor Aunt Augusta had been plagued by the three of them to the point where it was surprising that she was even willing to acknowledge them as relatives, much less stand their friend. But Aunt Augusta was a great believer in blood being thicker than water, and she was grudgingly fond of her wayward nieces besides.

"You're right, of course," she said. But while her tone was suitably meek, her smile must have lingered, because Aunt Augusta, who was nobody's fool, eyed her frostily.

"What's being said?" Claire asked. It was a welcome distraction. Aunt Augusta's gaze swung toward her.

"Apparently Lord Rosen told several

people that his and Miss Sauce-mouth here's engagement is to be announced to-night, which, as I have informed those who were impertinent enough to ask me, comes as a surprise to me. And then, as word of the impending happy news spread, people began to notice that both Lord Rosen and Beth had disappeared from the ballroom. When Lady Rosen started looking for her son and became clearly upset when she did not find him, the gossip took wing. Gabby is in the library with her right now, trying to keep her calm while the pair of you are located." Aunt Augusta's brows snapped together as she looked Beth up and down. "I take it there is a reason why you are up here in your wrapper with your hair around your shoulders, child, in the midst of the biggest ball of the Season?" Her gaze slid to Claire. "And why are you, the hostess of that ball, sitting in her dressing room chatting to her?"

"Miss Claire was looking for her sister," Twindle said, saving her favorite charge from having to lie.

"My dress ripped," Beth told her aunt. "I came upstairs to change."

Once again, it had the advantage of

being the absolute truth. As far as she was concerned, there was no need to acquaint Aunt Augusta with the details of exactly what had transpired between herself and William. The fewer people who knew the whole sordid story, the less chance it had of leaking out, and, anyway, Aunt Augusta was going to be upset enough when told of her broken engagement. There was no need to add details that would make her aunt go practically apoplectic. Though most of her anger would be directed at William, Beth knew that if the truth came out, she personally would be listening to lectures for years to come.

Neither Claire nor Twindle said anything to contradict her.

"So where is Lord Rosen?" Aunt Augusta asked, glancing around as if he might be concealed behind the washstand or the tall mahogany wardrobe.

Beth sighed, knowing that the time for confession was fast approaching.

"At home, I expect."

Aunt Augusta stiffened. Her eyes, which were focused on Beth's face, narrowed. Her lips tightened. Her complexion reddened. From the corner of her eye, Beth watched Claire wince in anticipation of the question they both knew was coming.

"I may be in my dotage, but I'm not quite a simpleton yet," Aunt Augusta said, her eyes holding Beth's. "You've thrown him over, haven't you?"

Beth braced herself. "We decided we should not suit."

"I knew it, I knew it! I knew we should not get through this Season without another horrid scandal. First Gabby sets the ton on its ear by falling in love with Nick, whom the entire world thought was your brother. Then we had scarcely recovered from that when you, Claire—well, you know perfectly well what you did, and just because dear Richmond married you at the end of it does not mean that people do not remember. The following Season there was still talk, but it was dying down, and when Beth got herself engaged to that nice boy Charles Amperman I thought we were set to come about at last." Her gaze, which had been briefly excoriating Claire, swung back to fix accusingly on Beth. "And then what did you do? What did you do? You cried off when you were practically in the church! And last year, you threw over Kirkby! Kirkby, who could look as high as he chose for a bride and yet chose you! And now—to jilt Rosen, of all people! A belted earl, with twenty thousand pounds a year. You must be *mad*."

"Beth may marry where she chooses." Claire rose to her feet in her sister's defense and faced their aunt with a dignity that, Beth thought, did her new station in life proud. "A title and fortune mean little when the man possessing them does not also possess your heart."

"Twaddle," Aunt Augusta snapped. "A title and a fortune mean a great deal as far as choosing a husband goes. Do you expect Beth to live with you for the rest of her life? Or with Gabby? Or to shuttle back and forth betwixt and between the pair of you?" Her gaze shifted to Beth again. "Is that what you want, miss? To be forever dependent on your sisters' charity, with no real home or family to call your own?"

"Aunt!" Claire said in outrage. Then, to Beth, "You know that you—"

"I know." Beth acknowledged with a nod what she knew would be Claire's disavowal of any charity, and a continuing pledge of a home with her or Gabby for the rest of her life if she chose.

"Because if you keep whistling suitors down the wind, that's exactly how you are going to end." Aunt Augusta glared at Beth. "And, believe me, being alone in your later years is no treat. A woman needs a family of her own."

Conviction born of experience colored Aunt Augusta's voice. Beth knew that before she and her sisters had appeared in her life, their aunt, though wealthy and respected, had been lonely. And she knew, too, that Aunt Augusta was right: she did want a home and family of her own.

The sad truth was, she just didn't want the one ingredient that was necessary to make that happen: a husband.

The thought of having to endure such brutality as William had visited on her for the rest of her life made her go cold all over. Once a female was wed, she was to all intents and purposes in bondage to her husband. Whether he was kind or cruel, it made no difference: there was no help for her anywhere.

"The key is to find the *right* husband."

Claire answered Beth's thoughts with un-canny accuracy. "The rest will follow."

Claire said that bravely, although Beth knew that her sister's failure to conceive the children she and her husband longed for was a growing dark spot in her other-wise bright existence. But her marriage was happy, as was Gabby's. They clearly demonstrated that all husbands did not turn into ogres once the vows were irrevo-cably said.

William's behavior tonight, as well as their own father's appalling treatment of his wives and daughters and Claire's first hus-band's cruelty, was not the fate of all, or even most women, and she knew that, at least with her head. Her heart, however, remained firmly unconvinced.

If truth were told, the idea of being sub-ject to a man, any man, irrevocably and forever, filled her with nothing short of dread.

"William was not the right man." Claire seemed to read her thoughts once again.

"Well, hoity-toity," Aunt Augusta sniffed. "That's three of the Marriage Mart's finest, then, that do not suit her ladyship here. Let me remind you, miss, that there are scores of eager young ladies out there all too willing to snap up your discards." She glared at Beth again. "And now you've got a new scandal-broth brewing besides. If you wish to have any reputation left to you—and, not incidentally, to spare the rest of us from having to hang down our heads whenever we appear in Society—you need to do your possible to salvage this debacle before word of it flies around the ton, which it will do tomorrow. Praise God there has been no official announcement of your engagement! I will put it about, quietly, that it was all a hum: Lord Rosen never actually came up to scratch. You, Beth, will cast down your eyes and say something along the lines of 'modesty'"—and here Aunt Augusta snorted expressively—"'forbids me to answer' if anyone has the temerity to ask you about Lord Rosen. You, Claire, will follow my lead: Lord Rosen never actually popped the question at all. There may be a few snickers at your expense, my girl, and some gossip along the lines of not counting chickens before they are hatched, but perhaps the worst of the scandal may then be avoided, and Beth may survive to become engaged another day."

Beth and Claire exchanged glances. It was clear to Beth that Claire was thinking the same thing she was: Aunt Augusta, while knowing only a fraction of the truth, had nevertheless hit on the best possible solution to bring them all about. The only thing missing from the scenario was William's and his family's cooperation, and she had little doubt that Lady Rosen, heartened by the news that Beth was not to become part of their family, would embrace the opportunity to keep gossip at bay.

There was, however, still one small problem.

"William sent notice of the engagement to the newspapers," Beth said in a small voice. "It will in all likelihood appear in tomorrow's editions."

Her aunt and sister stared at her, momentarily flummoxed.

"Of course I should have known we were not going to come about so easily." Aunt Augusta glared at Beth again. "Well. I am growing too old for this. You gels will be the death of me yet, mark my words."

"It isn't her fault," Claire said loyally. "We must just recall the notice at once."

"It is in all likelihood too late." Beth cast

a quick, hunted look at the clock on the mantel. "It's nearly midnight."

Claire's lips firmed with determination.

"One thing I have learned since becoming Duchess of Richmond"—Claire hurried toward the door as she spoke—"is that with money and position one can accomplish a great deal. Let me see what I can do."

"Why are you just standing there staring after your sister?" Having moved aside to let Claire pass, Aunt Augusta now clapped her hands sharply at Beth, who jumped. "If this is to work, you certainly cannot hide up here. Your absence has already been remarked, and the longer it lasts the louder the gossip will buzz. Twindle, you and I must help Miss Beth dress: she will be reappearing in the ballroom just as quickly as may be."

Reappear in the ballroom, when her knees felt shaky and her stomach had a knot the size of a fist in it, and a dozen growing aches and pains were vying with one another for her notice? But it seemed there was no choice. Between Twindle and Aunt Augusta, she felt like she had been enveloped by a whirlwind. She was pushed, pulled, brushed, pinned, powdered, perfumed, and exclaimed over to within an inch of her life, until, in the span of perhaps ten minutes, she was once again fully dressed, this time in an emerald satin gown that she had planned to wear to the Palmerstons' ball the following week. If the change in her raiment was noticed, as it almost certainly would be, that would be all to the good: she could then casually explain her prolonged absence by saying that she had spilled something on her gown and needed to change it.

"'Tis a good thing you've grown into a beauty." Aunt Augusta's tone made it clear her words were not a compliment as she surveyed her niece from head to toe when all was done. "That makes the world more forgiving. Come, we must go down."

"Here, Miss Beth, keep this about your arms," Twindle whispered, handing her a silk shawl with a significant glance at the aforementioned appendages as Aunt Augusta swept from the dressing room with the clear expectation that Beth would follow. "Bruises are starting to show."

Glancing down at her arms, Beth saw that Twindle was right: small discolorations just above her right elbow marked where William had grabbed her. Lips thinning at the memory, nodding thanks at Twindle, she draped the garment around her elbows and hurried in Aunt Augusta's wake.

Thank goodness I did not marry him. However great the scandal may be, at least I am free of him and every other man.

The knowledge lightened her heart just a little as she made her way down the ornate staircase to the guest-filled first floor in Aunt Augusta's wake.

Graham, Claire's stately butler, hurried toward them as they approached the foot of the stairs. From the worried expression on his usually imperturbable face, it was clear something was afoot. The hall, already warmed by its yellow walls and spectacular Oriental carpet, was bright as day as hundreds of candles blazing in the trio of huge crystal chandeliers overhead joined forces with others in wall sconces and tall silver candelabra in corners. Music and laughter and the scent of food and flowers filled the air. Out of the corner of her eye, Claire could just see the kaleidoscope of color that was the ballroom at the rear of the house. Against a backdrop of scarlet walls and masses of white flowers, gorgeous gowns of every imaginable description swirled and floated like windblown blossoms amongst the more soberly clad gentlemen as the dancers went through their paces.

"Miladies, Lady Rosen is—" Graham began, low-voiced, with the air of someone attempting to deliver an urgent warning. He broke off as the lady in question erupted from the direction of the library, stalking furiously into view with Gabby— slender and elegant in lavender silk, her chestnut hair piled high atop her head and her creamy neck and ears glittering with diamonds—following grim-faced behind. Gabby, with the children, was visiting for an indeterminate number of weeks, her husband, Nick, having had business abroad.

"We just must continue to trust that the gossip is not true." Gabby sounded as if her patience was being sorely tried. "Although I must point out that, if it were, the fault certainly could not be laid at my sister's door. Your son is a grown man, after all."

"One who has been cozened shamefully!"

Lady Rosen's riposte was sharp. Then, as she spied Beth, who was still standing on one of the lower steps with a hand on the elaborately carved banister, Lady Rosen stopped dead. "Hah!"

"Thank goodness," Gabby murmured as she discovered Beth in turn.

"I knew it! I knew he wouldn't have eloped with you." Relief combined with venom in Lady Rosen's voice. Dressed in magenta lace with a trio of plumes nodding in her upswept gray hair, William's mother resembled him in both build and coloring. Recovering, bosom swelling, she came toward Beth like a ship in full sail. "He, at least, is not so lost to all sense of propriety as to participate in anything so repugnant. I am not surprised you could not persuade him to it."

Beth's chin came up. "I never attempted to do so."

"Have Lady Rosen's carriage brought round," Gabby directed Graham quietly. Gabby's lips were tight and her gray eyes glinted with anger. Beth could tell that she was having a difficult time keeping a civil tongue in her head.

"Her Grace the Duchess has already

instructed me to do so." Graham slid back out of the way as Beth, her back poker straight now, stepped down into the hall beside Aunt Augusta, her eyes narrowing as she met Lady Rosen's accusing gaze full on.

"Where, pray, is my son?" Lady Rosen's eyes were fierce.

"William has gone home," Beth replied, pardonably proud of how cool her voice stayed. "It will no doubt comfort you when I tell you that we decided we should not suit."

"What?" A look of relief came over Lady Rosen's round face. "Thank heavens he came to his senses at last. I knew William could not be such a fool as to ally himself with one such as you."

Beth watched Gabby's eyes flash. Bright flags of color appeared in her pale cheeks. With the best will in the world for it not to happen, her own temper began to heat. Beside her, Aunt Augusta stiffened, drawing herself up to her full, formidable height.

"Lord Rosen is certainly to be admired for realizing in time that Beth is far too good for him." Gabby's reply was perfectly polite, with the tone of one agreeing with a previous statement. Her eyes, however, blazed.

Lady Rosen reddened alarmingly. Beth smiled at Gabby.

"You don't have the sense of a goat, Frannie, and never did." Taking full advantage of her superior height, Aunt Augusta glared down her nose at the much shorter Lady Rosen. "But that is neither here nor there, now that, thankfully, there is no question of our families being united by marriage."

Lady Rosen opened her mouth to give voice to what, judging from her expression, was certain to be a very pithy reply, but before she could say anything Claire swept into view, very much the grande dame with her beautiful head held high and her expensive skirts rustling, dragging her husband with her. In the face of finding herself the object of the Duchess of Richmond's snapping eyes and the Duke's intimidating frown, Lady Rosen bit back whatever she had been going to say. At thirty-four, Hugh, Duke of Richmond, was one of the most powerful men in the kingdom. Not even Lady Rosen's current spleen was enough to make her eager to incur his displeasure.

"I could hear the lot of you clear in the

supper room," Claire scolded in a hushed voice when she was close enough. Uncoupling herself from her tall, handsome husband, she thrust him at Beth. "Clearly it benefits none of us to make family matters common knowledge. Hugh, take Beth into the ballroom and dance with her, if you please."

"Your Grace, Lady Rosen's carriage is at the door," Graham murmured in response to a signal from a footman who had just hurried up the stairs from the ground floor.

"If you will accord me a few minutes of your time first, I promise I will not keep you from your carriage long," Claire said to Lady Rosen, who gave her a long, assessing look before acceding with an ungracious nod.

Her brother-in-law's gray eyes met Beth's. With Lady Rosen's attention focused on Claire, he gave Beth a quick, commiserating smile even as he offered her his arm.

"We've been given our marching orders, it seems," he said, low-voiced. "If you'll do me the honor?"

"Go on, Beth. Gabby and Aunt Augusta and I will sort this out," Claire promised. "You must just laugh and dance and appear as carefree as you can. Hugh, take care of her."

Understanding the role she needed to play if scandal was to be avoided, Beth tucked her hand in Hugh's arm and smiled back at him as they walked toward the ballroom, although the smile required considerable effort. He gave her hand an avuncular pat, then tugged one of the long red curls that cascaded over her right shoulder in the style that she habitually chose for evening, having learned over the years that there was no hiding her bright mane, and, thus, it was better to flaunt it.

"And here I was thinking Waterloo was dangerous," he murmured for her ears alone as they crossed the threshold into the ballroom and all eyes immediately turned in their direction. "If we'd just had the wisdom to dispatch our ladies to deal with him, Napoleon would have run screaming from the field before a shot was fired."

Beth laughed.

After that, smiling got easier. She was really very fond of Hugh, who treated her exactly like the little sister he'd never had and was amazingly good to Claire, and that helped her give an impression of ease as he bore her onto the floor and swung her into the steps of the dance.

Head held high, smiling brilliantly, pirouetting in her brother-in-law's arms as if she had not a care in the world, she set herself to facing the gossips down. By the time she went down to supper on the arm of Viscount Newby, with Claire dancing and Aunt Augusta gossiping on the sidelines and Gabby already in the supper room, she was fairly confident that they would be able to soldier through.

Chapter Six

THOUGH NEIL HUSBANDED IT carefully, Rosen's money disappeared like water in a desert. Three days after Neil had helped himself to it, he was down to his last few shillings. Leaving London was not an option: as he knew from recent experience, the continent was not far enough, and limited funds made next to impossible the kind of far-flung flight that would be necessary to preserve his life for any length of time. Anyway, running would provide only a short-term solution. London was where the heart of the problem lay, and London was where he needed to stay until the situation was resolved. The difficulty was, he could not stay in any one place for longer than was needed to grab a few hours of sleep, nor could he turn to any of his contacts in the capital or repair to any of his usual haunts. Although he had lost Clapham for the time being, he did not delude himself that the dogs had been called off and Clapham had given up and gone on his way. No, his fellow assassin was at present hunting him with all the skills he had acquired over the course of his very successful working life, along with the fervor of a strong personal animosity besides, and the only thing that was keeping Neil out of his hands was that he possessed the very same skills honed to a greater degree, plus the cunning of a predator now turned prey. People almost always returned to familiar places sooner or later. He knew that, and so did Clapham. Ergo, almost every person and place he might have turned to for help was denied to him.

Neil was also aware that it was quite possible, nay, likely, that there were others searching for him as well. Those who would order his death would be unlikely to rely solely on a single team of assassins.

They would send out multiple tools, who would do whatever was required to get the job done. An attack could occur anywhere, at any time. He was acutely aware that a gunshot or a thrown knife or any of countless other stealth techniques could do for him in an instant. He could die right now, or five minutes from now, or five hours or five days from now, with no warning whatsoever.

Which was a cheering thought indeed.

The hard truth was that, once set in motion, this kind of death sentence was both immutable and, ultimately, all but inescapable.

Unless he could outwit them, outrun them, or outkill them, the sad fact of the matter was that he was not long for this world.

To worsen the situation, he had a lowering presentiment that, if they succeeded in killing him, heaven was past praying for. He was going straight to hell. And since that idea didn't appeal, the only real solution to his problem was, simply, stay alive.

Which he was trying his best to do.

The best option he could come up with given his limited choices boiled down to cutting out the eye of the beast that sought him. Only a very few knew of his exist-ence, and only one of those knew enough about him to find him if he chose to go to earth. Not by happenstance, that was the man at the top of his particular food chain, one of the last who would have had to sign off on the order to eliminate him. By killing that man, he hoped to save himself.

And never mind that he had once, a very long time ago, counted that man as a friend.

The deed would have been done already were it not for a certain fiery-haired chit whose interference had ended most disas-trously. Since then, since Neil's escape from Clapham, his quarry had gone on alert. The man remained in London, at the heart of the organization as always, but he was be-ing careful, surrounding himself with guards, taking every precaution.

He knew better than anyone just how dangerous Neil, his former prized weapon, could be.

What he did not know was that Neil had discovered a weakness in his defenses, an Achilles' heel, as it were.

The taste of betrayal had long since

ceased to be bitter in Neil's mouth. As he had learned so many years ago that it seemed like another lifetime, it was simply the way the world worked. He expected nothing more.

The sad truth of his existence was, one killed, or one died.

"Come along, then, Florimond."

Neil heard her voice before he actually saw her, which wasn't wonderful considering that he was lurking concealed behind a nearly impenetrable thicket of thorny hollies that bordered the west edge of the ornamental dairy in Green Park. His horse—well, it was his horse now, as he had stolen it the night before—awaited him near the rarely used north entrance, tied to a tree.

"Hello, sweetheart," he said softly, way too softly for anyone save himself to hear. He had timed his arrival nicely, and had been waiting perhaps only five minutes. It was a beautiful morning, bright and breezy, with the promise of a warm afternoon to follow. Birds twittered cheerily all around him. Butterflies flitted. Insects buzzed. Abundant trees and bushes clothed in the fresh new green of spring added to the feeling that he had stumbled upon a small island of country right in the midst of town. The musky smell tainting the fragrant air—even ornamental dairy farms had an unmistakable aroma—served to underline the rural comparison. The magnificent outline of Devonshire House—a veritable palace—rising on the eastern horizon, its towers and turrets just visible from where he stood, provided a stark contrast to the bucolic surroundings. It marked the Clarges Street entrance that he had thought she was almost certain to use. At the realization that he had guessed right, he felt a quick rush of satisfaction.

Once again, his instincts had not failed him.

This wasn't the ideal solution, not by a long shot, but it was a workable one. As always, he would do what he needed to do.

Kidnapping was one of the few crimes he had never before committed, and under most circumstances he would have scorned to lower himself to it. But these were not most circumstances. His survival was at stake.

Therefore, kidnapping it was.

A couple of steps took him around

the thicket and brought his quarry into view, although—he was fairly certain—he remained concealed by shadow. The speaker, whose voice he was slightly surprised to realize he had recognized as readily as if it were one he knew well, was Lady Elizabeth, the remark was addressed to a stout, wheaten-coated little terrier that had stopped to sniff a willow trunk, and the tone was impatient. It was early, a few minutes or so past ten, and there were not many others about. Only a pair of unfashionable riders (the truly fashionable patronized Hyde Park, and at a much later hour) cantering away across the lawn and a nursemaid pushing a pram were visible from where he stood. Lady Elizabeth was, as she had told him was her daily custom, clearly out for her morning constitutional in the park. The dog (which would probably bark) and the bored-looking maid following her were impediments to his plan, but only minor ones that could be easily dealt with. The lady herself might prove more problematic, but he had done her a signal service and was reasonably certain that as a result he could persuade her to do what he wished her to do.

Which was, in a word, come with him. Persuading her to do so was so much more efficient than forcing her, although he was prepared to use force if he had to. Lady Elizabeth *Banning*—oh, yes, he had learned her identity during the past three days—was about to repay him for sparing her life by luring her brother-in-law the Duke of Richmond, now one of the directors of England's far-flung spy network and his own long-ago friend, to his death.

Only if Richmond died did he have any reasonable hope of living out his natural life span.

There was indeed, as his mother had once told him, purpose in all things. If he had killed lovely Lady Elizabeth as he should have done, he would not now have this most promising weapon to use in the battle to preserve his own life. He'd already made arrangements to have, on the following morning to give him plenty of time to get his prize safely away from London, a missive delivered to Richmond informing him that his most charming sister-in-law was in his quarry's hands. More instructions, he had promised, would follow. Neil had no doubt at all that he could lure the always heroically inclined Richmond into coming for the chit, and thus to his own death.

Watching as she strolled all unsuspecting along the gravel path toward him, Neil realized that he was feeling more optimistic at that moment than he had in the fortnight or so since he had learned that the organization that had made him what he was had turned on him with a vengeance. Lady Elizabeth, he was certain, was going to prove to be the surprise trump that took the game.

If Muhammad could not go to the mountain, then the mountain would be made to come to Muhammad, as it were. If he could not get to Richmond, then he would get Richmond to come to him.

With his lovely little sister-in-law as bait.

Savoring the thought, Neil waited for Lady Elizabeth to draw closer, and in the meantime enjoyed the view.

"Florimond, you may not stop to sniff every tree and bush and blade of grass in the park," she scolded the dog. "We are *walking.*"

The animal had brought her to a halt once again, and she addressed it with some exasperation. But she tugged only gently on the slender lead that stretched between her and it, and it continued sniffing around the base of the massive oak with impunity.

"Perhaps we should have left him behind, Miss Beth," the maid, a round-faced young woman with dark hair concealed under a mob cap and a sturdy body clad in a light blue dress and apron, said in a slightly wooden tone that told Neil that her own view of the merits of walking the animal was strong despite being dutifully suppressed.

"Oh, Rawlings, you know very well I promised Lady Salcombe I would look after him while Lady Anders is her house guest," Lady Elizabeth said. "Lady Anders breaks into the most dreadful fits of sneezing every time he comes near. And he's a very good dog, aren't you, Florimond? The trouble is that he has very little experience with parks."

"Or carriages, or horses, or children chasing hoops." The maid's voice had a long-suffering edge to it now. "'Tis a very pampered dog, Miss Beth. I doubt he has ever been beyond his own garden before."

"Then it's nice for him that we are broadening his experience. Come *on,* Florimond." Lady Elizabeth tugged on the lead, and the dog reluctantly abandoned the oak to toddle after her.

She regained the gravel foot path while the dog kept to the grass, its gaze now glued to the pair of ducks that flapped noisily overhead. She glanced up, too, and the bright morning sun struck the plethora of curls that cascaded out beneath the straw bonnet framing her face, making them gleam like a profusion of rubies and making her identity impossible to mistake even if he hadn't known from her voice who she was. No other woman of his acquaintance had hair like that.

Slender and graceful, she was clad in pale yellow, some filmy material that floated behind her in the slight breeze, with a matching fichu, and it struck him that she looked like a sunbeam herself, or certainly some bright, shiny creature that did not belong in the same world as the dark and desperate labyrinth he inhabited. Almost he hesitated. But then he remembered that if he didn't find a way to turn the tables on his enemies soon, he would be

dead. And the certainty proved very per-
suasive.

So he stepped out of the shadows onto
the sunlit path, still some distance ahead
of her but visible now if she chanced to
look his way.

But she didn't. At least, not yet. She
was wholly occupied with the uncoopera-
tive dog.

"No, Florimond!" she cried as the ducks
landed with a splash in the nearby pond
and the dog took off like a bullet toward
them, yanking its lead from her hand in
the process. For a moment Lady Elizabeth
stood aghast, looking after the yapping
little dog as it charged toward the ducks,
which floated with magnificent unconcern
in the center of the mirrorlike water. Then
she hiked up her skirts and raced in pursuit, putting a slight smile on his face as
he was treated to yet another view of slender, silk-clad ankles and calves.

As an afterthought, he noted that the
lady ran with the speed and agility of the
boy she most certainly did not resemble.

"Florimond! Florimond, come back
here!" she cried. "Here, Florimond!"

"Miss Beth!" The maid ran clumsily after,

then was sidetracked by the need to catch her mistress's hat as it went sailing, tumbling with the wind as it was whipped from Lady Elizabeth's head and blown toward the cow pasture.

"Florimond!" Lady Elizabeth raced on, her bright hair streaming out like a banner, her skirt bunched around her knees in front and billowing in the breeze behind, legs flashing, truly delectable bosom bouncing.

Thrusting his hands in his pockets and rocking back on his heels, Neil allowed himself to enjoy the sight until a stand of willows blocked his view.

Had she not been extremely fond of Florimond, Beth thought with aggravation, she would have left the little dog to his own devices when he darted toward the pond. She was almost sure he could swim—couldn't all dogs? She had never possessed one of her own, so she couldn't be positive, but she rather thought they could. Therefore, he would almost certainly have come to no harm as long as she made sure to collect him when he gave up his quest. But, not an hour since, the dog had been bathed by Tom footman on Graham's orders as a result of having rolled in something extremely malodorous in the garden when said Tom had taken him out first thing that morning. And since Florimond hated being bathed and made that abundantly clear with a series of howls loud enough to rouse the household, she had no wish to add to his, or Tom's, or anyone else's misery by putting him through the process again, should he decide to jump in the muddy-banked, reed-ringed, algae-infested pond.

"Florimond! Here!" she cried, hiking her skirts to indecent levels as she tried desperately to plant a foot on the trailing lead. The grass was slippery underfoot, and the ground was lamentably uneven. Falling flat on her face was a real possibility. Fortunately, a line of gracefully swaying willows between her and the path blocked the view of most anyone who conceivably might be watching. The riders she'd observed earlier, the nursemaid pushing the pram up over the hill—all those were out of sight. There was a closed carriage stopped on the road that led from the park entrance to the dairy farm, embarrassingly close to her projected path. Except for the horse, though, it appeared deserted. Perhaps the driver, instead of waiting for his passengers, had disembarked for a stroll of his own. In any case, she couldn't worry about it. She had more pressing concerns. Florimond, drat him, was picking up speed.

"Here, Florimond!"

The dog ran on regardless. Beth barely managed to swallow a most unladylike oath. Down in the dumps herself over the tide of gossip that had accompanied her nonengagement, which lurched between the glee of the camp that was sure Rosen had not come up to scratch and the disapproval of the camp that held she had jilted yet another fiancé, she had been profoundly sympathetic to his misery over the bath. Until now. Now she just hoped no one saw her running like a hoyden with her skirts bunched around her knees. As Aunt Augusta had made sure to tell her, her reputation hung by a thread. Much more talk, and she could rest assured that Rosen would be the last eligible suitor she'd be able to bring up to scratch. She would very likely end her days an old maid, living in her sisters' houses, caring for their children. And that, in Aunt Augusta's bluntly expressed view, would serve her just exactly right.

The gossip was certainly unpleasant, Beth had to admit, but she felt Aunt Augusta's view of the situation was too dire. Though some of the highest sticklers might look at her askance, the invitations had not stopped coming, and she still had a number of admirers whose attentions, now that Rosen had, in their view, withdrawn from the lists, were very flattering. The Earl of Cluny, for one, who was considered to be quite a catch, and the very rich Mr. Charles Hayden . . .

"Florimond, no!"

The edge of the pond was now close; it was a matter of seconds only until the dog reached it. He was flying, his little paws barely touching the ground. The ducks, ignoring Florimond's high-pitched threats, swam placidly toward the far bank. Florimond launched himself triumphantly toward the water . . .

And Beth's foot came down solidly on the end of the leash.

"Florimond! Stop!"

This time he did stop, brought down in

midleap by the sudden restraint of the leash. His high-pitched yelps cut off abruptly as he landed with transparent surprise on all fours, then fought to be free. Beth snatched the leash from beneath her foot, hanging on tightly to the leather strap until she reached the miscreant himself. He was practically hopping up and down with displeasure as she scooped him up with a sigh of relief.

"Thank goodness," she said, holding him tight in her arms while Florimond yearned after the ducks and squirmed to be free. "What were you *thinking*? Do you *want* another bath?"

Florimond paid no attention. He was still busily engaged in hurling threats and abuse at the ducks when a man spoke behind her.

"Be you Lady Elizabeth Banning?"

"Yes," Beth replied automatically, and was just turning to see who had so addressed her when something slammed hard into the side of her head. For the briefest of moments she saw stars. Then the world went black, and she crumpled soundlessly toward the ground.

Chapter Seven

IT WAS THE MAID who first alerted Neil to the fact that his plan had gone awry. Clutching Lady Elizabeth's hat, which she had finally managed to retrieve, the woman had hurried past the willows and down the slope and thus out of his sight in pursuit of her mistress. Now that the dog had been blessedly silenced, the morning's peace had been restored. Neil strolled into the middle of the path—the better for Lady Elizabeth to spot him when she resumed her morning's exercise—folded his arms over his chest, and waited with less tension than he had felt in days.

That is, until the maid's raised voice reached his ears.

"Miss Beth! Miss Beth!" The distress in the woman's voice was impossible to mistake. "Lawks, Miss Beth, where be you? Miss Beth!"

Neil frowned. His arms dropped to his sides. He moved, walking toward the pond, where the maid still called.

"Miss Beth! Miss Beth!"

Emerging on the other side of the willow stand, looking down the slope toward the pond, he saw the maid, her mistress's hat still clutched to her breast, running around like a madwoman, charting a rough zigzag course from the edge of the pond to every tree, bush, and tuft of ornamental grass in the vicinity that was large enough to possibly serve as concealment for a person.

What the hell . . . ?

"Are you hiding, Miss Beth? 'Tis not a funny game, if that's what you would be at. Miss Beth!"

In general, Neil was loath to let himself be seen, but in this particular case he realized it did not particularly matter: Richmond would know who he was dealing with as soon as he received Neil's message advising him of his sister-in-law's abduction.

Which should have been taking place just about now. Except he couldn't see the girl.

Anywhere.

"What's to do?" he asked, putting himself in the maid's path. He was unshaven—his razor was with his other belongings in the rented rooms he had been forced to abandon in Paris, and he had not cared to waste the few coins it would have cost him to acquire another—and his clothing was not in the best of conditions, which was not surprising considering that he had only a single change of apparel, acquired in a theft from a whorehouse floor while its owner was happily otherwise occupied, which had alternated with his own clothes since the eventful night a fortnight previously when an assassin had first tried to do away with him in his bed. But he had been the recipient of enough female attention over the years to know that he was generally accounted a very well-looking man indeed, and despite his current state the maid proved no exception. She stopped—she had no choice as he placed himself directly in front of her—and her eyes widened a little on his face. Then she gave him a lightning-fast once-over. Fortunately, there still remained enough of the gentleman in his speech and manner that her instinctive alarm at being addressed by a male stranger in a public place was almost instantly allayed.

"Oh, sir, 'tis my mistress," she gasped in obvious distress. She was flushed and sweating, and her eyes darted frantically around in search of the girl even as she spoke. "She has—she has disappeared, like. It was the dog, see, and . . . and her hat, and . . . and then she ran toward the pond and . . . Oh, sir, what am I to do? She is gone!"

As a result of this disjointed speech, Neil realized that he had been in the right of it. Except for himself and the maid, there was not a soul in sight. No flame-haired chit. No annoyingly loud dog. Only an oblivious cow grazing in its ornamental pasture and, bowling away toward the gate, a closed black carriage.

"Be silent," he said sharply to the maid, who was beginning to wail. As the woman, apparently scared into obedience, swallowed the sound with a gulp, he turned and walked swiftly toward the pond. A cold prickle of unease raced down his spine. Could Lady Elizabeth have fallen in? Was she even now drowning? Without so much as a ripple on the surface of the water, or a sound?

If not, where else could she be?

"Miss Beth swims like a fish." The maid, sniveling now, had followed him and appeared to have divined his thoughts as he stood scanning the murky surface. "Oh, sir, wherever can she be?"

He glanced back at her to find that she was gazing up at him as if she expected him to take charge and find her mistress for her. Again he looked around, taking in every detail of the verdant landscape, with no more success than before. To all appearances, Lady Elizabeth was indeed gone without a trace, and the dog with her.

Impossible.

"Lady Elizabeth!" His voice was far louder than the maid's, much deeper and far more authoritative. It was, in fact, the voice of a man who was accustomed to being instantly obeyed. In this case, it also had the virtue of being known to the one for whose ears it was intended. He had no doubt of an answer—if she was in any condition to make one.

Which she almost certainly had to be. What harm could she have come to in the few minutes she was out of his sight?

The only response came from the ducks: with a great flapping of wings, they took to the sky again, careening over the treetops and out of sight.

After that, silence reigned. Charged silence that was disturbed only by the pant of the maid's breathing and the rustling of the soft spring breeze through the tree-tops.

"Lady Elizabeth! Can you hear me?"

It occurred to him, too late, that by calling out to "Lady Elizabeth" he revealed to the maid that he knew exactly who her mistress was. Not that it mattered, given what he intended, or rather had intended, but caution was as much a part of his nature now as distrust, and he felt the breach of his customary anonymity like a physical pang. However, the maid didn't appear to notice anything amiss. Her face was red as a cock's comb now, and her mouth trembled as her head swung from side to side in a futile visual sweep of the little bowl of ground in which they stood.

"Could she have started for home without you?" Neil asked, without any real expectation that the lady had done so. If that had been the case, she would still be within sight, which she emphatically was not. In any case, to head for home without her maid, or her hat, for that matter, seemed senseless, and whatever else she might be, Lady Elizabeth had certainly struck him as a young woman of sense. Still, he frowned down the road that led past the pond toward the gate—and was just in time to watch as the door of the rapidly retreating carriage swung open. A bundle of some sort hit the ground. Inside the carriage, he caught a blur of rapid movement, a flash of vivid red and soft yellow, before the door was once again firmly closed.

For a brace of seconds he simply stared as his mind processed what he had seen. In the meantime, the carriage bowled through the tall stone gates and turned left onto the busy street beyond.

The red had been the same shade as

Lady Elizabeth's hair. The yellow had been the bright hue of her dress. And the bundle— even as he looked after the carriage, the bundle moved, shook and shed its mantle of gray to reveal a small tan animal—had been the dog.

"Florimond," the maid breathed, sealing the animal's identity for him.

Ye Gods, there was no mistake: for some unknown reason, Lady Elizabeth was inside the carriage.

Even as realization crystallized, he broke into a run, heading for his horse, cursing himself for having left it so far away.

"Sir!" the maid screeched piteously after him. "Sir, please, what shall I do?"

He had forgotten all about her. The dog, hearing her voice, turned its head in her direction, then started trotting their way, apparently none the worse for its experience.

"Wait here," he yelled over his shoulder, it being no part of his plan to have a rescue launched before he could secure the lady for himself. "She will undoubtedly return."

If the maid replied, Neil didn't hear it. He was already topping the slight rise that constituted the horizon at that particular spot and felt no need to respond. His thoughts were in turmoil even as his boots tore up the sod.

The more he replayed the scene in his mind, the more convinced he became that Lady Elizabeth was in that closed carriage, which presented him with two possibilities: either she had entered the conveyance of her own free will, or she had been forced inside. He really knew very little of the lady, of course, but just three days before she had been breaking off an engagement in the most final of manners. It seemed unlikely, therefore, that what he had just witnessed had been a clandestine elopement. The flash of movement he had glimpsed in the carriage had suggested to him there had been some sort of struggle going on inside. And the dog had been wrapped in something, thrown out, and abandoned. Given those facts, then, the most likely explanation for her presence in that carriage was an abduction.

But abducting her was *his* plan, and he had not been involved in any way, shape, or form.

Clearly, someone else had beaten him to the punch. His gut burned at the thought.

The question was, who? And why?

Pondering the possibilities was a waste of time. He knew too little about her life to even begin to speculate. All he knew was that his best hope of survival had just been rudely snatched out of his reach, and he meant to do his possible to get her back again.

Chapter Eight

WITH A PALE CRESCENT MOON floating high above the tallest of its many turrets, Trelawney Castle looked as starkly forbidding as any medieval fortress. Made of age-darkened stone, built perhaps three centuries previously, it was more visible than usual on this clear night because of the faint light glowing through its dozens of narrow, slitted windows. Isolated on a rocky island about a half mile off Tynemouth in the North Sea, the castle was a relic of an earlier time when landowners held on to their properties by might of arms. Besides the protection afforded by the expanse of water separating it from the mainland, it was surrounded on all sides by an immense stone wall complete with ramparts. Its location alone should have meant that visitors were few and far between. On this night, however, a ferry of sorts had been set up and the oarsmen had clearly been busy. Carriages climbed the winding road from the ferry landing up to the castle's massive gates, which were open, and inside the walls the courtyard teemed with activity as the carriages stopped, disgorged their passengers, and returned to the ferry for more. To a man—and they were all men—the guests who clambered down from the carriages hastened inside as soon as they arrived so as not to miss a moment of the promised entertainment. By this time—shortly before eleven p.m.— new arrivals had slowed to a trickle. Only a few passengers were gathered on the mainland dock to await the return of the ferry. A solitary horse and rider trotted along the narrow, rutted road, silvered now by moonlight, that led down to the ferry: a latecomer intent on joining the festivities, Neil had little doubt. In fact, unless he was much mistaken, he had seen the fellow before. The well-padded shape of him, plus the awkward way he bobbed in the saddle, were well-nigh unmistakable.

Viewing the scene from the crest of a wooded rise some distance above the hopeful rider, Neil snapped his spyglass shut. He'd been in place for a good hour or more. It had galled him to have to tarry so long, but with Clapham and his ilk hunting him, caution had to be his byword if he hoped to survive long enough to outwit them. He had needed to watch the road to make sure that no one followed. Now that caution found its reward: a mark whose fat purse he remembered from the inn in Durham, where Neil had ordered up a hasty meal to be eaten in the saddle and the rider had heaved himself down from his mount and pulled out his bulging purse to toss a handful of coins to the ostler who ran up to tend the horse. Up until this point, Neil's journey had been cursed by bad luck. His horse had stumbled and come up lame no sooner than he had left London behind, and he'd had, perforce, to exchange the beast for another. Without sufficient coin to purchase a fresh mount, the transaction (theft) had taken more time than he would have liked, and the new horse itself had proved to be the veriest bone-setter. As a result, the closed carriage with Lady Elizabeth inside was long gone before he had gotten anywhere near it. By dint of discreet questioning of the toll keepers along the Great North Road, various ostlers, and, later, when all indications were that the carriage had turned off toward the sea, certain select others he had encountered, he had managed to track it to its destination. But still he had not been completely certain that the carriage he was following was the one he sought until he beheld Trelawney Castle.

He knew this place. He knew what took place within its walls. Though he did not yet know who was responsible, he knew why they had brought her here.

The knowledge had caused a hard, cold knot of anger to form in his breast.

As a youth, he had witnessed the castle's depravities. He knew what would happen inside those walls, just as soon as the last guest had been admitted and the gates were once again closed. In his current incarnation, even if it had been played out in front of his nose, he would not have felt the slightest flicker of interest in what was occurring—that is, if Lady Elizabeth had not been inside.

But she was. He was as sure of it as it was possible to be given the fact that he had not as yet actually set eyes on her. He had, however, spent nearly thirty-six hours in the saddle tracking her down.

Somewhat to his surprise—it had been years since anyone else's welfare had mattered a whit to him—he found he disliked extremely the idea of the lovely bright warmth of her being subjected to the kind of use the men who frequented this place would make of her. In the days of his youth, the place had been the scene of such orgies and debauchery that it had become legend. Nowadays, as he had learned, on the third Sunday of certain months the so-called Bainbridge Society, a loose collection of scalawags who formed a social circle headed by the Earl of Bainbridge—ranging from the lowest of the low amongst the aristocracy, to certain wealthy Cits, to shadier figures whose identities were never revealed—purchased doxies here. Or, rather, what they were pleased to consider doxies. Most of the females were girls fresh from the country, young and chaste, who had been cozened or stolen into a life of prostitution with no idea what they were in for. Guaranteed virgins all, they brought a premium price amongst this lot, with the fear of the pox running rampant through London as it was. After a few days of vigorous deflowering behind the protective walls of the castle, the men would disburse and the girls would be resold, some to London abbesses for use in brothels, others in France and elsewhere abroad. When they were no longer young and fetching enough to earn their keep in a brothel, their most likely destination would be the streets.

It was a sad end that unfortunately befell many females in these hard times.

Someone had to have been paid, and paid well, to deliver one such as Lady Elizabeth into their hands. The who and why of it he would ascertain later. For now, his mission was to rescue the chit.

Having found what he hoped was the key to the castle, so to speak, in the person of the lone rider, Neil sent his poor excuse for a horse down the wooded slope toward the road. A thick layer of fallen leaves built up over countless autumns was treacherous under the beast's hooves. The animal almost lost its footing half a dozen times, sliding down the hill until he could pull it up. Coupled with the darkness, the new greenery budding throughout the woods was just about dense enough to provide concealment, he judged. And concealment was crucial to his plan: the last thing he wanted was for his mark to see him coming, take it into his head that he was in danger, and ride for it, shouting for help. Admission to the castle was by invitation only. No more than a select few even knew that the club existed, or what use was made of the old fortress by the men who flocked to it on nights such as this. Unfortunately, he did not possess the necessary invitation, and trying to force his way into the heavily guarded island enclave was likely to cause more havoc than he wanted to raise. Better to do the thing quietly, if he could.

When he gained the road, he was, as he had intended, only a short distance behind the solitary rider. Setting his heels to his mount's sides, he quickly caught up, alert and ready in case the man should sense danger and think to set up an out-cry.

"Well met, sir," Neil said, tipping his hat as the bag of bones he bestrode fell in be-side the other horse, a sleek chestnut that bore its rider's considerable weight with ease.

After no more than a startled glance, the rider—middle-aged, with a pronounced paunch and a bulbous nose that was all that was readily discernible of his features beneath his hat—seemed glad enough to see him.

"By jove, you snuck up on me! I thought I was all alone out here. Are you for the castle, too, then? I hear they've some prime articles this go-round."

By his accent, Neil judged him a York-shireman. The voice was thickened by drink and cheerful, no doubt as a result of the amusement he was anticipating when he gained his destination. A wealthy Cit, from all signs.

Neil's lip curled. Rapine as sport had never held any appeal for him, and he felt contempt for those who took pleasure from it. He had occasional needs, and he satisfied them as and when he could, but never with a partner who was less than willing.

"You've an invitation?" he asked.

"Aye, in my bag." The man patted the saddlebag on his right with clear satisfaction. "Are we late, d'ye think?"

"Not too late."

"The ferry takes no passengers after eleven, you know. My horse threw a shoe and I had to wait in Durham for it to be reshod, else I would have been here long since."

"We've time still."

The forest crowded close to the road on Neil's right, and to his left more tall trees marched with the steep slope of the land down to the gulley that culminated in, if he remembered his surroundings correctly, a creek. Though there were many sounds—rustling leaves all around, the distant cry of an owl, the steady clip-clop of the horses' hooves on the hard-packed road, the whisper of flowing water—none was such as to give him pause. The bend of the road that would take them the last three hundred or so yards down to the ferry was just beyond. For the moment, they were totally alone and out of view. The wind had risen, carrying the faint smells of woodsmoke and the sea on it, and the temperature had dropped enough to make him glad of his greatcoat.

"'Tis a cold night for a long ride, I'll be bound. Well, we'll soon be warm enough." From the Cit's lascivious chuckle, there was little doubt of his meaning.

"Indeed."

The moment was at hand. The simplest course of action—kill the disgusting old fool—was obvious. But it was one Neil realized he would be wiser not to take. The hunt for him would be on in earnest now, and leaving dead bodies about was somewhat akin to leaving a trail of bread crumbs for birds. If he killed, word of it would get back to ears he would rather it didn't reach, and then the search would hone in. To kill would be to make himself visible to those who sought him.

With that consideration in mind, the blow Neil dealt the Cit as he crowded his mount close beside his victim's horse was tempered: hard enough to bring instant unconsciousness, but not lethal. With nothing more than a surprised grunt, the man slumped sideways into his grip. After that, it was quick work to haul him down from his horse, and bind and gag him with his own garments. Finally he rolled him, still unconscious, down the slope, which was steep enough to prevent any easy return to the road when consciousness at last came back and he managed to free himself, which Neil anticipated should take the rest of the night and probably most of the next day.

Neil felt a moment of regret about the horse—though not a prime bit of blood, it was far superior to his own nag—but the chance that somebody might recognize it was, he judged, too great. Unsaddling it, he sent the beast running, then quickly rifled through the saddlebags. As he had hoped, besides the invitation, there was a plump purse. Adding its contents to his own, he discarded the purse itself, and tossed down the hill, too, the saddle and saddlebags, still stuffed with the various items of apparel that his victim had brought with him. Given the man's lack of height and immensity of girth, the clothes would be of no use to him. The exception was a black domino, made of fine silk but still far too ordinary to be identified. The garment would probably prove too short for him, but would otherwise serve his purpose admirably by providing a precautionary disguise.

When the Cit was restored to civilization, what had befallen him would be taken to be the work of a robber, or highwayman. Certainly there would be no tie to himself.

Sparing no further thought for his victim, Neil remounted his horse. No more than a few minutes had elapsed, and as he put his heels to the horse's sides he judged he would still be in plenty of time to make the last ferry to Trelawney Castle.

Chapter Nine

WHEN BETH OPENED HER EYES, it was because someone was slopping a cold, dripping rag across her face. The wet iciness
of it shocked her back to groggy awareness.

A middle-aged woman's raw-boned face
swam before her. Inhaling instinctively as
she tried to bring it into focus, Beth was
thankful to discover that she could now
breathe without impediment. The blanket
swathing her face was gone, as was the
gag. A curious smell—sweetish, heavy—
lingered in the air, making her nauseous
as she became aware of it. Of course, she

remembered now: she had been kid-napped. But why, and by whom, she had no idea. She vaguely recalled regaining consciousness in the carriage, kicking the doors furiously when it slowed at a toll booth in hopes of attracting attention, and being kicked into silence in turn, then drugged by a damp, horrid-smelling rag that was pressed to her face every time she stirred thereafter. That was the scent hang-ing in the air now. Upon her identifying it, her stomach churned and her head swam. She wanted to close her eyes again in the worst way, but dared not.

I'm in terrible trouble.

"Where am I?" she asked, blinking as she tried to get her eyes to focus. Coarse gray hair in an untidy bun, blunt, unre-markable features, a black gown of cheap, rough wool all coalesced to give her a fuller picture of the woman sitting on the side of the bed, who was clearly a servant of the lower sort.

The woman glanced at her, rheumy blue eyes engaging in a furtive peek, but vouch-safed no reply. The flickering candlelight that lit the small room didn't help matters as Beth fought to work out the answer to her question for herself. Everything seemed to shimmer when first she looked at it, which she hoped was an effect of the drug rather than the blows to the head she had suffered. How much time had passed since she had last been fully aware of her surroundings she had no way to calculate, but she had vague memories of being forced to drink a cup of broth, and of a midnight stop beside the road in which necessary business had been taken care of. Given that, she felt the time that had elapsed was long rather than short, perhaps as much as a full day. A desperate search would be under way for her by now; she knew that as well as she knew the sun lit the sky. Claire and Gabby would be frantic with fear. The combined resources of Hugh and Nick would be brought to bear, and no stone would be left unturned. They would find her. Of course they would. She must just keep herself safe until then.

If word of what has befallen me gets out, I'll be ruined.

At the moment, given the exigencies of her situation, such a concern seemed almost stupidly unimportant. Her life might very well be at stake. So far she had not been badly hurt, but her captors had shown an alarming willingness to abuse her. As a result, her head ached badly. Her ribs throbbed where the toe of a man's boot had landed in initial response to her kicking the carriage door at the toll booth. She was nauseous and dizzy from the drug they had given her. Her mouth was dry and her voice was weak as a result of being gagged for hours upon end. Her limbs felt weak, too—and were still bound, she discovered as she moved, although differently. At least, though her legs were still tied together at the ankles with what felt like rope—she moved them experimentally, just to test the bonds—her arms were pulled above her head. It took her a second or two to absorb the fact that her bound wrists, like her ankles, were fastened securely to the frame of the mean iron bed on which she lay. It clanked as she moved, but the bonds gave no sign of loosening. In other words, nothing substantive had changed: she was still, unbelievably, a prisoner.

Cold fear slid through her veins.

"Who are you?" she tried again, pulling

away from the woman's ministrations. This brought the pale blue eyes up once more.

"Never you mind who I be." The woman's accent was as coarse as her face. The rag was withdrawn and plopped down in a white crockery bowl half full of water, which rested on a spindly table beside the bed. Her reddened hands lifted the rag again and squeezed water from it with a practiced move. "You'd best be saving your worries for yourself, ducks. They'll be coming for ye soon enough."

"Who—who will be coming for me?"

Despite her best efforts at maintaining her composure, Beth could not quite keep her voice from cracking. Wherever she was—and her quick survey had told her only that she was housed in a tiny, dungeonlike room with stone walls, a beamed ceiling, a small slit of a window that no human being could possibly fit through and that revealed what seemed to be an impenetrably black night beyond—her situation was bad. Terrifying, in fact.

"Them that's in charge."

The slopping rag slid across her neck, then along her shoulders and over her décolletage in quick, practiced strokes that were as impersonal as if she were no more than a china doll. A remnant of damp chill about her person made Beth think that perhaps she had been given a sponge bath all over. A horrified glance down at herself brought the reassuring knowledge that she was still fully clothed. In fact, she was still wearing the lemon-colored morning gown in which she had been abducted. It was sadly crushed now and dirty, and her stockings felt loose about her legs, as if her garters were on the verge of giving up their grip, but nothing indecent met her gaze and she had no sense that any outrage had been committed upon her person while she had been unaware. Indeed, she was still wearing both shoes.

"Here, lift your head."

Beth complied automatically, to find that the woman had replaced the rag with a brush, which she proceeded to drag through the masses of hair that tumbled about Beth's face.

"What do you mean, them that's in charge? In charge of what?" Beth jerked her head away, and when it could retreat no farther she allowed it to drop once again to the flat mattress, there being no pillow. The brush followed inexorably, continuing its work. "What is this place?"

"'Tis not for me to say."

"Ouch!"

The brush caught on a tangle and was pulled on regardless. The tiny pain was lost in a swift uprising of panic. Glancing furtively around, Beth discovered that, even if she managed to somehow free herself of her bonds and evade her keeper, a heavy-looking wooden door that was closed and almost certainly locked also stood between her and escape. Even if she could somehow manage to get through the door, there was no telling what lay beyond. Whatever it was, she doubted that it was a clear path to freedom. Her gaze returned to the woman, whose attention was all on her task. Beth frowned with incomprehension as she realized what that task was: styling her long tangles of hair. The thick sausage curls the woman was coaxing to life by brushing them around her fingers and arranging them, one after the other, across her bosom, seemed to have no possible reason for being brought into existence. Likewise, the sponge bath made no sense.

"Would you tell me what's happening, please? Why are you doing this?"

Something—a quiver of fear, perhaps, in her voice, though Beth tried not to allow it—caused the woman to meet Beth's eyes with a degree of sympathy in her own.

"Listen, ducks. Ye do as you're bid and they'll not hurt ye over much."

Beth's stomach tightened. "What do you mean?"

"'Tis a hard thing to endure, to be sure, but still no more than what every woman must—"

"Open up!" The shout from outside the door, which was accompanied by a loud pounding on the thick wooden portal, made Beth jump. Her gaze shot toward the door. Her heart leaped. Her throat tightened. "'Tis time."

"Aye, just let me finish," the woman called in answer.

"Please, you must tell me what's happening." Panic that Beth didn't even try to hide any longer shook her voice as the woman replaced the brush with something—a tin of red-colored salve, Beth realized as the salve was rubbed into her lips and cheeks. To tint them, obviously. But why? Beth's eyes widened as the most horrible suspicion began to take shape and weight in her mind.

"The mercy is 'tis over fast." The woman was whispering now. "That's somethin' you just must needs keep tellin' yourself."

"What—what is over fast?"

"Woman, will you open this door?" The roar was accompanied by loud banging. Beth's heart banged with it. Her breathing quickened as her gaze flew fearfully toward the door.

"Please . . ." She breathed the entreaty, looking back at her keeper, who was no longer looking at her. "Please, you must just tell me . . ."

"Aye, I'm coming," the woman called, ignoring Beth now. She stood up, dropped the tin of salve on the table, and moved toward the door. For all the response Beth got to her continued whispered pleadings for information, the woman might as well have been suddenly afflicted with deafness.

When she pulled the door open, Beth instinctively went silent and still as a corpse. Her eyes were fixed on the door.

"Ye took yer own sweet time," the man

who walked through it grumbled, giving the woman a condemning look before striding to the head of the bed. He was middle-aged, with close-cropped grizzled hair and a lined face, a servant from his dress. A big, burly servant with a cruel expression. Battling the urge to scream for help, which she knew would be useless, Beth instinctively shrank into the mattress as he leaned over her. His rough hands brushed hers and then gripped her wrists. A moment later her hands were free, and she realized he had cut through the rope with the wicked-looking knife he now held.

He could have as easily slit my throat.

The thought was terrifying. It was followed by another one: did they mean to kill her?

No, she comforted herself stoutly, though her heart raced at the thought. If killing her was their object, she would already be dead.

In any case, cringing paid no toll. Taking a deep breath, she sat up.

"Who are you? What is the meaning of this?" she demanded, drawing on the last dregs of her courage in the faint hope that perhaps she could win her freedom through words alone. Grimacing at the tingles that shot through her arms and fingers as she shook them out, ignoring her swimming head as best she could, she cast a quick, calculating glance at the open door. If they would just unloose her ankles, perhaps she could make a run for it.

"Oh-ho! Talks like a duchess, this one does." Knife in hand, the servant addressed his words to the woman as he moved farther down the bed and slid a hand under Beth's skirt to grip her calf just above the bindings. Beth stiffened as the warmth of his pudgy fingers went clear through her stocking to her skin, and he must have felt her reaction because he smirked at her. "Well, you'll not be acting so high in the instep come mornin', and that's God's truth."

"I do not see how you can speak of God at the same time as you are taking part in such villainy," Beth said severely.

"I'll speak of God when and how I like, ye ken?" The man tightened his grip until his fingers dug painfully into her leg. Unable to stop herself, Beth caught her breath sharply.

"Ye'd serve yourself best by keeping your

tongue between your teeth," the woman, leaning forward, muttered hastily in Beth's ear as the man, satisfied that he had hurt her, lowered his gaze and roughly shoved her skirt and petticoats almost up to her knees.

The awful familiarity of it made Beth nauseous. She itched to box his ears at the very least. But such an act would be folly of the worst sort, she knew, and so she steeled herself not to react as he leered at her lower limbs. Still, she couldn't help her body's instinctive response: as his hand slid back around her calf, her insides shuddered with revulsion and fear.

"My family is quite wealthy. And they will pay well to have me back." Knowing the woman's warning was wise but feeling that she had to try anything and everything she could to gain her release, Beth addressed the man again with what she considered truly commendable composure, and played the strongest card she held. Then, as his eyes met hers with a gleam in them she could not mistake, she added hurriedly, "Unharmed. They will pay well to have me back unharmed."

Lingering hopes of perhaps somehow

still avoiding utter ruin kept her from revealing who her family was, or telling him her
name. If and when he showed an interest
in freeing her in exchange for money, there
would be time enough to announce that
she was Lady Elizabeth Banning, and provide him with her direction. Of course, her
kidnapper had known who she was: he
had asked if she was Lady Elizabeth Banning before hitting her over the head. But it
was possible that these miscreants did
not know, and she had no desire to bruit
her identity about to all and sundry. If she
could possibly keep what had befallen her
quiet, it was in her best interests to do so.

"Oh, unharmed, is it?" The servant
chuckled, looking up at her as he cut with
quick, deep strokes through the rope binding her ankles. "That's rich, that is. *Unharmed.*"

He could not be persuaded to help her,
Beth was suddenly certain, no matter what
lure she dangled before him. As he finished his task and straightened, the look
in his eyes as they ran over her made her
skin crawl.

I have to do something. The thought
brought panic with it, because she could

think of nothing, not a single thing, to do that might better her situation a whit. *Oh, Claire, Gabby, where are you? Hurry.*

"Up you get." The man sheathed his knife in his belt and moved toward her.

"Very well."

She acquiesced so readily because she could not bear the thought that he might touch her again. Dodging his reaching hand, she hastily slid her legs over the edge of the bed so that he could see she meant to obey. Her instinct was to hurl herself through that open door and run like a rabbit as far away as she could get as soon as her feet touched the floor, but the woman stood between her and the door and the man was close, and anyway her fear was that her legs would not support her through such an endeavor. She must just test them before tipping her hand. The consequences of failure would be nothing short of disastrous, she was certain.

A beating, she felt, would probably be the least of it.

"I've a pressing need to make use of the facilities," she lied as she cautiously stood up. The wave of dizziness that enveloped her was almost strong enough to override the pins and needles that attacked her feet as blood rushed into them. A pair of tottering sideways steps was the best she could manage before having to steady herself with a hand on the cold stone wall. Running was beyond her for the moment, and as she realized that she despaired. Her breathing quickened and her stomach roiled, and she fought desperately to clear her head.

I must just play for time.

Wetting her dry lips, she directed her plea toward the woman, who had at least shown her a glimmer of sympathy.

"Is there a convenience I might . . . ?"

"'Tis too late for such." Before Beth realized what he meant to do, the man grabbed a thick handful of hair at the crown of her head and hauled her after him toward the door. "You be wanted below."

Chapter Ten

WHILE SHE WAS BEING DRAGGED past the wooden platform at the far end of the Great Hall of what she had discovered over the course of the last few minutes was an enormous, ancient stone castle, Beth's heart stuttered and her blood ran cold. What she beheld was a hideously clear vision of what her fate would be unless she could somehow, by some miracle, save herself. Though help was undoubtedly coming, it was as certain as it was that leaves fall in the autumn that unless it arrived within minutes, it would be too late.

The knowledge brought panic with it.

Ruin is nothing. I'll gladly embrace it, if that's what is necessary to be delivered from this.

"Ye be sure an' give me a wave when it's ye up there, Duchess," her captor chuckled over the roar of the crowd.

"I am Lady Elizabeth Banning," she said clearly, although it was hard to force the words out past her constricted throat. "My brother-in-law is the Duke of Richmond. As I said, he will pay well to have me restored to him. You may also believe me when I tell you that he will punish you most severely if you fail to help me."

"Oh, a duke, is it?" The hand in her hair tightened viciously, making her cry out. "I don't care if he's the bloody King o' England. I got me job to do, and that's it. And if you don't quit flappin' your lips at me like you've been doin', I'll stick a gag down your bloomin' throat, see if I don't."

A scream snapped her attention back to the stage. What she saw made her knees go weak.

No, no, no. But Beth didn't say it aloud.

Horror and pity and a terrible clawing fear for her own fate combined as she came to the dreadful realization that the girl on the platform was being sold. Auctioned off to the highest bidder, for a purpose that was all too sickeningly clear. The shouts were offers of money, and the bidding had been whipped into a frenzy as the poor unfortunate's clothes were ripped away piece by piece until she was left to stand naked in front of them all.

"I've some gingerbread to spare. Mayhap ye'll get lucky and I'll bid on ye meself, *yer ladyship*." Her captor cast her a grinning look as he yanked her away from the platform and the sobbing girl into another hall.

Desperation had made Beth's mouth go dry. She had to swallow before she could speak. "By helping me get away from here, you'll make yourself rich. My family will see to it, I give you my word."

"Aye, and no doubt they'll pat me on me back while they're doing it, and thank me for my good services to their daughter." He stopped and rapped smartly on a door. "I've another one," he announced as it opened.

"No!" But without further ado Beth found herself thrust into an anteroom. As she stumbled forward, rough male hands grabbed her shoulders from behind to stop her, and she registered the presence of perhaps two dozen other young women cowering together in the center of the small room.

The door closed with a thud. Beth's hands were jerked behind her back. A scream, shrill with desperation, pierced the muffling door. It clearly came from the girl on the makeshift stage.

"What are they doing to her?" Beth demanded, unable to help herself. Jerking away from the man who held her, she whirled to face the door as the crescendoing shouts and cheers of the assembled men turned into an explosion of what sounded like approval. As another panicked scream followed the first, she shivered at the heart-wrenching timbre of it and glanced wildly around. "Will no one help her?"

"Shut yer trap and hold still." She was grabbed again, and this time her hands were securely bound behind her back. "Now get over there with the others."

The man who had just finished tying the rope around her wrists shoved her roughly toward the congregation of females huddled together in the center of the chamber. He was one of two men in the room. Like the man who had dragged her here, these men looked to be servants. Armed servants, or, more properly, guards. Hulking and mean-faced, pistols in hand, they stood between their prisoners and the door. That door was the only way out, Beth saw as she fetched up against a sturdily built blonde in garish red silk who took several steps back in response to the unexpected collision. Clearly an interior chamber, the room was small, with walls of raw, rough plaster and a single torch burning in an iron sconce beside the door. There were no windows. Escape appeared impossible.

The scent of cheap perfume enveloped Beth as the group of females rearranged themselves to absorb her into their midst. Regaining her balance, she fought to hold on to calm reason in the face of a situation that was growing ever more nightmarish.

How has this happened to me? What can I do?

It was not, she was becoming increasingly convinced, a random act. Someone had caused this to be done to her deliberately. But who? And why?

To that she could discover no clear answer.

Taking a deep breath, she fought to force back galloping panic. One thought formed cold and clear as ice: no matter what the consequence, she could not, would not submit to the hideous degradation that was clearly intended to be her fate. The very thought made her want to vomit. It was all she could do not to start screaming the roof down.

'Twill do no good to scream.

"Sure, and there's no help for any of us," an apple-cheeked brunette to Beth's left whispered as the screaming beyond the door was abruptly silenced. There was an Irish lilt to her shaking voice, and a tinge of red to her dark brown hair, which curled loosely past her shoulders. She wore a plain dress of coarse, dun-colored cloth, of unmistakably rustic origin. Her eyes were brown, and red-rimmed from weeping. Crude color tinted her lips and cheeks, and Beth realized to her horror that, like herself, like, as she discovered with a quick glance around, all the others, she'd been painted and primped. Painted and primped *for sale.* "If me poor mam could see what

I've come to. She thought I was to work on a dairy farm, she did, and she was that glad for me to get the position."

"We've all been right gammoned, and that's the truth with no bark on it." The blonde's ample bosom heaved with indignation. "I was working in my uncle's tavern when this swell who'd stopped in a few times offered to take me up to London and set me up in my own house. He swore I should have my own carriage and—"

"And ye believed 'im, lack-wit?" A tiny, pinch-faced, black-haired female in an ill-fitting black dress and white apron that bespoke a housemaid broke in, her voice dripping with scorn. "'Ow long was it afore 'e sold ye to this lot?"

"R-right away." The blonde's lower lip quivered. "He said beg pardon, but his pockets were to let."

"At least I was snatched off the streets," the black-haired female said with grim satisfaction. "Mary Bridger's not such a nodcock as to fall for some gent's plumpers."

"Silence!" The sharp command from one of the guards made them all jump as the conversation, which had been conducted in whispers that had been growing ever louder, at last reached his ears. His threatening move toward them was interrupted by a quick knock and the sudden opening of the door.

"We be ready for another," said a man's voice. Beth couldn't see the speaker, who stood just outside in the hall, but the women all drew in a collective breath and shrank closer together. It did no good. The guard who had tied her hands turned and grabbed the nearest female, a slender, fair-haired girl who cried out in fear as she was thrust just as quick as that from the room. The door shut once again, leaving the rest to stare at the thick wooden portal in stricken silence.

The thought that she would all too soon be the victim was written on every female face Beth could see. Acknowledging the harsh reality of that, Beth felt her heart flutter and her stomach cramp.

Please hurry. She sent the prayer winging toward her sisters, toward their husbands and the scores who she knew were desperately searching for her, knowing even as she did that help wouldn't come in time.

"Think we'll get a crack at the leavings?"

The second guard, the one who hadn't tied Beth's hands, ran lascivious eyes over the huddled prisoners as the crowd beyond the door, enlivened by a fresh victim, began to ratchet up their noise anew. Having wedged herself into the center of the pack and thus managing to put a small degree of distance between herself and the men, Beth nevertheless felt the weight of the guard's gaze. Swallowing, she kept her eyes focused on the smoke-darkened wall straight ahead, and tried not to think about what was even now, from the sound of it, happening in the Great Hall. So far, at least, there were no screams. "Me, I fancy the ginger."

Knowing that he was referring to her, to the color of her hair, Beth shivered inwardly as she pretended not to hear or be aware of his ogling stare. Her stomach clenched tight and her heart pounded like a parade corp's drummer as she faced the terrible truth: she was trapped, and helpless, and the fate of the girl on the stage would soon be hers.

And then, even more horrible to contemplate, some man would force himself on her.

Her bound hands curled into fists.

I can't bear it. I—CANNOT—bear it.

The other guard snorted. "'Tis lucky we'll be to see so much as an extra pint of ale at the end o' this, I don't doubt, much less one of yon toothsome females."

"Ah, well, as to that"—the first guard pulled a flask out of his pocket—"what do you say to a flash o' lightning now?"

Switching his attention to the flask, the second guard nodded and reached for it. "A nip'll help pass the time, for sure."

Passing the flask back and forth, they fell to talking and their attention shifted away from their prisoners, for which Beth was profoundly thankful. She felt cold all over, and she was breathing way too fast. Her legs were shaky, and her head ached abominably. The building roar outside the door was only marginally louder than the rush of blood in her ears. But her thoughts were now crystal clear, and focused on one thing: escape.

Even if they were to kill her for it, she was going to do her possible to get away. The plain truth was, she would rather die than submit.

"The next time the door opens, we must

rush it. All of us at once. Do you hear?" Her fierce whisper brought the widening eyes of the captives swinging around to her face. Behind her back, her hands curled and twisted, her fingers probing the rope, testing the strength of the bonds. They were knotted tight.

"We dare not," the brunette in the dun-colored dress breathed, with a frightened glance at the guards.

"They'll catch us," the blonde said with certainty.

"They can't catch all of us." Casting her own assessing glance at the guards to make sure they weren't paying them any mind, Beth dropped her voice even lower. By now she was the focus of every eye and ear in the group. Heads bent her way. "The hall and stairs behind the platform are unguarded. We must just run past the platform, into the hall, then fly up the stairs as fast as we can. If all of us branch out into different hallways and hide ourselves, some of us will surely escape."

"But the ones they find . . ." The brunette shivered. "Ach, they'll be so angry."

"What can they do worse'n what they already intend by us? Beat us?" The black-haired maid—Mary—looked at Beth and gave a decided nod. "I've the stomach for a good mill, I do. I'm with you."

"What about the rest of you? For this to have a chance, we must burst past them and flee as a group. Our only hope is in our numbers." Still plucking futilely at her bonds—it was heartening to discover that she was no longer the only one to do so— Beth looked from one frightened face to another, and saw determination dawn in several. A few nods and murmurs of agreement led to more, until the whole group was in.

"The next time the door opens we rush it," Beth whispered. "I—"

"No talking." The guard who had tied Beth's hands glared at them. "The next one to clap her lips be the next one to—"

He was interrupted by a knock at the door.

Beth's heart lurched. It was soon—too soon. But whether it was or not, the time was at hand. Exchanging quick, frightened glances with the others, she realized that they knew it, too. She could feel the sudden agitation in the bodies pressed close around her. A collective tension shivered through the air. All eyes fastened on the door as it was thrust open.

"We be ready . . ." the man in the hall began.

"Now," Beth cried, leaping forward, and to her relief the others fell in, rushing the door with her, barreling toward their only hope at freedom. The guards' heads came whipping around, but it was too late: they were charging past, through the door, knocking aside the man waiting in the hall, stampeding in a terrified, determined group past the platform toward the stairs at the back of the hall.

Chapter Eleven

NEIL ONCE AGAIN HAD A PLAN. It was a simple plan, elegant even, if he did say so himself, and virtually guaranteed to provide him with the desired result. Using the Cit's blunt, plus the contents of another fat purse he had knicked for insurance upon arrival at the castle just in case the price for a red-headed lady-born might soar to unprecedented heights, he would blend with the crowd until she was brought out, then bid like all the rest and ultimately buy Lady Elizabeth. After that, it would be easy enough to carry her away and then within a few hours spirit her out of the castle. His plan would cause no commotion and could be accomplished with only a minimal degree of risk in the early-morning hours, which he calculated would be the best time to leave the castle and convey her back to the mainland. By then, most of the forty-odd men who were at that moment crowded into the Great Hall cheering and drinking and bidding to the skies for the right to de-flower a frightened-out-of-her-mind wench could be counted on to be thoroughly jug-bit and sound asleep, and the majority of the male servants (so far he had counted nine, but he was certain there were more) would most likely be sleeping, too. Fortune only had to favor him a little to allow him to get the chit away without the slightest no-tice being taken of what he was about.

The more he thought it through, the more he perceived that the plan was really quite perfect. His first instinct, of course, had been to act at once, making use of as many of his considerable talents as were needed to rescue the chit by brute force. But that approach had drawbacks, includ-ing possible injury to the lady if he was not quite fast or thorough or lucky enough. Then there was the problem of leaving bread crumbs again. Word of such an assault would be bound to spread through certain circles like wildfire, and would undoubtedly come to the ears of Clapham and anyone else who might be hunting him. Having shaken his pursuers off, as he'd hoped, he was loath to give them so precise a fix on his whereabouts, to say nothing of an inkling of the existence of his prospective hostage to fortune, as it were. The less anyone knew of where he was or what he intended to do, the better.

Stealth was clearly the better course.

Propping a shoulder against one of the massive pillars that supported the Great Hall's soaring, smoke-blackened ceiling, draped in the black domino that, with its hood up, concealed all of him except the center portion of his face, which was in shadow, and the final twelve inches or so of his legs, Neil deliberately presented a picture of ease as he sipped a particularly fine Burgundy—the first decent wine he'd touched in nigh on three weeks—with real appreciation and waited for Lady Elizabeth to be brought out. His hunger had been appeased by a chicken drumstick that he had helped himself to as he passed the feast set up for the revelers in an adjoining room. His thirst he had slaked with a tankard of ale from the same source. Given that, and the wine, and the knowledge that he had only to wait and play his part to get what he had come for, no mayhem necessary, he should have been feeling relaxed as he watched the latest successful bidder count out his blunt into the hand of a genially smiling harpy with eyes harder than the stone against which he leaned, who seemed to be in charge of collecting the funds. But he was not. His anger at those who had brought Lady Elizabeth here was tamped down and carefully controlled, but it was there, no less dangerous because it had gone cold. Wariness lest he be taken unawares had become an integral part of his makeup, and it kept him completely alert. He might lounge against a pillar, but he was ready to move if necessary, if Clapham or his ilk should unexpectedly show up or, indeed, if any threat to his person or object for being in the castle arose. As a result, his nerves were stretched taut as a bowstring, although he gave no indication whatsoever of being on edge. As they always did when he was working, his senses had sharpened, attuning themselves by dint of long practice to the slightest threat. Closing his ears to the noise around him, he listened for other things: the whisper of a knife being drawn, the click of a pistol's hammer being pulled back, the too-purposeful tramp of feet. His eyes honed in on small, quick movements that struck him as being out of place. He had been in the business of surviving for so long that he could almost smell danger, or feel it in his bones like some people felt a coming rain.

But here, inside the Great Hall of Trelawney Castle, where the most dastardly of acts were taking place all around him, he felt nothing out of the way at all.

Safe, in fact.

He had taken care to secure a spot near the stage, which was momentarily empty as the bidding on the too-thin, flaxen-haired watering pot for whom the harpy was being paid had just ended. From his position he could see the first emergence from behind the wall of each female as she was led to the stage to be sold. That Lady Elizabeth was on the premises he'd had no doubt even before he had arrived at the castle: he'd thought he had recognized the carriage that had stolen her away amongst the vehicles being held in the stable adjacent to the ferry, and had subsequently confirmed with one of the ostlers on duty (how did not matter) that a red-haired lady, insensible from the sound of it, had indeed been taken from it and transported to the castle. Not too long since, he'd spotted the lady herself being dragged by the hair toward the holding chamber, a sight that had not sat well with him. But again, he had reminded himself of his plan, which was really quite the best solution in that it allowed both of them to get away unnoticed. That being the case, and knowing that the women inside that chamber must all be brought forth from it sooner or later, and with no cause for alarm in his immediate surroundings that he could perceive, he set himself to enjoying his wine.

And so it was that Neil was sipping Burgundy and idly looking over the crowd when the first inkling that yet another of his plans might go awry caused him to frown and glance to his left.

There was a disturbance in the hall

where the women were kept. The shouts and laughter and jumble of conversation all around him made it difficult to be sure, but he thought he was hearing sounds of discord, a rush of many feet. He was just straightening away from the pillar in reaction when an explosion of shrieks split the air and a bevy of females burst into view, bolting out of the hallway and toward the stage in a tidal wave of flying tresses and flapping skirts. He caught a glimpse of long red hair and a yellow dress at the head of the screaming tide and recognized Lady Elizabeth with that first astounded glance before the stage blocked her from his view as she flew past it out of sight. A jumble of shrieking females racing behind her likewise vanished from his sight behind the stage, and then he beheld, three yards or so behind the pack, a trio of burly, puce-faced, pistol-waving thugs giving chase. That was enough. Trouble was clearly at hand. He thrust his glass into the hands of the surprised roue to his right, who had turned to gape in obvious confusion at the goings-on, and took off after them.

"What's to do?" The bewildered question floated to his ears from somewhere behind him, from the not-yet-sure-what-was-happening audience.

"Is it part of the entertainment, do you think?" came the equally bewildered reply.

"By God, they're escaping!" A sharper knife hit on the truth.

"We can't let that happen! After them!"

"'Elp! 'elp!" a fleeing female screeched as he drew near enough to make out individual voices in the crowd he chased. "Lord amercy, somebody 'elp us!"

"Crikey, don't shoot 'em, Johnson!" one of the pursuing men just ahead of him shouted to another, who was leveling his pistol at the pack. "We wants 'em caught, not dead!"

"Don't shoot anybody! What if we hits one of the customers?"

"Run!" a female shrieked.

"Just catch 'em! Stop 'em!"

"Head for the door," a woman cried. This voice Neil recognized: Lady Elizabeth, without the possibility of mistake.

Pulse quickening with alarm, he rounded the corner of the stage in time to see that the women were headed true as a swarm of bees toward a shadowy open doorway in the rear wall. Just as the first of them, his red-haired charmer included, were about to reach it, a man stepped into the gap, fists on hips, grinning as he blocked the way. Wearing the white shirt and leather vest that marked him as a lower-order servant, he was almost as tall and wide as the doorway. His belly was round as a barrel, and his thick legs were planted wide apart.

In Neil's judgment, the women had about as much chance of getting past him as they did of breaking through the stone wall itself.

"Malloy, look lively! Grab 'em!" This shout from one of the men in front of him, presumably an exhortation to the behemoth in the doorway, pierced the tumult that was now so loud it echoed from the walls.

"What do we do?" Terror shivered in one woman's cry.

"Keep going! He can't stop all of us!" Lady Elizabeth yelled.

"Get the ginger! She be the ringleader! Grab 'er, Malloy!"

The ginger—Lady Elizabeth, without a doubt. Cold with fear for her, Neil closed the gap between himself and the three men ahead of him in a pair of bounds. Still some yards behind him ran a sea of others, the men in the audience combined with those employed at the castle in a great jostling horde, their pounding feet and shouted imprecations echoing through the vast space as loud as an oncoming army.

"Look at that! We got 'em now!"

"Hold fast there, Malloy! Troublesome gaggle o' wenches!"

"Aye, and when we get 'em back again we'll make 'em pay."

Neil reached the trio ahead of him in time to overhear that panted exchange. Knowing that his plan was well and truly out the window now, along with any hope of getting out of there with Lady Elizabeth unnoticed, Neil lunged forward, caught the slowest-moving of the three by the collar, swung him around, and flattened him with a single blow.

Startled, the other two whirled.

"What the 'ell?"

"Who . . . ?"

Even as the remaining two thugs jerked up their pistols, even as the shouts behind him drew closer and the sounds of more feet, many feet, rolled over him in a thunderous wave, a fresh round of shrieks from the beleaguered flock of females distracted him.

"Miss, no! Ye can't!"

"Keep coming! Fly past!" Lady Elizabeth cried. Then, louder, she added in what was almost a roar, "Stand aside, sirrah!"

Arrested, Neil was just in time to watch as Lady Elizabeth, her hands bound behind her, raced a little ahead of her companions. His eyes widened as she bent forward and charged the three-times-her-size man blocking the doorway like a small golden ram intent on bursting through a flimsy garden gate. Aghast, Neil could do nothing but observe as she head-butted him right in his ample gut.

"Oomph!" Clearly taken by surprise, the giant doubled over and took a staggering step back, but held fast in the doorway, grabbing for Lady Elizabeth, who'd bounced off. He caught a handful of skirt . . .

"No! Let *go!*"

"'Elp 'er!"

"We be trapped! We be trapped!"

With the pursuit closing off all possibility of retreat and nowhere else to go, the women were indeed well and truly trapped,

Neil saw. The swarm of females bumped to a confused stop just short of the doorway where Lady Elizabeth was now being dragged shrieking and fighting into the giant's hold. Just as Neil observed that, a pistol exploded almost in his face and a bullet whistled past his cheekbone, so close that its breeze tickled his skin. He was thus recalled instantly to the business at hand even as the shouts behind him crescendoed into what sounded like a single-throated bellow. The bullet careened over the heads of the pursuing crowd, causing the front-runners to duck and back-pedal and the whole to let out a mighty yell that was loud enough to put cannon fire to shame.

"Don't shoot 'im!" the man in front of him who had not pulled the trigger shouted to the other, who had. "Can't you see 'e's a bloody toff?"

Had he not dodged instinctively, he might now be dead, Neil knew, but his heightened senses had once again served him well. Angry for allowing himself to become distracted and thus nearly get killed, he fell upon his assailant, and his cohort, with controlled ferocity—he was still trying not to kill, which was what called for such careful control—and dispatched them with two swift blows. The second one was still falling unconscious to the ground as he snatched the man's presumably loaded pistol out of the air and, thrusting it into his waistband, whirled to dash to Lady Elizabeth's aid.

The giant now had a huge, meaty arm hooked around her waist, hauling her in as, screaming, she struggled to get free.

"Let me go! You let me go!" she cried. Kicking and squirming like a worm on a hook, she was nonetheless helpless, caught up in the giant's grip as she was. Still, she fought for all she was worth while a few valiant females tried to come to her assistance and the rest fluttered around in a tight little group that seemed to have screaming as its main purpose. The brave few threw shoulders and knees into the fray and kicked at the man's shins and in general did their possible to effect Lady Elizabeth's release. For all the good their efforts appeared to be doing, they might as well have been attacking an oak. Even in the throes of warding them off, the man managed to both hold on to his prisoner and block the door.

"Push past!" Lady Elizabeth yelled to her fellow females, and buried her teeth in the thickly muscled arm nearest her.

"Ouch! Ye little besom!" the giant bellowed, snatching his arm back only to grab her neck with a hamlike hand and use it to lift her clear up off her feet, shaking her like an enraged bull mastiff with an especially annoying rat. Lady Elizabeth, gasping for air, writhed desperately in an effort to escape the hand that was clearly in the process of crushing her windpipe. Just a few feet away from the shrieking knot of females now, sprinting toward them, toward the pair in the doorway, for all he was worth, Neil watched the giant bunch his free fist and draw back his arm, and he knew he was out of time: if her throat wasn't crushed in the next second or so, the punch that was coming would likely smash every bone in the lady's lovely face. "I'll kill ye for that, ye bloody trollop, see iffen I don't! I'll beat ye bloody senseless, I will!"

"Hold her, Malloy!" a man shouted from not too far behind, giving notice that the rest of the pursuit was closing fast. "Hold yer place!"

"Let 'er go!" one of the females, a tiny

black-haired mosquito of a woman, shrieked, flying at the man, while Lady Elizabeth, obviously on the verge of being rendered senseless, nevertheless struggled like a madwoman even as the big, anvil-like fist hurtled toward her face.

It never connected. Instead, the silver-handled knife Neil had snatched from his boot and thrown with a deadly accuracy that far surpassed that of any bullet found its mark, burying itself to the hilt in the giant's neck. Eyes widening in surprise, releasing the lady to clutch at his neck, the giant staggered back a pace, then collapsed just inside the doorway, rolling onto his back and kicking convulsively before lying still. Shuddering, Lady Elizabeth crumpled, dropping to her knees and doubling over. Her face, which Neil just glimpsed before it was buried in her lap, was now utterly white. She seemed to be fighting to breathe.

Sometimes killing was the only thing that worked.

"Malloy!" The shout came from behind him. "He's given way! Malloy!"

"Miss! Miss!" the loyal little mosquito cried at the same time, hovering over Lady Elizabeth. "We 'ave to go!"

Lady Elizabeth lifted her head and made an abortive movement that made Neil think she was trying to get up but could not.

"Keep going!" one of the other females screamed in warning as the bunch of them surged forward, surrounding her. "They be coming! Get through! Leap over!"

Taking heed, the women rushed the doorway, crowding through, abandoning Lady Elizabeth posthaste and leaping over the fallen giant like a herd of spooked deer even as Neil—acutely conscious of the yelling, onrushing crowd just strides behind him now, and in grim expectation of taking a bullet or knife to the back at any instant, if anyone had seen him throw the knife—reached her. Her glorious hair cascaded over her shoulders like silken flames. Her bountiful bosom heaved, threatening to overspill the bright confines of her bodice. Her beautiful face was both unnaturally flushed and bruised in places as it tilted up to his. For the space of perhaps a heartbeat, their gazes met. Fear shone out of her wide blue eyes, and he realized that with the hood shadowing his face and the desperate circumstances no doubt disordering her senses to a degree, it was unlikely that she recognized him. Her lips parted as if she would say something, but not a sound came out, and anyway there was no time.

"I'll see you safe," he promised, but whether she heard and understood over the tumult was impossible to tell. Scooping her up in his arms with barely a pause, registering her delicate scent and warmth and softness only peripherally, he ran through the doorway with her not inconsiderable weight clutched to his chest and leaped the giant just as a pistol spat behind him. The bullet he had been expecting splintered stone in the approximate place where his head had been a mere split second before.

He ducked reflexively, and the domino's hood fell back. Lady Elizabeth flinched in his arms, and he tightened his hold on her. The yards of silk that comprised her gown made her abominably slippery, and dropping her at this crucial moment would be disastrous for them both. Their eyes met again. Hers widened, and her lips moved.

"You!" she said. Or at least, he thought that was what she said, but he couldn't be sure because the women, many of whom were already flying up the narrow back stairs urged on by others who were pushing and screaming behind them as they fought to get up the stairs in turn, shrieked in window-shattering concert at the explosion of the bullet, nearly deafening him.

"'Ware ricochets!" a man cried behind him. "Demmed walls in the tower are stone!"

"Stop him! He's stealing a gel!"

"Don't hit the bawds, ye bloody idiots! The chase does but add spice, and the night's yet young!"

"Go! Go!" a chorus of females screamed, and go they did, pounding up the stairs in a riotous pack, with every footfall seemingly accompanied by a fresh volley of ear-splitting shrieks.

With only seconds left before the pursuers were upon them and knowing he needed at least one hand free, Neil threw Lady Elizabeth over his shoulder with a barked "Hold on!" to which he could not tell if she replied. He then paused only long enough to yank his knife from the fallen giant's blood-soaked neck, swipe it clean on the dead man's sleeve, and drop it in his own pocket.

He was already racing from the scene when he remembered she couldn't hold on, her hands were tied. He tightened his arm around her thighs, twisting his fist in the fine silk of her skirt for added insurance as he dashed down the corridor away from the stairs. With any luck, the pursuers would think he had run up the stairs in the midst of the fleeing women—or would be so intent on recovering the women that they wouldn't care about him. Too frightened or foolish to realize that silence would serve them better, the women were making so much noise that the path they had chosen was impossible to mistake.

"They be coming!" one screamed above the rest, clearly referring to the pursuing men.

"That way! Hide, hide!"

"Ah! They can see me! Move!"

The cries of the panicked females were all but drowned out by answering masculine shouts, clearer and closer than they had been.

"They're taking the stairs!"

"Malloy! Avast, ye lot, look ye at Malloy!"

"Get out of the way! They're getting away!"

"'E's been kilt!"

"Stand aside! Let me at the stairs!"

The first of the pursuit was through the doorway, Neil gathered from those cries, although having just rounded a fortuitous bend in the corridor that blocked both the doorway and the stairs from view, he could not confirm it with his own eyes. The thunder of feet seemed to be going up rather than following behind him, he noted with real gratitude, brought on by the knowledge that his defense of them would be hampered by the fact that he could use only one hand, and had to be careful of the lady besides. Had it not been for the twin distractions of Malloy's body and the fleeing women, coupled with the shadows in the narrow servants' hallway that grew darker with every foot that separated it from the Great Hall, this alternate way out of the tower stairwell would certainly have been spotted at once. Indeed, he expected someone who knew the castle to point out this possible escape route at any moment.

The saving grace was that he knew Trelawney Castle, too, not well but enough. Just a few strides farther on was a staircase that led down to the cavernous cellar, where long ago prisoners had been held and, more lately, potatoes, vegetables, and wine, amongst other less exceptional goods, were kept. The stout wooden door of his memory was missing, but he was relieved to discover that the steep stone stairs endured. Plunging into darkness that deepened with every step, he descended the twisty staircase that wound down into the cavernous rooms of the cellar as swiftly as he could, keeping careful hold on Lady Elizabeth as he took good care not to lose his footing.

Fortunately, the chit kept still, although the position she was in had to be uncomfortable, and probably frightening as well. With her hands bound, she had no way to brace herself, and thus slipped and slid with every step he took. Clearly, though, she had sense enough to realize that a fall from such a height would do neither of them any good, and lay still as a sack of potatoes as a result.

Finally, the screams and cries and pounding feet above them were barely audible, muffled by distance and the dense stone walls. From the now thick-as-pudding darkness and the earthy scent that increasingly enveloped him, he calculated they were nearing the bottom. Searching his memory, he tried to visualize the layout of the vast, labyrinthian space through which he must take them. They hadn't much time, he knew. Once their pursuers realized exactly what had befallen Malloy, they would be searching for him. The stairs to the cellar would be remembered. The hunt—this time for him—would be on.

Neil calculated that he had no more than two steps to go to reach the flat stone of the cellar floor when a sound—the faintest of scuffles, an indrawn breath—behind him caused every muscle in his body to tense.

Of only one thing was he certain: they were no longer alone.

Chapter Twelve

NEIL WAS GRIPPING HIS KNIFE AGAIN by the time his feet touched the floor. With one dead by his hand already, he was loath to add more corpses to the tally and thus draw more attention, but for the lady's sake he was prepared to do what was needed and count the cost later. Tightening his grip on Lady Elizabeth in anticipation of running hell for leather with her when the deed was done, Neil had just whipped around to dispatch their pursuers as quickly and silently as possible when, by the faint grayish light that filtered down from the top of the stairs, which rendered them into faint but unmistakable silhouettes, he saw that they were females. Four, no, five of them, unless he'd missed a bobbing head. Descending the stairs in an untidy rush, they had clearly followed him and his fair burden.

Just about the time he recognized that he was not going to be able to deal with this particular gaggle of pursuers as he had intended, an insistent toe prodded him firmly in the chest.

"Put me down," Lady Elizabeth whispered, just loud enough so that he could plainly hear her. But in case he didn't, her squirming coupled with her prodding toe underlined her words so that her meaning was unmistakable. "Put me down. At once, if you please."

Cursing silently at the turn of events that had given him pursuers he saw no easy way of getting rid of, he eased her off his shoulder and, his hands carefully gripping her trim waist until she found her balance, set her on her feet. No sooner had he done so than she was surrounded by women. Six, even more than he had feared.

Neil experienced a flash of true horror.

"Be ye all right, miss?"

"Yes, yes, and thank goodness so are all of you!"

"Sure, and ye were so brave!"

"We were all of us brave."

"I didn'a think we would win through, did you?"

"Did any of 'em follow us down 'ere?"

"What's to do now?"

"Are we safe, do ye think?"

"O' course we're not safe! We'll not be safe till we're well out of this great barn!"

"Aye, but who knows the way?"

To Neil's consternation, they all spoke at once, the volume of their voices rising alarmingly as each fought to be heard.

"Keep silent!" Neil commanded, speaking through his teeth even as he took the opportunity to wrap a steadying hand around Lady Elizabeth's arm. Thus holding her still, he sliced through her bonds. The women had been speaking in whispers, if increasingly loud ones, but any degree of noise was a risk. With so many of the prized females missing, the search would undoubtedly expand even sooner than he had supposed. Someone might even now be remembering the cellar. If they heard voices floating up the stairwell, the gig was up with no possibility of mistake.

"Well, here's a rudesby!"

"Who be he?"

"'Ow do we know 'e's not one o' them?"

"I don't think he can be. Else why did he save her?"

"May'ap 'e wanted 'er for 'imself."

Neil couldn't see the speakers properly—he could barely make out their separate shapes in the dark—but the increasing suspicion in their tones was unmistakable. He could feel their eyes trained on him even through the dark.

"Shh," he said, the syllable fierce.

"He's a friend," Lady Elizabeth intervened in a husky whisper, and he realized that she sounded hoarse. The giant had done damage to her throat, no doubt, and as he remembered how close she had come to being severely injured or even dying, he could only thank fortune that he had been in a position to secure her release before either occurred. Her hands freed now, she shook her arms, then scrubbed the back of her hand over her lips as if to remove something distasteful. They had been, he remembered, scarlet with paint. "You may trust him, I promise. He's a good man. Look, he's freed my hands. Come here, and he'll cut you loose, too."

Neil's lips twisted wryly. Her description of him was novel, if nothing else, but not necessarily true, especially as it concerned the others, who were most emphatically nothing to him and whom he had no desire whatsoever to make his concern. But with the women instantly crowding around and presenting their backs to him, twittering with murmurs of anticipation and inundating him with whispered variations of "Me next! Free me!" cutting their bonds seemed the simplest thing to do.

"Me fingers be tingling!"

"Rubbed my wrists raw, that did."

"Bloody bastards! I 'ope they gets what's comin' to 'em!"

"I was that scared, you wouldn't believe."

"Thankee. Oh, thankee!"

"Ye be a God-send, sir."

"*Quiet*," he growled. "Unless you *want* to be found."

All talk immediately ceased. He sawed through the last of the ropes with a feeling of thankfulness that the task was behind him before restoring his knife to his boot amidst a silence thick with swallowed words and nudges.

But at least it was silence.

Then with a quick movement he untied the now-useless-to-him domino and dropped it around Lady Elizabeth's shoulders. The cellar was cold and damp, the gown she wore was thin, and his scheme wasn't worth a farthing if the centerpiece of it sickened and died.

"Thank you." She looked up at him. He could see the gleam of her eyes through the dark. Her voice dropped so that it had just enough volume to reach his ears only. "What on earth are you doing here?"

"Life is full of strange coincidences," he replied drily. Then, before she could expand on the topic, he added, "Come," in a voice meant for her alone, and caught her by the hand, pulling her after him. The slender warmth of her fingers gripped his willingly, and she fell in behind him without protest— or, indeed, a word. The route he meant to try at least had the virtue of leading away from the steps where anyone searching for him—or the bothersome females—would almost certainly first appear. With the faint

illumination seeping down the stairs left behind after no more than a pair of strides, he
was unable to see even Lady Elizabeth,
who stayed close behind him and whose
fingers now twined securely with his, much
less anything or anyone else. It was dark
as pitch, so dark that he stumbled more
than once on the uneven floor and had to
feel his way along the clammy wall, and
trust to his memory besides, to get them
where they needed to go. But it was impossible to mistake that the women followed,
managing to stay with them despite the
darkness and the brisk pace that he deliberately set. Although they were clearly trying to be quiet now, their noise, from muffled
whispers to various dull thumps and thuds
to the rustle of skirts and the shuffle of feet,
was enough to give them away to a deaf
man, which he emphatically was not. It was
certainly enough to make him grit his teeth
and search his mind for a less-than-lethal
way to rid himself of them.

"'Tis so dark!"

"What be that?"

"Ow! I've bumped me head!"

"'Ware the overhang!"

"I can't see!"

"Mary, is that you?" This voice he knew: Lady Elizabeth, lagging a little as she spoke to one of the others. He could feel the drag of her behind him, realized she had slowed down, and tightened his grip on her hand, tugging to bring her along faster in hopes of losing the rest of them.

"Aye, it is."

Losing them did not seem to be working. That voice was even closer at hand than the rest.

"Oh! Watch out for the dip in the floor!"

"Where are we going?"

"Be they still looking for us, do you think?"

"Of course they are, ye great looby! Do ye think they'll—"

"*Quiet,*" Neil snapped, thoroughly exasperated now, and the talking stopped again. But that didn't obliterate the fact that the plaguey nuisances were trailing him and Lady Elizabeth like the tail on a dog. Having reached his immediate goal—a sturdy table resting against the clammy stone wall he'd been feeling his way along—he stopped, opened its single drawer, and by feel removed one of the many candles that he was pleased to discover were still kept

exactly where they had been since time im-
memorial, or at least since he'd become
acquainted with the castle, along with flint
and steel. The scraping of the drawer was
loud enough to make him grimace, but if
there was anyone nearby to hear, the wom-
en's noise would have already given them
away, so he assumed that his own noise
was a matter of little concern.

"Don't move." Speaking in her ear once
again, he directed the order to Lady Elizabeth alone, then let go of her hand and proceeded to bring flint and steel together to
light the candle. As the flame sparked to
life with a sulfurous smell and a small plume
of smoke, he glanced around. The cellar
was basically a series of chambers of various uneven shapes and sizes that had
been carved long ago from solid rock. They
opened into each other and wound snake-
like beneath the castle. Like the floor, the
ceiling was stone and in this spot scarce
higher than his own head. The rough-hewn
walls were shiny with damp. Centuries'
worth of detritus—barrels, trunks, coils of
rope, discarded furniture, and the like—
were piled high against the far wall, leaving
this side relatively clear. The candle was

something he would rather not have had to resort to, but continuing to feel his way along was more likely to bring them to grief than was risking a light, he judged, although if anyone came down the stairs their presence would now be apparent from a dangerous distance. But there was obviously no one within earshot, and probably no one in the cellar at all, else they would have been discovered by now. Anyway, too much time had passed, and too many things might have changed, for him to trust only his memory to guide them to safety.

"Do you know of a way out?" Lady Elizabeth asked as he looked at her. Still hoarse, she was pale but calm, her expression resolute rather than afraid. Her bright hair was as vibrant as the flame, and having tied the strings of the domino at her throat she was now swathed neck to feet in its concealing folds. She was also, he saw to his profound dismay, clasping the hand of the black-haired mosquito, who was clasping the hand of a comely blonde in red, who was clasping the hand of—well, it went down the line, all of them, plus Lady Elizabeth, linked together in a chain. Neil realized that all unknowing he'd been towing the entire group through the dark, and cursed silently again.

Seven pairs of eyes looked at him expectantly.

Will no one rid me of these pesky creatures? The line from *Macbeth*—altered to fit his present circumstances—popped unbidden into his head, proving yet again that even a bit of education is never entirely lost.

"Perhaps." The situation had to end. "Perhaps not. In any case, we'll fare far better on our own." He swept a frowning look over the gaggle of women. Raising his voice just enough to be sure of being heard by all, he directed his next remarks to them at the same time as he reached for Lady Elizabeth's hand, the one that clasped the mosquito's, meaning to pull it free and get on with getting her safely out of the castle as quickly as possible. But the more he tried to subtly disengage her grip, the more her hand tightened on the other woman's. "If you will take my advice, you would each do well to search out a far corner and hide yourself there. These cellars are vast. If you stay quiet, I doubt you'll be found."

"No," Lady Elizabeth said just as he succeeded in gaining sole possession of her hand at last, and jerked her hand away from his.

"Never say you're meaning to leave us, sir?" gasped a round-cheeked brunette in a dress the color of mud, her eyes wide on his face, as the women drew closer together to stare at him as one.

"'Iding be a fool's game," the mosquito said. "And Mary Bridger's no' a fool. I'll not be doin' it."

"They'll find us sure," said the comely blonde.

"Will ye not take us with ye?" begged one farther down the line. Tall, thin, and pale, with sandy hair straggling loose over her shoulders and her prim-necked blue gown ripped at the shoulder, she punctuated the question with what sounded suspiciously like a sob. In fact, he discovered to his dismay, she looked on the verge of tears. She was, however, no concern of his, none of them were any concern of his, and he meant to keep it that way. Neil once again reached for Lady Elizabeth's hand. She put it behind her back, which left him, most uncharacteristically, at a loss. He could, of course, reclaim it instantly if he chose to force the issue, but . . .

"Of course they're coming with us." Lady Elizabeth stood her ground, her expression mulish as she met his gaze. "I take full responsibility."

"You take . . ." Words failed him for a moment, probably because, in looking at her, he found himself irresistibly reminded of Old Hook Nose again. It was, he decided, something in the glint of the eyes, and the extremely decided set of the jaw. "Full responsibility?"

She nodded. "Yes."

Strong men shivered in their boots when they encountered the look he brought to bear on her. She put up her chin.

I'd kill a man who defied me so. Unfortunately, she was not a man.

"Please don't leave us," the thin female in blue begged, welling tears glinting in the candlelight.

"We'll be ever so quiet, sir," chimed in the round-cheeked one.

"And do just as ye say," promised the blonde.

Two more, a small, plump dove of a female with smooth wings of dark brown hair and a gray dress, and a taller, plainer one with an angular face, frizzy, lighter brown ringlets, and a dress that might have once been white, clung together, nodding vigorously as their eyes beseeched him. Only the mosquito frowned, and as his gaze fell upon her she sniffed in what he was clearly meant to know was disdain.

"We are staying together," Lady Elizabeth informed him as the women drew closer to their champion, huddling around her even as they looked at him. Her tone made it a statement of fact. Her eyes held his unflinchingly. *"You* may do as you choose." She looked at the others. "Let us but get another candle, and we'll be on our way."

"To where?" the blonde asked, casting him a sideways glance as if she might be pondering the merits of abandoning her fellow females to cast her lot with him, which, of course, wasn't an option.

"Never you mind." The mosquito was fierce.

"We will continue on in the same direction in which we're presently going in the hopes of discovering a way out," Lady Elizabeth said. Her manner cool and steady, she had already withdrawn another candle from the drawer and was reaching for the flint and steel to light it. Neil eyed the slender back she presented to him with mounting exasperation even as the group surrounding her darted speculative glances from her to him. He got the clear impression that they were waiting to see what he would do at this blatant challenge to his authority. The answer, arrived at after a few seconds' thought, was nothing. For one of the few times in his life, he had to acknowledge himself bested. While he was more than prepared to abandon the other women to their own devices, he wasn't about to let Lady Elizabeth get away from him. Though she had no idea of it, the plain truth was he needed her badly.

His lips tightened.

"Fine. You may have it your own way," he said, speaking to Lady Elizabeth, who had cast him a haughty glance over her shoulder when he began. Then his gaze swept the group. "But I tell you to your heads I've no idea what we may encounter, and all of us together make too easy a target. The best thing would be for us to separate. I'm warning each of you, you'll be safer alone." The thought of simply throwing Lady Elizabeth over his shoulder again, making off with her, and having done was tempting, but he doubted that the deed could be accomplished without a great deal of noise, on her part and the part of the other women. In fact, it wasn't difficult to imagine them screaming the walls down, all thought of concealment forgotten. Anyway, unless he physically disabled them, which he knew already he was not going to do because they were bloody harmless females after all, there was nothing preventing them from following. The knowledge was like a bitter pill he could see no alternative but to swallow. "Devil take it, this is foolish beyond permission, but we haven't time to debate. Stay with us if you will."

"Ye'll not regret it, sir."

"We'll be quiet as mice, you'll see."

"I'm ever so grateful, I am."

"We be in your debt."

"To my thinkin', we're no better off with 'im than we are without 'im." This, from the mosquito, was followed by another of those pointed sniffs.

"A man's protection—"

"No more bloody talking," he ground out as their clamor grew ever louder, casting a quelling look around the group, all of whom immediately clamped their lips together and stood totally mum.

Taking the unlit candle from Lady Elizabeth and dropping it and the flint and steel in his pocket, just in case it should be needed later, he grabbed her hand and started off again. Her fingers curled willingly around his now.

Of course they did. The minx had successfully called his bluff.

"Do you know a way out?" Meant for his ears alone, her voice, he was pleased to realize, was at least a little worried.

"'Twould be no more than your just deserts if I didn't, wouldn't it?"

"But you do."

"We'll soon find out."

She said nothing more for a moment. Then, her voice even quieter than before, she added, "That you would visit such a place as this is reprehensible, and I don't excuse you for it, but I do thank you most sincerely for saving me. Again."

That took him by surprise. Of course,

she had no idea that the only reason he was there was because of her, that he'd come for the sole reason of effecting her rescue. He started to tell her so, then thought better of it. Really, the less she knew, the better.

"You're welcome. Again." His tone was dry.

"Didn't somebody say there was to be no more bloody talkin'?" the mosquito asked acerbically.

No one said anything more. Moving carefully through the obstacles that littered the various chambers, Neil led the way as swiftly as he could manage toward the farthermost reach of the cellar, where, if things remained as they had once been, there was an iron door. That door opened onto a stairwell that led down to a cave with a small fingerlet of a cove that came right inside it, right in beneath the castle. Once used by smugglers to bring goods in from the open strait, it had been well guarded in his day. His hope was that that day was no more—and the door, stairs, and cove were still there. And, also, that there was still some kind of a boat.

Otherwise, the only alternative was to

swim out. As he recalled, the water was deep and cold, which would pose no problem for *him*. Few females could swim, but he seemed to remember the maid saying that Lady Elizabeth swam like a fish, and hoped it was so. If it was, and swimming was their only choice, it was possible that most of her companions would have to be left behind, not that he considered that a drawback. But whatever their numbers, swimmers would have to make their way around the jetty to where the rocks permitted access to the shore. Then, soaked and freezing, they must, if they wished to leave the island, walk around to the ferry. Where, because any searcher worth his salt would have considered that the ferry must be any escapee's goal, someone—probably many heavily armed someones—would almost certainly be keeping watch.

In which case, the battle would be well and truly joined.

He and an assortment of soggy females against a force of dozens.

He'd survived worse odds, but the thought of what a fiasco such a confrontation could turn into had him vowing to avoid the ferry landing at all costs. If there was not one in the cove, there had to be a boat concealed somewhere on the island.

"Oh, sir, I think there be a light coming behind us," one of the females whispered urgently just as he spied the door he had been seeking. Its smooth, iron-gray arch appeared at first glance as no more than a darker, stationary shadow amongst many shifting along the walls. If he had not known such a door existed and been looking for it, he would have missed it. "'Twas but a glimmer, but I saw it, I'm that sure."

The whole group looked around as one, himself included.

He saw nothing beyond the flickering yellow circle cast by his own candle. The way behind them was black as a tar pit, just as it had been all along. As far as he could tell, there was no change.

But he heard . . . something. What, exactly, he couldn't tell, only that it was a sound he couldn't identify, that struck him as being out of place. His senses leaped immediately to high alert. Unless the girl was mistaken, and he didn't think she was, whoever was back there had, upon spotting their light, immediately blown out his candle or shuttered his lantern.

Damn it to hell.

He did not dare risk doing the same, not yet. They were in the very last chamber, with nowhere to go except through the door. Hanging on like grim death to Lady Elizabeth, who still stubbornly towed the rest of the pack behind her, he took the few strides necessary to reach the door, then spent a precious brace of seconds surveying it by candlelight.

As far as he could tell, it was as he remembered.

Glancing around at Lady Elizabeth, employing a tone that even she should recognize was meant to be strictly obeyed, he whispered, "Stay right where you are and be ready to move when I tell you to move."

Then, dropping her hand, he blew out the candle. Impenetrable darkness dropped over them like a curtain.

Over the indrawn breaths of the females, from perhaps half a cellar away, he heard a man's muffled curse.

The chase was on, no mistake. There was a solution, of course, but it was in his best interests to cause no more commotion than that which had already occurred, and most certainly to leave no more telltale bodies behind. The object of the entire exercise was his own ultimate survival, after all.

Neil's hands were already tightening around the bar that secured the door. The noise it made as he lifted it made him grit his teeth, although he was counting on the cover of darkness to conceal their exit even if it did not muffle all sound. If things were as he remembered, the bar on the other side of the door should be unsecured. This secret entrance was always locked, one way or another. Fortunately, tonight it was locked on the castle side.

His luck held. Even as the smallest glimmer of a light—a lantern being cautiously unshuttered?—sprang to life in the distance to the accompaniment of the gasps and frightened muttering of the huddled women, the heavy door yielded to his determined efforts with only the slightest of creaks. The light—and thus the men with it—was already on the move toward them as he caught Lady Elizabeth's arm, propelling her toward the opening. Where they stood was still cloaked in utter darkness, but that would not last long. The probing tentacles of light would reach them well before the men did.

"Go down the stairs. *Hurry,*" he told her.

Chapter Thirteen

BETH'S HEART KNOCKED against her rib cage as she descended the broken-down, slippery stone steps at what felt like breakneck speed. Mary and the others crowded close behind her, although they no longer clasped hands, as each had to feel her way down the stairwell alone to keep from falling. She could hear their panicked breathing, and the shuffle of their feet. Enclosed by stone walls that were repellently slimy to the touch, the narrow passage seemed to have been chiseled out of solid rock. Having pushed them before him through a door he had somehow managed to open in the dark, her handsome housebreaker, whose appearance on the scene was proving as miraculous as it was astounding, was now bringing up the rear. She was in front, with no idea of where she was heading, other than down. Over the moldy scent of the walls, she thought perhaps she could smell the sea, and there was just enough grayish light seeping up from below to make her think—hope—that they were racing toward some sort of exit, a door or window that was open to the night.

She prayed it was so. Despite the closed and hopefully locked door that stood between them and the rest of the cellar, the sounds of pursuit were terrifyingly close. Thumps and bangs and clatters, so loud it was clear their pursuers were now in the chamber they had just vacated, echoed off the walls of the narrow chute they were escaping down.

"Where'd they go?"

"Hold that lantern high!"

"Bloody wenches have to be here somewhere."

"They're hiding, don't you know?"

"Search behind those barrels. See if any of those trunks open."

"'Ave a care. Whoever's 'elping 'em did for Malloy."

"Aye, well, shoot 'im and grab the bawds."

"Could they have doubled back?"

The barely muffled voices were sharp with frustration. The accents varied from gentlemanly to broad Yorkshire, with the gentlemanly one seeming to be in charge, which to Beth's mind indicated that the servants had now been joined by at least one of their masters. Knowing that they were mere yards away in the room at the top of the stairwell made Beth's blood run cold. From the voices, she guessed there were at least six, and possibly more. It could only be a matter of time until one of the band spotted the door. When that happened . . .

She shivered. They needed to be well away before then.

A moment later, just before she reached the ground, Beth could at last glimpse where they were headed as she looked out through the open door at the end of the stairwell. The place where she would emerge was night-dark rather than pitch-black, thanks to glimmers of moonlight that filtered in through the mouth of what appeared to be a large cave and glinted off the mirror-smooth blackness of a narrow finger of water. As she reached the bottom of the steps and ran out onto it, toward the water, the ground beneath her feet was rocky sand—a beach. Just strides away, the small inlet lapped at the shore. The arched mouth of the cave—for it was a cave she was in, with stone rising steeply all around to form a soaring ceiling over her head—must open to the sea beyond.

"Blimey, they be comin'." Mary rushed to join her, with the other women tumbling from the stairwell one by one to race behind her.

"They're coming, they're coming." The frightened warning rose from every throat.

Pulse leaping, whirling around to face the stairwell opening, Beth listened to the rattling and scraping that filled the air and identified it as the sound of someone attempting to open the door at the top of the stairs. Clustering together now in a tight group just a couple of yards from where the tide lapped at the shore, none of them knowing where to go next because, except for the mouth of the cave, which could only be reached by water, there seemed to be no way out, the women exchanged frightened glances.

"There's no damned boat that I can find, and the water just off the shore here drops to about twelve feet deep." The house-breaker caught up to them. Since he came from a direction other than the stairwell, she thought he must have been searching for a boat in the dark. "Can you swim?" His eyes were on Beth, and the question was clearly directed to her. He had been moving fast, but didn't seem even faintly breathless as he stopped in front of her.

"Yes," Beth answered, glad her voice sounded far calmer than she felt.

"No!" the blonde cried at the same time, clutching at his arm.

Shrugging her off, the housebreaker caught Beth's elbow. His large, warm hand slid beneath the silk to close around her bare skin. "That simplifies things. We must just . . ."

"I canno' swim either!" Mary grabbed a handful of Beth's domino, which billowed behind her as the housebreaker pulled Beth toward the water. Grabbing hold of the domino, too, and moving with them, the others chimed in together.

"Nor I!"

"Nor I!"

"I'm sorry for it." The housebreaker glanced around. He did not sound particularly sorrowful, Beth noticed. "If you hide, perhaps some of you will escape."

"There's no place *to* hide."

"'Tis sitting ducks we'll be!"

"I saw a boat in the cellar!"

"Bah, 'tis of no use to us now, is it, with them in the cellar with it?"

Beth could feel the frantic tug of their hands on the domino even as the housebreaker determinedly drew her on toward the water. She couldn't talk, and in fact could scarcely breathe. The prospect of leaving the others behind was terrible, but the alternative was something she knew she could not survive. The pounding from the top of the stairs turned into a drawn-out, metallic screech that cut through the night. Beth's already racing heart thumped even harder. There was no possibility of mistake: their pursuers were now attempting to force open the door.

"What be that?"

"They're forcing the door."

"Cor, what do we do?"

The panic in the other women's voices flayed at her like a whip.

"The water will be cold," the housebreaker warned in her ear. "I'll stay beside you in case you need help."

"I don't need your help."

A lightning glance at the mouth of the cave confirmed it: the distance was not that great. With the water so smooth, Beth knew that, cold or not, she could swim it with ease.

"Ye'll not leave us! Please, please!"

I won't be taken. Just thinking about what she would endure if that happened made Beth shake like a blancmange inside. *I can't endure it. Never, never.*

They were just a couple of paces from the edge of the water. She must needs kick off her shoes and untie the domino . . .

The metallic screeching from the top of the stairs was so loud now that it almost drowned out the other women's frantic voices. Its increasing volume underlined that they had only precious minutes or even seconds left in which to escape.

The water gleamed black before her.

From the corner of her eyes, she saw Mary, her mouth moving in a plea that the pounding of Beth's pulse in her ears would no longer allow her to hear, and the faces of the others, too. Terrified faces . . .

Terrified, just as she was terrified.

Fear tasted like vinegar on Beth's tongue. The temptation was almost overwhelming. But to leave them without any protection at all, to abandon them to their fates while she saved herself, was something she discovered she just could not do.

Swallowing, squaring her shoulders, she dug in her heels hard just one small step away from the water's edge. When the housebreaker looked back at her inquiringly, she shook her head.

"I can't go without them." Her voice was hoarse, raw.

"What? Oh, yes, you can." His hand tightened on her arm, and she realized that he was about to pull her into the water by force majeure if necessary. "When we reach safety, we can send the constable back for them. He should arrive in time to—"

"No." Beth wrenched her arm free and leaped away from him to the accompaniment of what sounded like a collective female moan of relief. *He* would not leave without *her,* they all knew, although why that was so she wasn't quite sure. Her thoughts flew to that stolen kiss. Was he helping her escape only to secure her for himself? She didn't know—but he *was* helping her, and for now that was enough. His motive she would worry about later. Clearly the others' fear wasn't so much that she would leave them, but that he would. They looked at him as the best source of protection they had. She remembered the knife, flying out of nowhere to lodge in the throat of the huge man who was choking her. Remembered, too, how he had dealt so handily with William, and realized they were right. He was strong and able, handy with his fives and, if the knife was any indication, with weapons, too. But he would be so badly outnumbered . . .

"Damn it to hell and back, we've no time for this folly. That door will not hold forever." The housebreaker's ire was evident in his tone as he advanced on her. Surrounded by the others, who fell back with her, Beth backed away. Even as their voices swirled around her unheeded, she held his gaze. He was clearly angry, clearly bent on imposing his will on her. She'd had personal experience with his strength, and had no doubt that she stood little chance of withstanding him if he chose to simply pick her up and bear her off. First, though, he had to lay hands on her again.

A sudden sharp *pop* and a triumphant male cry punctuated the terrifying groans of metal being systematically pulled apart.

Heart in throat, Beth glanced back toward the stairs.

"They're breaking through," Mary gasped. Some of the others clutched at Beth, their expressions fearful.

"What do we do? What should we do?"

Making a harsh sound under his breath, the housebreaker reached Beth with a single stride that was far longer and swifter than anything she had foreseen and caught her by both arms, frowning down at her. His hands were large and incredibly strong, and he held her in a grip that this time she knew she couldn't break. The others fell back a little, looking from one to the other of them with both fear and indecision plain in their faces.

Beth knew what they were thinking very well: Should they attack the man they hoped would help save them? From their expressions, she could see the answer was clearly no.

"Let me *go*." Beth had visions of being borne away into the water willy-nilly, and scowled right back at him. "If you force me, I'll not swim a stroke."

"Please, sir . . ."

"Help us."

"Oh, please."

"We be beggin' ye."

As the chorus of pleas continued disregarded around them, his eyes took on a dangerous gleam as they bored into hers. His mouth thinned and his jaw hardened to granite. His grip tightened cruelly, and he pulled her up onto her toes while Beth stared right back at him with undeterred defiance.

"I mean what I say," she told him.

After a brace of seconds in which the issue hung in the balance, some of the hardness left his eyes and his mouth twisted into a wry sort of grimace. His grip eased. He glanced around at the women, who were now gathered in a circle around them both. One tugged at his sleeve, another laid a beseeching hand on his arm;

all implored him with their eyes as well as their voices. Watching his face, Beth got the impression that he was, at the very least, wishing them all at Jericho.

"God save me from all bloody women." His tone was harsh, but Beth recognized the words as capitulation and felt a rush of relief. His hold on her loosened enough so that she was once again standing flat on the beach. She smiled at him. He did not smile back. It didn't matter. Though he was obviously less than pleased with the prospect, she knew he would do what he could to help them withstand their pursuers, who were, from the sound of it, in the last stages of tearing the door from the wall. But would it be enough? Not likely. He was only one man, after all. But if they all worked together, perhaps . . .

"We can help you fight them off," she said, and the others chimed in eagerly.

"There be rocks . . ."

"We can throw sand in their eyes when they gets close."

"Sand? I'll scratch their bleedin' eyes out for 'em, I will."

"Rocks and sand against guns? We must—"

"No." He sent a quelling glance around. "If you lot want to help, then you'll do what I damned well tell you. Nothing more, nothing less." His eyes gleamed blacker even than the nearby water as he looked down at Beth again. As she met them she was suddenly, forcefully put in mind of a predator. "That goes especially for you, my girl. Do I have your word that you'll do exactly as I say?"

"Yes," she promised.

There was a change in him that she couldn't quite pinpoint. It was too dark for her to read the fine points of his expression, but he seemed now to emanate a savage energy that spoke more of beast than man. His hands had tightened on her arms again, and she was perfectly sure that unless he chose to release her, she wouldn't be able to get away.

"Then hide, damn it. All of you. *Now.* Get down behind the rocks and stay there. Keep your heads down. Do not make a sound. Do not come out until I come for you. Do you understand?" His eyes were on Beth.

"Yes." Beth answered along with the rest.

"Go, then." Releasing her, he made an imperious gesture that sent them rushing away.

Beth ran with the others toward the clumps of rocks that rose perhaps hip-high from the sand. Even as the women split up into groups of different sizes to accommodate the sizes of the rocks they crouched behind, another sharp *pop* followed by a victorious yell and, within seconds, the dull thud of boots pounding on stone told Beth that their pursuers had broken through at last, and were rushing down the stairwell toward them.

Oh, no.

Her heart leaped into her throat. Her gaze fastened on the mouth of the stairwell.

"Ayee." The soft cry came from the apple-cheeked brunette, who immediately clapped her hands over her mouth to stifle further utterance. Along with Mary, she was hunkered down with Beth. No one else made a sound, but the fear in the air was as palpable as the smell of the sea.

Swallowing hard, Beth searched the shadowy darkness for the housebreaker. There he was, running flat-out toward the stairwell. Her eyes widened in disbelief. What was he thinking, to race straight toward a charging force that was both numerically superior and presumably well armed? Beth's stomach tightened in fear and guilt. Were it not for her refusal to leave the others, he would be well on his way to safety now. He alone faced death if they were overrun. She had not realized until now that her actions were putting him so dreadfully at risk.

Please, God . . . She sent a hasty prayer for his safety winging skyward.

"There 'e is!" a man shouted as the group burst from the stairwell in an untidy knot. "Shoot 'im! Shoot 'im!"

The sharp bang of a pistol caused them all to duck. Beth swallowed a cry. She suspected the others did, too.

Then the cave exploded into a firestorm of gunfire. Cowering behind the rock, Beth covered her head with her arms. Shouts and screams of pain and the sounds of running feet mingled with the gunfire, the whole so loud that it was almost impossible to discern any individual sound. Heart racing, occasionally peeking around the rock because she absolutely could not help herself, Beth saw dark shapes racing about and bright flashes as the pistols were fired, and little more. It was a battle of shadows veiled by night, and the fine points of it were impossible to discern.

But she was sore afraid that she knew what the outcome had to be.

Glancing compulsively over her shoulder at the water as the battle raged, she recognized something lowering about herself: if the moment were truly at hand, if it came to the point where they were to be retaken, she would save herself after all, plunging into the water and swimming for all she was worth.

I am a coward.

But she couldn't help it. The other prospect was too dreadful to be borne.

Silence, when it fell, was absolute. Suddenly there was nothing at all beyond the ringing in her ears.

After a moment or so of this, the women stirred restively. Beth felt the brush of nervous movement on either side even as she dared raise her head above the rock for another quick look. It was so dark. She could see nothing—nothing moving—at all. Her heart threatened to pound its way out of her chest as she strained to see through the dark.

"Wot's 'appened?"

"Do ye see ought?"

The other women, she saw with a glance, were peering around the rocks, too.

"I can't see anything." Beth squinted as she searched the shadows near the stairwell. Where were their pursuers? Where was *he*? She could see no one at all, not a single solitary soul, and that was growing increasingly terrifying. "We must stay hidden, and be very quiet until we—"

A footstep crunched behind them. Gasping, head whipping toward the sound, Beth jumped like she'd been shot.

The housebreaker stood there. A tall, imposing figure in his long greatcoat, he thrust a pistol into his waistband and looked up as her gaze found him. His face was in shadow, but the savage energy she had sensed in him earlier seemed to have lessened.

Beth felt a flood of relief.

"You're alive." Standing, she hurried toward him. That she was glad showed in her voice and the beaming smile with which she met his narrowed gaze.

"Did you doubt I would be?" He caught her arms again, his hands warm and strong but surprisingly gentle now as they curled just above her elbows. His eyes slid over her face.

"Perhaps. Just a trifle," she admitted, still smiling up at him. Her hands came to rest on his chest, and she absently noted the smooth texture of the waistcoat he wore, and the width of his chest in relationship to her hands. "Though I'm very glad to be wrong, of course."

"Are you indeed?" His voice was dry.

The others reached them in a flurry of footsteps, swishing skirts and questions.

"Did they hare off, then?"

"Wot 'appened?"

"Be we saved?"

"Is there a way out?"

"What do we do now?"

"Where'd the buggers go?"

"Never tell us you've single-handedly slain the lot?" The tone of Beth's question was less than serious, because she didn't see how that could be possible. What was likely, in her opinion, was that their pursuers had fled upon encountering determined opposition.

A twist of his lips was her only reply.

"We've not much time." He glanced around the group. "The gunshots will have been heard, you may be sure, and someone will come to investigate. Did one of you say you saw a boat inside the cellar?"

"I did." The speaker was the girl with fuzzy brown ringlets in the stained white dress. "It was lying against the wall in the last chamber before we came down the stairs."

"We must needs fetch it." Releasing Beth, he turned away, speaking over his shoulder. "As quickly and quietly as we can. I may require your help to get it down the stairs."

They all rushed after him. As they ran toward the stairwell, Beth spied a dark shape in the sand that hadn't been there before, and recognized it for what it was with a quiver of dismay: a man, lying prone. Not a foot away lay another. This one was on his back. Yet another lay curled on his side, a growing dark circle spreading through the sand around his head. None of them so much as twitched a finger.

"Be they dead, d'ye think?" Mary asked, her voice low. She was at Beth's elbow.

"I don't know," Beth replied.

"They look dead to me," the apple-cheeked girl murmured from Beth's other side.

"Cor, 'e did for 'em all," Mary breathed, awe in her tone. "All by 'is lonesome, like."

Glancing around, following the direction of Mary's gaze, Beth saw that she appeared to be right. Three more bodies were scattered around the curve of the inlet. Until now, they had been hidden by the dark. That meant six motionless bodies in all lay on the beach.

Dead? If some amongst them were not, from the look of them they were close enough as to make no difference.

Beth's breath caught in her throat. A cold little thrill of horror snaked all the way down her spine from her nape to her toes. Widened and wary, her eyes sought the housebreaker's broad-shouldered form as he disappeared into the stairwell. She could not be sorry she and the others were saved, of course, but it was terrible to realize he had indeed almost certainly killed six men. Plus the giant above stairs.

Seven. Single-handedly. Without apparent compunction.

What manner of man is this?

That was the appalled thought that twisted through her mind even as she and the others ran after him up the stairs.

Chapter Fourteen

THE BOAT WAS a small open rowboat, probably intended to be occupied only by two and certainly no more than four. It was old and creaky, and looked barely seaworthy, but it had oars and it floated under all their weight, which as far as Beth was concerned was all that was required of it. Piling aboard under the housebreaker's terse direction, they managed to cram themselves in. Pulling off his boots and greatcoat and thrusting them at Beth for safekeeping, he pushed them out and then jumped aboard himself. Now he sat in the forward seat facing them as he rowed, sopping wet from the knees

down, his long legs in their black pantaloons and white stockings stretching out
almost to the aft seat. The rest of them
crowded together, filling the boat to overflowing, wincing at every dip of the bow
and groan of the wood. They were huddled on the floor of the boat, crammed together on the aft seat, wedged in at the
stern, in quarters so tight that it was almost impossible to move. The boat rode
dangerously low in the water, but with the
inlet as smooth as it was their progress
was swift. The housebreaker worked the
oars with a will. They had almost reached
the mouth of the cave when another band
of men spilled out of the stairwell.

Beth heard them before she saw them.
The hum of excited voices, the drumbeat
of running feet, were loud enough to be
audible even over the slap of the oars and
the disjointed conversations and rustling
movements around her. Her heart, which
had been slowing down to a near-normal
pace, recommenced thumping wildly. Curled
in a cold puddle in the bottom of the boat
beside the housebreaker's left leg (Mary
was crunched near his right leg, and his

boots, standing upright, took pride of place between his knees), Beth felt him stiffen even as she cringed at the unmistakable sounds of the chase being taken up anew. With fresh fear in her eyes, she glanced back at the beach they were steadily leaving behind just in time to watch as a running clump of men burst into view.

"Hell and the devil." The housebreaker's muttered imprecation told her that he saw them, too. The muscles of the thigh against which she leaned tightened, and he began to row with even more vigor than before.

There were indrawn breaths and murmurs of fright and warning as the others saw the men. Beth could not tell how many there were. Only that a number of faceless pursuers were now on the beach—and had spotted the small boat scudding through the mirrorlike water toward the mouth of the cave.

One pointed. "Look at that!"

"There they go!"

"Don't let 'em get away!"

Their shouts made her shiver.

A pistol spat toward them with a bright yellow flash. The sound exploded off the walls of the cave, the volume amplified by the enclosed space. That shot was immediately followed by another and yet a third. Beth saw a white spurt in the dark water as a ball skimmed the surface not a yard off the starboard side, and ducked, pulling the silken folds of the domino closer around her as if the garment could somehow protect her.

"Keep down!" the housebreaker roared, but they needed no warning. Huddled into a frightened mass now, holding on to each other and the boat for dear life, those at the rear sheltering under his greatcoat, which they shared, the women got as low as they could as a volley of gunfire rattled down around them. Beth could feel the tension in his muscles as he feverishly worked the single set of oars. Fear stabbed her as she realized that he could not follow his own advice and still row. Whatever he was—and she was still trying to reconcile her instinctive trust of him with the fact that he had so easily and without apparent remorse killed so many, and broken into her brother-in-law's house for an unknown but certainly unlawful purpose besides— she did not wish him to be hurt, or killed, and sitting upright in the midst of a fire-storm of bullets seemed a good way to accomplish both.

"Jenkins! Hawks! Run toward that—by God, look here, it be Loomis. And Fielding. Jesu, they're all dead!"

They were not so distant that they could not plainly hear the cry from shore as the bodies were discovered. A plethora of shouts and curses punctuated with another burst of gunfire aimed their way had Beth burying her head against the housebreaker's hard-muscled thigh. She was ashamed to discover that she now had her arms wrapped tight around his leg. But there was nowhere else to go, nothing else to hold on to, and the bullets whizzed by in such numbers and so close, they whined like a horde of angry insects as they passed. A spray of water as one hit particularly near splattered her averted cheek with cold droplets and made her catch her breath.

"*Ah.*" The housebreaker made a quick, pained sound that stopped just short of a groan, and the rhythm of his rowing faltered. Lifting her head in the teeth of the gunfire, Beth looked up at him, wide-eyed.

"What?" she demanded.

"Nothing. Keep your head *down*."

Bullets peppered the water nearby. As one sang past her ear, she flinched reflexively, but didn't duck. If he'd been hit . . .

"Are you hurt?" Her eyes ran over him from head to toe, encompassing as much of him as she could see. Silhouetted by moonlight as he was, his expression was difficult to read. But his eyes were narrowed. His mouth had thinned. His jaw was set. Even as she looked him over he was already rowing strongly again, the powerful muscles of his arms and shoulders working in a steady rhythm, his leg still warm and strong and firm against her. He remained his handsome, inscrutable self, and there was no damage to him that she could see. But the darkness, which, coupled with his black frock coat, waistcoat, and pantaloons kept her from seeing any real details beyond the broad outline of his person, was most concealing, so there was no way to be certain. As far as she could tell, he was unharmed, but under the circumstances that meant little. The odd little sound he had made troubled her, as did the corresponding hiccup in his rowing. His expression as their eyes met was certainly grim, but then the situation was dire and grimness was called for. And he undoubtedly blamed her for finding himself caught up in it, because she had refused to leave the others. Refused so often he hadn't even bothered to argue about the merits of piling so many into so small a boat, as she had half expected him to do.

"I *said,* get your bloody head down."

"And I asked if you were hurt."

"If you wish to take a ball through the brains . . ."

"I could just as easily be hit in the back, or the side. Besides, I feel we are now out of reach of all but the luckiest of shots."

"Oh, setting yourself up as an expert on the range of firearms, are you? And it takes only one lucky shot, I assure you."

"Were you hit back there?" She put it to him directly.

"No."

"You made a sound as if you were suddenly in pain."

"Doubtless you were squeezing my leg too tight."

That reminder of how she had clung to him had the potential to be mortifying, which was no doubt what he intended, but Beth, who fortunately was no longer holding on to his leg for dear life, but instead had wrapped her hands around the edge of the seat, chose not to be embarrassed.

"That is not it and you know it."

His mouth tightened still more. That was his only reply as with strong strokes and in the teeth of the near-continuous barrage of gunfire—which, just as she had said, was beginning to fall short—he took them on through the mouth of the cave. Just that quick and the most immediate source of danger was left behind. The moonlit night into which they emerged seemed almost bright to Beth's thankful eyes, and the brisk wind that blew from the sea smelled sweet and fresh as the rarest perfume. Towering above them was the castle, an enormous turreted relic with innumerable windows that glowed like narrow, malignant eyes against the night sky. Even as she looked up at it her hair got caught on an updraft and flew everywhere, streaming across her eyes, whipping into his face. Gathering it up and securing it with a couple of practiced twists, she knotted the ends into a cumbersome bun at her neck. Another volley of gunfire and threatening shouts echoed futilely in what was now the distance as the cave was slowly but surely left behind. Cloaked in the castle's ink black shadow, the boat began to rock over the small, choppy waves of the open strait.

"Tell me, do you ever follow orders?" He looked down at her, his tone caustic.

"Until I become a junior member of a military company, I see no need to do so, at least without thought."

"While you're under my protection, you'll do as I tell you, however."

"Will I, indeed?"

"If you know what is good for you, my girl."

"I am not your girl—and it is precisely because I do think I know what is good for me that I do not just blindly follow orders, even when they are issued by so estimable a personage as yourself."

"For a young woman who is in trouble every time I see her, you seem very sure of the infallibility of your own judgment."

"I've learned to rely on my own judgment. And speaking of being in trouble, every time I've seen *you,* you've not exactly been a pattern-card of rectitude. Far from it, in fact."

"The cases are not the same."

Now that the need for ducking was indisputably past, she took the opportunity to look him over with more care. They were out of the shadow of the castle now, and the moon was a slim crescent soaring high overhead. By its silvery glow, his lean cheeks looked much paler than she remembered, but then, that could be an illusion caused by the vagaries of moonlight. There was a new thinness to his mouth, though, and a tension to his jaw that she did not think was caused solely by the exigencies of rowing. His eyes seemed more hooded than before, and she thought—it was impossible to be sure in the darkness—that there were lines around them that she had not previously observed. Lines of pain?

"You *were* hit," she said.

"You know, you are beginning to be a dead bore."

"Now, isn't that a coincidence? For I was just thinking exactly the same about you. And, while we are speaking of coincidences—I find it hard to believe that your being here on this night is pure chance."

"Pure *lucky* chance, as far as you're concerned, do you mean? And you are welcome to believe what you will."

"Saints be praised, we be out of it!" A tremulous voice from the rear of the boat distracted Beth. His greatcoat, which had formed a kind of roof over much of the boat, as all the women who could fit under it had used it to cover their heads when the shooting started, stirred. Several cautious faces peered out.

"We're out of the cave!"

"It's all right, everyone, we're safe."

"It's safe, did you say?"

"Oh, aye. The bullets can't reach us, more."

"Cor, we be in a leaky boat on the bloody sea, and none of us save miss and 'is worship there can swim a stroke. 'Tis not what I would call safe, precisely."

Even as the coat was cast aside, Mary's trenchant speech had the effect of dampening the others' incipient giddiness as effectively as a deluge of cold water. All fell glumly silent as they sat up and looked about them at the waves of black water curling past. White-knuckled hands gripped the sides of the boat and the edges of seats and each other as they took stock of their position. Some caught their breath. One or two mouthed silent prayers. Nervous glances shot everywhere.

"Mary, you've no need to call me 'miss,'" Beth said, in an effort to turn the others' thoughts in a direction more cheering than the prospect of imminent drowning, which now appeared to be occupying them almost exclusively. "I am Beth."

Mary shook her head. "I knows a member of the quality when I see's one, and you be quality, miss. And 'is worship, too."

The housebreaker said nothing as he continued to row, but Beth realized that Mary had discerned something that had not until this moment consciously registered with her. His speech, his manner, his carriage, a certain air about him that was indefinable but recognizable nonetheless, all marked him as being a man of a certain birth. Casting a curious glance at him—whether he was listening was impossible to tell from his expression, but she didn't see how he could have missed hearing the exchange—she decided to save her questions about his origins for a later time, when they could be asked in private. Although she suspected she probably wouldn't glean much from his answers, if he even deigned to answer at all. That he might have reasons for wishing to keep his own secrets was already abundantly clear.

"I'm Beth," she repeated firmly, turning her attention back to Mary. Mary shook her head, indicating her inability to address Beth so familiarly. Beth gave it up for the moment, and glanced at the apple-cheeked girl in dun who was wedged in between Mary and the aft seat. Her face was now pale as the froth on the waves, and she clutched the side of the pitching, creaking boat with both hands. "And you, what is your name?"

"Peg." Her name emerged between deep breaths. "Ach, I've no love for boats."

"We'll be all right," Beth said, hoping it was so, and looked at the pair on the only available seat: the blonde in red silk, and the fair-haired girl in the ripped blue dress. With the greatcoat now wrapped around both their shoulders, they sat huddled together with their backs hunched and their arms curled around each other's waist, their posture clearly indicating fear that an unanticipated dip or roll would send them instantly tumbling into the surging water.

"I'm Dolly." With a semicoquettish dip of her head, the blonde addressed the information to the housebreaker. "Dolly Ivers. From New Bingham."

If she was hoping for a response from that quarter, none was forthcoming. Beth, who glanced at him to check, could not detect so much as the flair of a nostril to indicate he had noticed Dolly's unmistakable interest in him, or that he cared if he had. His eyes were hooded and dark as he looked back at the island they were leaving behind. His movements stayed strong and steady as he continued to row toward the mainland. The distance was not that great; the increasingly turbulent journey could not last much longer. To keep all their minds off the growing waves, she next turned her attention to the thin girl sheltering under the coat with Dolly.

"And you are?"

"Jane Meadows." This one's lips quivered as if she would burst into tears even as she spoke. "From D-Dover. And I'm mortal afeared of water."

"It will be all right," Beth said again. "Look, we are past halfway there."

The remaining two were crammed into the stern. Beth looked a question at the plump girl with smooth wings of brown hair just as an errant plume of icy water sprayed over everyone, herself included, on the starboard side of the boat. The waves, she saw with dismay, were picking up.

"I be Alyce," she said. "I work at a weaver's in Macclesfield. Or I did. Before."

Before she was snatched away to the castle was what she clearly meant. Dashing the salty droplets from her face, Beth nodded. Trying not to notice the rising waves or the increased pitching of the boat, her gaze moved on to the frizzy-haired girl in the stained white dress.

This one was busily occupied in looking around in obvious fear at the peaking whitecaps, and didn't speak until Alyce, beside her, elbowed her in the ribs.

"Say your name," Alyce hissed.

"Eh? Oh!" She clutched her side as her attention was brought back to them and she realized everyone was looking at her. "My name's Nan Staub."

Nan spoke through chattering teeth. Beth

realized that now that the island no longer stood between them and the open sea, the wind could reach them at full strength, and had turned almost biting. Even wrapped in the voluminous folds of the domino as she was, she was getting cold, too.

"My dad owned a shop in Donnington," Nan continued. "He passed on not a fort-night since, leaving nothing but debts. Everything had to be sold. We lived over the shop, him and me, so when they took it to sell I was cast out. A gent who'd been a customer of ours heard of my troubles, and was kind enough, as I thought, to offer me a position as a companion to his old aunt. At the time, it seemed a God-send. O' course, it turned out to be no such thing."

"You're in the same case as I am, then," Jane said. "With nothing to your name, and no place save the workhouse to go."

She sounded so forlorn that Beth's heart was touched.

"Don't concern yourselves, any of you, with what is to befall you once we are out of this," she told them. "We'll see to it that you're each restored to your homes, or if

you've none, to a place of safety, I promise you." A restive movement on the housebreaker's part had her glancing up at him
for endorsement. "Will we not?"

The look he gave her fell sadly short of
that which she was hoping for.

"I don't deal in promises."

A sudden, boatwide silence was the response.

"Well, I do," Beth said, rallying. Then,
glancing around at the others, she added
stoutly: "You will not be abandoned, I give
you my word."

"'Tis a right trump you be, miss," Mary
said. Some nodded agreement, while
others gave the housebreaker the same
kind of nervous looks they had been casting toward the waves. It was easy to see
they remembered how eager he had been
to leave them behind, and drew their own
conclusions from that as to his future behavior toward them.

"It would not have hurt you to have
agreed with me, you know," Beth said with
some asperity when the others' attention
was no longer on them.

"But I *don't* agree with you. And, apparently unlike you, I have no power to predict the future. Circumstances may very well dictate that this lot will have to fend for themselves before this folly reaches its conclusion."

"You would leave them?"

"Easily."

"And I suppose you would abandon me, too?"

"No, not you."

"And why is that?" Beth demanded, incensed at the evident unfairness of it.

He didn't reply. His face was unreadable.

He was once again looking back the way they had come. Beth, following his gaze, saw why: a jumble of bobbing lights raced away from the castle toward what she thought must be the jetty where the ferry was docked. She had been conscious only briefly when she'd been carried onto the island, but she was good with direction and she was almost certain that the jetty was where they had come ashore. Just as she was almost certain that the lights were lanterns, and the reason they were bobbing and moving so fast was because they were being held by men on horseback who were racing toward the ferry. That being so, she had little doubt of their object: to cross the strait in time to cut the escapees off.

Her head swung around and she measured the distance they still had to go before they reached shore. They were now about two-thirds of the way across.

The chase was still on. If the horsemen reached their destination before they did . . .

Her now-comprehending gaze met the housebreaker's. From his expression, it was clear that he had been aware of the danger long before she spotted those bobbing lanterns. Probably from the time they had left the cavern behind.

If the others hadn't seen, or realized—and there was no reason to think they had, because this was not a group that held silence to be a virtue—Beth saw no point in worrying them with the news.

"Sir, what should we call you?" The bold voice served to return her attention to the group. The look the blonde—Dolly—gave the housebreaker was unmistakably coquettish this time. And once again, he appeared to fail to notice her interest. Indeed, it wasn't clear that he even heard the question.

"I would know, too," Beth said softly.

The ensuing pause was so long that Beth thought he wasn't going to reply. As the answer interested her exceedingly, though, she was, like the others, looking at him with expectation by the time he did, with a glance down at her as she curled at his feet.

"My name is Neil."

There was something about his voice—was it starting to sound more labored than before?—that Beth found concerning. Rowing in such conditions was exhausting, she had no doubt, but he was an exceptionally fit and strong man. Despite his denial, she was almost sure that he had been at least grazed by a bullet. Perhaps he was losing blood, and weakening as a result?

The thought was so alarming that her heart beat faster.

"Are you all right?" she asked almost under her breath, so that only he could hear.

Their eyes met. His were now as remote as the night-dark sky.

"Leave it alone," he said.

"Water is coming in back here right through the wood," Alyce cried in obvious fright. "'Tis rotten, I fear."

Instantly diverted, Beth saw that Alyce was looking down at something between herself and the side of the boat, her face a study in horror.

"Indeed, she is right. The pair of us are already awash." Beside Alyce, Nan scrambled onto her knees, holding on to the far side of the boat for support, her eyes wide as she glanced at the rolling waves surrounding them. The boat rocked ominously at this shift in weight, and several cried out and clutched at each other and anything else they could grab hold of.

"Sit down and stay still," Neil said. "You'll swamp us else. And bail. Use your cupped hands to throw the water out."

"We will drown," Jane cried, while Nan, her arm having been caught by Alyce, sank down again, although her terrified expression did not change. Already it was apparent that the boat was starting to sink lower in the back. Although she was positioned well forward, Beth could see the dark gleam of water as it climbed incrementally higher inside the stern. Alyce and Nan, in the rear, began frantically bailing with their cupped hands. There was nothing any of the rest of them could do. Shifting around in an effort to help might well overset them all.

"How big is the hole?" Neil demanded, rowing more strongly than ever. The shore was growing nearer, Beth saw with a frantic glance around. But not, she feared, near enough. Seeking out the bobbing lanterns, she saw that the lights were now rolling in unison rather than bobbing about individually. That, and their position, told her that those chasing them were now on the ferry, and already more than halfway across.

"About the size of sixpence. Oh, water is gushing in now!"

"'Tis a regular fountain!"

"And cold! 'Tis cold!"

"Stick something in the hole to plug it up," Beth recommended in as steady a tone as she could muster. Water was sloshing past the rear seat, and would in only a matter of moments reach her and the others in the bow, she feared.

"Use this! Use this!" several voices chorused at once, as various items were produced for possible use.

Beth could not see precisely what was jammed into the hole, but from Alyce's actions it was clear that something was.

"Did that stop the water?" Neil asked, very calm.

Alyce looked up. She was so frightened that the whites of her eyes showed.

"It slowed it some, but some be still seeping through." Her voice shook. Beth felt an icy gush of water around her legs and looked down: the thinnest layer of black water was washing toward the bow.

"Put your hand over the plug and hold it there." His gaze swept the group. "The rest of you, bail."

Thus adjured, they all started bailing with a will. The water was almost half an inch deep around Beth now, and the depth in the stern was much worse. Her legs and bottom were now soaked to the skin and freezing cold, but she barely noticed. The boat was riding ever lower, and it seemed that every other wave showered them with spray. Along with the other women, she used her cupped hands to fling the sea back where it belonged in a frantic rhythm, and prayed that they would reach the narrow, rocky beach that provided egress to the mainland before the craft completely sank beneath them. But as a long, cold shadow fell over the boat, a questioning glance around to find its cause showed her that they were no longer in line to land where she had supposed they must. From the force of the wind or a strong current or for some other reason she couldn't immediately fathom, they'd been swept around past the promontory that marked the end of the beach. They were now heading straight toward the black granite cliffs that towered some fifty feet high and marked the little bay's convergence with the sea. With the waves driving them on, unless a change of course was made they must be dashed against the rocks within minutes.

Beth's eyes widened with horror. Was Neil so intent on his rowing that he had not realized? Did he not know they were now wide of the mark and on the brink of disaster?

"We've missed the beach!" she cried. But as soon as they left her mouth her words were caught and flung away by the wind that had risen precipitously, and it seemed neither he nor anyone else had heard. More spray pelted her. The cold drops stung, and she could taste their salt on her lips. Abandoning bailing, she put a desperate hand on his thigh and shook it to get his attention. Rowing with what now seemed to be fierce determination, he looked a question at her.

"We've missed the beach!"

But even as she screamed it at him it was too late. A wave caught them up and sent them hurtling straight toward the sheer face of the cliff.

Chapter Fifteen

GASPING, BETH GRABBED the cold, wet nankeen of Neil's pantaloons with one hand and the edge of the seat in front of her with the other in simultaneous death grips. Twisted away from her now, he, too, stared at the cliff.

The boat will be smashed like an egg, and we'll be the first to hit.

But she didn't say it, or anything else, because she was suddenly so terrified she couldn't make a sound. The waves immediately preceding the one that had caught them up crashed into the looming wall of smooth vertical stone with roars and boiling explosions of seething white foam. With no possibility of turning aside, they flew inevitably toward the same fate.

Please, God, please . . .

At the last minute, as the boat hurtled like a thrown javelin toward the towering wall of granite now immediately before them, the others saw their danger and loosed a chorus of screams. Those sounds, too, were caught up by the wind until they were barely audible over the booming of the waves.

"Hold fast," Neil yelled, rowing manfully as the wave crested. With their boat riding atop it like a cork in a maelstrom, frozen with terror as she realized that they must within seconds be dashed to their deaths against the rocks, Beth did as he said— and found herself looking in astonishment at a narrow opening in the cliff face. Seconds after she saw it, the boat sailed through the fissure with the slimmest of margins, only to plummet downward like a kite falling from the sky and wash up seconds later in a churning, ink black pool.

There was a long moment of dead silence as Beth, at least, processed the fact that she was still alive.

"Scared me near witless, that did. I thought I'd be cockin' up me toes for certain sure." Mary was the first to recover her voice as Neil once again began to row, but with much less urgency now.

"'Tis a bloomin' miracle," Peg said devoutly, looking back at the opening. They all followed her gaze. With its bottom edge some twenty feet over their heads, the jagged crack allowed them a view of the slenderest slice of the star-studded sky. Then a wave hit the outside of the cliff with a muffled roar and echoing boom, and a torrent of water cascaded down toward the pool. They were too far away to be hit by it, but it helped drive their now badly listing boat on toward shore.

"You were absolutely *smashing*." All admiration, Dolly once again directed her words to Neil. "To find that crack in the cliff and get us through like you did! You saved us all!"

As the others echoed that sentiment in their various ways, Jane burst into noisy tears and buried her face in her hands.

"Oh my God." Neil's disgusted response was just loud enough to be heard by Beth. She fixed him with a censorious look while the ones who could reach Jane and were so inclined comforted her with pats and reassuring words.

A moment later, with a gritty sound, the bow slid up onto what a quick glance around showed Beth to be a narrow eyebrow of pale sand surrounded by a line of tumbled rocks. Like the cave beneath the castle, this one was a cathedral-like stone hollow, only the water it sheltered was more properly a small salt lake rather than a cove. Inside the cave it was dark and shadowy, but not quite pitch-black thanks to the moonlight streaming in, and quiet save for the sound of the sea, which continued to burst, roaring and spewing froth through the fissure that had just admitted them.

"Saints be praised, we've made it to dry land at last," Peg said in a shaky voice as Neil pitched his boots and the oars away from him onto the sand, then rolled out into foaming black water that was scarcely higher than knee-deep now and pushed the boat the rest of the way in.

"Aye, but where be we?" Mary asked darkly, glancing around. "'Tis not Lunnon, that's one thing sure."

"'Tis another cave," Nan said.

"Any rate, 'tis a sight better than where we were," Alyce pointed out.

"I was mortal afraid we was done for." Jane's head was up now, and her sobs had deteriorated into the occasional hiccuping gasp. "I'm that sorry I cried." Her tone was apologetic. Alyce patted her consolingly on the back.

"We were all afraid," Beth said. "But we're safe now."

I hope. But she wasn't about to voice any doubts.

"Everybody out," Neil ordered. Having made sure the boat was more or less securely lodged on the beach, he held it still as he waited for the women to disembark.

Getting rather awkwardly to her feet, Beth clambered out last. Her toes were so cold she could barely feel them, and water sloshed uncomfortably inside the poor bedraggled half boots that had once been so cunning. Her legs felt about as solid as jelly, and she wasn't surprised to discover that her knees shook. Stopping to take a deep breath once she was on solid ground, she tried to get a better look at her surroundings, but it was too dark to see anything beyond the beach area, so she gave it up. She was soaking wet from almost the waist down and freezing with it, her throat hurt, and her heart was still beating like a scared rabbit's. But she was alive and relatively unharmed; they all were. And that was what mattered.

There were murmurs of exhausted conversation as the others staggered toward the nearest rocks and sank down upon them, but she was too far away to make sense of anything that was said. Following in their wake, leaving a dripping trail like some just-emerged sea creature, she stopped to untie the strings of the wet domino, which was dragging from its own weight. Wringing it out, she draped it over her arm, then got sidetracked by Neil. He had been dragging the boat farther up onto the sand, and dropped it with a soft thud just a couple of feet away.

"You knew that opening in the cliff was there, didn't you." Her tone made it more of a statement than a question as she joined him. In retrospect, it was obvious that he'd been maneuvering the boat toward it when she'd been speechless with terror from thinking they were about to crash into the solid granite wall and die.

"I knew it used to be there." He picked up the oars and tossed them into the boat, where they landed with a clatter. Then he went to retrieve his boots, which lay on their sides in the sand.

Gathering up her sodden skirts in both hands and wringing them out as she went, she followed. "How?"

"Credit a misspent youth." Boots in hand, he stopped to look at her.

"Did you grow up around here, then?" She stopped, too, and they stood facing each other as she continued to wring streams of briny water from her skirts.

"What is that saying about curiosity?"

"It's obvious to me that the cave beneath the castle, and this one, are used for illicit activity. Probably smuggling."

"Recollect, if you will, what happened to that curious cat." He moved past her toward the rocks.

Beth's lips firmed in aggravation as she followed.

"I could not care less whether or not you are, or were, involved in smuggling. What I am asking is, are we safe here?"

"Probably not, or at least not for very long. For tonight, it seems we are. At least, I see no signs of anyone else around save ourselves."

"What about those men from the castle who are at this moment undoubtedly riding over the top of these very cliffs hunting us?"

"As we had no light, I doubt that they ever even saw the boat once it left the cove under the castle, so unless we're very unlucky, they should have no idea where we went. In any case, as far as this place is concerned, there are only two ways in. One is the way we just came, and as you've experienced for yourself, making use of it is damned tricky. The other— I doubt they will risk the other."

"It's more dangerous than what we just did? What does it involve, slaying a host of fire-breathing dragons?"

He laughed, but broke off abruptly, the sudden change in his expression making Beth frown. Then, having reached one of the clusters of stumplike rocks that ringed the sand, he sat down on the nearest available surface.

Or, more properly, dropped his boots in

the sand and sank down on it as if he badly felt the need to sit.

Beth remembered her conviction that he had been shot.

"Does it hurt very much?" she asked, with what she considered truly commendable cunning.

"'Tis the sting of the salt that's the worst of it, I think," he answered, then caught himself up as he realized what he had been tricked into admitting, and looked up at her so warily that despite his size and style, he reminded her of nothing so much as a guilty small boy.

"Are you just going to sit there and bleed, or do you want me to take a look?" Her tone was tart. From the way he was sitting, and the long, questing hand that he pressed to the area not far above his right armpit, it wasn't all that difficult for Beth to guess the location of the wound. She tried to see if she could discern the wet blackness of blood on his damp black coat, but it was impossible to make that kind of distinction in the shadowy gloom.

"I've no need of a ministering angel, thank you very much."

"That's fortunate, because I have no

wish to be one. However, you must see that if you were to bleed to death or some such thing, the rest of us would be left in a pretty fix. We don't know the way out."

The smallest of smiles just touched his mouth.

"And here I was thinking you were worried about me."

"Devil a bit," Beth replied with far more cheer than she actually felt. "However, I have no wish at all to be trapped forever in this cave, which I fear we might be if you were to die."

That brief shadow of a smile appeared again.

"I won't die, I assure you. It's the merest flesh wound"—with that he seemed to read something in her expression that caused his voice to become more forceful—"which I will see to myself when it suits me."

"You may certainly do as you please, of course."

Dropping his hand, he looked down at it. Beth followed his gaze to discover a dark stain that was certainly blood on his broad palm. He glanced up as if he felt her gaze on him, frowned as he met her eyes, and wiped his palm on the rock.

"Perhaps this would be a good time to ask if you have any idea who bears enough of a grudge against you to have arranged to have had you kidnapped?"

Beth folded her arms over her chest. "I've been thinking about that, believe me. The only possibility I can come up with is William. Lord Rosen."

"Ah, your forcefully dispatched suitor. He certainly has to be a strong candidate. Tell me, are there many others who bear you a similar grudge?"

Beth's eyes narrowed at him. "As I don't usually go about knocking men unconscious, the answer would be *no*."

"William stays at the head of the list, then."

"Are you sure you don't wish me to do something to try to stanch the bleeding? It seems foolish to do nothing."

"Nonetheless, nothing is what you will do."

Clearly, there was no more to be said.

"Fine." She glanced around. "Shouldn't we be moving on, then? Please tell me we don't have to get back in that benighted boat to get out of here."

"No, we must walk out, which should

take about four or five hours. But for what remains of the night, while the hunt for us is white-hot above ground, I think we are best off staying where we are. We can get some rest and move on in the morning, in the hopes that by the time we're topside again, the search will have died down."

"Would you mind just pointing in the direction in which we are to go, in case you should be insensible when the time comes?" Her voice was dry.

"Head due west, away from the sea, and keep bearing right."

"Thank you. I am now much easier in my mind."

"You shouldn't be. Without me, you have no chance of finding the way out."

Her expression must have been something to see, because he laughed, only to break off with a wince, which Beth found worrisome, although nothing would have induced her to admit it. Another thought had been troubling her, and though she was almost sure she knew the unhappy answer, she posed the question to him.

"Is there the least hope of getting help back to those poor girls still imprisoned in that terrible place?"

"Information can be laid with a magistrate and a constable can be sent back to do what he can. Of course, that's after we reach some place that has a magistrate. We have no chance of going back that way ourselves, and I wouldn't do it if I could." Once again he must have been able to read the expression on Beth's face, because his own tightened impatiently. "Don't tease yourself about it, for God's sake. Without your intervention, none of this lot would have escaped. I'd no notion of rescuing a bevy of troublesome females when I came after you, believe me."

"You . . . came after me?" Beth looked at him in wary astonishment. Their eyes met. His mouth twisted. Once again he looked guilty, like a small boy caught out in a misdeed.

"I did, yes." He must have seen the question in her face, because he continued after only the shortest of pauses, "Remember the payment you promised me for the signal service I performed for you in regards to the villainous William? Though I was admittedly a few days late, I appeared in Green Park at the appointed hour to collect. I encountered your maid, who was screeching to the four winds about your having been abducted. As I had just seen a carriage bowling away at a surprisingly fast clip, I made the connection and followed it. After a long and arduous journey, the details of which I don't propose to bore you with, I found the castle, and you. I was just waiting to liberate you with the least amount of commotion when you"—he hesitated and gave her another of those faint smiles— "precipitated events, as it were."

"And just how were you planning to 'liberate' me?"

"By that time, I had secured enough funds to be fairly confident that I could cover your purchase price."

"You were going to *buy* me?" For a moment additional words failed her. She thought of how frightened she had been, of what she had endured, of what she still would have had to endure once she'd been forced onto that stage. The ultimate horror might have been spared her, but . . .

"It seemed easiest." His tone was apologetic.

"Not for me!"

"Possibly not."

Beth had been doing more thinking. "So

you were not there to . . . to . . . ?" Words failed her again.

"Despoil some unfortunate girl?" he supplied. When she nodded, he shook his head. "No, I was not."

Beth frowned. "You went to a prodigious amount of trouble, and put yourself in extreme danger besides, to rescue me. Why did you not just immediately inform my family and have done?"

"Surely, if you will cast your mind back to how we met, you will appreciate why I might have been reluctant to approach your family. Making myself known to all and sundry is really not conducive to what I do."

"Which is?"

"Any number of things," he said. "Just be glad I came after you, my girl. You would have been in a sad case if I hadn't."

"Yes, I am aware of that, and I thank you most sincerely, but—"

"So, miss and yer worship, what's to do now?" Mary called to them. Breaking off, Beth glanced her way. Mary was perched with Peg and Alyce on a clump of nearby rocks. All three were busy wringing out their soaked skirts. Jane and Nan, fixed on more distant rocks, were doing the same.

Dolly stood near them, combing her fingers through her wet hair.

"We take what remains of the night to rest, and then we walk out." Neil raised his voice in answer. Beth got the impression that he was glad of the interruption. "We should be above ground again before dark tomorrow."

"So long as it does not involve a boat," Peg said. "I be game for anything. Anything else."

The others shudderingly agreed.

"If you could keep silent about the very slight wound I seem to have suffered, I would appreciate it," Neil said quietly to Beth. "The prospect of six more females fussing over me is more than I can bear."

"I am not fussing over you." Her brows snapped together. To her surprise, he handed her a candle, and she realized that he must have retrieved it from his pocket. "But your injury is certainly yours to reveal. Or not."

"Thank you. Pray hold still."

A spark flared in the darkness, and he used it to light the candle. She realized that he'd kept the flint and steel from the castle in his pocket, too.

"Praise be! A light!"

"Me feet feel like dead mackerels. Could we be 'avin' a fire while we rest, d'ye think?"

"And what would we make it with?"

"Driftwood? Won't there be some here-abouts?"

"Wouldn't the smoke be seen?"

"We'll catch our deaths, without."

"Better to catch our deaths than to be taken again."

"Oh, *aye.*" They all agreed.

While this conversation was going on, Neil touched another taper to the one Beth held. The wick caught. This candle, the one that he had used previously, she thought, he kept himself.

"There's another chamber beyond this one. It once held firewood, and lanterns, and trunks containing things such as changes of clothing and blankets, as well as other necessities. In case someone, for what-ever reason, should wish to pass the night, or several nights."

Tucking his boots under his arm, he stood up. Even with him in his stocking feet, her head just cleared the top of his shoulder, Beth realized. His height alone was enough to make him intimidating, to say nothing of his broad-shouldered, narrow-hipped build, or the steely muscularity of his body, or the sudden icy opaqueness that could drop over his eyes like a curtain when he was displeased—or the fact that he had just killed seven men without a qualm, and had broken into her brother-in-law's house besides. As clearly dangerous as he was darkly handsome, he was the kind of man that any female in her right mind should be at pains to avoid. But she wasn't afraid of him, not in the least, and he didn't intimidate her either. As surprising as it was, there existed a kind of affinity between them that made her feel almost comfortable in his company.

"Almost" being the operative word.

"It served as a hideout, in fact," Beth said, for his ears alone.

"Possibly." As they started to move toward the others, he glanced down at her. "We must just hope it is empty tonight."

"No doubt you could deal with whoever is in there if it isn't," she replied. "Just as handily as you dispatched all those men back there in the castle."

"Just as handily as I killed them, you mean." His voice turned silky as he faced the subject she skirted around. "But had I not, I would be dead now and your fate would be something that I am sure you would rather not contemplate."

As they passed them, the others got to their feet and, talking amongst themselves, fell in behind them in a ragged procession.

"That is very true," Beth admitted. "And once again I thank you for the rescue. But . . ."

Her voice trailed off.

"Again with one of those troubled 'but's of yours. What is it?"

"You seem extremely skilled at killing."

"I am skilled at any number of things."

Out of nowhere, Beth remembered the kiss he had pressed on her. His lips had been warm and firm, and in retrospect really quite expert. Was that, perhaps, another of the things he considered himself skilled at? The thought was so bothersome that she was once again temporarily silenced.

A breath of fresh air made his candle flicker, and he put up a hand to shield it. The whisper of it on her face promised that somewhere ahead of them was indeed access to the outside. Shielding her own candle and lifting it high, Beth observed that they had reached another fissure in the granite wall of the cave. This one served as a door into an adjoining chamber, she saw as she followed him through it. Irregularly shaped, festooned in shadowy darkness, which the flickering candlelight barely penetrated, it had stalactites and stalagmites reaching toward each other like the teeth of a feral cat. The ceiling was lower and more rounded than the soaring cathedral peaks of the chamber they had just left. Shelves of flat stone that reminded her of agricultural terraces ascended partway up the walls. The ground was stone, worn smooth and almost shiny by the passage of many feet over the years. Trunks and barrels and stacks of firewood, amongst other miscellaneous items, were piled against one wall. Deep in the gloom at the far end of the chamber, the glint of moving water caught Beth's gaze.

"Is that freshwater?" she asked, for the stickiness of drying salt on her skin had already begun to bother her.

"A spring-fed stream. 'Tis safe to drink. And if—just if, mind you—I should be insensible when the time comes, you may follow it all the way out."

That made her laugh. "I will remember."

Then the others joined them, and for some time afterward they were occupied with the minutiae of setting up a makeshift camp.

By the time a fire had been built, a barrier consisting of the domino and Neil's greatcoat had been strung between stalagmites to protect the women's privacy, and they had stripped to the skin, rinsed out their clothes, and bathed, Beth was exhausted. It did not help to reflect that she had now been missing from her home for above three days, and her family would be frantic with anxiety even as they searched for her. Dwelling on the possibility of ruin paid even less toll, so with some effort she dismissed both from her mind. She was snuggled in a rough wool blanket over a man's too-large shirt, which was the only piece of dry clothing she had managed to secure for herself when the contents of the trunks, which contained very few garments and all of them men's, were parceled out. With her clothes steaming on rocks near the fire along with everyone else's, and her shoes filled with hot rocks and placed rather closer to the blazing embers in the probably vain hope that they would dry by the time she had to put them back on, she was seated on a stone shelf raking her fingers through her hair, which was loose and wet and curling sadly as it dried, when Peg, who sat beside her, nudged her with an elbow.

"A right baggage that one is and no mistake." Peg inclined her head toward Dolly, who was wrapped like the rest in a blanket and stood with her back to them at the makeshift barrier. From her posture, it was clear that she was peeping at something beyond it. "I've little doubt what she be lookin' at."

"Ogling 'is worship, is she?" Sitting on the ground nearby, swathed to her chin in a blanket as she pulled on the pair of mismatched wool stockings she had claimed as her share of the booty from the trunks, Mary shook her head. "Well, she'll catch cold at that. 'Tis plain as the nose on your face that 'e wants no part of 'er. 'E only 'as eyes for miss."

"Beth," Beth corrected automatically, frowning as Dolly was joined by Nan. Both peeked around the barrier and giggled softly. "And he does not have 'eyes' for me, Mary. It is just that we were acquainted *before*."

Mary made a skeptical sound.

"He be a fine figger of a man," Peg said. "But he gives me the shivers, and not in a good way. His eyes be—be *cold*."

Although she was conscious of a strong desire to, Beth could not in good conscience argue with that. She had encountered that deadly look of his herself, more than once. Fortunately, it never lasted long.

She started to say as much, only to break off as Dolly and Nan, wide-eyed and giggling still, turned and fled toward them.

"He saw us! Oh, my!"

"'Twas because you *would* laugh so!"

"Mayhap you ought to go round there and offer to help him." Nan plopped down on the ledge beside Jane and Alyce, who shared a blanket and sat next to Peg. Dolly stopped before them, glancing around in indecision.

"Do you think I should?"

"He'd be positively grateful for an extra hand, I should think."

"An extra hand to do what?" Beth asked.

"He must have an injury, don't you know, because he's pouring that bottle of spirits he took from the trunk over his back. Why else would he do that, but to clean out a cut or some such?" Dolly giggled again. "Unless he likes to bathe in spirits."

"That be about as likely as 'im wantin' your 'elp," Mary muttered.

"Oh, you should have seen." Ignoring that, rolling her eyes around at the rest of them, Dolly fanned her face with her hand. "La, I'm still all atwitter."

"From what?" Alyce inquired, a little wide-eyed.

"He's unclothed to the waist. All those muscles . . ." She pretended to swoon. "I just adore a well set-up man."

"Probably he'll be wanting to bandage that injury up, next." Nan gave her a sly smile. "That's where he could use the extra hand, you see."

"If either of ye 'ad the sense the good Lord gave a goose, ye'd leave 'is worship alone," Mary warned. "Bein' that 'e seems not best pleased with yer company anyway. Or any of ours, for that matter."

"If he upped and left us," Peg added, "we'd be properly in the suds."

"But what if he's hurt sore?" Jane, who'd been silent until now, looked frightened.

"What if he's *dying*? What would we do then?"

That was the question that had been teasing Beth. Alone amongst them, she knew that he had been shot. Given that, and the weakness he had exhibited when he'd sat so abruptly on the rock, and what Dolly and Nan had just seen, the possibility that he might be seriously injured was more likely than the rest of them knew.

"I'll check on him," she said, standing up.

"Why should *you*?" Dolly frowned at her, her face a study in affront. "Why should I not be the one to go?"

"'Cause 'e'll send *you* away with a flea in your ear," Mary told her flatly. "Miss should go."

Except for Nan, the others nodded agreement.

"I am going." Beth's tone brooked no disagreement, and though Dolly pulled a sour face, there was none. Barefoot, her steps silent on the smooth stone, she approached the strung-up garments that separated the chamber into two distinct areas. He'd built a fire on his side, too, and the cave was almost warm as a result. The light from the blaze limned the makeshift barrier in orange. As she reached it, her courage wavered, knocked a little askew by the thought that she had no way of knowing what he might be doing, or just how indecent he really was.

Conscious of the weight of the others' eyes on her back, she stopped just this side of the barrier.

"Neil," she called, though his name felt strange on her tongue. Still, she had nothing else to call him, "housebreaker" being clearly ineligible. "'Tis Beth. I need to talk to you, if you please."

She waited. Nothing. No reply.

"Neil?"

Still nothing.

Dear Lord, has he fainted? Has he died?

With a quick glance back at the others— Mary made encouraging motions, while Dolly still frowned—she peered around the barrier.

And saw a small fire burning near one of the tiered shelves, and deep shadows doing a sinister dance across the walls and ceiling. His white shirt and cravat were in plain view, hung from a stalagmite near the fire, and his black frock coat and waistcoat adorned more stalagmites nearby. Then she saw his stockings, and his pantaloons, hung out to dry like the rest. Amongst other items, he'd taken some breeches from one of the trunks, she recalled, and the memory helped quiet the dismaying thought that he might be completely nude even as it occurred.

But he was nowhere to be seen.

Her heart beat a little faster.

"Neil?" she tried once more. When there was still no answer, she took a deep breath, squared her shoulders, and stepped around the barricade.

Chapter Sixteen

BETH WAS ONLY A FEW PACES into her search when she saw him. For a moment she stopped, halted in her tracks by the sight of so much bare male skin. His lack of clothing, combined with his dazzling good looks, was unsettling in the extreme. Her first impulse was to turn back at once and leave him to his fate.

Don't be a fool, she scolded herself, and pressed on.

"Neil?"

He didn't so much as twitch. Fortunately, she realized as she drew closer, he did not appear to be dead. Wearing only his boots and the breeches he had scavenged from the trunks, he was obviously breathing. He sat on one of the terrace-like shelves in an alcove area that was not visible from the barricade. Probably, she thought, he had moved when he realized he was being spied on by Dolly and Nan. He leaned against the wall, his long legs stretched out before him, his head tipped back against hard stone, his black hair, loosed now from the ribbon in which it had been confined, hanging in waves to his shoulders, his eyes closed. Despite his natural swarthiness and the stubble that darkened his cheeks and jaw, his face seemed pale. His arms lay limply at his sides. There was no expression, absolutely none at all, on his face that she could discern.

He has *fainted,* she thought with a thrill of alarm, and hurried to his side.

"Neil?" Even as she said his name and tentatively laid her hand on a warm, smooth-skinned, hard-muscled upper arm that felt so disconcertingly male that she drew back immediately, she took in more details. As Dolly and Nan had said, he was in possession of a bottle of spirits, and he smelled of them. The squat glass bottle was open, half empty, and sat on the stone beside him. A battered brass dish with water and a crumpled bit of rag in it was nearby. His left hand gripped a candle that, as evidenced by the wisp of smoke wafting from the wick, had been recently snuffed. The smell of burning was strong, stronger even than the scent of alcohol. It was difficult to look at his nakedness, at his wide bare shoulders and broad chest with its wedge of curling black hair, at his muscular arms, without flinching or turning away out of modesty. But look she did, and with a gathering frown, too, because in that first comprehensive glance she saw something that should not have been there: a black sear mark on his flesh in the general vicinity of where she would expect the wound to be. A closer inspection revealed that in its center was a round hole sealed with darkened congealed blood.

Beth was just registering what that meant when he opened his eyes and looked at her.

"What do you want?" His tone was disagreeable. His eyes were narrowed. His mouth and jaw were tight.

Too conscious of having just touched

his bare skin, she folded her arms protectively across her chest. The knowledge that the blanket, which she wore draped over her shoulders, concealed the extent of her considerable deshabille from his view was strengthening.

"I thought you might need help."

"I don't."

Her gaze dropped to the blackened wound, which was high in his upper right chest. "That is no mere flesh wound."

"And what would you know of bullet wounds, my girl?"

"I know enough to know that a hole like that means a bullet went into your chest."

"And came out my back again, missing all vital organs on the way. I'll live, never fear."

"You relieve my mind," Beth said politely. "You cleaned it with alcohol and cauterized it with the flame from the candle, didn't you?"

"The one prevents infection, the other stops bleeding."

"You sound like you've done this before."

"Upon occasion."

"Are you in pain?"

"Nothing to speak of."

But the shadow in his eyes, and the continued tightness of his mouth and jaw, belied his words. There were smears of blood on his chest and down his side, she saw, and since he had bathed in the stream before turning that section of the cave over to the women, she knew they had to be of extremely recent origin. Then she realized that some of the blood she was seeing on his side was scarlet and fresh, and that it was trickling down from the exit wound in his back.

"Your back is still bleeding."

"I'm aware of it."

From the position of the wound, she didn't see how he was going to be able to cauterize the hole in his back himself, although from Dolly's description he had already poured spirits over it. And if he was to continue without sickening or weakening from blood loss, cauterization was clearly what was needed.

"It will be difficult for you to reach. You'd best let me do it."

His eyebrows lifted as he looked at her skeptically. "You? Hold a flaming candle to the hole in my back? No, I thank you."

"You cannot reach it yourself."

"I told you, I need no ministering angel."

Her brows snapped together. "Now who is being foolish beyond permission? And it is nothing but folly when stupid male pride and mule-headed stubbornness combine to prevent you from allowing me to do something that obviously needs to be done."

"I should perhaps take this opportunity to tell you that I find managing females particularly unattractive."

"Amazingly enough, I feel precisely the same way about stupid, stubborn males. Which makes it most fortunate that I am not concerned with finding you attractive, only with preventing you from dying before you can get us out of this devilish maze of caves."

"I repeat, I'm in no danger of dying."

"Weakening from blood loss, then. You're putting me out of all patience with you, you know. Give me the candle and have done."

"You'll faint, or worse."

"I never faint." Beth took the candle from his unresisting hand. "I'm quite strong-stomached, believe me."

"Now that I believe."

"Well, then." Moving over to the fire, she held the candle to the flame. The wick caught. Protecting it from drafts with a cupped hand, she returned to stand in front of him. When he continued to look at her without moving, she added in an encouraging tone, "It would probably be best if you were to lie down on your stomach. That way, if *you* should feel faint, there will be no chance of you falling and injuring yourself more."

The derisive sound he made told her his opinion of that. He eyed her a trifle grimly, then appeared to see the sense in letting her do what he could not, because he moved sideways, lifting his right shoulder away from the stone and turning so that she could see his back. Here the bullet had exited just above his shoulder blade. Untreated, it was a jagged-edged hole the approximate diameter of the end of her thumb, and dark around the edges with dried blood; more blood oozed from the center to run in scarlet rivulets down the sleek planes of his back.

"Do it, then," he said.

"Certainly. Pray hold still."

Hitching the blanket more firmly into place, laying a hand on his wide shoulder (which was as disconcertingly warm, smooth-skinned, and heavily muscled as his arm) to steady herself, she gritted her teeth and put the flame to his flesh with no more roundaboutness. There was a horrible sizzling sound and a smell like some sweetish meat being cooked as the hole was sealed and the blood bubbled and stopped flowing. He stiffened and, she thought, caught his breath. But he made no sound and, except for the steel-like hardening of the muscles of his shoulder beneath her hand, gave no other sign of the pain she knew he had to feel.

"There, it is done." Blowing out the candle, she bestowed a comforting pat on his shoulder. Her voice was perfectly steady, just like her hand had been throughout the whole nerve-shredding ordeal. But her heart beat faster, and a surge of nausea made her grimace and swallow; fortunately, with his back to her, he could not see.

"Thank you." His voice was a shade grittier than usual, and there was a new hardness around his eyes, she saw as he shifted around so that he was once again facing her. He was careful to keep the injured portion of his back away from the wall even as he leaned against it for what she guessed was badly needed support. Once situated to his liking, he looked at her from beneath half-lowered lids. "I make you my compliments: you ministered most admirably."

"And you were very brave," she replied. He made a sound that might have been an aborted laugh, grimaced, and reached for the bottle of spirits. Laying the candle on the stone beside him as he put the bottle to his lips and took a long drink, she forbore to give him so much as a disapproving look. Instead, she took in the beads of sweat that had popped out on his brow, the whiteness around the corners of his mouth, and the overall pale tinge to his skin, and felt sorry that she'd had to hurt him.

He might not show pain, she thought, but he felt it.

"Don't concern yourself, there isn't enough left in this bottle to make me even the slightest bit bosky." Lowering the bottle, he encountered her frowning gaze and put his own interpretation on it.

"I wasn't thinking about that. I was wondering what to use for bandages." Having spied what she needed, Beth busied herself gathering it up. First his neckcloth, and then the slender knife that was lined up with a pair of pistols within easy reach of his hand. Remembering the use to which the knife had most recently been put, she picked it up with some reluctance, but pick it up she did. The circumstances were such as to preclude any tendency she might feel to indulge her sensibilities.

"Bandages?"

"The wound has been sealed, but it might very well open up again if it is subjected to friction from, for example, your shirt. Protecting it with bandages seems only prudent."

"You may be right, but—hold, are you cutting up my neckcloth?"

"Since I see no bandages about, it seemed the best choice."

"I should perhaps point out that it's the only one I possess."

"It was that or your shirt. And your shirt is wet, and liberally stained with blood besides."

He made no reply, but watched her in silence as, having begun by slicing into the fine linen, she proceeded to rip it to shreds. He once more rested against the wall in the position in which she had found him, and from his very stillness she guessed that he was feeling much worse than he was willing to let her see. The notion made her anxious, and not only because she and the other women would find themselves in the basket if he were to be incapacitated or worse. She was also, she was somewhat surprised to discover, genuinely concerned about him. Fashioning the torn cloth into two small pads and then knotting the remaining strips together until she judged they were long enough to serve the purpose, she moved to stand in front of him once more.

"This won't hurt a bit," she promised as he looked up at her with a frown, and his mouth twisted in wry response. "'Twould be better if I had some basilicum powder, but there is none, so we must hope the spirits did the trick. If you could just hold this in place for a moment?"

Having gently placed the pad over the wound in the front of his chest, she waited until he obediently covered it with his hand. Then she wrapped the strip of linen across his chest, over his shoulder, and, as he shifted to accommodate her, around his back, inserting the pad over the exit wound as she did so. He said almost nothing during this operation, while she, most uncharacteristically, ended up chattering nonstop, finally describing every step of what she was doing in a too-bright tone that was meant to disguise the growing discomfiture she could not help but feel. She only hoped her nonsense didn't sound as artificial to his ears as it did to hers.

". . . and I will just loop this around one more time, if you will but lift your arm again . . ."

The operation required that she get very close to him, far closer than she had ever been to any unclothed male, wrapping her arms around him, ducking under his, touching him with a degree of intimacy that, to her own annoyance, left her flustered in the extreme. Everything about him, from the truly impressive width of his bare shoulders and chest to the flexing muscles in his arms and back when he shifted position in response to her prompting to the very scent of him, was unmistakably, rampantly male. Although she tried to remain as mentally disassociated from her task as possible, and carefully refrained from meeting his eyes when they would have normally made contact, there was no way not to be acutely, even embarrassingly, aware of him.

"I will just thread this between the folds of the pad so it will not shift, or at least so we must hope . . ."

Her fingers could not avoid brushing the thicket of hair on his chest, and unwillingly she learned that it was crisp to the touch and wanted to curl around her fingers, and did not quite hide a pair of flat nipples. His skin was warm and sleek over well-honed muscles, and his abdomen was muscular, too, and firm above a too-large waistband that would have allowed her gaze to follow the narrowing trail of black hair down to his belly button, and perhaps even beyond, had she not refused to look. Finishing off with a sense of relief the knot that would hold the bandage in place, she straightened away from him only to discover that he was looking at her quite expressionlessly.

"You're blushing," he observed as their eyes met.

To her horror, Beth realized that she

was indeed. She could feel the heat burning in her cheeks. To cover up, she looked around for something else with which to occupy herself, and discovered the bowl and rag within easy reach. The dried blood on his chest and side she could leave for him to deal with, but he wouldn't be able to reach the blood on his back on his own. Wiping it away would also provide a convenient excuse to look away from him while she recovered her countenance.

"'Tis the curse of all redheads," she said lightly, knowing that a denial would only make the condition, and possibly its cause, more obvious. Picking up the rag, she dipped it in the water in the brass bowl and wrung it out. "Anything, the least exertion, an overwarm fire, even a too-spicy dish, and we turn rosy as pigs. I would wipe some of the dried blood away for you. Would you turn your back, please?"

"You must find that most inconvenient at times." He shifted his shoulder away from the wall so that she could reach the dried smears on his back.

"I've learned to live with it."

Rubbing the damp rag over the smooth contours of his back was not as disconcerting as practically wrapping her arms around him to bind up his chest had been, but it was still not a comfortable experience, she discovered. She was too acutely aware of him, which she did not like. Even his back was breathtakingly attractive. Wide at the shoulders and tapering to a narrow waist and lean hips, it was heavy with muscle and straight of spine beneath smooth tawny skin, and so foreign in comparison to her own pale, slender back that it might have belonged to another species altogether. Finishing the task quickly, conscious that her pulse had quickened and little curls of something she refused to put a name to had taken up residence deep in her stomach, she took a moment to press her damp fingers to her still-warm cheeks in the hope of cooling them before saying in a decided tone, "There, that's done. There is still some water left if you wish to wipe the rest of the blood from your chest."

Returning the rag to the bowl, she glanced up to find that he was looking at her again even as he eased back into his previous position.

"And your face is *almost* its normal hue. I own, I wonder that you would put yourself within my orbit if the sight of me without a shirt disturbs you so."

He said that casually, as if it were the most commonplace of observations, but there was a glint to his eyes that made her almost as uneasy as touching him had done. Lying was useless, Beth saw clearly. Anyone of the meanest intelligence— which he decidedly was not—must guess what had brought on her blush.

"All right, I confess it: I am not in the habit of dealing with gentlemen who are at best only half dressed and I found it a trifle embarrassing. Although I am quite recovered now." In an effort to turn his thoughts in another direction, she glanced around and added, before he could reply: "Have you no blanket, or at least a dry shirt to put on? At this juncture it is important that you stay warm."

"I'll be fine." He wiped the dried blood from his chest and abdomen as he spoke. Beth could not help but watch, then felt her cursed cheeks heat all over again as he glanced up and caught her at it. His eyes narrowed on her as, the job done, he returned the rag to the bowl. "You should run away now, and this time stay away.

Did it not occur to you that you might be putting yourself very much at risk by coming to me as you did?"

"It might have occurred to me, had I thought there was the least need to be wary of you, but I don't think that. I trust you."

"You should not."

Before Beth realized what he meant to do, he hooked his arm around her waist and pulled her down into his lap.

"Oh!" she gasped, but she didn't scream, and mindful of his injury, she didn't struggle beyond a compulsive grab at his waist—which she quickly released because the feel of warm smooth skin over sinewy muscles was far too disconcerting—to steady herself. Instead, she sat where she had landed on his taut thighs. Resecuring her blanket, which had slipped most lamentably, she lifted her chin and glared at him as he held her easily in place.

"Really, you are behaving like the veriest child," she said in a scolding tone, keeping her composure even though her heart was suddenly beating way too fast. "I am not frightened of you in the least, so you might as well let me up."

"You should be frightened of me." His

voice was thoughtful rather than threatening as his eyes slid over her face. There was a glint in the hard, black depths that made her breath catch. "Believe me, 'tis not to your credit that you have not the wit to see it."

At that, she stiffened.

"Did you just call me a want-wit, sir?" she demanded, outraged.

He smiled.

"A want-sense, rather," he said, and kissed her.

Chapter Seventeen

AS HIS MOUTH TOUCHED HERS, Beth went very still. His lips were warm and caressing, tender even, and the hand that cradled her jaw was gentle. He tasted of spirits, a taste that she would have said she abhorred, but not in this case. The hint of it on her lips made her feel almost dizzy. She could easily pull her mouth away, and even jump off his lap with scarcely more required than a shove on her part. He was not holding her in such a way that she could not escape if she chose. But as his mouth moved on hers, coaxing her, and his tongue feathered between her lips, she didn't move at all, because she couldn't. Her pulse raced, and her heart pounded, and her blood heated. The little curls in her stomach tightened and twisted wildly. It was all she could do to remain upright and breathing. His kiss awakened the most exquisite sensations she had ever experienced in her life.

He kissed her only briefly, then drew back to look at her through hooded eyes. Dreading to think what she must look like—she was once again flushed, she knew, because she could feel the heat in her face; her breathing had quickened, and no telling what he could read in her expression—she kept her composure as best she could, returning his gaze with a coolness she was far from feeling.

"Tell me," he asked in the tone of one engaging in the most idle of conversations, "do you ever kiss back?"

Beth bristled. "Certainly I kiss back—when the gentleman is someone I want to be kissing."

"Ah. Like your former fiancé, for instance? Or should I say, your three former fiancés?"

"Though it is very unkind of you to bring

that up *again,* I will answer: as a matter of fact, yes."

"You kissed them all back." Skepticism was plain in his voice.

"Who I kissed—or did not kiss—is no concern of yours."

"But I am curious. Did you kiss them back? Or more to the point, did you enjoy kissing them back? Any of them?"

"Again, that is none of your concern."

"Then I am left to draw my own conclusions. Obviously you did not, or you would have wanted to take kissing a step further—several steps further, in fact—and, being a gently bred lady, that would have required you to marry the fellow. As you did not marry any of them, I must conclude that you had no desire to venture beyond the kisses you must have exchanged. Ergo, you could not have enjoyed them."

"You may conclude anything you like."

"I'm right, aren't I?"

"Absolutely not."

"Telling me lies is a waste of time, you know. I can read the truth on your very expressive face. You, my girl, are a hardened flirt who cannot handle the passions you provoke in the breasts of susceptible males. You do not enjoy kissing, or anything else of that nature."

He had hit on the truth, but she would die before she let him know it.

"I'll have you know that I am *not* a flirt— and I am extremely fond of kissing," she said haughtily.

"Are you indeed?"

It occurred to her that she was still sitting on his lap. His thighs were firm beneath her. His bare chest was so close that her shoulder would have brushed it had she not been protected by folds of blanket. His arm encircled her waist only loosely, and he was leaning back against the stone and regarding her with a lazy interest that she found most provoking. What she should do, she knew, was get up at once and take herself back to her side of the barrier. He would not prevent her. But the sad truth was, no matter how shocking it was that she was sitting on this dangerous near-stranger's lap, she did not want to leave.

"In any case, this is a most improper conversation to be having," she said, cross at herself for not doing what she knew she should do.

"Sweetheart, we have by now gone so far beyond the point of what is proper that I recommend that you not concern yourself about it."

That was so true that she was left with nothing to say. She frowned at him instead, and he smiled.

"If you are extremely fond of kissing, as you claim, then please feel free to indulge yourself: kiss me."

"I have not the slightest wish to kiss you."

"Then there's where we differ: I find I have an almost overwhelmingly strong desire to kiss you. But I won't if you don't wish it, of course."

With the best will in the world to do so, Beth found that she could not find the words to tell him to stop as he moved his shoulders away from the stone and leaned toward her, watching her all the while, clearly intent on kissing her again. Feeling a little helpless, and more than a little excited and nervous, too, she made no effort at all to evade him. Instead, she sat perfectly still with her hands in her lap while her breathing quickened and her mouth went dry. She did not tell him no or make any attempt to get away because she wanted him to kiss her, and as she faced the truth of that, her heart pounded a mile a minute and her blood heated until she was sure it must steam. Their eyes were still locked as his mouth found hers.

Then she closed her eyes.

This time the pressure of his lips was firmer. His hand came up to cradle her jaw, caress her cheek, and at the same time tilt her head so that their mouths fit together perfectly. The slightly roughened texture of his fingers and the rasp of his stubble against her own soft skin made her go all light-headed. He kissed her with a slow, unhurried finesse that erased the thought of everything else from her mind. When his tongue came out to trace the line of her closed lips, she parted them for him. As it slid inside her mouth, she met it shyly with her own. Fire shot through her most unexpectedly at the hot, slick contact, and she made a little sound of pleasured surprise. When his grip on her tightened and he took total possession of her mouth in response, she instinctively slid her arms around his neck and leaned into him and kissed him back as passionately as if she liked kissing after all.

"Oh! I'll hurt you!" Remembering his wound almost immediately, she opened her eyes in alarm, pulled her mouth from his, and sat up straight again so that her arms looped only loosely around his shoulders. For the briefest of moments she took it all in, his lean, handsome face scant inches from hers, the bright fire of her hair spilling over the powerful biceps of his upper arms, the gray wool of her blanket just brushing his broad chest, the pale silkiness of her slender arms draped across his wide bronzed shoulders. The bandage hugging his right side served as a stern reinforcement of her impulse to call a halt. But despite her best intentions, her lids felt surprisingly heavy, her lips seemed to tingle, and a rhythmic quickening deep in the very center of her being made her feel shivery all over. She was breathless and quivering with all the unbelievable things his kiss was making her feel, and some of that must have been obvious to him because his eyes were suddenly hot.

"You won't hurt me." His eyes blazed at her as he leaned toward her again. "Believe me, at the moment I'm suffering no pain at all."

This time, when he kissed her, he wrapped his arms around her and turned her so that her head fell back against his uninjured shoulder. Her neck arched in longing and her toes curled as he once again took full possession of her mouth. Tightening her arms around his neck, she kissed him back with a newfound hunger that would have amazed her had she been in any state to consider it. But she was not. When she kissed him, her head swam. Her bones turned to water and her body to fire. Her insides melted like butter. Her breasts tightened and swelled. In that deep-inside place that she had never before had any real cause to think about, her body throbbed and ached.

It was only when she heard the rattle of metal on stone and felt herself being tipped back that she surfaced a little. The rattle, she realized, was him clearing his pistols out of the way with a sweep of his arm. The tilting sensation was the result of him laying her down. Her back settled onto the shelf; her blanket served to cushion the hard stone. She realized that he had shifted positions, easing her down as they kissed so that she now lay on the shelf with her legs draped over his lap and him looming possessively above her. Still she kissed him with a passionate abandon that until now she would have said was as foreign to her nature as placid obedience. She was almost senseless with the taste of him, the feel of him, the wonder of her own response. But in the tiny part of her mind that was still marginally functional, she registered the coolness of the open air on her legs that she just in that instant remembered were completely bare. Then the warm slide of his hand down her throat and over the fine lawn covering her upper chest set off alarm bells in her mind.

"I can't."

The merest breath, her protest was uttered as she turned her head aside to pull her lips from his. It coincided almost precisely with the feel of his hand finding and caressing her breast.

Hard warmth, delicious pressure, a jolt of instinctive pleasure: the sensation was electrifying. It was also galvanizing.

"Oh!"

Her eyes popped open. She was breathing hard, and her heart pounded so fiercely she could hear its drumbeat in her ears.

The first thing she saw was that the blanket had fallen away, to trail down the side of the shelf. She was looking at her own very feminine shape, inadequately veiled by the thin shirt, which was high-necked and long-sleeved but so nearly sheer that the round globe and jutting nipple of the breast he wasn't favoring with his attention were mortifyingly visible, as were the outlines of her delicate rib cage and flat abdomen. Even—and she shuddered to see it—the shadow of the triangle of curls that was the hallmark of her sex could almost be discerned. There any scant protection afforded by the cloth stopped. Although the shirt, when she had put it on, had reached almost to her knees, it was now rucked up clear to the tops of her thighs. Which was no wonder, as her bare legs were bent at the knee and curved over his. His hand, unmoving now, covered her breast. The sight was stirring: her legs, slender and pale, draped over his muscular, black-clad thighs; his hand, long-fingered and swarthy-skinned, resting on the white shirt that was all that lay between his palm and her breast.

As a study of the contrast between the masculine and the feminine, the sight was all that could have been desired. Unfortunately, Beth did not find it the least bit edifying. Rather, she looked on it with growing horror. Worse still, she could feel the firm heat of that hand burning through to her skin. Her nipple, foolish, unknowing thing, butted eagerly up into his palm, as if it wanted his caress.

"You're beautiful." There was a husky quality to his voice that made her shiver and look up at him. His eyes were pure obsidian now. His lips were slightly parted. His breath came just a little too fast. "There's a great deal I could teach you about lovemaking."

"No." From somewhere Beth drew the strength to make herself heard. Her body might be weak, and most unaccountably melt and tremble at his touch, but her mind knew better. Memories of her father's profligate treatment of her mother, of his lecherous friends always trying to force themselves on her and her sisters, of Claire's hideous first marriage, crowded to the fore as they always did, along with her firm conviction that for men, the conquest of a female's body was just that, a conquest, with a victor and a vanquished. Suddenly she felt as if she were suffocating. Taking a deep, unsteady breath, she caught his wrist and shoved his hand from her breast as if it were a loathsome thing.

"Let me up. At once."

"Certainly, if you wish it."

As he sat up, she scrambled pell-mell off the shelf, pulling the blanket with her and wrapping it around herself as if it were an enveloping shield. Her knees felt weak, and her stomach churned. Her first instinct was to flee, but pride stopped her. Holding herself rigidly erect, she turned to face him. She could barely bring herself to look at him, but not to look would be to let him know how truly shaken she was.

His face was still dark with passion and his eyes were bright with it, but there was another expression in them, too: a kind of comprehension that made her feel more naked than if he had stripped away all her clothes.

"You're afraid, aren't you? Of sex."

Her breath caught. "Just because I am not so depraved as to offer up my virtue to a brigand does not mean that I am afraid of"—she couldn't say the word—"that." She was proud of how cool her voice sounded. Unfortunately, she could do little about the color that flooded her cheeks.

"But you are afraid, nevertheless. I saw it in your face when I put my hand on your breast. Why, is what I would know."

Her face flamed hotter at such plain speaking. "I'm going back to the others now. Good night."

"Beth."

He caught a fold of her blanket as she turned away. Frowning, she looked back at him.

"It was only a kiss," he said softly.

"Let *go*."

Jerking the blanket from his hold, she stalked—there was no other word for it—toward the barricade. She was angry at him, furiously angry, although she was still fumbling through her emotions to figure out why. Certainly she could not blame him for the kisses, or even the hand on her breast. At least, not precisely. In any case, she hadn't told him not to kiss her, or touch her, and as soon as she had protested he had let her go. A few steps short of her goal, she remembered that the others would be waiting, probably breathlessly, for what they were surely hoping would be a blow-by-blow account of everything that had passed between her and Neil, and stopped short. Fobbing them off would not be a problem—except for her telltale cheeks. And the angry sparks that were doubtless shooting from her eyes. And her clenched fists. And gritted teeth.

Taking a deep breath, she deliberately relaxed her jaw and unclenched her fists. Pressing her fingers to her cheeks, she tried to summon cheerful memories, and latched onto an image of the grand ball the Duke of Clarence had given last Season for a cherished niece, and herself in a favorite silver-spangled ball gown twirling about the floor. She'd been in quite her best looks, if she had to say so herself, and the crowded ballroom had been a veritable fairy land of blazing chandeliers and massed flowers and the ton's crème de la crème in their most splendid finery. A lovely night—but as she thought on it further, the arms she'd been dancing in had belonged to Lord Kirkby, and just a fortnight later she had accepted his very flattering proposal.

Which had unfortunately ended in . . .

"Very wise," an all-too-familiar voice

murmured behind her, making her jump. "Had you returned to your flock of fluttering hens with your face ablaze, they would have been agog with curiosity."

Whether she found having herself and the other females compared to a flock of chickens or his reference to her flaming cheeks more annoying, it would have been hard to say. In any case, she had no time to sort out the answer, because he walked on past her. With a single surprised glance she registered that, clad in breeches and boots and her bandage only, he was still as indecent as when she had left him, and most unwillingly admitted that thus attired he was magnificent. Even as she acknowledged that, he reached the barricade. For a moment she thought he meant to continue on and join the women, shirtless as he was. Instead, he stopped and, plucking his greatcoat from the duty to which it had been put, shrugged into it. Having hung it up between the stalagmites herself, Beth recalled that it had been barely damp, and guessed that it was probably, by now, quite dry.

"We need be on our way in no more than six hours, and the trail ahead of us is rough. I suggest you cease your chatter and get some rest." Raising his voice, he addressed the others, whom Beth still could not see, although without his greatcoat to serve as a barrier there was only the stretched-out domino to block her view of the rest of the shadowy cavern. His tone was one of command, and the answers he received sounded abjectly obedient to Beth's jaundiced ears. Then he turned and came back toward her.

Their eyes met. She regarded him with chilling hauteur, while, with every bit of willpower she possessed, she tried to keep the heat from rising to her cheeks.

Most unexpectedly he paused, smiled, and chucked her under the chin, in a fashion that was most maddeningly avuncular.

"Sleep well, Madame Roux," he said softly, and moved on past.

Milady Redhead. As she translated that, Beth's anger, like her cheeks, flamed anew, and she was forced to exercise considerable self-control to keep from blistering him with a few well-chosen words by way of reply. Instead, holding her head high, placing her whole dependence on the hope that Neil's unexpected appearance would have provided the others with enough to talk about so that she would not be pounced on the moment she appeared, she walked with a truly admirable degree of dignity to rejoin the rest of the women for what remained of the night.

Chapter Eighteen

DESPITE THE DAMNABLE STIFFNESS in his shoulder, an increasing degree of hunger, a slight but noticeable bodily weakness, and the irritation of having been put in the position of bear-leading a gaggle of bothersome females toward a destination he had no wish to revisit, Neil found that he was almost enjoying himself as he waited at the foot of a nearly perpendicular granite wall that rose some thirty feet to the trail's next level. Like amusement, enjoyment had been a rare commodity in his life for more years than he cared to think about, and he discovered to his own surprise that he had missed it. He did not have to look far to find the cause: Beth. Since they had arisen, eaten their execrable meal of water and hard tack from a tin in the trunks, and begun their trek some six hours before, she had been short to the point of curtness the few times she had been forced to reply to something he'd said. The looks that had accompanied those replies had been frigid, leaving him in no doubt that she was mortified by what had passed between them the previous night and, in the way of women everywhere, angry at him as a result. Still obviously intent on giving him the cold shoulder, she showed him her profile now as she stood beside him watching one of the wenches— the lachrymose one; Jane, he thought her name was—make her careful ascent. Madame Roux made quite a pretty picture with her delicate nose firmly in the air, her eminently kissable lips primmed into a forbidding line, and her big blue eyes taking care to look at everything but him. The flickering light of the torch he held brought the fire of her hair, which she had bundled into a loose knot at her nape, to vibrant life. Dressed once again in her yellow gown, which had to be sadly damp around the hem although she had answered with a brief "'Tis fine" when he had inquired as to its state, she looked like a flame herself.

A most beautiful, feminine flame.

Who was sadly out of charity with him and taking care to let him know it.

It had been a long time since a woman had been in a snit with him. People in general tended to be frightened of him, and as soon as they had a chance to take his measure usually gave him a wide berth. Women typically fell into one of two categories: attractive, round-heeled, eager wenches who fawned over his looks and fell into his bed at the snap of his fingers, and the rest of them, whom he barely noticed.

Madame Roux was something new.

"I—I can go no higher," Jane gasped. Glancing up, he saw that she had stopped dead some three-quarters of the way to the top. Flattened against the wall, her toes wedged in a barely visible crack and her arms stretched above her as she hung on to a craggy outcropping, she looked for all the world like a large, bedraggled bat— complaining of the cold, she had been offered the domino and was wearing it at that moment—that had lit on the cliff face and clung. Shadows leaped across the walls and shrouded the soaring ceiling, throwing elongated images against the stone and making her position look far more precarious than he was almost sure it actually was. With his burning torch and the one in the passage above as the only sources of light in an encroaching darkness as absolute as the tomb, it was hard to tell if she was in imminent danger or not. Much had changed in the caves since he had last passed through them. So far they had encountered ample evidence of flooding and rock slides, and in places water seeped through the walls, making them damp to the touch, and dripped from the ceiling. But even if the rock crumbled and she fell, the distance was not all that great. And he would, of course, do his possible to catch her.

"Don't look down," Beth warned, as Jane's frightened face tilted their way.

"Ye great looby, ye can't stop there. Not unless ye means to 'ang on to that rock till Judgment Day." Mary-the-mosquito, on her hands and knees inside the upper passage, looked down on Jane with a frown. Clustered behind her, the other women peered over the edge, their faces studies in concern. "Ye must either come up, or fall down. There be no other way."

Jane whimpered. Her eyes sought Neil's. "You'll catch me, sir, if I slip?"

Although he had climbed the cliff first, demonstrating how easy it was in the teeth of their collective skepticism, showing them each handhold and foothold, promising to catch them if they fell had been the only way to induce the majority of them to make the attempt. If he had not made such a promise, they would be standing at the base of it arguing still.

"You won't slip. Lift your right foot out of that crack and move it about ten inches up and a little to the side. There's a ledge, and once you are standing on it you'll find the going much easier," he instructed her. His patience was being sorely tried, as a trek that would have taken him at most three hours alone had now stretched to twice that, with another hour or more at the rate they were progressing to go, and his hope of arriving at their destination in the early hours of the day, when few if any people would be about, quite ruined. But he had discovered already that his unwanted charges were best handled like skittish horses, with a calm voice and steady demeanor, and the occasional firm hand on the bridle.

"Sure, and if the rest of us can get up here you can," the Irish farm girl—Peg—encouraged her as Jane, visibly shaking, lifted her foot the required distance. A shower of pebbles accompanied the movement, and as she gained the safety of the ledge a paper-thin layer of shale dislodged beneath her and slid down toward the bottom in a slithering rush. Gasping, Jane flattened again. The gasp, and the rattle of the pebbles and subsequent crash as the shale reached the bottom and shattered, echoed hollowly off the walls.

"Keep going," Neil said. To his relief, after a frozen moment in which the issue hung in the balance, she did. A moment later her hands touched the lip of the passage, and the others, with much chatter and many exclamations, pulled her up amongst them to safety.

"Thank goodness," Beth said. The remark wasn't addressed to him, precisely, but he was pleased to take it as conversation and reply.

"She would have had no trouble at all if she hadn't stopped."

The look she shot him in return told him clearly that he was still in her black books and conversation wasn't on the agenda.

"Miss, when you come up, have a care when you put your foot in that crack. It felt like it wanted to give way," Jane called down to Beth. They'd all taken to calling her "miss," just as they called him "sir." Except for Mary, who most ironically persisted in addressing him as "yer worship," as though he were a bishop or some such.

"I'll watch out," Beth called back.

"If you're afraid . . ." Neil began in a low-ered voice, because she could be forgiven if that sliding layer of shale had given her cause for concern. Then he remembered the last time he'd suggested the possibility that she might be afraid of something, and smiled.

"I'm not," she answered curtly. From the look she gave him, she was remember-ing, too, and, unlike himself, not fondly.

Only he and she were left below, which, as he had determined the order of ascent, was how he had intended it, given that it was difficult to coax her out of the sullens with six pairs of nosy ears listening to every word he said to her and every snippy reply she made to him in turn. Unfortunately, having the others up while he and Beth were down did not provide them with the privacy he had hoped to achieve. Having all too quickly gotten over the excitement of Jane's arrival, the women were all looking down at them from the passage, once again ably fulfilling their roles as the duennas from hell.

There was nothing for it but to adjust to adverse circumstances. He couldn't make them vanish with a wish, and, as he had already discovered, he couldn't just leave them behind, either. And not solely because Beth wouldn't like it. It was a shocking thing to discover about oneself after all these years, he reflected, but he found that abandoning six helpless women inside a cave system that they would almost certainly never find their way out of alive was beyond him. Even if he was hoping for a private moment or two with the woman beside him, and they were, once again, decidedly in the way.

"Your turn, then." With an inner sigh that signaled capitulation to forces beyond his control, he wiped the smile from his face and turned to face Beth, with—truly!—nothing any longer but the business at hand on his mind.

She gave him an evil look. Under its influence, his determination to stick strictly to the business at hand wobbled. Unfortunately, at least from her point of view, the first foothold was some five feet off the ground. His role had been to boost the ladies up to it, and the process clearly required more contact than she was in a mood to allow him.

"Come," he said, beckoning.

Looking as if she tasted something sour, she stepped closer.

"Well?" she prompted when he didn't immediately make a move to boost her up.

"You've forgotten to tuck up your skirt," he pointed out. Just as she was, her fellow females were once more wearing their gowns, and they had most sensibly tucked the fronts of their skirts into their waists so as not to catch their feet in them as they climbed. He expected that she would tell him to close his eyes, as some of them (really, all except the brazen blonde) had done, but she did not. Instead, with an expression that clearly told him that she trusted him not an inch, she turned her back. Despite her precaution, he was treated to a pretty glimpse of a froth of ruffled petticoats and elegant calves in white silk stockings, along with a tantalizing flash of bare thighs. Having seen the lady's legs in their lovely entirety only the night before, he was already acquainted with their slender shapeliness. Still, his body responded with appreciation, and as nature intended.

Having arranged her skirts as modestly as she could under the circumstances, which meant that a considerable amount of leg was still on display should anyone— ahem!—care to look, she turned back to him, shooting him a wary glance.

"Are you just going to stand there?" she demanded testily.

"Certainly not."

Thus summoned to his task, he thrust the torch down between two rocks to hold it steady and stepped up to her, grasping her by the waist and lifting her clean up off her feet before she had a chance to guess what he would be about. She was no feather, but she wasn't heavy, either, and he liked the way she felt beneath his hands.

"What . . . ?" She looked down at him in surprise as her hands flew to his shoulders for support. Their eyes met, she glared at him, and he had a sudden, almost overwhelming urge to let her slide down into his arms and kiss her until the glare was replaced by another expression entirely. Only the thought of their by now probably wide-eyed audience above caused him to refrain.

"Is ought amiss?" he asked, as innocent as if he had no idea what the problem was. Without waiting for a reply, he shifted into a better position vis-à-vis the wall and at the same time lifted her incrementally higher despite a warning tightness in the vicinity of his wound.

"You know there is!"

Given that he had hoisted the others upward by means of their feet in his cupped hands, her reaction was not unexpected. But the mood of devilry that seemed to have taken possession of him over the course of the morning and in the face of her ill-humor was really quite irresistible now, almost as irresistible as the lure of putting his hands on her again had been. He'd been forbearance itself since she'd first greeted him with a lift of her chin and a dismissive glance when he'd come to wake the ladies that morning, only to find her already up, dressed, feeding the fire, and in no mood to talk to him. But the desire to tease her a little had grown with every cold glance and curt syllable she'd thrown his way. Now he had his chance, and he made the most of it. Lifting her slowly, his hands tight around her waist, his fingers splaying across her lower back and pressing into the resilient flesh beneath layers of silk and muslin, he measured the trimness of her waist and the gentle flare of her hips with pleasure while she eyed him grimly. She was tense and her muscles had tightened as a result, but he remembered the normal softness of her curves very well. It had been a while since he'd had a woman, so perhaps his memory of his own usual response had grown dim, but the heat that last night's relatively chaste exchange had engendered in him seemed truly quite remarkable, now that he thought back on it. A few kisses and a caress of her not-quite-bare breast should

not have left him riven with lust, nor should
the memory of it have stayed with him the
way it had. But, like the memory of their
first encounter when he'd been treated to
a full, unobstructed view of the luscious
globes of her breasts, it seemed to have
lodged indelibly in his mind. Even feeling
the fully clothed shape of her waist beneath his hands now was engendering a
salutary response, he discovered. Last
night had shown him that she was far
from indifferent to him, too. Under the
right conditions, and given sufficient privacy, which he hoped to achieve at some
point, helping her overcome her apparent
aversion to physical intimacy would provide him with a great deal of gratification.
He would never take what she was not
willing to give, of course, but once they
were on their own he was confident of his
ability to seduce her with her full cooperation.

Are you really that big of a bastard?

That disgusted inner voice belonged, he
was astonished to realize, to his own conscience. Having been almost completely
silent for a number of years, its interfer-

ence was unexpected, unaccustomed, and most decidedly unwanted.

"Can you not lift me up there any faster than this?" Her eyes shot sparks at him.

"Would you have me hurt my shoulder?"

His shoulder repaid him with a decided twinge for his mendacious response, but he ignored it. As the veteran of numerous wounds from bullets, knives, and various other assorted weapons, he was accustomed to functioning through far more pain than this mere bagatelle of an injury caused him. But under the watchful eyes above them he could only stretch out the moment for so long, so with regret he lifted her high enough so that she could gain a toehold on the rock that was the starting point, held her while she got her balance, and finally, reluctantly, let her go. Clinging to the rock face now, she shot him a fulminating look.

"Having failed to mention it last night, may I take this opportunity to tell you that your legs are truly lovely?" he said, his voice pitched to her ears alone, his eyes sliding admiringly over her legs, one of which was on charming display from midthigh down as a result of her tucked-up skirt. "Almost as lovely as your beautiful breasts."

"Oh," was her indignant reply. Situated as she was, she was unable to cover herself, or to reply as she might have wished. But the temper in her glance said everything she was clearly biting back. "I'll have you know that a *gentleman* wouldn't look, and certainly would have better taste than to comment on anything he might accidentally have seen."

"Leaving me to once again reflect how fortunate I am that I'm no gentleman."

"Come on, miss, there be nothing to it atall," Mary called down in response to what she clearly interpreted as Beth's hesitation. The dove gray girl—Alyce—thrust the torch she held out into the cavern so that more light fell on the cliff face, and the others offered advice and encouragement in such a vociferous tangle that he, for one, could not make out one word in ten of what they said. But it quickly became apparent that Beth needed no help from anyone. Though he stood watchfully below, most fully prepared to catch this particular female without fail should she slip, there was little danger of that: fueled no doubt by anger at him, she scaled the wall with ease, and without mishap.

Once her hands reached the lip of the passage, the others pulled her in and out of sight.

Snuffing the torch, which he then did, added the odor of charred wood to the pervading scent of earthy dampness. With the thing still smoking, Neil called up to the women to stand back, and threw the blackened stick up amongst them. The flint and steel had already been carried up by Mary in the pocket of her dress, and used to light the torch that Alyce now held, which he had thrown up to them earlier. Without any light, the caves would be black as the most impenetrable night, and practically impossible for even someone who had knowledge of them, such as he himself, to navigate. With light so critically important, he kept the candles by him, in the pocket of his greatcoat, which he wore. He'd had to abandon his frock coat and waistcoat because of the hole that had been blown through them and the blood that had soaked them as a result. His shirt he'd likewise had to leave for the same reason, but at least he'd managed to exchange it for another, though ill-fitting one. His decimated neckcloth now adorned his shoulder rather than his throat, but he was wearing his own trousers and boots. His greatcoat was a trifle heavy, and the length of it occasionally got in his way, but he was loath to abandon the perfectly good garment. Aside from the growing paucity of his wardrobe, it was quite possible that, given the uncertain spring temperatures, either he or his unsuspecting hostage would be glad of its comfort as soon as the caves were left behind, and their flight—sans her de trop companions—resumed. He might be safe from Clapham and his ilk for the moment—only a select few even knew of the caves' existence, although he had little doubt that his pursuers would learn of them soon enough if he didn't resurface elsewhere—but as soon as he was above ground again he would be in mortal peril once more. Those who were chasing him would not stop until either he stopped them or they saw him dead, and that was the hard truth of the matter.

"Can you not reach the first foothold? 'Tis not so *very* high." Beth's taunting voice, calling down to him, made him look up. They were all looking down at him, he discovered, but hers was the only face he saw. Her expression, he discovered to his delight, was pure mockery.

By way of a reply, Neil smiled and began to climb.

As he did, it occurred to him that he had smiled more since meeting her than he had in years. Amusement, enjoyment, even an urge to tease—he had almost forgotten what those felt like. They belonged to his all-but-forgotten youth, and feeling them took him back to a place he wasn't sure he wanted to go. Toying with this innocent young woman was making him feel almost like a stranger to himself, and he wasn't sure whether that was a good or a bad thing. For a moment he played with the notion of abandoning his plan to use her as bait, and instead considered just trying to remain in hiding—in the caves, perhaps—until, hopefully, his existence was forgotten. She was, quite simply, a darling, and to cause her pain, which killing her brother-in-law might reasonably be presumed to do, was something that he would prefer not to do could he avoid it. But there was no choice: Richmond was the only one who knew the truth of his identity beyond the fearsome assassin who killed on the government's command. And beyond that, it required only the briefest reflection to know that he could not remain hidden away in the caves, or indeed anywhere, forever, or even for very long. Besides, even were it possible, he had no wish to live for months or years constantly looking over his shoulder. If he was going to live, then he wanted a *life,* and to have that he was going to have to eliminate the largest obstacle in his path: Richmond.

Although, strictly for Beth's sake, he was sorry for it.

"Have we much farther to go?" Dolly asked as he climbed into the passage and straightened again to his full height, which meant the top of his head almost brushed the low ceiling. The buxom blonde stood the closest to him, while Beth, of course, stood the farthest away, with her back turned to him—deliberately, he was sure—as she appeared to study something absolutely fascinating on the plain stone wall of the tunnel. Even though Dolly was looking tired and unkempt, she wriggled and batted her eyelashes at him and essayed a hopeful smile. She was comely enough, and might, at some other time, have stirred his interest sufficiently to earn a brief sojourn in his bed. But at the moment she held no appeal for him at all.

"Not far," he said, and brushed past her.

"Not that I mean to tease ye, yer worship, but 'ow far's not far?" Mary asked.

"Two miles. Three at the most," he replied, his eyes on the ground as he looked for the torch he'd thrown. Finding another such stick would be well-nigh impossible until they were out of the caves, so he had no intention of just leaving it behind.

"I don't think I can travel such a distance," Jane said, wringing her hands. "The air is so close in here—sometimes I think I can't breathe."

Mary gave her a disgusted look. "So what do ye plan to do, sit 'ere and 'ope a wind blows through?"

Peg, who had apparently picked the torch up before he'd reached the passage, handed it to him.

"Fresh air be what we need, all right," she said. "We must just walk to reach it."

"Where will we come out?" Nan asked,

and all eyes fastened on him as they awaited the answer.

"An inn." His response was brief, but that was all they needed to know. The caves opened into the cellar of an inn that was the lowest of the low, a place where criminals ranging from murderers to smugglers to grave robbers to pickpockets came and went without ever a question being asked. Outsiders were not welcome; the too curious might never be seen again. It was notorious enough that it was left alone even by the local constabulary, yet secret enough so that only those who needed to knew of its existence.

"An inn!" The prospect appeared to energize Jane.

"We can get a hot meal." Nan clapped her hands together.

"Oh, and a wash!" Dolly exclaimed.

"And then go home," Peg said. Then she looked at him, suddenly less certain. "Can't we?"

Lighting the torch from Alyce's, hesitating over the answer, he looked at the circle of expectant faces around him with grim acceptance: for the moment they were his responsibility, whether he liked it or not. What he *wanted* to do was continue his dalliance with Beth, who was now standing a little way back from the others and once more regarding him with a frown, while putting as much distance as possible between himself and those who would kill him. What he was *going* to do was lead this gaggle of gooseberries out from underground, see them safe, and then rid himself of them forever before proceeding with the previous agenda.

"Why not?" he answered, and they all seemed satisfied except for Beth, who still frowned at him. When she found out that she would be accompanying him to a destination quite remote from London, instead of remaining with the other females in some quiet country inn until her family could fetch her, or returning home under his aegis, she was sure to treat him to fireworks aplenty. And that, he discovered as he set off once more with the chatterboxes in tow, was something he was actually looking forward to.

It would be a most pleasant interlude—until he killed her brother-in-law and made her hate him.

"'Tis getting narrower," Peg observed in a nervous tone as they had to pick their way over piles of rock and squeeze one by one past a fallen slab. "I'll be that glad to get out in the sunshine."

Dolly sneezed. "It smells of damp."

"Doesn't water weaken rock?" Nan asked, glancing around uneasily. Neil, knowing the answer, didn't reply. When he'd last passed this way, this passage had been clear. Now it wasn't. From the evidence, it seemed there had been any number of rock slides over the years, some of them quite recent.

"What happens if the way out be blocked?" Jane's voice quivered. "What will we do then?"

"Find another way out," Beth said shortly. It was such blunt good sense that the rest were silenced. Her brows were knit, and she seemed to be in such a brown study that Neil let Alyce take the point with the other torch and fell back to discover what— besides her snit with himself, of course— ailed her.

"Does being kissed *always* make you angry?" He'd come up behind her to murmur wickedly in her ear when, thanks to the remains of a rock slide that partially blocked a passage, they found themselves momentarily alone. Just as he had expected, her head came up and her shoulders squared and she, who had been studiously ignoring him since he had fallen in behind her at the end of the line, shot him a killing glare over her shoulder.

"I have no idea," said she, with her nose in the air and icicles dripping from every word, "what you are talking about."

And marched on.

"Well, there was Rosen: I'm not saying he didn't deserve it, but he definitely roused you to anger. Then there was my poor self, who, after having done you the not insignificant service of assisting you in that matter, chose to take payment in the form of one paltry kiss. You were furious, you can't deny it. And after last night . . ."

"Hush." Her whisper was fierce as they caught up to the others. "You will be overheard."

Smiling to himself as he watched that slender, now ramrod-straight back, Neil waited until another tunnel blockage left them once again to all intents and purposes alone.

"Almost you make me afraid to kiss you again," he said pensively when the others were out of sight. "Almost."

She was right in front of him, facing the outside wall with her hands flat against the rock as she began to traverse the severely narrowed passageway. Her head snapped around so that she was looking at him. Her brows practically met over her nose and her eyes shot sparks at him.

"You dare . . . !"

"Daring is certainly required, but then I've always considered myself a fairly daring fellow," he agreed in the mildest of fashions, and barely controlled a smile when she made an infuriated sound under her breath and turned her head away from him again. If the passage had been wide enough to allow for flouncing, he was quite sure she would have flounced away.

"Come, Beth, cry friends," he said to the back of that red head when he caught up to her again. "You really have no reason to be so vexed at me, you know. I at least let you go without having to be forced to it by aid of a fireplace poker."

Her head whipped around again. "You

are never going to let me forget that, are you?"

He grinned. He couldn't help it. "I admit, at the moment it seems to be claiming a place at the top of my most cherished memories. Right along with how you looked that night clinging to the balcony, your breasts bathed in moonlight . . ."

"Oh!"

The passage was really very narrow, he discovered when, turned sideways like the others, he attempted to catch up again as he followed her through it. But then, he was a great deal larger than any of them, which accounted for at least some of the reason she was managing to move much more quickly than he. The rest of the reason could undoubtedly be attributed to her desire to escape his teasing.

By the time he had won free, she was bunched in the middle of the other females. He was content to let her go. Later, when he truly had her alone, there would be plenty of time to engage more in the promising pastime of causing her cheeks to heat until they matched her hair color.

"Be they still hunting us, do you think?"

Alyce asked as they emerged from the tunnel at last into a chamber almost as large as the one in which they had passed the previous night. Like that one, it had a soaring ceiling, a goodly number of stalactites and stalagmites, and curved walls terraced by flat stone shelves. At the opposite end was a solid granite wall with the entrance to the last of the tunnels situated some twenty feet above where they now stood. This tunnel would take them directly into the cellar of the inn. Unless, as Jane had so depressingly suggested, the way was blocked. Which he trusted it wasn't, although the deteriorating conditions in this end of the passage suggested that of late it had gotten very little use.

"Unless they—" Mary began, but her reply was interrupted by a sudden sharp crack that made the hair on the back of Neil's neck stand up. He barely had time to glance up in the direction of the sound before the ceiling came crashing down.

Chapter Nineteen

ONE MOMENT BETH was standing there looking at Mary, who was talking. The next there
was an ear-splitting *boom,* and the world
seemed to cave in on top of her. Something slammed into her with the force of a
runaway carriage and dashed her to the
ground to the accompaniment of a thunderous roar. The back of her head smacked
into stone, the air was forced from her
lungs as a huge weight crashed down on
her chest, and everything went black.

But she wasn't unconscious. She knew
she wasn't, because her head ached and
her ears rang and she saw stars despite

the blackness, and she had to be conscious to be aware of that. Plus she could hear terrified screams that sounded somehow muffled, so that they seemed to come from a little distance away, and more crashes, smaller crashes, as if brittle objects were hitting the ground one at a time and shattering just beyond where she lay.

"Beth? Beth, are you all right?" Neil spoke urgently in her ear. She was so glad to hear his voice, so relieved to know that she wasn't alone in the terrifying darkness, that she completely forgot that she had been feeling vexed with him scant moments before. She let out her breath in a long sigh. It was only then that she realized she had not been breathing at all.

"Beth? Are you hurt?" His hand slid across her shoulder to her neck, where his warm fingers pressed into the soft flesh below her ear. "Answer me, damn it."

She couldn't see him, although her eyes were wide open and straining with the attempt. The blackness was more absolute than anything she had ever experienced. She could see nothing, absolutely nothing at all. Not even Neil, whom she realized must be lying almost completely on top of her. His hard body was the smothering weight crushing her down into the unyielding stone beneath her back; he had thrown her to the ground and fallen on top of her. Even as she regained enough of her wits to become aware of that, and registered that his fingers on her neck were checking her pulse, he shifted so that he was no longer lying on her, but stretched out against her side. Even though she couldn't see him, she turned her head to follow his movement, desperate not to lose contact.

"What . . . happened?" she managed, wheezing a little as she pulled air into her lungs.

"Thank God." The relief in his voice was palpable. "The roof collapsed. We're damned fortunate to be alive."

"You tackled me." Reaching out, she tried to find him, making clumsy contact with smooth wool—his greatcoat. Her hand was on his broad chest, she realized as her fingers splayed out and discovered a button. With her hand flat on his chest, she moved a little, turning toward him. "I think you might have saved my life."

"Saving you is getting to be quite a habit with me, so think nothing of it. Stay still for a minute. Are you bleeding anywhere? Can you move your limbs?" As he spoke, his hands ran lightly over her face and neck, her arms and legs and body, checking for injuries. Even when he skimmed her breasts and other private areas, she didn't think of protesting because it was so clearly designed to make sure she was all right.

"I'm not hurt. What about you?" Except for a slight ache where she'd struck her head, nothing felt out of the ordinary.

"I'm fine." His tone was impatient. His fingers were sliding through her hair now, and when they touched the tender spot at the back of her skull she winced. "You've got quite a bump coming up here."

"It's nothing. It barely even hurts. What about the others?" Remembering the screams, her pulse quickened with alarm. "I heard them screaming."

Only then did it occur to her that the silence was now profound. There were no screams, no crashes, nothing at all. Suddenly terrified, she started to jackknife upright, ready to call out to the others, to start searching through the dark for them, only to have him press her back with a restraining arm across her shoulders.

"No, don't do that. You want to watch your head. We're under one of the shelves, so there's a stone slab about three feet above you. And I don't know about the rest of them. When I saw the ceiling coming down I dived for you, and we ended up under here. What happened to everyone else I have no idea."

"But you heard them screaming, too." Unable to help herself, Beth reached up as she spoke, and sure enough her fingers brushed stone. Pulling her hand back, she took a deep, steadying breath.

"Yes, I heard them."

"They might be hurt. Or—or dead."

"They might be."

"Oh, dear God."

"We have to see to ourselves before we can help them."

She felt him moving, felt him reaching across her, and got the impression that he was also testing to see what was around them. Experimentally, she, too, reached out toward the side that should have been open, only to discover what felt like a wall that seemed to cover the entire space. Squirming around, careful not to lose contact with his body because to be alone in the pitch-blackness would be the most horrifying thing she could possibly imagine, she tried to find an opening—any opening—and failed. As far as she could tell, there was solid stone all around: floor, ceiling, four walls.

Her heart pounded like a cornered rabbit's.

"It feels to me like we're trapped under here." She was trying not to sound as afraid as she felt. "I can't find a way out."

"We'll get out somehow, never fear."

The fact that he didn't contradict her she took as terrifying confirmation of her worst fear: they were walled into a space not much larger than a coffin.

Her pulse thudded against her eardrums. Her mouth went dry.

"We're trapped, aren't we?"

"It seems so, yes."

Her nails dug into her palms as she tried to hang on to at least a semblance of outward calm. The complete absence of light coupled with the chilly dankness of the air enfolding them was oppressive in the extreme. Beth took another deep breath, greedily filling her lungs, then had a thought that caused her stomach to drop: Would they suffocate? What if there was only a limited amount of air?

"Neil. What if the air runs out?"

"It won't. Don't trouble your head about that."

"How can you be—" "Sure" was what she meant to add, but was interrupted before she could finish.

"Oh, please, can anybody 'ear me?" The desperate-sounding shout came from the cavern beyond, and Beth instinctively looked in that direction, although of course it was useless: she saw nothing but that terrible, intense black. But she recognized the voice instantly, and was so glad to hear it she felt almost dizzy.

"Mary!" she cried. Turning impulsively toward the sound so that she was now lying on her side with her back to Neil, she pressed both hands against the cool stone slab in front of her. It stayed solid and unmoving; she thought about shoving at it with all her might, but then was afraid to. It felt huge. What if it was only precariously lodged, and she brought it down on top of them? The prospect made her shiver, and she withdrew her hands as quickly as if the stone had suddenly turned red-hot.

"Miss! Miss, be that you?"

"Yes! Yes, it's me!"

"We're here," Neil yelled. "Beth and I, under the rocks that fell against the wall we came in through."

"Yer worship! Are either of ye 'urt?"

"No. What about you?"

"Nothin' to speak of, or Alyce either. Oh, Alyce be 'ere with me."

"'Tis just me and Mary left!" Alyce cried, her voice high-pitched with fear. "Everybody else be gone! What do we do?"

"Do you have a light? Can you see what's on top of us?" Before he spoke, Neil put his hand over Beth's topmost ear, presumably to keep her from being deafened by the volume of his shout. Although she was facing out toward the cavern, she could not see the stone blocking them in. All was total, unrelieved darkness. She could see nothing of Neil, who was so close she could feel his body pressed against her back and his breath feathering across her cheek. If she'd held her hand directly in front of her eyes, she would not have been able to see it.

"Alyce dropped the torch, but we be tryin' to organize a light," Mary answered.

There was a moment of silence. "I tore off a strip of me bleedin' dress and lit it on fire, but we just 'as a moment afore . . . Ah, there be the torch! Alyce, there!"

"Dolly! Look, it be Dolly!" Alyce cried.

More silence. Beth strained to hear, but beyond her own and Neil's breathing there was silence. His arm was around her waist now, and she folded her own on top of it, glad of its solid comfort. Terror, cold and creeping, was inching through her veins. If Mary had managed to kindle a light and they hadn't seen so much as a flicker penetrate the gravelike darkness in which they lay, then the rocks imprisoning them had to be solid, and thickly layered.

The hideous truth hit her like a blow to the stomach: they might never get out.

"What's happening out there?" she cried, battling back panic.

The arm around her waist tightened. "They are undoubtedly rendering aid to the others," Neil said in a voice as prosaic as if they were standing in the middle of Green Park discussing the weather. But she was glad of his calm, because it steadied her.

Breathe in, breathe out. Don't panic.

"We found Dolly. She be under some rocks, but we're getting her free," Alyce reported.

"We 'ave 'er!" Mary cried, while in the background Beth heard Alyce calling for the others. "She got a good knock to the 'ead, but she be all right! And Jane and Nan be yellin' to us from under the rocks over 'ere, but we can't get to 'em. Just like we can't get to you, miss, and yer worship. There be a positive mountain o' rocks on top of ye, some of 'em big as a bed!"

Beth's heart thumped harder at this information. *We're trapped.* Although she'd suspected it, known it really, the confirmation was terrifying. Her stomach clenched. Cold sweat broke out along her hairline. But she couldn't, wouldn't give into fear. There had to be something they could do . . .

"Steady." Neil must have been able to sense some part of what she was feeling, because his voice was cool and calm in her ear. "We're going to be all right, you know."

Her mouth was so dry she had to swallow and wet her lips before she could speak.

"Do you think, if we both kicked against

this slab that's lying in front of us, we could . . . ?"

"No, I don't. You heard Mary—there is no telling how many rocks are piled on top of the slab. The last thing we want to do is bring the whole mess down on us."

They would be crushed instantly. She knew it, although he refrained from being quite that graphic.

Her palms had grown damp, and her hands had curled into fists. She was breathing way too fast. Her heart raced like she had run for miles. She was sore afraid that they were going to die.

But there was, simply, nothing to do.

"Peg! Peg!" Alyce's voice could be heard more clearly now, and Beth guessed that she and Mary must be walking around the chamber as they searched for the girl who was still missing. "Answer if ye hear me! Oh, she's here! She's moving! Mary, come help me get her out!"

"That's all of them, then," Neil said. "If Jane and Nan are talking, and Peg's moving and they're digging her out, then everyone's alive."

"Do you think they'll be able to get us out?" She was cold, so cold, freezing really, but not because of the coolness of the air or the less than warm temperature of the unforgiving stone on which they lay. Shock and a burgeoning fear that she wasn't able to keep completely tamped down despite her best efforts coursed through her body in waves, mangling her nerves, freezing her blood. But panicking was clearly worse than useless, and she battled back against it with every ounce of courage that remained to her. At least Neil was with her. His arm around her, and his solid warmth against her back, served as an effective antidote to the abject terror that threatened to consume her.

"Probably not," Neil responded. Once again the measured calm of his voice robbed the words of some of their power to frighten. "If the rocks are as large as Mary says, they're going to need help to shift them."

"Where can they find help?" A fresh burst of fear wobbled through her voice as she realized that down here in the caves there was absolutely no help to be had.

Neil didn't have a chance to answer as Mary yelled, "We've got Peg out! Oh, she be bleedin' bad."

The voices then lowered to what, to Beth's ears, sounded no louder than murmurs. Straining to hear, she thought she detected the sound of someone noisily weeping: Peg, probably, if she was injured.

"I'm getting ready to shout again," Neil warned as he put his hand over her ear. Then, true to his word, he raised his voice to near-deafening volume: "Mary, I need you to listen to me."

"I be listenin', yer worship."

"One of you needs to go for help. See that passage on the far wall? It's the last one. You must climb up into it, and follow it, and it will take you directly into the cellar of the inn I was telling you about. I once knew the proprietor very well. His name is Creed. Find him, tell him what has happened, and inform him that his old friend Hume begs his immediate assistance."

"Tell Mr. Creed—'ume begs assistance," Mary repeated, as if fixing the words in her mind. "Aye, yer worship."

"Will he come, do you think?" Beth asked, conscious of her heart knocking against her ribs and trying to stay as calm as possible despite it.

"Of a certainty." Incredibly, Neil almost

sounded as if he was smiling. "The last time we met, I absconded with a very large sum of his money."

"Oh." Beth was reminded of the criminal tendencies of this man she'd come to feel she could utterly rely on in the most terrifying of circumstances, and knew she should by rights be recoiling in disgust at his cheerful confession of this newly revealed crime. Instead, she felt a spurt of thankfulness that the inn's proprietor would have such an excellent reason for hastening to their aid, and decided that her recent adventures must have addled her brain.

"Yer worship, there be a slight difficulty." Mary was still shouting, but she sounded as if she was closer to them now.

Neil covered Beth's ear again. "What's that?"

"We've only the one light, and none of us wishes to stay 'ere in the dark. We're that scared, like. And if we was to encounter some difficulty in the passage . . ."

"You may as well all go. You can do us no good here, after all."

Beth shivered at the idea of being entombed in the dark without anyone to watch over them. But there was a torch burning in the cavern already, and the blackness where she and Neil lay was still absolute. And there was no help Mary or Alyce or the others could give those who were still trapped. Therefore, it could make no possible difference whether one or more of them stayed in the cavern. Better that they should go for help, although the thought of them leaving made her chest feel tight.

"Be sure to tell Nan and Jane that you're going for help, and you'll be back," she called, summoning up all her fortitude in an effort not to appear as weakly frightened as she felt.

"Aye, we will. And we'll 'urry as fast as ever we can, too."

"We won't fail ye, miss." Alyce already sounded like she was farther away. Beth pictured them, heading toward the tunnel opening that she had just glimpsed high up in the far wall before the ceiling fell.

"Do you think they'll be able to climb up without assistance?" she asked Neil. Keeping her voice steady required considerable effort, but she thought she managed it very well.

"I think they'll do what they need to do

to get help. Mary is nothing if not tenacious, Peg and Alyce both strike me as being quite intelligent, and Dolly—well, Dolly will do whatever she has to do to save herself."

That was all so true that Beth felt the tiniest bit better.

"How long do you think they'll be gone?"

"It will take them some time," he admitted. "Several hours. All we can do is make ourselves as comfortable as possible, and wait."

Chapter Twenty

"So—your name is Neil *Hume*?" Beth asked after an interval of near silence, which she had spent calming herself while listening to the increasingly difficult-to-detect sounds of the four who were going for help making their way, as she assumed, across the cavern, up the wall, and into the passage. But she'd heard nothing of them for several minutes now, and hoped—prayed!— that they were far enough along in their journey as to put them out of earshot. Up until that moment she had been situated so that she was facing the cavern. Now, in a convulsive move that said volumes about the panic she refused to let surface, she turned over so that she was facing Neil as she asked the question. Unable to see him, although she could feel his long body brushing against hers, she reached out for him to get her bearings, and found herself touching the smooth cambric of his shirt. Beneath it, the solid warmth of his chest was a further welcome reminder that she was not alone.

If she had to be trapped in what amounted to a stone crypt, it occurred to her that there was no one else she would rather have with her. The idea of Neil simply surrendering to these dreadful circumstances was unfathomable. Whatever happened, he would fight hard to survive. But for now, there was nothing either of them could do.

"I've answered to many names. That was certainly one of them." Neil capped what should have been, for her, a most unsettling confession by draping something heavy and warm—his greatcoat—around her shoulders. "Here, put this on."

"What about you?" Although she would be glad of the coat's protection, she hesitated. Depriving him of his own garment seemed unfair.

"I'll survive quite nicely without it, believe me. Just do as you're told for once, would you, please?"

Beth responded to this crisp directive by making a face at him, which of course he couldn't see, then sitting up as best she could, sliding her arms into the sleeves, and wrapping herself in his greatcoat. The garment was enormous, cozy as a blanket, and smelled indefinably of him. As she settled into it she realized how cold she was, and how bruising the ground was beneath them. Her thin dress, with its low neckline and tiny puff sleeves, might be the height of fashion, but it had never been designed for conditions such as these.

"Thank you," she said.

"Mm."

It was impossible to see him, so she reached out for him again, suddenly desperate to make sure of his presence in the dark, and found her hand once more resting on his chest. He wrapped long fingers around her wrist, holding her hand in place. The sturdy heat of his body beneath his shirt brought solace with it. Had he not been there in that hideously confined space with her, she thought, she would have been beating her fists against the imprisoning stone walls, or at the very least screaming herself hoarse, by now.

Instead, she was managing to maintain a really quite impressive measure of calm.

"We've a deal of time to pass, so talk to me," he said, tugging on her hand to pull her down beside him. With no objection to make, she slid down obediently. By the time they were situated comfortably, he lay on his back and she curled against his side. He had an arm around her and her head was pillowed on his uninjured shoulder. His other arm, presumably, was curved beneath his head. It was still black as pitch, they were still trapped, and the situation was still so dire that she couldn't think about it without feeling sick. But she felt infinitely better lying there in his arms. "I know that you are Lady Elizabeth Banning of the flaming hair and hotter temper, that you've whistled three fiancés down the wind, at least one of them quite violently, and that you're afraid of sex. I would know more. Let us start, say, with how old you are."

Feeling her temper heat, Beth willed

herself not to think about where they were anymore. It helped that he couldn't have hit on a more annoying speech if he had tried. Or perhaps he was trying to distract her, in which case his ploy was certainly working. Her eyes narrowed at him.

"If we are to get on, I should perhaps warn you that I do not care to have the color of my hair constantly thrown in my face. Also, it would probably be best if you stopped bringing up the number of fiancés I've had, or the way in which my last engagement was broken. And I am *not* afraid of—of . . ." She couldn't say it. Instead, she ended, lamely she knew, with ". . . that."

"All duly noted." He sounded as if he was smiling again, and she was suddenly sure that he'd set out to ruffle her feathers deliberately. "But you haven't answered my question."

"I am twenty-one. How old are you?"

"Thirty-one, a whole decade your senior. Are you going to tell me why you're afraid of sex?"

"I am *not*—" She broke off. "You are the most complete bounder, and I refuse to let you bait me. Let us rather talk about you. If your name is not Hume, what is it?" Then a thought occurred to her, and her tone turned severe. "Is it even really Neil?"

"Yes, oh doubting one, my name is really Neil. My surname is"—he seemed to hesitate for the briefest of seconds—"Severin."

"Is that the truth?" she asked suspiciously.

"I give you my word."

She snorted.

"What? My word's good. When I give it, which I must tell you is something I don't often do."

"So I should feel honored that you are giving it to me, is that what you're saying?"

"You should, yes."

"Neil Severin," she said, weighing the sound of it. "You are English by birth, then?"

"My father is English, my mother was French. And beyond that, my origins are something I prefer not to discuss."

"Oh, ho! Very well, then, if your origins are out of bounds, then so, too, are my hair color, my fiancés, and—all the rest of it."

"You mean the reason why you are afraid of sex?"

She glared at him, although of course

he couldn't see. "You devil, you know perfectly well what I mean."

He laughed. "Very well, consider the
deal struck."

"Then would you care to tell me how it
came about that you stole Mr.—What was
his name? Oh, yes, Creed—how you stole
a large sum of Mr. Creed's money?"

"That's quite a tale." She could feel him
settling into a more comfortable position.
"Are you sure you want to hear it? It might
sink me utterly in your eyes."

"I'm already aware that you're a housebreaker and probably a smuggler as well,
besides being horrifyingly proficient at killing our fellow human beings. Oh, and that
you are purse-pinched enough to show up
in Green Park some days after we agreed
to meet to collect a sum that I no longer
owed you, because you saw fit to extract
immediate payment from me by way of a
snatched kiss. I have also had time to reflect on your subsequent pursuit of me for
long enough to arrive at the conclusion
that you probably hoped to profit from restoring me to the bosom of my family. Bearing all that in mind, I can quite easily assure

you that *nothing* you can tell me could cause you to sink any lower in my eyes."

"That's put me in my place." His tone was appreciative. "But there is one point of your most chastising narrative that you have got all wrong."

"And what would that be, pray?"

"I am no longer in the least purse-pinched. On the contrary, I am presently in the possession of two extremely fat purses. You may check the pocket of my coat if you don't believe me."

Beth realized that she could, indeed, feel heavy weights pulling down the fabric in the area of one pocket. Thrusting her hand inside it, she felt two, as he'd said, full-to-bursting purses, along with the pair of candles she knew about. A quick moment's reflection sufficed to reveal to her how odd it was that he should have two very plump purses that were, from the feel of them, different in every particular.

"These are not yours, are they? Did you steal them?"

He laughed again. Listening to the brief bark of amusement, Beth realized that she was almost having a good time despite everything. And she owed that to the fact that she was with Neil.

"One of them is mine, although the contents may once have belonged to someone else. The other I stole," he admitted. "It seemed like the best thing to do at the time. Though I'm very sorry now, of course."

"You are not in the least bit sorry, and I know it, so you may as well not try to humbug me. Instead, I wish you will tell me about Mr. Creed's money."

"You are most persistent," he complained. Then, after the briefest of pauses, he continued: "Very well, if you feel you must know. At the time I was deeply involved in—ah, expediting—shipments of various types of highly desired goods into this country from our bloodthirsty neighbor across the channel."

"You were a smuggler," Beth interjected with relish. "I knew it."

"Yes, well, be that as it may, Mr. Creed and I and a small number of others were working in concert, and doing very well for ourselves, when Mr. Creed, who was our leader, had a flash of uncharacteristic brilliance. Instead of paying for the large load of brandy that was delivered one night, right through this very passage, by the way, he determined to keep it, as well as his money, by killing the men who made the delivery. This he did, in the coldest of cold blood, with, as he thought, since he had told none of the rest of us the shipment was coming, no one to know. Only as I was working in the taproom at the time—Did I mention that I was seventeen years old? Yes, I was, and I worked in the inn's taproom when I was not uh, expediting the delivery of goods—I saw Mr. Creed go down into the cellar and I followed him. I saw all that passed, and I saw, too, where he hid the money. His intent, I think, should any of the unfortunate victims' associates have come to inquire for them, was to say that the delivery was never made. If something had befallen them, how was he to know? But as I had a most pressing need for a large sum of money, and little interest in the fate of those who had brought it, I left their misfortune to the concern of others and made off with the money. As I said, it was a large amount, and that Creed knew it was

I who had taken it was borne in on me when, a year or so later, I happened to pass this way again. He was extremely wroth, believe me. I was fortunate to escape with my life."

"Will he not try to kill you when he comes to free us? Or"—the thought made her stomach clench—"will he not just be content to leave us—you—here to die?"

"Creed won't leave me here. He was ever a vengeful man, and satisfactory vengeance requires face-to-face retribution. That, and the hope of recovering some of what he lost, will ensure that he pulls me out."

"Won't he then try to kill you? Or"—oh, happy thought—"will what's in these purses be enough to repay him?"

"Not nearly enough. And he probably will try to kill me, but not until he assures himself that he has wrung all the blunt he possibly can from me. At that, he is liable to catch cold. Much has changed since we last knew each other, the chief of which being I am no longer a raw youth."

That was so very true that Beth was reassured.

"So why did you need such a large sum of money?" she asked.

He didn't reply right away.

"Neil?" she prodded.

"That is a very old story that I am persuaded you don't want to hear."

"Then you are persuaded wrong. I very much want to hear it. Pray tell me."

"I hoped to use the money to free my mother and sister."

Beth waited, but he didn't continue.

"Free them from what?"

The ensuing pause lasted so long that she wasn't sure he meant to reply. Finally he went on, but she had the sense that he was almost reluctant to do so.

"The French. As I told you, my mother was French, and she and my sister were living in France. They were arrested for crimes against the state, probably simply because my sister was half English and my mother was married to an Englishman, and locked away, along with thousands of others, in prison in Paris."

Again he stopped. From the very expressionlessness of his tone, Beth began to get a most horrible feeling.

"And were you able to free them?"

"No."

"No?" Her voice faltered. Unable to see

anything at all, she nevertheless looked up at him through the dark.

"No. They were tried and convicted before I could reach them. I stole the money to try to see if I couldn't use it to get them free. I had some thought of bribing the authorities, or paying restitution, or—well, whatever it took."

"What—became of them?"

"They were executed." His voice was very even. "On the guillotine. My mother first, and then my sister, one immediately following the other. My mother was terrified—you could see it in her face, her eyes—but stoic. My sister—Isobel, she was only twenty, a beautiful girl with long black hair that on that day was twisted up on top of her head in a clumsy knot so, I can only presume, it wouldn't get in the way of the blade—my sister screamed. Screamed and screamed. All the way up until that thrice-damned blade fell."

His voice was absolutely bereft of intonation, but Beth could feel the long-denied pain buried deep beneath his words. Her heart turned over. Her stomach clenched. Her hand, which rested on his chest, slid around him. Holding on to him tightly, she looked up at him through the darkness, although she could see nothing of him at all.

"That is—just horrible. But how could you know those things? Anyone who would have told you such details . . ."

"I was there. In the crowd, battling to get to them. I'd done everything I could, talked to everybody I could think of, bribed the guards at the prison, who took my money and laughed at me, tried to break them out of the cell where they were being held, to no avail. I knew they'd been sentenced to death, but I'd no notion they were to be executed so soon. I thought I still had time, you see. I was begging for an audience with Ambassador Whitworth when I got word that they were amongst those who had been loaded into the tumbrels that morning. And then I arrived too late. I would have shot the damned executioner if I could've gotten close enough. But they pulled them out of the tumbrel, shoved them beneath the guillotine, and . . . it was over. Just like that. A matter of minutes only. My mother—they caught her head in a basket. Isobel—they held my sister's head up high, held it by her beautiful hair for all to see. And then they tossed their bodies away like trash and went on to the next poor unfortunate."

His voice did not break. Beth's heart did instead. She pictured the lean, handsome boy he would have been, imagined the horror he had endured on that terrible day, the horror that had been visited upon the mother and sister he had clearly loved, and felt hot tears well into her eyes.

"Oh, Neil. I am so sorry." Her voice broke. She snuggled closer, hugging him tightly, her cheek pressed against his chest. "So terribly, terribly sorry."

"It was a long time ago." He almost seemed to shrug. The indifference in his voice tore at her heart, because she knew it was assumed, or rather constructed over the course of many years to mask a fathoms-deep well of anguish. "I never think of it anymore, so don't imagine I'm still grief-stricken, or anything of that nature. The brutal truth is, it was just one atrocity out of tens of thousands that came out of those years. I would it had not happened, of course, but it did and it can't be changed, so there's an end to it."

"You must have suffered so much," she

whispered, because a sudden lump in her throat kept her from speaking any louder. The welling tears spilled over to run in scalding tracks down her cheeks. "What a hideous, horrible—"

She broke off because she couldn't continue. The lump in her throat had grown too large.

"Are you *crying*?" His fingers were on her face, sliding over her cheeks, discovering the telltale wetness of her tears for themselves.

"Yes." Beth gave a defiant sniff, which was meant to serve as punctuation to her uncharacteristic display. Its purpose was ruined when her breath caught on a sob and more tears leaked out despite her best efforts to hold them back. "Oh, the devil take it, I never cry. It's only—thinking about you there, in the crowd watching—" She broke off, swallowing hard before she could continue. "Well, why wouldn't I cry? Anyone would. It is just . . . so . . . *sad.*"

"I think," he said slowly, and there was a note in his voice that Beth had never heard in it before, "this has to be the first time anyone has ever cried for me."

Beth took a deep breath, trying to rally

her defenses, trying not to make an utter cake of herself even though her heart ached for him.

"If that's true, then that has to be almost the saddest thing of all," she said, striving for cool composure. But her voice shook on the last words, and she wasn't quite able to stop more tears from coursing down her cheeks.

He brushed them away. His touch was incredibly gentle.

"Did you know, Madame Roux, that you are really quite a darling?" he whispered.

Then he moved, shifting onto his side, and as she looked up at him with blind questioning his mouth found hers.

Chapter Twenty-one

HIS LIPS WERE FIRM, and warm, and sure, and they felt so right on hers that she responded instantly. Her head fell back onto the steely resilience of his upper arm. Her lips parted under his. His mouth was wet and hot and he tasted faintly of spirits and his unshaven cheeks felt bristly against her smooth skin—and she loved all of it. She kissed him back with an ardor that would have surprised her had she been in any condition to consider it, which she was not. She was lost in the moment, in the upswelling of emotion, in the increasing urgency of the kiss. She kissed him as she had never imagined she would kiss a man, answering the hungry demand of his lips and tongue with fervent caresses of her own, sliding her hands up over his chest to twine her arms around his neck, pressing herself against him with abandon. The folds of the greatcoat parted so that she could feel every blatantly masculine inch of him against her. The solid wall of his chest invited her breasts to swell and tingle as they flattened against it, and they did. The lean, hard cradle of his hips lured her to press close, and she did. His hand slid beneath the coat to cup her bottom, exploring the taut roundness he found there, squeezing her softness so that she felt the long strength of his fingers clear through the fragile layers of her clothes, then pulling her closer yet until she was pressed so tightly against him that she could feel the shocking contours of that part of him that had grown amazingly large and rigid with wanting her. The electrifying intimacy awoke tremors of passion that set her to shaking in his arms. Deep inside, a series of quick, instinctive contractions began to spiral ever tighter until they became a clamorous throbbing that was like nothing she had ever felt. She clung to him, intoxicated by the unfamiliar sensations, on fire now as she responded to his kisses, to his touch, with a rising hunger of her own.

He licked into her mouth, claimed it, possessed it so thoroughly that she was no longer sure where his mouth left off and hers began. His hand on her bottom rocked her against him until that most secret part of her ached and wept. But instead of reacting to such a gross assault on her person as she would have expected herself to do, instead of protesting or whisking herself out of his arms or responding with anger or fear or any of the myriad emotions she knew she should be feeling, she made a little sound of surprised pleasure into his mouth and tightened her grip on him and kissed him harder, kissed him as if she never wanted to stop, which she didn't. Knowing it was wicked, knowing it was wrong, she pressed even closer against the hardness of him, moved against it, experimentally, tantalized by its bold promise, wanting to get closer, to deepen the contact, to keep the delicious tremors of excitement that radiated from that place where he pressed most firmly into her, building until—what? She didn't quite know. All she knew was that the prospect made her dizzy. When his hand slid from her bottom down the length of her thigh and lifted it so that her leg curved atop his in the most wanton position imaginable, she let him do as he would, allowing him to pull her skirts out of the way without protest, even, if she was honest, with a shameful eagerness for what would come next. If she was going to die, which with every minute that passed seemed more and more likely, why should she not first experience this dark, forbidden thing he would teach her? The very thought of it filled her with longing. That, along with the sheer outrageousness of feeling the smooth cloth of his pantaloons and the long, muscular legs they sheathed intertwining with the soft bare skin of her thighs, made her heart pound and her toes curl. Then one thigh pushed fully between her legs. It lodged possessively against her, on purpose she judged, moving in the most arousing fashion against that secret place at the juncture of her thighs, which, as she wore nothing beneath her petticoats save her chemise, was naked and thus left totally vulnerable to his machinations. The muscular invasion made her squirm against it quite without volition, and the resulting jolt of fire caused her to go all light-headed as her insides liquefied in a burning rush.

Almost mindless with sensation now, kissing him fervently, she moved against him with an instinct she had never realized she possessed. She was barely aware of anything besides the fiery passion he was awakening her to as he turned her onto her back and slid her arms free of the great-coat, which then acted as a cushion for the unyielding rock beneath them. Clinging to him, answering him kiss for torrid kiss, she realized dimly even as his weight set-tled on top of her and her thighs spread willingly apart to accommodate his that this was what she had avoided for so long, what she had dreaded, what she had shuddered at the prospect of being forced to endure. If she was going to die, though, she did not want to do so without knowing what this ultimate experience was like. Caught up in the moment, in the danger and the heat of it, in the strange, unimag-ined but delicious urges that he had roused in her, she surrendered utterly. The now-driving demands of her own body, the physical cravings she had never dreamed existed inside her, the thought that this brief time with him might be all she would ever have, seduced her past the point of reason, and she recognized with a flicker of amazed acceptance that she was his to do with as he would. He kissed her, and she kissed him back. He rocked against her, and she arched and moaned and moved in the most lascivious response. It helped that it was darker even than the darkest midnight, that she couldn't see that they were twined so closely that their bodies were almost one, that she was returning his kisses and caresses with an abandon that spoke far more of strumpet than of lady, that her skirts were pushed up around her waist and he was lying between her thighs in the most debauched of positions. But even if it had been broad daylight, even if they had been caught out in the open air with legions of onlookers to gasp and point, she thought she would not have been able to summon the will at that point to call a halt. This hot, urgent quaking, this most unexpected onslaught of the earthiest of passions, was like nothing she had ever in her life expected to feel, and to her own amazement she discovered she was now completely powerless to resist.

When his mouth slid from hers to trace a searing path down the tender cord at the side of her neck, she gave a tiny gasp and clutched at the long, crisp waves of his hair. He was settled firmly between her legs now, rocking fully clothed against her nakedness, and she writhed helplessly at the delicious torment.

"Neil . . ."

"Mm?" It was a sensuous murmur, uttered as he pressed a necklace of scorching kisses around the base of her throat.

"I—*oh.*" Her mind went fuzzy with shocked pleasure as one of those large, strong hands she had made mental note of before slid inside her bodice to find her breast. He caressed her, so lightly, cupping his palm delicately over her breast as if it were made of spun sugar and would melt, then dipping beneath the soft globe to hold it in place as his thumb brushed her nipple. That brief, barely there contact shot through her like a lightning bolt. She shivered and clutched at his shoulders and tightened her thighs so they pressed beseechingly against either side of his. Her lips parted, but only to breathe erratically as his hand then made itself at home inside her bodice. It felt big and warm and possessive as he thoroughly fondled first one bare breast and then the other. Instinctively she arched against him, offering herself up to him with a voluptuousness she would have said was absolutely not in her character, moving beneath him in silent, urgent entreaty as the insistent quaking deep inside her tightened and intensified until she could hardly bear it. She wanted— she wanted—she wanted—*more.*

"I love the way you taste." His mouth slid along her collarbone. His voice was husky and low. "So sweet."

She realized he was tugging at her bodice, pulling it down farther, pulling it completely out of his way to bare her breasts for his kisses, for his mouth, and barely swallowed a moan.

"I mean to love you, Beth."

Her heart beat so fast that she thought he must feel its frenzied pounding against his lips as they traced their way up the first gentle swell of her breasts toward her nipple, which was upright and quivering in anticipation. Still fully clothed, he pressed himself solidly against her, down there between her legs, pushing into her harder than before, moving against her in a rhythmic way that left her in no doubt whatsoever of what he intended. She caught her breath in a part-frightened, part-bedazzled gasp as she regained enough reason to understand what he was telling her, what he meant to do to her next unless she forbade him. *You should tell him to stop,* she thought, but she didn't, not by word or gesture, because the truth was, she didn't want him to stop. She wanted him to love her, wanted him to keep doing what he was doing until the fever pitch to which he had roused her broke at last.

"I—know." She whispered her acquiescence. The hot, honeyed, melting feeling she was experiencing was more potent than any libation could ever be. She was intoxicated with need now, burning up with it, her body no longer her own to command, her mind clouded past the point of reason by the wondrous things he was making her feel. The sad truth was, in the state she was in he could do what he would with her, anything at all, and she would rejoice in the doing. Regrets, which she knew there would be as certainly as she knew there were fish in the sea, were something she would deal with later. If, that is, she survived, and they got out of this terrifying prison, and there was any reason to feel regret about anything.

But she would not think about that. For now there was only him, and the blazing desire he had so unexpectedly ignited inside her. She would lie with him because she simply did not have the strength to draw back, because her quaking, burning body would not allow her to do anything else, because she hungered for his full possession in a way she had never imagined she could hunger for anything, and, if needed, she would count the cost later.

Then his mouth found her breast, and any lucidity that had remained to her, any hope of cold, sober caution winning out was lost. He kissed her nipple, caressed it with the scalding heat of his tongue, then drew it into his mouth with a carnality that made her cry out and arch against him and hold his head to her breast like the loosest of women.

He favored both breasts with his attention, then finally lifted his head.

"Not afraid anymore, sweetheart?" His voice was hoarse but his tone was tender as his hand slid with warm surety up the silken skin of her inner thigh. The purposeful caress made her tremble. She knew where he was going, knew where he meant to touch her next, and the prospect drove her wild. Her breasts swelled, begging eagerly for his kisses. Her thighs trembled and fell open with wanting. She could feel his hand on her skin like a brand, moving so slowly, too slowly, toward that part of her that was dying for his touch.

"Not with you." From the unevenness of her voice, she realized that her breathing was ragged.

Most unexpectedly, she heard an unfamiliar sound and realized to her surprise that it was his teeth snapping together. At the same time his hand stilled on its silken path, his fingers tightening suddenly on her thigh so that she could feel the full size and strength of them as they burned into her flesh. For the briefest of moments he didn't move, but stayed perfectly still, as if he had turned to stone between one instant and the next. The harsh rasping sound she heard was, she realized, his breathing.

"Neil?" Perplexed, she strained to see him through the darkness.

As if her voice broke whatever spell had been holding him frozen in place, he swore, horribly, then lifted his hand from her thigh and rolled away from her, just like that, as though she had suddenly broken out in a rash of thorns. Though she gaped in his direction, she might as well have been blind for anything she could see. But she could feel him beside her, mere inches away because the confines of the space they were in would permit nothing more, and got the sense that he was now lying on his back with his arm flung over his eyes. Desire had turned the small space warm, steamy even. The greatcoat on which they lay felt plush as a rug. Tension hummed between them like an invisible, electrifying force. Every instinct she possessed bade her close the scant distance separating them—but she hesitated.

"Neil?" Instead, she laid a questioning hand on his arm. To her surprise she felt a tremor rack the hard muscle. "Is something wrong?" Her voice turned small and uncertain suddenly, and she hated the way it sounded. Hated the vulnerability she detected in it.

He pulled his arm free of her touch. "What did you mean, 'not with you'?"

"What?" The sense of his words barely registered. Her heart still pounded, her blood still raced, her body still burned. The almost unpalatable truth was that she wanted him to keep on with loving her—though he, apparently, had no such intention.

"I asked you if you were not afraid of sex anymore, and you said, not with you. I want to know what you meant by that."

"Oh." Remembering her own words, Beth flushed. Praise the Lord he could not see! In fact, that was the only saving grace in the whole situation, she decided. Taking a deep breath, she suddenly became aware that her skirts were twisted around her waist. Her bodice had been pulled down well past her breasts. She was to all intents and purposes naked, lying on her back with her legs sprawled indecently apart and the wetness from his mouth drying on her breasts. As she realized the enormity of what she had let him do, the full scope of the intimacies she had allowed him to take, the heat in her face intensified and spread until she was certain she must be blushing all over. Mortified, she quickly and quietly did what she could to restore herself to decency, then scooted as far away from him as it was possible to get, until she was on her side with her back pressed against the stone slab that blocked them in. She, who had so dreaded physical intimacy that the very thought of having to endure the marriage bed was enough to make her turn sick to her stomach, had almost given herself to this man—this unrepentant criminal. It was unbelievable, but it was true. Disgracefully, her lips still yearned for more kisses, and her body yearned, too, for more kisses and caresses and everything else he had done to her. No, everything they had done together. There was no point in pretending that he had forced her, or that she had been anything less than a willing, nay, eager participant. And the worst part of the whole thing was, she wasn't even glad he had stopped. Not yet. Not while her heart still pounded and her blood still raced and her body still hungered for his taking.

"'Oh' is not an answer." He sounded testy. They were no longer touching in any way, but she could feel his presence as acutely as if she were plastered against his side. "And I would have one, if you please."

"Very well, then. I meant what I said." The honesty that had always been one of her foremost virtues—or besetting sins, as Twindle would have had it—combined with pride to rise to her rescue, infusing her with a slightly defiant courage. Indeed, she scorned to try to turn what had just happened between them into anything less than the truly momentous revelation it had been. Whatever this most unexpected attraction that had sprung up between them owed its existence to, the fact was that it did exist. Because of that, because she could not rid herself of her fear that they were never going to get out of there, and because even now where she most wanted to be was back in his arms, she would give him the truth with no bark on it, and to the devil with the consequences.

"Would you care to explain that so it's a little clearer?"

"I would have thought it was perfectly clear, but if you need it spelled out for you, then fine: Just as you guessed, I have not cared to be kissed, or"—and here, despite her determination, she stammered slightly— "or handled, by any gentleman. Except, for some reason I am at a loss to explain, I don't seem to feel that aversion with you."

"God in heaven." Her confession did not seem to please him.

She frowned, affronted. "You asked me a question, and I answered it. If you didn't want the truth, you shouldn't have asked."

"I don't think you quite grasp what almost happened here. A few moments more and I would have had your damned virginity." Instead of merely testy, he now sounded downright angry. "What you ought to be doing right about now is slapping my face. At the very least."

Chapter Twenty-two

"WHAT GOOD WOULD THAT DO? Anyway, you did nothing I wasn't willing for you to do." With that gruff admission, Beth folded her arms over her chest. "Besides, if we are going to die, whether or not I am a virgin when it happens doesn't much matter, does it?"

Neil gave vent to a series of soft but fluent curses. By the time he finished she was glaring at him through the darkness.

"And what was that in aid of, pray?"

"We are not going to die, damn it. And you need to understand this: You were willing because I made you willing. I know what pleases women and I knew what would please you and I did those things to you deliberately so that you would let me have my wicked way with you. If you would know the truth, I've been contemplating seducing you almost since I first set eyes on you."

"Then why did you stop?"

There was a pause.

"Because I have a shred of decency left to me, it seems. And you should thank your lucky stars I do. Otherwise you would now be my mistress, and utterly and completely ruined."

"If we survive, I am probably ruined anyway. I doubt my credit will survive this."

"Am I to understand from that that I need have no scruples?" he asked sardonically.

"None at all."

Dead silence greeted that.

"You, my girl, are a menace." She got the impression that now he was speaking through his teeth. "Fortunately for you, I've discovered a most unexpected aversion to deflowering virgins, however bloody-minded they may be."

"Are you calling *me* bloody-minded—" Beth broke off as the sense of what she had just heard penetrated. "Wait, are you saying you've never, ah, um"—the unaccustomed frankness of the conversation caused her to stutter again, to her annoyance—"deflowered a virgin?"

"What I have or have not done in that area is nothing I mean to discuss with you."

"You haven't, have you?"

"Damn it, Beth, leave it. The subject is closed."

By now her heart had slowed to something approximating its normal rhythm, and her blood flowed through her veins more or less as it was wont to do. The carnal desire he had most astoundingly roused in her was easing, and she had little doubt that if nothing more occurred to feed it, it would soon fade to a delicious memory. But what she would carry with her always, for however long or short always was, was the knowledge that she could feel that way, that she could contemplate the marital act with delight rather than dread, that rousing a man's lust meant experiencing it along with him rather than subjecting herself to it.

His abandoned seduction had, in fact,

freed her of the shackles that had kept her from fully living the life she wanted to live.

The key, of course, as Claire had repeatedly told her, lay in finding the right man.

"Neil," she said softly into the silence that, disturbed only by their uneven breathing, had spun out between them, "thank you."

"Thank you?" He sounded wary.

"Yes."

"You're welcome. You should know that stopping when I did was damned hard. In fact, it's probably one of the hardest things I've ever done in my life."

Beth smiled into the darkness. "Oh, I wasn't thanking you for stopping when you did, although I do see now that it was probably for the best. But you've changed everything for me: if we get out of this alive, if by some miracle I am not totally ruined, if I can go back to London and my life continues on as before, I can actually marry the next gentleman to whom I become betrothed. That's why I was thanking you: I see I need no longer avoid marriage for fear of—of the intimacies of the marriage bed."

"Oh my God." It was a groan. "That is not what I needed to hear." He moved restively, and Beth got the feeling that he was in the throes of doing battle with some inner demon. "I see why I've never acted the gentleman before now: it's too damned difficult."

"Is it?"

"Hell, yes. And you are not helping, and you know it. You think I don't want to love you so much that denying myself is well-nigh killing me? 'Tis your well-being I'm thinking of here." The rough edge to his voice sent a delicious shiver racing over her skin. "And then you go and tell me that I've made it possible for some other man to—"

A sound from somewhere beyond their small prison made Beth stiffen. Even as her senses went on alert and her head swung questioningly toward it, a familiar, devoutly welcome voice pierced the darkness.

"We be back! We brought 'elp!"

"Thank God." Eagerly, Beth turned over to face the cabin and raised her voice in answer. "Mary!"

"Miss! Be ye and 'is worship all right?"

"We're fine," Neil yelled. "Is Creed with you?"

"No," Mary replied, but before she could continue a strange male voice shouted cheerfully, "Mr. Creed's away, but it don't matter. There's a group of us here, and we'll get you out right and tight. From the looks of things, it'll be takin' some time, though."

"Who are you?" Neil called back. Beth thought she heard a hint of wariness in his voice, and a different kind of tension emanated from him now. Of course, they were no longer insulated from the outside world. Was it possible that the cheerful voice belonged to one of their pursuers from the castle? At the thought, Beth's heart started to beat a little faster for an entirely different reason than before.

"Name's Tandy. We'll be getting the others out first, acause you're under a heaping pile o' rock, and them, not so much. You just hang on, you and the lady, and leave all to us."

There seemed nothing else to do. Frowning out toward the cavern where she could hear faint thuds, as if of rocks landing after being flung aside, Beth heard a smaller, metallic sound directly behind her and glanced back toward Neil.

"What are you doing?" she asked. Her voice was scarce louder than a whisper, and she realized it was because she feared being overheard by their rescuers. Which was ridiculous. She could hear none of their conversation or noise beyond those muffled crashes. Still, some atavistic instinct made her cautious.

"Getting the pistols. I took them out of my pocket before I gave you my greatcoat and tucked them out of the way. They're empty, curse the luck, but no one needs to know that. I've used empty pistols to back men off before."

Beth's stomach tightened. "Do you think you'll need to back them off? Who do you think they are?"

"In all likelihood, honest men. But it pays to be prepared." He reached out for her, hooking an arm around her waist and pulling her back against him. "From the sound of it, they're not being overly careful. 'Tis safer here in the back against the wall, in case they should trigger another rock fall."

That was a frightening possibility Beth hadn't yet thought of.

"Neil . . ."

"Worrying is a waste of time. At this juncture there's nothing to be done but wait until they dig us out, then deal with what we find." His arm was hard around her waist, and she could feel the slight rise and fall of his chest against her back. Then he moved, changing positions, taking her with him. Once again they ended up in the most comfortable position they could find, with him on his back with his arm around her and his chest pillowing her head. Lying against him, listening to the continuous low thunder of noise that now emanated from the cabin, Beth found herself craving fresh air, and longing for the moment when they would be freed from the claustrophobic space.

And yet . . . and yet . . .

"London seems a long way away," she observed, thinking that if these were indeed honest men, she would be back there in short order, probably by the following night. "I must go home, of course, and I want to, just as soon as may be, but—" She broke off as it hit her that once she was back in her world he would be out of her life. "Once I'm home, I won't be seeing you again, will I?"

"Do you wish to see me again?"

"I own, I think I do."

"That's quite an admission." There was an inscrutable note to his voice that made her frown and tilt her head in an instinctive bid to look up at him, which, of course, was useless in the dark. "Whatever happens, I doubt I'll be disappearing from your life any time soon."

Beth's frown deepened. "But . . ."

"Again with your troubled 'but's." He silenced her with a kiss, to which she instantly, instinctively responded. As hot and hungry as it was brief, it drove everything else out of her head. "Aren't you glad now I stopped when I did? We will both live to see another day, and you still have your damned virginity."

"I suppose I must be. But, you know, I find I quite like kissing," Beth murmured reflectively. Her arms were looped around his neck, and her chin rested against his chest. Her eyes were open, but of course she couldn't see him, or anything else.

"Among other things. With you, in any case."

A moment of electrically charged silence followed her remark.

"Fortunately for my barely surviving gentlemanly instincts, I find the presence of so many strangers just on the other side of these rocks most inhibiting," he said at last, sounding slightly out of breath as he removed her arms from around his neck and settled her against him again. "Suppose you distract me further by talking to me. You can start by telling me about your childhood. What of your parents?"

Though it cost her an effort, she had enough pride to rise above the dizzying effects of that kiss, and managed to reply with a creditable assumption of gentle raillery. "Oh, your origins are off-limits, but mine are to be explored?"

"Exactly so," he said, and she thought he smiled. Certainly the tension she had felt in him seemed to ease a little. As for herself, her heart pounded and the delicious melting feeling was back, but she, too, was conscious of their rescuers' nearness. She was relieved to discover that under the circumstances she had enough proper feeling left to her that she was content to lie close and talk, and nothing more.

"Unfair," she protested, but then at his insistence proceeded to tell him what he wanted to know, starting with what little she had managed to glean over the years about her mother, a clergyman's daughter named Elizabeth like herself, who had become the Earl of Wickham's fourth wife only to die in an accidental fall when Beth was so young that she could not remember her. She spoke guardedly of her father, whose brutality toward and lack of love for his offspring she did not care to dwell on, even in her thoughts, and of her father's friends, who considered making sexual advances toward the earl's unwilling daughters a form of sport. Gabby and Claire she described lovingly, the one as the mother figure who had raised her, the other as her dearest friend. Their husbands, Nick and Hugh, she spoke of with affection, both for their own sakes and for the happiness they had given her sisters.

"Fond of Richmond, are you?" Neil asked. Once again, there was an inscrutability in his tone that she couldn't quite account for. It struck her as peculiar for him to specifically mention Hugh rather than include both her brothers-in-law in the question, and with that Beth was reminded of the circumstances under which she had first set eyes on him.

"Hugh's been very kind to me, and he's amazingly good to Claire. I love him, and Nick, too, as if they were my own brothers," she said firmly. Then she added, "You know, you never did tell me precisely what you were doing in Hugh's house the night we met."

"Did I not?"

"No. I assumed you were there to rob us, but—"

Before she could finish, a cheer went up from the cavern, distracting them both. The sounds that followed made it clear that Nan and Jane had been successfully rescued. Beth heard their joyful cries thankfully. Moments later, a series of thuds far closer at hand than any they had heard before was their first indication that now it was their turn. Relief and anticipation mingled with apprehension as she realized that their hours of imprisonment would soon be at an end. She wanted to be free in the worst way, of course, but she had no idea who awaited them in the cavern, or what circumstances they might find themselves in once they were freed. And Neil had said he wouldn't be disappearing from her life, but she wasn't foolish enough to think that once she was home in London things between them would be the same.

"Shifting this bloody enormous pile o' rocks is lookin' like it'll take us all night, or more," Tandy announced from what sounded like just outside their prison, his raised voice making it clear that he was talking to her and Neil. "I've a better plan: We'll be putting a bit of a lever under this great slab that's lying against the wall like, and lifting it. Then we'll pull you out beneath it quick as can be, with the lady coming out first, o' course."

Beth felt Neil's sudden tension, but after only the briefest hesitation he yelled back, "All right."

"Make ready, then." Tandy's shout was accompanied by a loud, metallic grating. "When we've got the thing up, you'll need to move fast."

"Do you think we can trust them?" Beth whispered as, at Neil's urging, she scrambled into a crouching position near the slab. Beside her, she could feel him making movements that she thought meant he was thrusting the pistols into his waistband for easy access if needed. Apprehension made her stomach flutter. She wet her suddenly dry lips.

"We have no choice. We sure as hell can't stay here." Neil's voice was grim. A glimmer of light between the ground and the slab suddenly appeared, seeming to Beth to shine bright as the sun. As she blinked at it, dazzled by what seemed like the sudden brilliance, it widened. Then without warning Neil's hand slid around the back of her neck and he kissed her, quick and hard.

"Get the lady in position," Tandy yelled. Neil let her go, and Beth, heart pounding, glanced rather dazedly at the crack to discover that it now formed an angle that was nearly a foot wide and growing at its widest point. The shaft of light beaming in was almost as blinding as the darkness had been.

"I'll be right behind you," Neil promised.

"Now!" Tandy yelled, and two meaty male hands appeared through the opening, fingers outstretched as he reached for her. "Lady, you grab on to my hands."

With a lightning glance back at Neil—she could see him now, just barely, as a dark, crouching shadow beside her—she grabbed Tandy's hands.

"Go," Neil cried, his hands on her waist as he added his impetus to Tandy's fierce yank. Ducking her head, she found herself being whisked out beneath the precariously balanced sheet of rock.

Quick impressions—dazzling torchlight; armed men in numbers sufficient to practically fill the cavern, all with their weapons pointing at the wedge of space that had just been opened up beneath the tower of rocks; Mary, Nan, and Jane in a huddled group, seemingly under guard—hit her even before she was all the way through.

Her eyes widened. Her mouth popped open. Her heart lurched.

Dear God, I have to warn Neil . . .

But before she could make so much as a sound, a hand clapped down hard over her mouth and she was hauled to her feet, to be restrained by a pair of tall, solidly built men who each clutched one of her

arms. They weren't dressed in military uni-
forms, and their faces were hard and
etched with years, but the impression they
gave was of military men.

"Don't you be afeared, milady," the rough
voice of the man whose hand covered her
mouth whispered in her ear. "If that mur-
dering dog who kidnapped you so much
as breathes wrong, we'll kill him out of
hand. We was sent by His Grace the Duke
to find you and take you back home again."

Even as the last word left her captor's
mouth, Tandy was reaching under the slab,
one end of which, Beth saw, was being
held perhaps two feet off the ground by
four sturdy men wielding iron poles. A half
dozen men armed with rifles moved silently into position around him, ready, from
the look of them, to shoot Neil on sight.

"Grab on, then, sir," Tandy yelled into
the opening, sounding every bit as cheerful as before.

Her mind raced as her blood turned to
ice in her veins.

Jerking free of the hand covering her
mouth just as Neil's head and shoulders
appeared, she said in a cold, clear voice

loud enough to be heard throughout the chamber, "He has pistols, but they are empty. Do not kill him, I order you in the name of my brother, His Grace the Duke. He will be extremely angry if you do, I promise you, because I would see this scoundrel hang."

Still prone but scrambling to get out from under the slab, his hands still grasping Tandy's, Neil looked up sharply at that. Their eyes met for no more than a split second before a rifle butt crashed down on the back of his head.

Chapter Twenty-three

HIS HEAD ACHED LIKE BE-DAMNED. The nauseating pain was what made him aware that he was once again fully conscious. Suppressing a groan out of instinct—the same instinct for danger that had saved his life many times before—Neil stayed still and kept his eyes shut as he strove to get mind and memory to the point where both were functional. His first thought was, *This time I'm in trouble.* His second was to remember exactly how he had come to be so. Wherever he was, the temperature was cold enough to make him aware of the chill, cold enough to penetrate his clothes.

He seemed to be fully dressed, at least to the point where he was wearing shirt, pantaloons, and stockings. His greatcoat was missing, which was not surprising considering the contents of the pockets, as were his boots. A pungent smell he couldn't quite place teased his nostrils. The surface on which he lay prone was both soft and damnably prickly at the same time. His arms were shackled behind his back. He could feel the iron cuffs fastened crushingly tight around his wrists, along with the heavy weight of the chain looped around his forearms. His ankles were shackled, too, also painfully tight, with more chains wrapped around his legs. There was noise in the distance, raised voices, laughter. Strident female voices. Raucous male laughter.

And—this was the detail that got his heart pumping—certain stealthy sounds much closer at hand made him think that someone or something was attempting to creep up on him, almost certainly to no good purpose.

Not by the slightest rattle of a chain did he reveal that he was now aware, although it required all of his considerable self-control to remain unmoving, except for the opening of his eyes the merest slit. Dizziness immediately assailed him; he gritted his teeth and ignored it.

It was night, and his surroundings were dark and full of shadows. He was in a stable, in a stall, lying facedown in a pile of straw, which accounted for both the prickliness and the smell. The wooden sides of the box were rough, with uneven boards, and from that he knew that this was a humble place scarce better than a cow barn. The partitions between the stalls rose to only about shoulder height, so that he could easily hear the stamps and snorts of the horses occupying the surrounding boxes. All this he absorbed in an instant, aided by the flickering light cast by what was probably a lantern affixed to a nail in the stable's center aisle.

In that instant he also saw that someone was in the stall with him. Someone who was easing the door closed in the clear hope that no one would hear. Someone who was careful to stay too low to be observed by anyone who might glance her way across the tops of the stalls.

Because it was a woman. Even before, bending nearly double, she turned to sneak toward him and the lamplight touched her bright hair, he had no doubt as to her identity: Beth.

Some of the tension immediately left his body. He could not think she meant to harm him. Still, he regarded her narrowly. The last words he had heard her say before someone had most viciously struck him down replayed with vivid exactitude in his mind.

Betrayal on every hand was no more than he had come to expect in this world, of course, but—Beth? No, she would not betray him. He was—almost—willing to bet his life on it.

"Are you in league with my captors, then?" he asked, craning his neck to look up at her as her skirt—no longer the flimsy yellow silk, but some dark color and made of sturdier stuff—swept to within a foot of his head.

She jumped, frowned down at him, and hissed urgently, "Hush!"

"'I would see the scoundrel hang'?" Discovering that besides the shackles confining his wrists and ankles, he also was chained to the wall in such a way that it precluded him from sitting up or rolling over, or, indeed, moving very much at all, added an edge to his voice as he threw her words back at her.

"Would you keep your voice down? 'Twas but a ploy to keep them from killing you out of hand, as any but a complete bonehead would know." With a rustle of skirts, she knelt beside him. Her hair had been put up in a proper lady's style, he saw. Her dress was severe in cut, with a high neck and long sleeves. "There are armed guards everywhere, and I doubt they will hesitate to shoot you if the need arises. They seem to feel you're a most dangerous man."

She was leaning over him as she spoke.

"They're right." Craning his neck in an attempt to keep her face in view was making his head ache worse than ever, he discovered. "What are you doing?"

"I have the key. If you would but hold still, I might be able to fit it into the hole and unlock the shackles."

With that promise as bait, Neil held still. Chained as he was, even all his skill and experience in the art of killing did him no good. Much as he hated to admit it, he was as helpless as a fish in a barrel. He could be shot, stabbed, strangled, or otherwise disposed of at an attacker's will. The thought sat ill with him. Vulnerability was not a state he was familiar with, and he didn't like the sensation. The subsequent clink of metal on metal as the key went home was, thus, music to his ears. Even better, the knowledge that he had been right about her trustworthiness was balm to his wary soul.

"Where did you get the key?"

The iron band around his right wrist opened. Neil immediately pulled his hand free. "Mary stole it from Mr. Tandy's coat pocket while he was having a wash. She is the most redoubtable girl."

The band around his left wrist sprang loose, and Neil pulled that hand free and started to shake off the chains that wrapped his arms. The resulting clanking caused Beth to grab his shoulder in alarm.

"*Shh.* Do you *want* to be hauled off to Newgate?"

Newgate was not the fate he faced; summary execution was. Probably the only reason he was not dead already was because of her presence on the scene, or perhaps the men who had captured him were waiting for someone else—someone like

Clapham—to arrive to do the job. But his intended fate was something she obviously didn't know, and he didn't see any reason to enlighten her. Feeling much better now that his hands were loose, Neil flexed his fingers, ignoring the pins and needles that shot through them as proper circulation was restored. Having no wish to be discovered before he was free, though, he quit wrestling with the chains in favor of waiting until the last of the locks constraining him was opened. He was still lying prone, because, as he had discovered, a chain that had been passed around his chest was secured somehow to the wall. Another chain similarly constrained his legs. Clearly, his captors were careful men who knew what they were dealing with and weren't prepared to take any more of a chance than leaving him alive past the point of first encounter, which in retrospect would no doubt be judged to have been a grievous error: bad for them, good for him.

"Who are these men?" he asked. "I can't imagine Creed letting them on his property, much less showing them the way down into the caves."

"From what I've gathered, they're a band

of retired soldiers under the direction of Mr. Tandy, who's a Runner. Apparently there are a dozen or more groups just like them even now scouring the countryside in search of me. When Mr. Tandy got wind of the murders at the castle, and learned of the auction and the shambles it turned into, he and his men thought the escape might have something to do with me and conducted a search of the area. They came across this inn just as Mary was trying to persuade Creed's nephew—Creed is dead and his nephew owns the inn now—to come to our aid, which she says he was less than willing to do. Fortunately, Tandy and his men proved willing. At least, it seemed fortunate until they clouted you over the head and told us they were placing you under arrest for murder."

Neil grunted by way of a reply, wondering how much of what Beth had been told was actually true. Very little, probably, but then it didn't matter: thanks to her, he—and she, because he would be taking her with him—would soon be on their way.

Beth made quick work of the numerous locks, and in no time at all he was sitting up and throwing off chains like so many scarves.

Let them come at him now, by God.

"Thank you, by the by," he said, preparing to get to his feet.

"You're welcome. We must— Oh, there are your boots."

Reaching into the dark corner behind him, Beth retrieved his boots, which had obviously been removed to facilitate the placing of restraints on his ankles, as she spoke and passed them to him. After thrusting a hand inside each in a quick, although not particularly hopeful, search for his knife—as he had expected, it wasn't there—he pulled them on.

"You don't by chance see my greatcoat, do you?" Having looked around the stall himself, he was disappointed but not surprised by her negative answer. With two fat purses and the same number of pistols in the pockets, he would have been astonished if they hadn't stripped him of it as quickly as they could.

Grimacing at the pain in his head, he stood up despite the rush of dizziness that reconfirmed what he had suspected: the blow that had struck him down had been a mighty one. What he saw out the open barn door as he glanced over the tops of the stalls toward the yard explained much. The stable, built since his time, was in the backyard of the inn he had described to her, the inn he had worked in as a youth. It was called the White Swan, and from what he could see of it, the rambling stone build-ing he remembered had not changed by so much as the thin plume of smoke pour-ing out of the kitchen chimney. All re-mained the same, from the location of the scraggly kitchen garden to the tumble-down well to the chickens scratching in the dirt to the sputtering bonfire that lit the night. There was even, as there had ever been, a fight going on in the yard, which was the source of the female shrieks and male shouts and laughter filling the air. Perhaps a dozen armed men—including those who were meant to be guarding him at that very moment, he had no doubt— were gathered in a circle around a pair of combatants they were cheering and egg-ing on. Neil's eyes widened as he caught a glimpse of the fighters: Mary and Dolly. To all appearances they were going at

each other tooth and nail. As he watched,
Mary caught a hand in the neck of Dolly's
gown, ripping it clear to the waist, and received a mighty slap for her pains.

"Holy Mother of God." The exclamation
was not entirely under his breath.

"Keep your voice down," Beth admon-
ished in a sharp whisper. "Come, we must
go out the back. I've saddled a horse, for
you must fly from here as quick as you
can."

Having skirted around him, Beth already
had the stall door open and was moving
into the center aisle.

"Mary and Dolly . . ." He was still
shocked and sounding it as he followed.
The stall's threshold seemed unaccountably high, catching him unawares, and he
all but tripped over it.

"They're shamming it, of course. To give
me time to free you, and you time to escape. If you would *hurry,* it might even work."

Making an impatient clucking sound
when he apparently didn't move fast
enough to suit her, she grabbed his hand
and pulled him toward the back of the stable, where the big door to the outside was
closed. Behind him, outraged shrieks and

encouraging shouts amidst much laughter told him that the fight went on. Compelled to glance over his shoulder, ignoring the thick throbbing that attacked the base of his skull as he moved his head to such a degree, he saw that Dolly had thrown Mary down into the dirt and was pulling her hair.

The sight was staggering.

"'Tis the biggest farce I've ever seen," he muttered.

"Five quid on the blonde!" A gleeful yell separated itself from the general hubbub outside.

"Ten on t'other! She be tiny, mebbe, but she's a fighter!"

"Open the back door. *Quietly,*" Beth instructed him as she dropped his hand and disappeared into the last stall on the left. He did as he was told, glad the wooden panel opened easily and was not barred, because the task seemed to him far more difficult than it should have been. It was beginning to occur to him that perhaps he was not operating quite as efficiently as was his wont when she came up behind him leading a big roan gelding by the bridle.

"When it's discovered that I've escaped, they'll know Mary and Dolly and the rest helped." Frowning, he looked back toward the fight again. It was a curious thing, but he found that he was actually concerned about the safety of the plaguey nuisances. Who were, most unaccountably, putting themselves in danger to help him get away.

"And what do you propose to do about it, try to kill all twenty guards that are here to take you to gaol?" Her tone tart, she pushed him through the door. "In case you haven't noticed, you're practically staggering as you walk. Such a feat is beyond you at the moment, not that I wish to encourage you in such bloodthirstiness anyway. Come, we must just make it into the woods and then you can mount and be away. Leave us to take care of the rest."

"Killing all wouldn't be necessary. Men lose their fight when they lose their leader."

"Come *away.*"

Now she was practically dragging him and the horse through a grassy meadow toward the woods, that most determined expression that he had come to know all too well on her face. Once again she reminded him of Old Hook Nose, taking control of a tricky situation most masterfully. For the moment, with his senses still in some slight disorder, his body something less than fully functional, and this ridiculous, nagging sense of responsibility toward the females he had never wanted to be saddled with in the first place afflicting him, he reflected that the wisest course would probably be just to fall in with her plan. At least, for as long as he could.

"Thank goodness," she sighed, which he took as an expression of relief as he quickened his step in response to her urging.

The outer edge of what was, if memory served, several thousand acres of mixed evergreens and hardwoods stood stalwart as a stockade and blacker than the night just a few hundred yards away. Once they had gained that, they would be safe from an unlucky glance over a shoulder, a snapped-off shot, which was the most acute danger they faced at the moment. Fortunately, he realized, the glow from the bonfire only served to make them blend in more completely with the shadow-laden gloom enveloping the tall grass through which they were moving. The shouts and shrieks and laughter behind them drowned out any small sound they might have made.

Another round of shouts made Neil suspect the fight might be ending, and his step slowed again.

"What are you doing *now*?"

"I can't allow harm to come to them because of me."

"They'll not harm us, I tell you. Did you not understand that they were employed by Richmond, who they assure me is even now on his way? Indeed, once he arrives and I explain the whole to him, it's very likely that he could have been persuaded to let you go. But Tandy *would* call you a murderer, and insist you must be hauled off as soon as may be to gaol, so I thought it best not to dispute with them, or trust entirely in Richmond's coming, in case releasing you should be beyond his power. This way, there is no possibility of mistake."

"Very wise."

"And you must see that the message Tandy sent to Richmond telling him that they have recovered me, along with his pending arrival, assures our safety despite your escape?"

Thinking the matter over, wishing his head would quit pounding so that the process would not be so unaccustomedly, damnably slow, Neil realized that the immediate reaction of his captors upon discovering his escape undoubtedly would be to mount up and ride after him in furious pursuit, leaving no time for retribution against the women even if they were so inclined.

Which reflection reassured him sufficiently to allow him to keep going.

"I do see that, yes."

Reaching the edge of the woods, they stepped into the velvety darkness beneath the trees. Immediately the sights and sounds and smells of the forest—low-hanging limbs reaching toward them like bony arms, tree trunks straight as sentinels stretching away as far as the eye could see, rustling leaves, the hoot of an owl, a pervasive scent of damp earth and pine—swallowed them up like Jonah's whale.

Beth stopped, passing him the reins.

"You must go," she said urgently. Then her voice changed. It was such a small change, an infusion of reserve so slight as to be almost undetectable, that only someone highly attuned to everything about her—which, he realized, described himself—would notice it. "I will be at Richmond House when—if you wish to contact me. And I will make it a point to always walk in Green Park at ten in the morning."

He realized then that the change in her voice was because she thought they were at the point of saying good-bye. He could just see the lovely pale oval of her face tipped up to his, in perfect position for what she no doubt expected to be his farewell kiss. Her eyes shone with welling tears. Her bright hair was muted, her shape lost in shadow. Her voice was husky and low. He had no doubt, if he were to leave as she expected, the tears now swimming in her eyes would start to fall before he was out of sight. His lips tightened as he looked down at her. Fortunately for his peace of mind, her pretty display of reluctance at parting from him was emotion wasted, because he had not the slightest intention of leaving her behind. The question was, could he persuade her to go with him willingly?

He rather thought he could.

"As reluctant as I am to admit it, I suspect that riding for any distance is beyond me just at present. My head throbs like the devil, and I confess to feeling damnably dizzy." That last sentence, at least, was true. "The sad fact is, I am quite likely to come toppling out of the saddle before I've gone a mile."

"Oh, no. I never thought of that." Her eyes widened with dismay. Clearly considering that the magnitude of the problem called for a response other than weepiness, she blinked, then sniffed determinedly. Knowing himself for a fool, Neil realized that he found the prosaic sound charming. "What's to be done?"

"Perhaps you could come with me for a ways, to lend support. If I grow weak, you could take the reins."

"Yes. That's probably a good idea. If you were to be taken again—" She broke off as a man's exclamatory shout, loud enough to be heard even where they were, pierced the night. "Oh dear, I very much fear your escape has been discovered."

Another shout and various muffled sounds indicative of general confusion reached their ears.

"Sounds like it." Gathering up the reins, he swung onto the roan's back, then kicked his foot free of the stirrup and held his hand down to her. "Will you come with me?"

In answer, she caught his hand and put her foot in the stirrup and let him pull her up behind him. Then he put his heels to the horse's sides, and they were off.

Had he not known the terrain as well as he did, they would have been overtaken many times. The pursuit was, as he had predicted, immediate and furious. The exigencies of escape made him forget all about the headache and dizziness that had plagued him. Riding hard, he headed roughly north, sending the horse galloping ventre à terre through the silvery moonlight, staying well away from the roads and villages. Several times, as he set the roan plunging up hills where no trails existed, or down steep gorges where the slightest misstep would have meant a fatal fall, or took shelter in a hollow hidden by undergrowth, their pursuers passed so close that he could hear them cursing and blaming one another for the laxness that had permitted his escape. But by the time dawn broke, they'd seen or heard nothing of those who chased them for an hour or more. With the sun just peeking above the horizon, and pink and orange streamers spinning through the purpling sky announcing day was at hand, they were about to lose the cover of night, which would make hiding more difficult. Having climbed to the top of a towering, wooded hill and coming at last to a cliff overlooking the countryside, as well as, at some distance, the road from Tynemouth, and seeing nothing more alarming than a herd of grazing cows as he scanned the moors stretching out below them, Neil felt it safe enough to dismount and stretch their legs. Reining in the horse, he said as much to Beth, who for some time had been resting rather heavily against him, arms clasped around his waist, silent as a shadow.

"Tired?" he asked as she slid to the ground. Her hair had fallen from its knot during the night, and now hung down her back in a riotous mass of curls. Her face was pale as milk, her eyes smudged underneath with shadows.

"Sore, rather," she said with feeling, holding on to the stirrup as if not certain her legs would support her.

Neil smiled, knowing full well what part of her anatomy she was referring to.

"If you laugh, I'll not be answerable for the consequences," she warned, frowning up at him most direly.

"I'm not laughing." He dismounted to stand beside her, then frowned, too, but not at her, his attention having been caught by movement on the road.

"What is it?"

"Riders." A group of them, moving north at a brisk pace. Neil counted a dozen men. It was impossible to be certain, of course, but he would be willing to place a substantial wager that so large and fast-moving a party was out at such an hour for no other purpose than to hunt them.

"Why, I believe it's Hugh. It is! In the front there. I would know his horse anywhere! They must be searching for me."

"Wait." Neil caught her arm when she would have waved and, he thought, shouted.

"But it's *Hugh,*" she said, as though he didn't understand. "My brother-in-law Richmond. He'll know how to sort this out, I'm sure of it."

"No." Neil's tone was brutal, and his grip tightened on her arm. Although the confrontation with Richmond was what he had planned from the beginning, what he needed to set himself free, what he desired, he had no wish for it to occur *now*. Beth stiffened at his unaccustomed usage of her; he could feel the sudden tensing of her arm beneath his hand and, all at once conscious that his grip was too tight, loosened it apologetically. He looked down at her, his lips compressing at the sight that greeted him. The soft glow of the just-rising sun turned her glorious hair to fire. The silky black wings of her brows had twitched together in a manner he knew well. The delft blue eyes looked back at him unblinkingly. Her soft and eminently kissable lips had firmed into a frown.

"Why not?" she asked in an ominous tone.

Why not, indeed. As he opened his mouth to tell her yet another lie, Neil had an earth-shattering epiphany: *Betrayal works both ways*.

Chapter Twenty-four

NEIL'S HAND DROPPED AWAY from her arm.

"Because if you summon him here, I'll kill him, and I don't wish to do that in front of you."

The blunt statement robbed Beth of breath. For a moment she stared at him, hoping that the words would take on some other meaning if she allowed them enough time. But they didn't, they kept their unpalatable form, and finally she could no longer deny it and said faintly, "What?"

"I said I mean to kill Richmond."

Under her wondering gaze, his mouth hardened into a thin, cruel line. His eyes as he looked down at her became the piti-less jet she remembered from their first meeting. His handsome face set in sav-age lines. His tall, muscular body seemed to expand and tighten into something truly formidable. She'd glimpsed this side of him before: the predator.

Beth felt very cold suddenly. "Why?"

"Because if I don't, he's going to kill me. One or the other. There's no other way out of this."

Breathing remained difficult. Thinking was harder. It was as though the safe, familiar landscape she'd thought she was traveling through had changed in an in-stant into something out of a nightmare.

Keeping her voice even cost her a con-siderable effort. "And what is 'this,' pray?"

There was a flicker in his eyes as they slid over her face.

"Something far too dark and ugly for me to sully your ears with." His tone was curt. "Suffice it to say that I find I can no longer make you a part of it, and will drop you off at the next village or farmhouse we come to."

Tightening his hold on the reins, he turned back to the horse, giving every indication he meant to once again mount up. Beyond him, on the road far below, Hugh and his men rounded a bend and disappeared from sight.

"Oh, no, you don't." Beth walked several steps away before turning to scowl at him. She was very much shocked still, but her wits had recovered enough to realize that what she was hearing from him was the truth. The man she saw before her, the predator, was absolutely real, and, she had no doubt, absolutely ruthless. She also did not doubt that he meant to do exactly as he said. But she was not, she discovered, frightened of him in the least. He might look as savage as he chose, but she knew as well as she knew anything that he would never harm her. "Do you actually think you can just tell me you mean to kill my brother-in-law, and if you don't he's going to kill you, and that's an end to it? No more questions, no discussion of any kind, just *'I'll drop you off'*?"

He was watching her, slapping the reins across his palm impatiently, his expression grim. Behind him, the horse dropped its head and began cropping at the dew-drenched grass, the homey sound an odd juxtaposition to the tension spinning out between them.

"I'm sorry for it. Believe me, I would not cause you pain if I saw any other way out. But I don't. And if one of us has to die, I mean to make damned sure it's Richmond and not me."

Beth thought of Claire, and her heart lurched. "You can't do this."

"I have no choice."

"Why? Forget that fustian about sullying my ears and give me a round answer. I love Hugh as dearly as any brother, and he is my sister Claire's whole world. If you kill him, she will be destroyed. Our whole family will grieve forever."

"Would you rather I be the one who dies instead?"

Beth's heart lurched a second time. The world seemed to spin around her as she realized how that possibility made her feel, and then it steadied again as she faced the knowledge head-on. Her shoulders squared. Her head came up. Her eyes held his without flinching.

"No. I can't bear that either," she said.

He stood looking at her for a moment

without saying anything more. Then he turned away, pulling the horse's head up.

"Come." His tone was curt as he tossed the reins over the horse's head and swung into the saddle. Behind him, the sun was limning the horizon with gold, and casting the blackest of long shadows across the countryside below. It backlit him so that he appeared as nothing more than a big, sinister silhouette on horseback as he rode toward her. "It's time to go."

Beth watched his approach with growing resolve. Reaching her, he reined in, then held his hand down to her, clearly meaning to once again pull her up behind him.

Chin jutting, she backed several paces away and folded her arms over her chest.

"Oh, no. I'm not going anywhere with you. Not until we talk this out."

"Talking pays no toll." His voice turned harsh as he withdrew his hand. His face was the hard, expressionless mask she'd seen only once or twice before. But he didn't set the horse to following her.

"Nevertheless, I wish to talk."

"Do you think I can't compel you to come with me, my girl?"

That made her bristle. "I think you'd be well advised not to try."

"I warn you, you are beginning to test my patience."

Her eyes flashed. "Behold me all aquiver."

His eyes narrowed dangerously at her. "You should be all aquiver. If you had the sense God gave a goose, you would have been from the beginning."

"Pooh. You don't frighten me in the least." She held his gaze, not backing down an inch, even as the truth broke over her like a particularly icy wave and her eyes widened at the force of it. "That's why you came in the window. You meant to kill Richmond that night. Didn't you?"

"Yes."

"I must have been damnably in the way!"

"You were. And don't swear."

"Don't swear? *Don't swear?*" Her voice rose precipitously, so much so that the horse threw up its head in alarm. She was suddenly so angry at Neil she could practically feel steam rising from the top of her head. *"You* to tell me that, who doesn't so much as blink at murder? I'm surprised you didn't just kill me, too, that night. Then there would have been nothing to stop you getting to Richmond."

He said nothing.

Her eyes widened. "You thought about it. Didn't you?"

"I thought about it," he admitted.

"You don't even have the grace to lie," she marveled.

"I'm done with lying."

"Having lied for so long, the difficulty of that must be on the order of an alcoholic adjuring drink!" Her brow knit as she cast her mind back over various things he had told her. Then she looked at him with growing horror. "Dear Lord, you came after me for a purpose, didn't you? You saved me from that unholy castle so that you could use me as bait to lure Richmond to you!"

Once again he sat silent. Then he said, way too calmly for her liking, "Before you attempt to slay me with any more dagger looks, I suggest you take a moment to reflect again on what your fate would have been had I not rescued you."

"Are you looking for *gratitude*?"

"I'm looking for nothing. Damn it to bloody hell and back anyway, I've had enough of this." With that, he swung down from the horse's back, tossed the reins over a nearby branch, and stalked purposefully toward her.

Every self-protective instinct she possessed screamed at her to run, to put as much distance as possible between herself and this formidable man who was clearly quite capable of breaking her in two and looked like he would enjoy doing it, but then she'd never been much a one for turning tail, and anyway her temper was heating.

"I forbid you to kill Richmond. Forbid you, do you hear?" Her tone was fierce. "Just as I mean to forbid him to kill you."

He gave a derisive laugh. "Forbid away. It will make no difference."

Then he was upon her, towering over her most disconcertingly. Knowing him, Beth read his clear intention in his expression of putting her on the back of the horse by brute force if necessary.

"I certainly can't prevent you from behaving like the veriest bully, but I guarantee you'll not keep me behind you for long. I'll jump off the first chance I get." Holding his gaze, she scorned to retreat so much as a step.

"I give you thanks for the warning. I see I must set you up in front of me instead." Lip curling mockingly at her, he scooped her up with such ridiculous ease that, angry as she was, Beth was forced to acknowledge that physically she was all but helpless against his strength. Fuming silently, glowering at him, she scorned to struggle as he carried her like a babe in arms the necessary few feet and plopped her down sideways in the saddle, clearly meaning to mount behind her.

"Hah!" Taking no more than a split second to swing her leg over so that she was astride, she snatched the reins from the branch and drove her heels into the horse's sides, then clung for dear life as the startled beast leaped forward and bounded away into the undergrowth as if a pack of wolves were nipping at its heels.

"Beth!" he roared after her, and commenced to swearing. She delighted in every profane word.

Chuckling, in full control of the horse now, Beth took her time circling back toward him, being careful to keep well out of his reach. Bathed in the rosy glow of the brightening dawn that pinkened his white shirt and cast a long shadow at his booted feet, his eyes snapping with anger, his lean cheeks flushed with it, he left off swearing as she came near in favor of fixing her with a hard stare that must, she thought, have curdled the valor of many an opponent.

Pulling the horse to a halt in the lee of a just-greening larch, she smiled at him seraphically, triumph plain in her eyes.

"Piqued, repiqued, and capoted," she said.

"So it seems." He was still angry, she knew he was, but he had it well in hand now and, had she not known him so well, it wouldn't have shown. His tone was deceptively mild.

"Why must you kill Richmond, or he you?" she demanded, keeping a wary eye on the distance between them. "Unless you wish to be left to walk, you'll tell me. The truth, mind!"

"'Tis fortunate, then, that walking suits me well enough."

To her surprise, with that he turned his back on her and walked away, striding off into the trees along the narrow path that wound down the hill. Most unexpectedly thwarted, Beth stayed where she was, frowning after him. He kept going until his tall form was almost lost amidst the forest's early-morning gloom.

The devil fly away with him!

Only for a moment did she consider just turning about and riding away. Abandoning him when search parties scoured the countryside hunting for him had never been what she intended. Despite everything, she had no wish to see him recaptured. A little anxious, entirely wrathful, fearing a trick, she nudged the horse forward and followed, keeping him in sight, staying carefully back. Once in the woods, it quickly grew almost as dark as though dawn had not yet broken. A wash of deep charcoal gray lay over everything. Mist rose like fingers of smoke from the ground. The air smelled of damp. The twittering of just-waking birds was punctuated only by the jingle of the bridle, and the rhythmic plodding of her mount's hooves.

A branch, wet with dew, brushed her cheek. Ducking, she pushed it away. When she once again looked at the path, she realized that he had increased the distance between them. Or, at least, she thought he had. That was he up ahead. Wasn't it? No, it was a thick branch half fallen across the path. Surely she hadn't lost . . .

A flurry of movement from behind caused her eyes to widen with fright. A grunt, a rush of air, the landing of a weight heavy enough to jar her and make the horse throw up its head and lunge forward in surprise, followed before she quite knew what was happening. She barely had time to gasp and tighten her grip on the reins to steady the plunging horse before a strong arm clamped around her waist and a hard body slid into the saddle behind her and another hand—his hand—caught the reins in a steely grip that took instant control. Stunned, she realized he had leaped onto the horse from behind, and both cursed and marveled at herself for not having foreseen it.

Stiff with indignation, Beth didn't even bother to struggle as he settled more comfortably into the saddle and took the reins from her unresisting hands. With his thighs pressing against hers and his wide chest supporting her back, she might as well have been sitting on his lap.

"What now, Madame Roux?" he said in

her ear, with just the smallest hint of gloating in his tone.

Knowing herself bested for the moment, Beth scorned to put up what she knew would be an entirely useless fight.

"If you think you are just going to drop me off where it suits you and go off and kill my brother-in-law without any hindrance from me, you are sadly mistaken, and so I take leave to tell you," she flung at him over her shoulder. "I will raise the mightiest outcry you have ever heard. I will scream for help until the windows shatter as far away as London! I would sooner see you recaptured than permit that."

"Ah, but that's because you don't perfectly understand the case." He continued to guide the now understandably skittish horse down the trail with an expert hand. "If I'm recaptured, I'll be executed as close to immediately as they can manage. Without trial. On, I might add, Richmond's orders. Or at least, with his concurrence."

"But *why*?" He was telling the truth. She heard it in his voice, and her stomach tightened in fear. Her fingers clenched on the pommel. "Neil, please, I'm begging you. Whatever the truth is, I deserve to know it."

"Believe me, you are much better off not."

She skewed around to look at him. His eyes were inscrutable, his mouth hard. Lines she had never seen before etched his skin, and she realized that, for all he gave no outward sign of it, he must be as weary as she.

"I have developed a—fondness for you, you know," she said, a trifle gruff. "Nothing you tell me, no matter how terrible it is, will change that."

His arm tightened fractionally around her waist. A quick glint in his eyes was as quickly gone.

"I thought it wouldn't be much longer before I was treated to a display of feminine wiles. The last trick in a woman's arsenal, are they not?" His tone was light, purposefully, she believed. "Egad, you'll be fluttering your eyelashes at me next."

Giving him a pert grimace by way of a reply, she faced forward again. "I mean what I say. Whatever dread secret you're harboring, I will not think the worse of you for it, I give you my word."

He laughed, the sound utterly mirthless. "Are you so sure I care for your good opinion? That's mighty conceited of you, my girl."

"Yes, I think you do."

She felt him tense. The arm around her waist went suddenly hard as iron.

"Very well, then, if you will have it. I'm an assassin." He practically bit off the words. "A hired killer who has dispatched so many souls over the course of my career that I've lost count. A government-sanctioned murderer who, in one of life's smaller ironies, now finds my own kind unleashed on me."

The truth was terrible, but, Beth realized, not altogether surprising. It explained much.

"So where does Richmond fit into this? He is not an assassin, too." That last wasn't even a question. Impossible to imagine Hugh in such a role.

"What, no hysterics? Not even a delicate, maidenly shrinking at finding yourself trapped in the arms of a killer?" His tone was bitterly satirical. His arm remained hard about her waist.

"I can't see that either would be the least use, and hysterics might further frighten the poor horse."

Almost, she thought, he laughed. Certainly he made a quick, choked sound, and some small degree of tension in the arm around her eased.

"Thus speaks my unshakable Beth! You've been a rare delight to me, you know." They reached the meadow at the bottom of the hill, and he set the horse at a canter through the mist that now glimmered in the rising sun. "Making your acquaintance has been like encountering a ray of sunshine in the darkness."

She gripped the pommel tighter. "You say that almost as if it's a farewell. You should know I don't mean you to be rid of me that easily."

"But you will be rid of me nonetheless, as soon as I can contrive to set you down somewhere safe, because I would not kill Richmond in front of you. And kill him I must, for all I own I would rather not. Afterward, I imagine the fondness you profess to feel for me will be at an end."

Her heart clutched. "There must be some other way."

"There isn't. A death sentence like the one hanging over me is all but impossible to elude. The only chance I stand lies in vanishing from the face of the earth. And the only way I can do that for as many years as it will take is by resuming my true identity. I kill Richmond, then am never seen again, while the Marquis of Durham lives quite comfortably into what is hopefully a ripe old age."

Beth took a deep breath. "Are you saying you . . . are the Marquis of Durham?"

"Do I detect skepticism in your voice, Madame Roux? I am indeed. And unfortunately for him, Richmond is the only one who knows it."

There came the briefest of pauses. Beth thought that over, then came to a most eye-opening realization.

"No," she said softly, "he isn't. Because now I do, too. And even if you hadn't told me, our paths would have crossed sooner or later, if you are who you say and you mean to take up that identity again. I would ever have recognized you."

There was a long silence broken only by the creaking of the saddle and the horse's muffled hoofbeats.

"I must be more tired than I had supposed. You're quite right, of course."

"So do you now feel compelled to kill me, too?"

"It seems the obvious solution, doesn't

it? Yet I believe I must make an exception for you."

"You cannot expect me to keep silent if you kill my brother-in-law."

"I wonder if I meant to spike my own hand?" There was a musing quality to his voice. "I won't kill you, and I can't expect you to keep quiet. What does that leave to me, then? Clearly I must now flee the country at the very least, and do my poor best to deal with whoever catches up."

Unspoken between them hung the near certainty that sooner or later, someone who caught up might very well deal with him instead.

"I have a better solution," Beth said. "One that I believe will save us all. I will marry you."

Chapter Twenty-five

A SMALL VILLAGE in the south of Dumfries-shire, Gretna Green was less than four miles from the River Sark, which served as the dividing line between England and Scotland. It was a notorious place, the scene of many a scandalous marriage, because the law provided that a couple need only show up in town and pledge themselves to each other in the presence of another person, and the deed was done. To wed over the anvil, as it was called, was such a disgraceful act that the shame of committing it made Beth shudder inwardly. Adding to her dismal spirits was the knowledge that she was submitting to a yoke from which she would find it most difficult, if not impossible, to ever free herself. From the time the vows were said, her life would no longer be her own. When a man and woman wed, they became one person according to the law, and the man was that person. To all intents and purposes, she, Lady Elizabeth Banning, would cease to exist. The lure of becoming a marchioness—if indeed Neil was telling the truth about the title, which she rather thought he was but could not be sure about—did not tempt her in the least. Yet she stood in the marriage room of the village blacksmith's house—a half-timbered cottage with chimneys at each end, the smithy's workplace behind, and a single window that looked out onto the cobbled street in front—and with outward calm said the words that would make her Neil's wife.

Her blood drummed so hard in her ears that she scarcely took in a thing after that, or heard what he replied, or what the smith—*the smith!*—said to them. All she knew was that the whole exercise—from the time they walked in the door, said the words, and signed their names to the registry and the marriage lines, to the time they walked out again—took less than five minutes.

Then she found herself outside again, standing on the smithy's stoop in the cold starry quiet of a Scottish night, dressed in the same plain blue gown that had been lent to her by Creed's nephew's wife at the White Swan, and worn now for more than twenty-four hours straight. Her hair had been groomed by a borrowed brush, and, although she had done her best to put it up properly before the ceremony, tendrils had already escaped to curl around her face and straggle down her back. She had washed her face and hands, but longed badly for a bath, and her own—or at least fresh—clothes. In the last twenty-four hours, she had napped for perhaps a total of two hours, wrapped in Neil's arms in a leafy copse after they had stopped to share a purloined lunch basket that a farmer busy plowing his field had left unattended. Exhausted, hungry, wearing a sadly crumpled dress, Beth shuddered inwardly at what she had done. Shorn of the trappings that she had never before realized meant so much—wedding gown, flowers, church,

society's approbation, her sisters' support—
she was nonetheless a bride. She was also
freezing cold, sick to her stomach, and, save
for her new husband—*husband!*—now
standing silently on the stoop at her side,
utterly alone.

She had never felt so low in all her life.

This is my wedding day.

"Well, 'tis done," Neil said, and walked
on down the steps. Dry-mouthed, Beth
watched him descend. Wearing a buff coat
and a cravat he had purchased from the
smithy, who was fortunately a large man
himself, along with the previously borrowed
shirt and his own pantaloons, he, too, presented less than a creditable appearance.
But as handsome as he was, an unshaven
jaw, disheveled, poorly fitting clothes, and
mud-spattered boots lent him a raffish air
that a fair number of people might have
found added to his attraction. Certainly,
over the course of the day's journey, Beth
had caught more than one female, including the smith's plump wife, looking him
over with appreciation.

"Yes," Beth replied, following him, for
there was nothing else to do. More build-
ings of various descriptions lined the broad

street, which was the main one for the village. Except for the inn, which possessed a lively taproom and where they were to pass what was left of the night, the world seemed asleep. They dared not tarry much past daylight, because the threat of their pursuers catching up was ever present, if remote, for who would expect to find them in Gretna Green? Already it was late, and moonlight cast a pale glow over all. He waited for her in the street, watching her come to him with an absolutely expressionless face. Without touching, without another word exchanged between them, they turned and walked side by side toward the inn. Walked, because he'd had to sell the horse to pay the half-guinea cost of the smithy's services, and provide sufficient funds for their night's lodging, and meals, and various other sundries, and to hire a carriage to convey them back on the morrow to London, where at Beth's insistence they were to go immediately to Richmond House and thus seek protection in the very belly of the beast who sought Neil.

But first they had to get through this night.

This is my wedding night.

Her stomach dropped clear to her toes at the thought. If she had been prone to fits of the vapors, she would have had one right then. But she was not so prone, she was distressingly unhysteric by nature, and so she just kept walking, feeling all the while as if she were trapped in the unreal landscape of a bad dream.

I'm married.

Her heart knocked in her chest.

"I bespoke dinner, upon our return," Neil said as they passed through the inn's arched doorway into the warmth and light inside. He bestowed a curt nod on the inn-keeper, who had come out to greet them and showed them into a private parlor. The innkeeper was a round little man, with a florid face, white hair, and a look in his eyes as they slid over Beth that was far from what she was accustomed to. Drawing herself up in response to it, Beth returned his gaze with some surprise, then realized that of course that less-than-respectful look was because she had just contracted a clandestine marriage at Gretna Green, putting her quite beyond the pale, and she felt even more wretched.

The private parlor was small, made dark by wood-paneled walls and tight shuttered windows despite the fire in the fireplace and the bunches of candles guttering in their sconces, and smelled of smoke. Noise from the taproom next door made conversation all but impossible, which Beth didn't mind because, thanks in some part to the listening ears of the innkeeper's stout wife, who waited upon them and cast numerous surreptitious but avid looks over the newlyweds whenever she thought herself unobserved, she seemed to have lost her tongue. Uttering the few commonplaces that occurred to her, jumpy as a cat on hot bricks, she responded to Neil's unexceptional conversational gambits almost at random while picking at her capon and broccoli without ever tasting the few morsels she put in her mouth. In the end, she sat sipping tea while he made a hearty meal.

It was all she could do to keep her hand from shaking. Despite her efforts, though, the china cup rattled more than once in its saucer as she set it down.

"I—believe I will go upstairs now," she said when the port was brought in and the dishes cleared. At the thought of what going upstairs implied, her heart fluttered and her stomach knotted so tightly that even the little she had eaten was in danger of resurfacing. She badly needed a few moments alone, a few moments to settle her racing mind and calm her shredded nerves, a few moments in which to come to terms with this drastic change in her estate.

A few moments to come to terms with the notion of being married.

"I'll join you in, say, half an hour," was his reply. It was rendered no less dismaying because it was spoken in a perfectly calm voice. He sat there in front of the smoking fire, looking quite at his ease, pouring himself out a glass of port, his long legs disposed carelessly beneath the table, his broad shoulders blocking most of the fireplace from her view. There was nothing of the lover about him. Indeed, there had not been since, after a great deal of spirited argument, he had been brought to see that—because Beth knew with certainty that Richmond would do all in his power to protect one who had become, irrevocably, a member of his own family no matter how much he might dislike the necessity—wedding her was the only rational answer to their dilemma. But still her knees were practically knocking together as with a murmur of assent she escaped his presence and all but fled up the stairs toward their—*their!*—chamber.

A maid emerged just as she reached it.

"I've made all ready, mum, just as the gentleman ordered," she said, bobbing her head.

"Th-thank you," Beth stuttered, unable to contemplate with anything approaching equanimity the idea that this sturdy Scotswoman knew that she would be sharing a bed with her new, most scandalously married husband. Managing to preserve her countenance for long enough to pass into the room, Beth closed the door behind her. Then, leaning back against it, she surveyed the scene before her with nausea-inducing anxiety.

Lit solely by a fire burning low in the grate, the room itself was well enough, with a carpet in muted colors covering the floor, a single shuttered window that looked out, she thought, on the stable yard, a washstand, a dressing table, a wardrobe, a pair of mismatched chairs, and a large bed practically smothered in quilts and hung with heavy, tawny gold velvet curtains. Beth could barely look at the bed, and the other comforts awaiting her, though welcome, were no more calming.

Steaming gently in the firelight, a bath stood before the hearth. Beside it, a night rail had been laid out across one of the chairs. There was also a portmanteau and what looked like a dress and the appropriate undergarments, along with a brush and other necessities. Those would be for the morrow, of course, and had doubtless been scrounged up by the landlady at Neil's request, in return for some small sum.

The bath and night rail were for tonight.

The hollow feeling taking up residence in the pit of her stomach was, she decided, at least preferable to the sickening churning that had previously occupied it.

This was your idea, she reminded herself. *You talked him into wedding you, and must now stick to the bargain.*

But marrying had seemed so much easier in the abstract.

For a moment, no longer, Beth remained where she was, back pressed against the door, wishing with all her heart she was safe back in her own spacious chamber in Claire's house in Cavendish Square. Then she realized that a goodly number of the minutes that Neil had promised to allot her had already ticked past, and this galvanized her into moving.

The first thing she did was turn the key in the lock so that she could be certain he would not take her unaware.

The second was to scramble out of her clothes, which presented her with some difficulty as the hooks in the middle of her back proved difficult to reach, and the strings to her stays had knotted.

The third was to climb into the bath.

The hot water felt heavenly. Closing her eyes, she sank down into it, letting it soothe muscles that ached from the hours she'd spent riding pillion, enjoying its silken comfort against her skin for a long, luxurious moment before the specter of Neil's imminent arrival once again reared its demoralizing head. Sitting up, making liberal use of the soap, she scrubbed herself until her skin glowed, rinsed, and climbed out again, all much faster than she would have done if she had not feared hearing his knock on the door at any second. Shivering a little, she dried herself and pulled the night rail over her head. Long-sleeved and high-necked, it was of white cambric, a deal too large for her, and, except for a few rows of pin-tucking around the neckline, completely plain, but it was clean and fresh-smelling and covered her, and that was what mattered most. Ears straining now as she listened with growing trepidation for Neil's footsteps approaching the door, for surely he would arrive at any second, she unpinned her hair and brushed it out. Although she usually slept with it in a long braid, that didn't seem appropriate. Perhaps he would prefer it loose?

I've given him the right to have a voice in how I wear my hair.

The thought so appalled her that she twisted it up with more haste than care, scraping the hair back from her face anyhow, thrusting pins into the unwieldy bun at her nape with such speed that more than one stabbed into her scalp. Having finally tamed every last wayward tendril, she then discovered as she finished that after all she would have been better served by leaving it loose: with the firelight shining

through it, the night rail was all but indecent, and, loosed, her hair would have at
least covered the most private parts of her
anatomy. Horrified by the discovery, she
was still staring at herself in the mirror over
the dressing table in some shock when the
knock she had been dreading came.

It was a soft, most discreet rapping,
which for the effect it had on her could have
been a furious pounding of fists.

She jumped, stared at the portal, took a
step toward it, paused as the impossibility
of opening the door clad as she was im-
pressed itself upon her, then quickly
snatched the topmost quilt from the bed.
Wrapping it around herself, setting her
teeth, she went to open the door.

Neil stood on the other side of it. Their
eyes met as she pulled the panel wide, and
at the same time as she was once again
registering just how very tall and broad-
shouldered he was, his gaze slid down her
quilt-wrapped body. When their eyes met
again, she could read nothing at all in his.
Clutching the quilt tighter, feeling hideously
self-conscious and so nervous she could
scarcely breathe, she stood back to let him
enter.

He did so, then took the door from her cold fingers, closed it, and turned the key in the lock. The click would have made her jump had she not managed to control the impulse just in time.

Then, finally, they were utterly alone. He was her husband. She was his wife.

Icy curls of panic chased each other through her system as he turned to look at her.

Barefoot as she was, her head just topped his shoulders. With the best will in the world, she found she couldn't quite meet his gaze, and instead ended up looking steadfastly at his chin.

"You shaved." The surprise of it saved her, unglued her tongue from the roof of her mouth, where she had feared it was permanently stuck, gave her something to focus on besides the fact that they were *married*. It was, she realized, the first time she had seen him completely clean-shaven. Without the scruff that had darkened his jaw for most of their acquaintance, he was even more wickedly handsome than she had known.

"Totally in your honor." He gave her the faintest of smiles. "Having purchased a razor and other essentials from the landlord"—he held up a small traveling case that she had not previously seen, and which she assumed contained the newly acquired items—"I thought I might as well make use of them. I called for a can of hot water and some soap, and the deed was done. Although the water I was provided with was cold. I trust your bath was not?"

"Yes. No. I mean, it was wonderfully warm. Ththank you for thinking of it."

"Considering your comfort must always be an object with me, of course."

He crossed to the fire, set the traveling case down beside the portmanteau, then glanced around the room. She, meanwhile, stayed where she was, watching him. Rather like, she realized to her own annoyance, a frozen-in-place rabbit might watch a dog it feared had found its scent.

You are not such a coward as this.

She put up her chin.

"The situation is a trifle awkward," she said. "But we need not let it be. We are married, and must just make the best of it."

"The ceremony isn't binding until it's been consummated," he reminded her, coming back toward where she still stood by the door. It took a great deal of determination, but Beth neither moved nor flinched as he stopped in front of her to regard her with a gathering frown. "You realize that, don't you? There's still time to change your mind. You have only to say the word, and I'll take myself off."

"I don't wish to change my mind." She wanted to wet her lips because her mouth was excruciatingly dry, but refrained because she felt the gesture would reveal too much about the state of her nerves. "Do you?"

"No."

"Well, then." Swallowing, she met his gaze head-on. Despite her brave words, she was conscious of teetering on the brink of developing the coldest of cold feet. "Oh, the devil! Could we please just get on with this? Bed me and have done."

His eyes widened fractionally, and then he laughed. "Such a romantic as you are!"

"Don't laugh. I'm not funning. I need this to be over with. Quickly, if you please."

Girding herself as if for battle, she let go of the quilt. It slithered to the floor. Stepping out of the puddled folds, she took the few steps needed to put her right up against him and determinedly put her arms around his neck.

"Hold a minute." His hands spanned her waist, holding her back when, with great resolution, she would have risen on her toes to kiss him. His eyes glinted in the uncertain firelight as he looked down at her. "You're white as paper, and as cold to the touch as a corpse. It's not me you're afraid of, I'll swear, and if my memory serves, you recently assured me you did not fear having sex with me. So what's all this dread in aid of?"

Beth made a face as the truth burst upon her. "Marriage, I suppose. The idea of willingly making myself some man's chattel, subject to his orders, my happiness dependent on his benevolence, or lack of it . . ." It was all she could do to repress a shudder. "I confess I find the prospect daunting."

Though she had told him only the broadest outline of her childhood, comprehension dawned in his eyes.

"I doubt the man exists who could rule you against your will, Madame Roux. You may believe me when I tell you that I would never make the attempt."

Despite the anxiety that now had her insides tied up in knots, that made her smile. "What a bouncer! When you have done nothing but try to impose your will on me for days!"

He smiled, too. "With, I must point out, a notable lack of success. I've since learned my lesson, I promise."

She took a deep breath and realized she was starting to feel a little less unnerved. His hands were still on her waist, but they were no longer keeping her at bay; instead, his grip had eased enough to allow her to rest comfortably against him. The length of their acquaintance was brief, and the facts she knew about him were so terrible as to appall anyone. This was certainly nothing like any marriage she had ever envisioned for herself. But the situation was desperate. Marriage was the only way out she could see. And she had, just as she had told him, developed a decided fondness for him. A kind of camaraderie had sprung up between them from the first that made her, in the usual way of things, amazingly comfortable in his company. However improbable their relationship, she considered him, in a word, as a friend. A dizzyingly handsome friend whose lovemaking she found exciting rather than repugnant. Certainly—and this was the clincher—she could not bear to think of him being killed.

On the other hand, marriage to him was something she felt she could survive.

"Sooner or later, I must have wed somebody," she said, as much to reassure herself as him. "And I would sooner be married to you than William or—any of the others."

"Careful. You'll unman me with your compliments." His voice was dry. His eyes slid over her face. Then, with no more warning than that, his hands tightened on her waist and he kissed her.

Chapter Twenty-six

HIS KISS WAS SEARING, and possessive, and not at all gentle. Beth was briefly surprised at the fierceness of it, but then she surrendered to the hot, wet invasion, closing her eyes, tightening her arms around his neck, kissing him back without reserve. The rush of heat he always managed to ignite in her made her body quicken, and she welcomed the familiar sensation with true thankfulness. Now if she could just close off her brain . . .

Marriage is forever.

Even as she had the near-paralyzing thought, he swept her up off her feet, carrying her as if she weighed nothing at all, to lay her down on the bed. When she felt the give of the mattress against her back, another craven pang assailed her.

If you go through with this, there's no turning back.

But there was already no turning back, and she knew it. Even as he lifted his mouth from hers and she resurfaced enough to begin to think about what she was doing again, he was pulling off his boots and shrugging out of his coat. Her hair had fallen down, she discovered. It tumbled over her shoulders and across the quilt in a wavy cloud, and as she quickly raked her fingers through it to remove the remaining pins, then swept it to one side, she saw that his shirt was following his coat. She gazed wide-eyed at the muscles flexing in his back as he pulled his shirt over his head, then took in the smooth, bronzed expanse of his shoulders that was marred only by the puckered circle of the wound she had cauterized for him, as he dropped the shirt on the floor and turned back to her. His wide chest was utterly masculine in its beauty. Remembering how warm and sleek his skin was, how firm the muscles beneath it felt, how the hair on his chest tried to curl around her fingers, made her catch her breath. Excitement flickered at the idea that she could now touch him as she would. Almost immediately, it was followed by an ardor-freezing corollary: *After this, he'll have the right to touch you whenever he likes. To bed you whenever he likes.*

Before her wayward thoughts could coalesce into an attack of full-blown fright, he was stretching his length beside her on the bed. Bare to the waist, his wide shoulders and muscular arms outlined in orange by the fire that glowed behind him and picked up red highlights in his black hair, he looked formidable. There was a dark intensity to his face that she'd never seen there before. His jaw was set. The curve of his mouth was harsh.

The way he looked at her sent a shiver down her spine. The expression in his eyes was almost grim.

Propping his head on his hand, he caught her hair where it spilled over her shoulder, winding it around his fist in a gesture that shrieked to her of ownership.

"I don't know if I've ever mentioned it,

but I'm extremely partial to red hair," he said softly, and lifted his hair-wrapped fist to his mouth, pressing the silken strands to his lips.

Butterflies fluttered in her stomach even as her heart started to pound.

"Neil . . ." Some of the apprehension she was feeling forced its way to the surface despite her best efforts, and almost she gave in to it and snatched her hair from his grip and shot off the bed. But instead she bit back what she had been going to say and steeled herself. Her hands, which lay flat against the mattress on either side of her, curled into the quilts for support. "Love me."

Her voice was low, but it did not shake.

"I mean to."

Then his mouth was on hers again, and she was glad, fiercely glad, because the heat and hunger of his kiss clouded her thoughts, sent them whirling away, made her dizzy and weak and unable, finally, to do anything but kiss him back, her hands sliding over the broad expanse of his shoulders to fasten around his neck, her body arching up against his hard bare chest like a flower seeking the sun. His hands found her breasts through the thin cambric, causing her nipples to tighten, and the quickening his kisses had awakened to intensify into a full-blown ache, but lingered only briefly before sliding down her body, purposefully tracing the curve of waist and hip and thigh, trailing fire in their wake. Almost she panicked again as she realized that he was gathering her night rail up in his hands as he went. But she let him, she didn't protest, even when a moment later he broke off the kiss to pull the night rail over her head so that she was left without a stitch to cover her.

"You're beautiful." His eyes slid over her even as the cool night air whispered across her nakedness.

Following his gaze, she saw herself as he did, skin smooth as satin and painted pale gold by the firelight, the lush roundness of her breasts topped by strawberry nipples that strained most embarrassingly erect, slim hips flaring from a narrow waist, flat stomach leading down to the fiery triangle of curls at the apex of lissome legs. Even as her blood heated and her cheeks flushed at the knowledge that he was seeing her thus, he dipped his head to kiss her breasts, bestowing a single scalding wet kiss on each vulnerable nipple. His hand, big and dark and masculine against her creamy skin, rested on her belly briefly and then slid down, warm and faintly rough as it stroked over the nest of curls, covering them, before moving between her thighs with a surety that made her shudder.

"Oh!" It was a gasp, having been surprised out of her by the jolt of pure sensation that shot through her as he unerringly found the most delicate, sensitive part of her. Quivering at the thrill of his touch, shocked at the sight of his hand moving between her legs, mindful that they were in a public inn where anyone might hear, she set her teeth against giving voice to more utterances, closed her eyes tight, dug her nails into the quilt, and let him do what he would. She could feel him watching her as he played with her breasts and touched and rubbed and explored between her legs, but despite the mortification inherent in that, she was helpless to do anything but respond as that first delicious shaft of pleasure tightened and twisted into a spiral of urgent desire.

"I've wanted to do this to you since I first

set eyes on you," he said, his voice thick as she writhed most shamefully beneath his ministrations. Then he kissed her again, his mouth hard and hungry, and at the same time slid his fingers inside her, pushing deep, withdrawing, pushing in again, until she responded with feverish abandon, until he had her boneless and mindless and melting for him. On fire for him, gritting her teeth against the moans that tried to escape, she welcomed his weight as he eased on top of her. The feel of the hard wall of muscle that was his chest coming down on her swelling breasts made her tremble with anticipation. When his warm bare thighs parted hers—When had he removed his pantaloons? She didn't know—she was ready. When she realized that what was pushing inside her was no longer his fingers, she was, if not eager, at least burning to discover what came next and thus totally acquiescent.

"Hold tight," he muttered as, gripping his damp shoulders, she instinctively arched against him in response to the invasion of her person by that part of him that she had not expected to be quite so huge, or hard, or hot. She was just trying to make sense of what he was telling her when he most unexpectedly gave a quick thrust that hurt like the devil and felt like it must rip her in two, then with a groan kept on pushing until he was deep inside her.

"Oh!" It was a cry of pain this time, uttered as her eyes flew open, and she stiffened as if she'd suddenly been turned to wood.

"That's it," he said. His voice was rough, his breathing ragged. His eyes had opened, too, and met hers. They were black and opaque as coal in the firelight. "It won't hurt again, I promise. Close your eyes now, and kiss me."

A dark flush stained his cheekbones. She could feel a fine tremor shake the strong arms that held her.

There's no going back now, she thought, feeling a little sick.

With the die cast, she could see no help for it, so she gritted her teeth and did as he bade her, hoping that the nameless yearning only he seemed to be able to awaken in her would soon return, so that she could lose herself in it again. Kissing her mouth, her jawline, her neck, her breasts, with a torrid sensuality that she discovered to her dismay she seemed to have quite lost her taste for, he came into her again, filling her once more, then kept doing it, in and out, more and more until she thought it must go on forever. He heaved and panted over her in the grip of a raw passion that she recognized he was doing his best to keep under some sort of control, taking her with a savage rhythm that now she only wanted to end.

"Ah, *Christ.*" With that, and a last deep plunge, he shuddered and went still, his big body hot and damp and heavy as a dead horse as it lay atop hers.

This is what I'll be subject to for the rest of my life.

That was the appalling thought that ricocheted through her brain as Beth slowly let out her breath and eased out of the embarrassing position he'd coaxed her into. She then lay still and flaccid as a doll in his embrace, although his weight was crushing her into the mattress, and what she wanted more than anything in the world was to get out from under him and off that bed.

Without warning his head came up from where it had been buried against her neck.

Before she could regain enough of her wits to close her eyes—meeting his gaze in the aftermath of what they had just done was the last thing she wanted to do—it was too late.

He frowned, squinting at her in the firelight, and she realized that he was trying to read her expression. Regret was useless. They were now married past redemption. Certainly presenting him with a woebegone face or reproaches would serve no useful purpose. With that in mind, she resolutely managed to give him a small smile.

"Oh God!" With that pained utterance he dropped his head against her neck again, seemed to gather himself, then rolled off her, coming lithely to his feet beside the bed and turning to scoop her into his arms before she had the least idea of what he meant to do.

"Wh—what . . . ?" she began, stuttering under the onslaught of senses that were being all but overwhelmed by the fact that he, utterly naked, was carrying her, utterly naked, in his arms. But before she could finish demanding an explanation, or do anything else except try to cover herself, he stepped into the tub with her, then sank down into the still-warm water with her on his lap.

Squeaking in surprise, Beth snatched her hair out of the way so that it would not get soaked, then splashed hastily around so that she was facing him as he lounged back against the rolled rim of the tub. Twisting her hair up into a precarious knot, she eyed him warily. The water covered him to midchest only, and droplets glistened on his wide shoulders and brawny arms like diamonds, and were sprinkled throughout the wedge of curls that covered the muscular breadth of his chest. With his hair having escaped from its ribbon sometime during the course of their late, unlamented exertions, he looked the veriest brigand—and so handsome he took her breath. Huddled at the narrow end of the tub, her knees almost touching her chin, she had to scrunch down to keep her breasts beneath the surface. Given the way the fire reflected off the water, she hoped her position was enough to preserve some modicum of her modesty. Certainly he didn't seem to be troubled by such concerns. Having discovered the soap, he was lathering himself with every evidence of enthusiasm, which she watched with an emotion very much akin to disbelief. It was all but impossible to grasp that she was engaged in something as indecent as sitting naked in a bath with him, and even more impossible to believe that she was married to him.

But she was. They were. And he, at least, seemed to be enjoying himself.

Her brows snapped together.

"That's better," he said.

"What's better?" she asked suspiciously.

"You're no longer looking at me like I imagine an early Christian martyr might a lion."

She bristled. "If you're implying that I'm afraid of you . . ."

"Not afraid. Just being very, very brave."

"Is there something wrong with that?"

"Other than the fact that it makes me feel like the biggest rogue unhung? Not a thing."

She was quiet a moment.

"I don't blame you for"—she hesitated, unsure of how to put it—"any of this. Getting married was my idea to begin with, after all. And as I told you times out of mind, there was no other way."

"So you still have no objection to making a human sacrifice of yourself?"

"I'm wed, not dead." Her tone was tart.

His eyes softened.

"I'm sorry I had to hurt you," he said. "The first time is always difficult for women, I believe."

"It was necessary. I'm perfectly aware of that."

"It gets better. You may take my word for it."

Her lip curled at him. "I'm sure you would know."

He laughed, but forbore to reply. Which was as well, because something extremely daunting had just occurred to her: was it possible—would he expect to have sex with her again, after they rose from the bath? She knew, from things her sisters and other married women of her acquaintance had said, that gentlemen could sometimes go on all night.

Oh, I can't.

Almost she shuddered, but caught herself in time, not wanting him to see, not wanting to reveal how nerve-racking she found her situation. But still, something must have showed in her face.

"Regrets?" Cocking an eyebrow at her, he passed her the soap.

"About marrying you, do you mean?" Her feelings could only be described as severely conflicted, but she gamely shook her head and took refuge in washing her face and hands. She could not, she discovered when that was done, possibly actually bathe with his eyes on her. The best she could manage was to discreetly rinse off a little. Fortunately, she had already had a very thorough bath not much more than a quarter of an hour earlier. Certainly no more than that, because the water had barely cooled at all.

Funny how the world could change in such a short period of time.

To her own surprise, she yawned, then sat regarding him a little owlishly, having raised a hand to her mouth just a fraction of a second too late.

He smiled. Then without warning he stood up and stepped out of the tub, completely flustering her. Her first good look at a naked man was brief, but it was enough to make her avert her eyes and send hot color flooding her face. Fortunately, or unfortunately, depending on how one chose to look at it, she was almost instantly distracted by the exigencies of her own situation: with his exit the water sank a full foot, leaving most of her person mercilessly exposed.

"Ah!" she gasped, and hugged her legs closer as she cast a wild look around in hopes of discovering some means of covering herself within reach.

"Come on. Out you get."

Even as, with some apprehension, she looked at him again, he stopped beside the bath holding the quilt she had discarded earlier open wide to receive her. Around his waist was hitched their only towel. It covered only the most vital part of his muscular frame.

Suppressing the impulse to insist he close his eyes—she'd had time now to recollect that he had already seen, and more than seen, as much of her person as there was to see, and had no wish to appear ridiculously missish—Beth stood up with as much dignity as she could muster, stepped over the side of the bath, and was immediately wrapped in the quilt and his arms. Not quite fast enough, however, to prevent him from having an excellent view of her dripping body. That he had taken full advantage of the opportunity to look was obvious from the gleam in his eyes as she glanced back at him. Holding the quilt close, she stepped away—he made no attempt to keep her—then turned to regard him a trifle nervously.

The expression on his face set her heart to knocking. The only word she could use to describe it was: hungry.

"Neil." She wet her lips as she sought a tactful way to say that which wanted to burst from her lips. "I would rather not— that is, I wish to go to sleep now." Then, anxious to make sure he understood, she tacked on hastily, "Just sleep, and nothing more."

His expression changed on the instant, but before she had a chance to try to work out what that change meant, he spoke.

"And so you shall, Madame Roux." He turned away, only to return a moment later with her night rail, which he handed to her. "I'm not going to pounce on you, you know, or do anything you don't like. You wed me to save my life, and Richmond's, and I am quite aware that I stand in your debt, and also that you now find yourself in an awkward position as a result. But you needn't be afraid that I'm going to require you to act the wife in bed, or anywhere else. Once this matter with Richmond is settled, you may arrange your life to suit yourself, with my goodwill."

"Neil . . ." She regarded him with a little trouble in her eyes.

"Go on to bed, Beth. We'll sort the rest out on the morrow."

He walked past her to the fire then and crouched in front of it, threw another log on the glowing embers, and prodded it with the poker. All the while, firelight played over the broad planes of his bare back. By the time the fire was settled to his apparent satisfaction, she was dressed in the night rail again and tucked up in bed with her eyes tight shut, because she really was very tired, and because her emotions were muddled and she thought that sorting the rest out tomorrow, after they'd both slept and their heads had cooled, was probably the wisest course. But even after he slid under the covers beside her and almost instantly gave every indication of having fallen deep asleep, she remained awake, despite being so tired she ached with it. Though she stayed carefully on her edge—not side; sprawled on his stomach, he took up too much room for that—of the mattress, she could not but be acutely aware of him. To begin with, his stertorous breathing fell just short of snoring. His weight caused the mattress to sink toward him in such a way that if she moved just a little bit out of her spot, she would roll willy-nilly toward him. The heat of him, the force of his presence, an occasional slight move-ment all made it impossible for her to pre-tend that he wasn't there, even though she lay on her side with her face resolutely turned away from him and willed sleep to come to her.

Dear Lord, what have I done? was the panicky thought that, try though she would, she couldn't get out of her head.

Exhaustion finally claimed her. She knew it did, because she had to have fallen asleep to be subsequently awak-ened. And she was awakened, though by what she knew not: a sound, probably. An especially loud pop from the fire? The wind rattling the window? Opening her eyes, blinking bemusedly into a thick gloom rife with shadows cast by the dying fire, she was stunned to see one of the shadows move.

At first she could hardly credit her own eyes. But it moved again, stirring from its position near the door and seeming to creep toward the bed. Heart pounding, watching it with widening eyes, afraid to move or reveal that she was awake lest she provoke she knew not what, she realized something even as the shape drew nearer and solidified into a crouching man: she could no longer hear Neil's harsh breathing.

Just about the time she registered that, a violent shove sent her flying from the bed to fall tumbling to the floor.

Chapter Twenty-seven

THE ENSUING BATTLE was fast and furious and absolutely, unmistakably lethal in intent on both sides. Beth had no sooner hit the floor than she heard the sounds of it, and realized to her horror that Neil had leaped from the bed the instant that he shoved her from it and was from that moment engaged in a deadly fight with an unknown assailant.

"Beth, get out of the room," Neil roared, but she was already screaming like a banshee and on her feet and diving for the poker, because she was not about to let him face this threat alone. Grabbing it up, fueled by a rush of adrenaline, snatching her night rail out of the way of her flying feet so that the too-long hem would not trip her up, she darted back toward the grappling men, thankful for the firelight that let her tell them apart. They were much of a size, but Neil was naked and the man he fought so closely was not only fully clothed but armed with a wicked-looking knife that gleamed as the light struck it, and so she had no trouble knowing where to aim her blows.

"Goddamn it, Beth!"

Ignoring Neil's groaning curse—he must have seen her flying approach over the attacker's shoulder—she brought the poker down with a satisfying thud on the fellow's back, having aimed for his head but been thwarted when he dodged just in time. She then commenced to whacking him frenziedly when at the first blow he did no more than curse and flinch and try more ferociously than ever to spit Neil on the end of his knife.

The end came as quickly as the beginning. A flurry of movement sent the knife flying. There was a soft crack, and then the assailant crumpled silently to the floor at Neil's feet.

"Dear God!" Panting with exertion, Beth stood over the inert man, the poker poised ready to strike as Neil bent to check his pulse. His head lay at an odd angle in relationship to his body, and she guessed that his neck had been broken.

"Is he . . . dead?" she asked as Neil straightened.

The face Neil turned on her was as tightly furious as anything she had ever seen. He was once again in predator guise, and as she realized that, she felt her heart skip a beat. This was the part of him she scarcely knew, and didn't want to know.

"You may thank your lucky stars that he is." He growled the words at her. "What the bloody hell do you think would have happened to you if he'd killed me instead?"

Before he could say more, there was a loud knock on the door.

"What's to do in there?" It was the innkeeper, calling through the panel.

"Thank God." Beth felt some of the tension leave her body at this timely arrival of reinforcements.

"Stay," Neil hissed when she would have hurried to open the door. "A thousand pardons. My wife had a nightmare," he called back, and shot Beth a speaking glance.

"A nightmare?" Disbelief was plain in the innkeeper's voice. "I never heard of no nightmare sounded like that!"

So they were to lie, were they? Beth didn't understand it, but she was willing to follow Neil's lead.

"Indeed, I'm very sorry," she chimed in, trying to keep the breathlessness out of her voice. "It must have been something in the dinner that disagreed with me. It was a most terrible dream."

"Hmmph. This is a decent establishment, I'll have you know, where decent people expect to be able to get a good night's rest. If I hear any more noise out of the pair of you, I'll cast you out of doors no matter what hour it is."

"There'll be no more noise," Neil promised.

"I'm very sorry," Beth called again.

With another unhappy "hmmph," the innkeeper took himself off. For a moment they both stood unmoving, listening to the faint sounds of the innkeeper's retreating footsteps.

"Well played." Neil's voice was low.

"Is there a *reason* we don't want anyone to know someone broke into this room and tried to kill you?" she asked, her tone a shade too polite despite her hushed voice, her gaze swinging from the door to him.

"It makes for far too many unpleasant questions."

Beth looked down at the man at her feet. He was, indisputably, dead.

"Who is he?" she asked in a hushed voice.

"He's known as the Butcher. His name is Hector Bunn." Neil was searching the dead man as he spoke.

"Why 'the butcher'?" Beth couldn't believe she was speaking so calmly about a corpse that lay newly murdered almost at her feet. Shock, she expected.

"Because he likes to use his knife to carve people up. It's quick and silent, I grant you, but messy, and there's always risk involved when you work in close with a knife. For myself, I prefer a clean pistol shot when I can, and when I can't I'll use my hands."

Beth caught her breath. "Dear Lord, he is what you are, isn't he? An assassin."

"One of the best," Neil agreed. He straightened, and Beth saw that he was holding a pistol and a wad of cash he had taken from the dead man.

"What do we do with him?" she asked, looking down at the corpse again, the practical problem posed by having a dead man in their chamber having just occurred to her.

Neil made a sound that was almost a snarl. As she glanced up in surprise she discovered that he was walking—no, stalking—toward her, having disposed of the pistol and cash by tossing them on the end of the bed. Now that she was no longer in fear of either of their lives, his nakedness caught her notice, but she was still too agitated by the situation to pay much attention beyond registering that his private region was as large and impressive as the rest of him, and that he seemed totally unconcerned with his state of undress. What was more to the point was that he was looking angry again, and was bearing down with evident purpose on her. Tension and an almost tangible field of dark energy seemed to emanate from him like rays from the sun, electrifying the air around him. Her instinctive response was a tiny little frisson of unease (never say fear!), but this was Neil, she reminded herself stoutly, and stood her ground.

"Most females would be having hysterics about now." He didn't sound like he was complimenting her on her fortitude. His eyes were once again as shiny black as pieces of jet as they held hers. "They would be terrified at what they had just witnessed, and shrinking away from me, and they for damned certain wouldn't have started walloping a professional killer who could slice them open with one swipe of his knife with a damned ridiculous poker, which, by the way and for future reference, makes for a piss-poor weapon."

Having delivered himself of that speech, he took the poker, which she had tucked up under one arm, from her and threw it on the bed, where it landed with a bounce. Then he caught her arms just above the elbows in a strong grip that stopped just short of hurting her. When she raised her brows at him with what she meant to be quelling hauteur, he pinioned her with a look that should, by rights, have made her cower.

She put up her chin at him.

"You say that as if you *wished* I was such a puling creature."

His face tightened dangerously. "What I *wish* is that you had enough sense to recognize that you would be better off far away from me. Bunn came after me, but he would have killed you without a qualm. And I—I'm no better than he. This whole situation—you, me, married—is nothing short of utter folly. I'm a killer, damn it, by inclination as well as training, as ruthless as they come, with no conscience at all. You think I'm sorry for all the lives I've taken? I'm not. This is what I am. This is what I do. Underneath this thin layer of civilization I've shown you, I'm a savage, a vicious animal who's no longer fit for any but the lowest of human company. You may rest assured the devil has a special place reserved in hell for those of my breed."

Beth felt her heart lurch as she realized that he truly believed what he was saying.

"Oh, pooh!" she said. "What nonsense."

For the merest instant something flickered in his eyes—disbelief? admiration?—and then he pulled her up onto her toes and took her mouth in a kiss that was as savage as he claimed to be. The sheer force of his mouth on hers caused her lips to part instantly beneath the onslaught; his tongue took fierce possession of her mouth. Lips hard and cruel, he kissed her as if he wished to reinforce his words, to frighten her, to cause her to pull away from him, but instead she kissed him back just as fiercely, her lips clinging to his, her tongue clashing with his in a war that she was afraid, for his life, to lose, because if she did she was as certain as she'd ever been of anything that he would thrust her away from him and vanish into the night, to take his chances on his own.

When he lifted his head at last to glare down at her, she matched him furious look for furious look.

"You may try as you will. You can't scare me," she said, though her heart pounded and her breathing came way too fast.

His eyes flamed down at her. She held his gaze without flinching.

"Oh, can't I just?"

Lips twisting, he released one arm at last—his grip was hurting her now, though she would be boiled in oil before she would give him a sign of it—and then, before she guessed what he would be about, he locked his fingers over the neck of her night rail and yanked downward. The sound of ripping material was as shocking to her ears as the sudden breath of night air on her skin.

"What the *devil* do you think you're doing?" It took her a second to recover from the shock, and then she glanced down at herself, aghast. The night rail, ripped past her navel, was already falling from her shoulders. Her breasts, her waist, the curve of her hips and belly, were all laid bare to his view. Only his grip on her arm kept it from dropping away entirely.

"Teaching you the truth about what I am." Reaching inside the edges of the ruined garment, he fondled her breasts, not gently but crudely, handling her as if she had no say in this at all and he could do with her as he would. To her surprise, her nipples responded to his roughness with shocking eagerness, hardening and thrusting against his palm. Her knees grew weak. Her pulse drummed in her ears. Glancing down at herself, at the full pale slopes of her breasts from which her nipples thrust, now quiveringly erect, feeling the heated tightening in the pit of her stomach that was becoming almost familiar to her now, she knew that there was no mistaking the desire he had roused her to, and that he recognized it as well as she did. One look at the expression on his lean, handsome face as his eyes raked over her told her that.

"I know what you are." Embarrassed at the physical evidence of her own response, she yanked her arm from his hold and whisked out of his reach, grabbing for the edges of the ruined night rail before it slithered to her feet and pulling them together. His unfamiliar aggression had ignited her temper—ordinarily, no man, not even he, would use her so and live to tell the tale!—but for once in her life she tamped it down. The stakes were too high. She was determined to keep him with her, to keep him safe, no matter the cost. "A gentleman. A kind man. And a good one. Though you try to hide it, that's what you are at heart."

He laughed, the sound harsh and grating, with no amusement in it at all.

"You won't long think so," he promised.

Then he came after her, his face hard, moving as swiftly and silently as a panther, catching her around the waist and lifting her clean up off her feet when she disdained to retreat before him, then stripping away in a single ruthless stroke the ruined night rail, which fluttered down to land on the carpet, white as a flag of surrender in the darkness. Suddenly as naked as he was himself, shocked to feel his arm curling beneath her bare bottom as he lifted her up against his solid, muscular warmth, she gave a squeak of surprise. Grabbing his wide shoulders for balance, her eyes locked to his, which burned into hers, Beth found her back pushed up against the cool plaster wall near the door. He crowded against her, both hands on her bottom now, forcing her legs to open as he positioned himself between them, pulling her hard against the cradle of his hips. Even as her thighs obediently parted to straddle him he thrust inside her, impaling her without warning, hot and turgid and every inch the conquering male as he filled her to capacity and beyond.

"Oh!" She cried out at the shock of it, at the sense of sudden harsh violation, at the force of his penetration. Giving her no chance to do anything but capitulate, he clamped his mouth down over hers to stifle the sound, kissing her with a deep, almost barbaric intensity that made her instantly weak and dizzy. Then he took her there against the wall with a single-minded ferocity that she would have resisted with every fiber of her being had it been turned on her by anyone else. Clinging to him, legs wrapped at his silent direction around his waist, she endured the hard thrust of his hips crushing her into the wall, the carnality of his hot, wet mouth on her lips and neck and breasts, the fierce possession of his hands cupping her bottom and holding her captive for his pleasure, until suddenly shocked endurance no longer described what she was experiencing at all. This lovemaking was rough, it was atavistic, it was as far removed from the gentle caresses she imagined she desired as anything could possibly be, but all at once she found herself melting inside, on fire with need, moving with him, wanting, wanting . . . *more*.

"This is sex, my girl," he whispered into her ear as he rocked himself inside her. "It's dark and dirty, nothing like that pretty parlor game we've been playing up 'til now. How do you like it?"

"Doubtless—I shall become accustomed." Her voice was ragged, but her tone was defiant.

Her answer seemed to drive him wild. He made a harsh sound under his breath and drove into her, pinioning her against the wall with deep, hard thrusts that seemed to reach to her very core. Trembling, back arching, holding on to him now for all she was worth, kissing him as if she would die if she didn't, she felt him come into the hot liquid center of her again and again and again. Eyes closed, breathing erratically, heart pounding, in the grip of an urgent throbbing tension that seemed to be winding ever tighter, she realized that she would not free herself even if she could. She didn't want him to stop. Not now. Not yet. Oh, God, not ever. There was no sound except for the harsh rasp of his breathing and the frantic coupling of their bodies. The scent of what they were doing was all around them. His skin was smooth and slick with sweat and so hot it seemed to burn her everywhere they touched. They were joined together, one flesh, and he took her as thoroughly and as furiously as if he had every right, which, she realized with the tiny part of her mind that wasn't dazzled with heat and shock and a tide of rising passion, he did, because she had given it to him.

Married past redemption. Instead of regret, the thought was accompanied by a quaking wave of heat.

"God in heaven," he groaned at last, his voice thick and tormented. He ground into her one more time, holding himself inside, spilling his seed in a scalding burst that liquefied her bones.

"Neil," she whispered in shaken answer, but he was kissing her again and the sound of her voice was swallowed up by his mouth, so she knew he didn't hear.

Just as suddenly as it had begun, the onslaught was over. He held her captive for only a moment longer before disengaging their bodies and allowing her to slide to her feet. She still breathed like she was dying, though his breathing was already under control. Her arms still wrapped around his neck, although he was already putting her away from him. Her body still burned and yearned and ached for him, for something that she sensed still eluded her that he could give her, although his passion had clearly been spent.

It was over. She had survived.

"Now run away, little girl." His voice held a jeer. "Run, while I'm still willing to let you go."

Beth's eyes snapped open. As shaken as she was, she had not yet lost sight of the goal. She could not let him drive her into sending him away into the night.

"Running away may be in your nature. It isn't in mine."

Their eyes clashed.

"You're a fool, Beth Banning." His expression was as unpleasant as his tone. She moved away from him, and he let her go. She could feel his eyes following her as she crossed the room on tremulous legs, feel the weight of his gaze on the sway of her bottom beneath the tangled fall of her hair, but she kept her back straight and refused to look around or try to cover herself in any way. The Butcher's body still lay on the floor, she saw, and realized with a twinge of surprise that she had forgotten all about it. Sparing it only the briefest of shuddering glances, she snatched a quilt from the bed, wrapping it around herself as she turned to face him. The issue still hung in the balance, she knew, and whether he stayed or went would, she feared, be a perilously near run thing.

"That's as may be. And it's Beth Severin now, as you may recall. There, you have shown me your worst and I still hold you to the marriage, so perhaps you could leave off trying to give me a distaste for you while we put our heads together and decide what's best to be done about that." A nod of her head indicated the body on the floor.

"Your life is in danger every moment you're with me."

"You've done a fine job of keeping me safe so far. From everyone except yourself, that is." The merest hint of humor, with which she hoped to lighten the atmosphere, underlay that last.

"I didn't hurt you." It was a statement more than a question, but there was something of penitence in his frown, and the curve of his mouth.

"You know full well you didn't. You took good care not to, in fact, which I am perfectly aware of."

His face darkened. "I wish you would rid yourself of this conviction of yours that a decent human being is lurking somewhere deep inside me. It's no such thing, you know."

With his own glance at Bunn, he walked toward the window. Following him with her eyes, Beth was treated to an excellent view of his small, tight derriere. It was, as she recalled, wonderfully firm to the touch. The recollection of how she came to know that made her cheeks crimson, and she turned away.

"I take it I may expect more visitations like this one?" she asked, her voice commendably composed, she thought, considering all she had recently gone through. Her heart was just now slowing to a normal beat, and her knees were just regaining their strength. Her body felt softer and more malleable than usual, and she still tingled and burned in the most embarrassing places, but that, she felt, was something she was better off ignoring. With his back still turned, she splashed water from the washstand on her face and gave herself the quickest of sponge baths. Her hair spilled about her shoulders in an unruly mass, and, once again tucking the quilt securely around her, she occupied herself with retrieving her scattered hairpins and twisting it up. The corpse on the floor was a problem, but it was one that was probably not going to fall to her to solve, so she ignored it in favor of concentrating on persuading him to stick to the plan.

"I don't know. I hope not. Bunn worked alone, so I believe we need not fear to encounter his confederates lying in wait in the shrubbery outside. He must have got on my trail yesterday and followed us here. Until the dogs have been called off, though, another attack is always a possibility." He was, she saw with a quick glance, looking out the window, from which he had drawn back the shutter a crack. "The best course to follow would be for me to put you in the carriage and send you on your own to London, and perhaps meet you there."

"Oh, no." Beth recognized prevarication when she heard it—if she got in that carriage alone, she was as certain as it was possible to be that he would head in the exact opposite direction from London, never to be seen again—and her voice was sharp. When he turned to look at her, she planted her fists on her hips and glared at him. "We're going to London together. You'll be safe in Richmond House, because that's the last place anyone would look for you, and a message will be sent to Hugh, and as soon as he arrives and the situation is explained to him he will, as you put it, call off the dogs, and neither you, nor he, nor anyone else will be killed."

He looked pained. "Beth . . ."

"That is what we agreed to!"

"I never realized until this happened what danger I'm putting you in. If you're with me and something goes wrong . . ." He slowly shook his head. "Well, I won't do it. The risk to you is too great."

The finality in his voice awoke something very akin to desperation in her. With every ounce of strength and cunning she possessed she would fight letting him ride off to an almost certain death.

"If I travel alone to London, what's preventing the carriage from being attacked by someone who mistakenly thinks you're in it with me, pray? If he"—she gestured at the dead man—"could find us here, what makes you think that someone won't learn that you hired the carriage and come after it? Without you beside me, I would be defenseless. Or if, perchance, they discovered that you had married me, could they not then hold me as a hostage in hopes of luring you to come after me?"

Neil's arrested expression told her that her words had struck home. Encouraged, she didn't wait for him to reply but pushed the advantage.

"Our best course of action—the one that is safest for me as well as for you—is to stick to our original plan. We have only to get to London, and Richmond, and the thing is done: there will be no more danger for either of us. For any of us."

"Damn it to bloody hell and back!" He ran his fingers through his hair and frowned at her. "Was there ever such a damnable coil?"

With that she knew she had won. Relaxing a little—she was only just realizing how dreadfully afraid she'd been that he would disappear, leaving her behind—and thinking it better not to reply, she watched him come toward her again with some interest. But he stopped before he reached her, picking up his pantaloons from where they lay crumpled by the side of the bed and pulling them on.

"Get dressed," he flung at her as he sat on the side of the bed to pull on his stockings and boots. "I want to be on the road at the first crack of dawn, which doesn't give us much time."

Thus adjured, clinging to the shreds of her modesty because she was simply unable to help herself, Beth retired behind the one high-backed chair and, using it as a makeshift screen, exchanged the quilt for the fresh chemise and petticoat that had been laid out for her, then slipped into her stays. The laces on these proved difficult, and no amount of jerking sufficed to loose the tangle they'd worked themselves into. Though his back was turned to her, Neil must have seen her struggles through the dressing table mirror, because, fully dressed now except for his coat and standing in front of the mirror as he tied his neckcloth, he made a disgusted sound under his breath and came to her assistance.

"Turn around," he directed, his eyes sliding over her as he stepped behind the chair that she'd hoped would serve to shield her to some degree from his view.

It was ridiculous to feel shy after all that had passed between them, but she did. Trying to disguise it, she presented her back to him.

"You must just get the tangle out, then start at the top and tighten—"

"You've no need to tell me. I'm a dab hand at stays," he broke in, and she could feel him separating the component parts of the tangle as he spoke.

Surprised to discover that she didn't particularly like what that implied, Beth stiffened and cast him a narrow-eyed look over her shoulder. "Are you indeed?"

He must have felt her eyes on him, because he glanced up from what he was doing to meet her gaze. For a moment he looked surprised. Then he grinned.

"As I believe I told you before, I am skilled at any number of things."

The reply that sprang to her lips was, she discovered to her disgruntlement, on the order of the landlord's disapproving "hmmph!" But she bit it back, not caring to reveal that she had just been pierced by a stab of something that she feared must be very akin to jealousy. The emotion was wholly new to her. She was accustomed, rather, to provoking jealousy in her admirers. Certainly she did not like it.

"How very handy!" she said brightly instead. Having succeeded in remedying the tangle, he was already tightening her laces for her. She waited until he secured them with a knot, then stepped away from him with a brief "thank you" to put on her gown. It was high-necked, long-sleeved black bombazine, probably laid aside when a recent widow had put off her mourning, and was loose where it should have been tight and tight where it should have been loose. But under the circumstances, she realized she was lucky to have a fresh gown to wear at all, and so she accepted it in that spirit. The tiny buttons at the back were difficult to do up without assistance, and she half expected to feel his hands brushing hers aside at any moment. When he didn't come to her rescue, she glanced around to see what he was doing.

He was, she saw, at the window again, with the shutters fully open now. Indeed, the window was open to the night, with the sash thrown up and crisp air blowing into the room, and he was leaning out.

Even as Beth saw that, she realized that there was no longer a corpse in the center of the carpet. Eyes widening at the discovery, blinking in dismay at the thought of what she must have missed, she hurried toward the window.

"What are you *doing*?"

Reaching him just as he pulled back inside the room, she didn't wait for an answer but looked out and down herself, ignoring the purpling sky and the cold wind in favor of searching for the missing body. At first all she saw below the window was a thicket of leafy bushes, which were part of the shrubbery that hugged the walls. Then she realized that in the bushes she could see a boot and part of a leg, and withdrew into the room so swiftly that she almost bumped her head on the sash.

"You dumped him out the window!"

"Shh!" Clearly unabashed, he closed the window and the shutters over it. "What would you have had me do? If he'd been discovered in this room, we would have had hue and cry after us before we reached the border."

"You surely don't mean to just leave him there!"

"I don't. I'm going to go down now and bear him off to the woods yonder, where, if and when he should be discovered, it will most likely be assumed he suffered some sort of accident. Certainly there will be no way to link him to us."

Beth couldn't like the scheme, but she could think of nothing better, and she had to admit that in this area, at least, his judgment, due to vastly more experience in disposing of corpses, was likely to be better than hers. She said as much, in a decidedly acidic tone, as he shrugged into his coat and added the dead man's cash and pistol to his pockets. Then, putting on her second shoe as she went, she hopped after him as he headed for the door.

"Wait! I'm coming with you." Just in case he had it in his head to flee once he was out of her sight.

With his hand on the knob, he looked back at her. Whatever he saw in her face must have told him that arguing was useless, which it was because there was no way that she could see that he could prevent her from doing just exactly as she chose, at least not without risking a deal more noise than he wanted.

"Be quiet, then, and stay close" was all he said, and left the room.

At this very early hour of the morning, with dawn just on the verge of breaking, the old inn was full of shadows and creaks. Only a dim oil lamp hanging from the ceiling at the top of the stairs lit the way as they moved quickly but silently down the narrow steps toward the dark passage that ran between the taproom and coffee room and various private parlors, and led to the front door. Beth's heart thumped at every sound. She was breathing way too fast. Following close behind Neil, she stayed hideously on edge lest they be attacked again, or, as seemed more likely, were discovered and called to account for themselves by the suspicious innkeeper or his wife. Even before they reached the foot of the stairs, they were swallowed up in gloom, and the drafty passage was dark enough to make her shiver and long to be out of it. Keeping close behind Neil, having to school herself not to take a firm grip on the tail of his coat, she already had her eyes fixed on the front door when a man unexpectedly stepped out of the taproom into their path.

"Stop right there," he growled, but in that first moment of heart-leaping shock Beth barely registered the words because her attention was riveted on the pistol in his hand. A glance sufficed to tell her that it was cocked and aimed at Neil's head. His menacing words were addressed solely to Neil. "Get your hands in the air. *Now.*"

Chapter Twenty-eight

"HUGH!" A SPLIT SECOND LATER Beth was almost giddy with relief as her worst fears vanished between one heartbeat and the next. "Oh, thank goodness! I am so glad to see you! We were coming to find you!"

The instant she had looked past the pistol to the man holding it, she recognized her brother-in-law, looking handsome as always but tired and out of temper. Recovering from the fright he had given her, she beamed at him in delight. Feeling as if a huge weight had been lifted from her shoulders, she almost acted on her first impulse, which was to run forward and cast herself into his arms. The grim look on his face and the sight of that loaded gun pointed unwaveringly at Neil, who had, like herself, stopped short at his advent, reminded her that these two were deadly adversaries and held her back. Neil knew better than to try to murder Hugh, but Hugh as yet remained unenlightened about the change in the situation. Until everything was explained, wild horses weren't going to drag her away from Neil's side, so she executed a neat dance step that positioned her between the two men and faced Hugh even as, behind her, Neil slowly raised his hands.

"Hullo, Richmond." The unmistakable note of mockery in Neil's tone was not, Beth felt, what the situation called for.

"Walk toward Hugh, Beth," said another, deadly voice behind her. Beth glanced around in surprise to discover Nick, possibly even handsomer than Hugh but looking equally tired and every bit as unpleasant. He was standing a yard or so behind Neil, holding a pistol on him, too. The shadows lining the passage seemed to move. As Beth blinked at them bemusedly they resolved themselves into more armed men, a half dozen at least, fanned out behind Nick. Every gun was trained on Neil.

"Nick! I'm so glad to see you, too! I declare, I could hug you both! But you don't need those guns, so you might as well go ahead and put them away. Neil isn't going to hurt anybody, I promise you. Oh, Neil, this is Gabby's husband, Nick DeVane."

"Oh, ho, the fabled spy-catcher! Well, well! No wonder you were able to find us, Richmond! Rather beyond your powers, I would have thought it," Neil said.

"You are not helping," Beth told him, aggravated.

"Come here to me, Beth." Hugh's voice was sharp. "You're perfectly safe now. There's not a thing in the world he can do to hurt you. And as for you"—his tone changed, becoming fierce, making it obvious he was now talking to Neil—"though I'd hate to kill you in front of her, all you have to do is breathe wrong and I will."

"You really think you could?" Neil made the words an obvious challenge.

"With all of us here? I know it."

"No one is going to kill anyone!" Beth took a step back so that her back pressed protectively against Neil's chest. Conscious of Nick and the others behind Neil, terribly aware of how inadequate a shield she was, suddenly uncertain of the outcome, she glared at Hugh. "Do you hear me?"

"Step away from him, Beth!" Hugh ordered.

"You won't persuade her to leave me, Richmond." At the continued baiting note in Neil's voice, Beth was conscious of a strong desire to box his ears. He was being the opposite of conciliating, which under the circumstances she considered plain foolish. The two men bristled at each other like angry dogs, and she knew that if she hadn't been there one of them probably would have been dead already. "She's mine now. You may be sure I took good care to make her so."

"What?" Hugh and Nick barked almost in unison. Hugh's face, already hard, turned to stone. His eyes blazed with outrage. Although she couldn't see Nick, she could imagine he was having much the same reaction. The most maddening part about it was, she had no doubt that infuriating them was exactly what Neil had intended.

"Oh, for goodness' sake! Neil, would you

stop being so provoking? What he means is, we were married last night," Beth said. "We—"

"By God, you slimy bastard!" Hugh interrupted, starting forward. "That tops everything! To force an innocent—"

"Mind yourself, Hugh," Nick warned sharply. "Keep well out of reach."

Hugh stopped. The pistol was now aimed directly between Neil's eyes. Beth felt a shiver of alarm at her brother-in-law's expression. Although she didn't dare glance back, she had the most lowering suspicion that Neil was answering that murderous look with a taunting one of his own.

"Of course he didn't force me! He didn't force me to do anything! Getting married was my idea, because—" She broke off, suddenly remembering the many listening ears that did not belong to family members. "You are a pair—no, a trio!—of complete *idiots,* and I am fast losing patience with the lot of you! Hugh, Nick, please, if you love me, put your guns down, and Neil, you keep your tongue between your teeth. What we are going to do, all four of us, is repair to a private parlor, just there"—she pointed toward the room she and Neil had dined in the previous night—"where I will explain the whole thing."

"Purely in the spirit of brotherly cooperation, I give you my word that I won't kill either of you for at least the next half hour. Plenty of time to hear the lady out." Mockery still laced Neil's voice. Out of patience, Beth elbowed him smartly in the ribs.

He flinched. "Ow!"

"Stop it!" she ordered.

"Keep your hands up!" Nick snapped.

"Other than a pistol, which he has in his pocket, and which I am going to fish out and give to one of you, he is totally unarmed." Beth turned and fixed Neil, who had his hands up and the remains of a pained grimace still twisting his mouth, with a darkling look as she reached into his coat pocket for the gun. "Pray don't shoot him. I realize he is being difficult just at present, but that's probably because he feels you have the advantage of him and he doesn't like it."

Neil narrowed his eyes at her, and she made a face at him in return. Retrieving the pistol, she turned just in time to note Hugh's arrested look, and the glance he exchanged with someone behind her, whom she presumed was Nick.

"Take that pistol from her, Barnet," Nick directed.

"'E don't need no pistol to do what 'e does, Colonel. You just remember that." A familiar gravelly voice addressed the warning to Nick as the speaker stepped carefully around Neil to relieve Beth of the pistol. George Barnet, a giant of a man with the squashed features of a former pugilist, had served as Nick's batman during the war, and as his right-hand man since. Beth had known him for as long as she had known Nick, and liked him very well.

"Hello, Barnet." She gave him a quick smile.

"'Ello, Miss Beth." Nodding at her, he cast Neil a wary glance. "We was that worried about ye, miss."

"I'm sorry." This reminder of the distress her disappearance must have caused everyone who cared about her brought her sisters instantly to mind.

"I reckon it weren't your fault," Barnet replied as, bearing away the pistol and shooting Neil a poisonous look even as he took care to give him a wide berth, he returned to his position at Nick's shoulder. "'Twas 'im."

"No! No, it wasn't! You have it completely wrong, all of you!" At their collective intransigence, she felt like stamping her foot. "Hugh, Nick, unless you want me to tell you this very private story in front of everyone, we should step into the parlor now." Relying on her status as a beloved little sister, she resorted to giving both beseeching looks. *"Please,* won't you hear me out?"

Once again Hugh and Nick exchanged looks.

"Or you could just shoot me out of hand," Neil suggested.

Beth shot him a killing glare.

"All right, we'll listen. *You"*—the abrupt change in Hugh's tone once again made it clear that he was addressing Neil—"keep well ahead of us."

"We'll be right outside this 'ere door, Colonel," Barnet said grimly as Beth led the way into the private parlor. "Ye or 'Is Grace only need to give a shout."

By the time Nick closed the parlor door behind them, Neil had propped a shoulder against the fireplace and turned a sardonic face to the room while Beth, seeing how dark it was with the shutters closed and the fire having died to an orange glow, lit a candle on the embers and touched it to the tapers in the wall sconces on either side of the fireplace. Nick and Hugh, she noted, stationed themselves well apart along the back wall. Both kept their pistols trained on Neil.

Returning the flickering candle to its holder in the middle of the table, she moved to stand beside Neil. Not that she truly thought he needed her protection, now that there were only the four of them, but just in case.

"How are Claire and Gabby? Are they much overset?" she asked.

"As you may imagine," Hugh answered drily. "Claire was beside herself with anxiety when last I saw her. Gabby, while bearing up, was white as a ghost and unable to eat. I doubt they've improved any while we've been scouring the countryside in search of you."

"Oh, no!"

"We promised we'd get you back safe," Nick added. "We left them together, along with my children, under guard at Richmond House in case your abductor"—here he shot a sulfurous look at Neil—"should have decided to target them, too."

"But Neil didn't abduct me," Beth objected. "He rescued me, rather! I think it must have been William—Lord Rosen— who arranged to have me kidnapped."

"Is that what he's led you to believe?" Hugh thrust a hand into the pocket of his greatcoat and pulled forth a folded sheet of paper. As he unfolded it, Beth, from the corner of her eye, thought she saw Neil respond with a nearly imperceptible wince.

"What is that?" She looked from the paper to Hugh.

"This was written by him, and delivered to me after you disappeared. Allow me to read it to you." Glancing down at the paper, he began: "'My dear Richmond: It is my pleasure to inform you that I have in my possession the Lady Elizabeth Banning, who I propose to keep until you should present yourself, in person and quite alone, to reclaim her. At that time, I am confident that our differences can be settled. Please accept my profound assurance that if you do not follow my instructions to the letter, and arrive in good time at the location I shall subsequently acquaint you with, the consequences to the lady will be, shall we say, unfortunate.'"

He stopped, but Beth had already turned her attention to Neil, who met her shocked gaze with a rueful look that advertised his guilt as loudly as a shouted confession.

She frowned. "But you *didn't.*" Her conviction gained strength as she mentally reviewed events to see if she could possibly have misinterpreted them. "You had nothing to do with kidnapping me."

He sighed. "No, I actually didn't. But only because someone—I agree that it was most likely your spurned suitor—beat me to it. The dismal truth is, I went to the park that morning to carry you off with me, by persuasion or, um, whatever means was necessary, with the intention of using you to draw Richmond to me. For what purpose I imagine you can guess."

She regarded him indignantly. "What a shabby thing to have done!"

"Shabby?" Hugh choked out as Neil shrugged in silent apology. "Dastardly, rather."

"Beth . . ." Nick began.

She rounded on them. "But don't you see, he *didn't* kidnap me. He may have—most reprehensibly!—formed the intention of doing so, but instead he rode after me and saved me from the most dreadful—Oh, let me tell you the whole story, and you may judge it for yourselves."

Which is what she did, starting with their first encounter in the library at Richmond House and ending with Hugh and Nick's arrival on the scene, glossing over only the most personal moments. When she finished, Neil's arms were folded over his chest and his countenance was absolutely expressionless, while Hugh and Nick seemed to waver somewhere between astonishment and horror.

"First things first." Hugh was the first to recover. "Are we to understand that there is even now a dead body lying concealed in the shrubbery at the back of this inn?"

Beth nodded.

"It's not that well concealed," Neil told them. "I was on my way to move it when you showed up. Unless you want to have to answer a number of awkward questions presently, I suggest you have someone convey it to the woods behind the stable before the sun's well up."

With a speaking look at Hugh, Nick moved, opening the door and saying something inaudible to, Beth presumed, Barnet, who was, as promised, just beyond the door.

"You don't need to worry about the marriage. It won't be allowed to stand." Finished giving his orders to Barnet, Nick closed the door again, rested his back against it, and looked at Beth. His tone was comforting. For all his soft words, his pistol was once again trained on Neil. Hugh's had never wavered, and she wondered with despair if they had heard a word she'd said.

"It's perfectly legal," Neil drawled. "No grounds for overturning it whatsoever."

"You made sure of that, didn't you?" Hugh's expression turned ugly. "Whether it can be overturned or not doesn't matter, you bounder, because Beth will, in any case, shortly be a widow."

"But I don't wish to be a widow!" Beth said before Neil could reply. She shot a quelling glance at him, to find that he was once again looking mockingly at Hugh. Frowning him down, she looked at Hugh again. "I don't wish to have the marriage overturned, either. I am not saying that it is precisely what I would have chosen, but if fate had not forced my hand in this way, I daresay I never would have married at all. I— Believe me when I tell you that I would as soon be married to Neil as anybody."

"Thank you." Neil gave her a small, ironic bow.

"Beth, don't think we don't understand how it must have been." Nick's voice was incredibly gentle. "You've been through a shocking experience, and are naturally inclined to regard the man who saved you from the worst of it as a hero, but . . ."

"I am not such a fool, Nick, and you know it!"

"Indeed, that passel of females I en- countered at the White Swan told much the same tale," Hugh said reluctantly. "That was before you came up with us, Nick. They claimed he rescued them from all manner of dangers."

"Oh, did you see Mary, and Peg, and Al- yce, and the rest, then?" Beth asked Hugh, eager for news of them. "I assured them that if they assisted me to help Neil escape from that dreadful Tandy and his men, you would see to their safety."

"I did." His voice was dry.

"Enough of this. Beth needs to know the truth about what he is." Nick, looking impatiently at Hugh, cut that line of conversation short. "She's built up this image of him in her mind, and the only way to counter it is to tell her the truth. She has *married* him, for God's sake. But you're the one here who has the authority to break the confidentiality of the War Office, not me, so it's your call."

"If you mean to acquaint me with the fact that he is an assassin, you needn't bother," Beth said. "He told me himself."

"Clever of you," Hugh said to Neil. "But I fancy you didn't tell her the entire truth." His attention shifted to Beth, and his expression softened fractionally. "In the world he inhabits, he's known as the Angel of Death. He got that sobriquet because of the sheer number of people he has killed, and because of the ruthlessness with which he does the job. Once he is set on a target, the target is as good as dead, along with anyone who happens to get in the way. He is the best at what he does, and in this case to be the best is a terrible thing. With the war over and our men coming home, it was the unenviable task of the War Office to acknowledge that some operatives we were forced to use to secure victory could not be reintegrated into the populace. I promise you that only a very few were deemed impossible to rehabilitate. He was at the top of the list, judged an extreme danger to society."

"And did you make that determination, Richmond?" Neil's voice was very soft, while his eyes gleamed diamond hard.

Hugh returned his look steadily. "No, but I agreed with it. I still agree with it."

"But it's *wrong*," Beth burst out. She glared at Hugh. "Did you not kill anyone during the war? Of course you did! Claire says you will not say much about your time on the continent before you met her. Indeed, I feel if I, or Claire, knew the full total of your activities there, we would feel quite as much horror toward you as you expect me to feel toward Neil now." As Hugh's mouth tightened in silent acknowledgment of a hit, she rounded on Nick. "And as for you, Gabby has told me some of what you did.

You were instrumental in the capture and execution of a great number of spies, weren't you? Just because you did not generally kill them yourself does not make you any less guilty, you know."

Nick's expression changed, too, and Beth knew she had scored there as well.

"I would have expected better of you than to try to hide behind a woman's skirts, Durham." Hugh's voice was harsh.

"Now, there you mistake, my old friend. It's you who have been hiding behind a woman's skirts. I would have killed you the night I entered your house had I not encountered Beth instead, and I would have killed you today had it not been for her."

"You might have tried!"

"I would have succeeded."

"Stop it, both of you!" Grabbing hold of Neil's sleeve to shush him, Beth flashed a furious look at Hugh. "The point is that neither of you—none of you—is lily white. I doubt anyone who served in that frightful war is! But it's over, and you moved on"— then her gaze shot to Nick—"and you moved on, and Neil is going to move on, too. If there is some kind of death order out against him, you must just rescind it."

"Even if I wished to, I don't have that power," Hugh said.

At the look on his face, Beth felt her stomach drop clear to her toes. The arm beneath her hand tightened, and her hand clamped onto the hardening muscle. Unless Neil wished to be stopped, however, she knew her grip was useless. With a terrible sense that events were beginning to spin out of control, she felt Neil gathering himself beside her, and knew to what purpose.

"No! You can't do this, either of you! By God, after all those bloody years of war, aren't you both sick of killing?" It was a cry straight from Beth's heart.

"Hold a minute." Straightening away from the door, Nick looked at Hugh. "I know it's not in your power to rescind the order. Indeed, I wouldn't be willing to wager much on the chance it could be rescinded. But it might be circumvented."

"How so?" Though Hugh replied to Nick, his eyes never left Neil.

"We have a dead body on our hands, I apprehend. If we claimed it was his, who, outside of those in this room, would know the difference?"

Silence greeted that.

Hugh frowned thoughtfully at Nick. "Your men."

The fact that he allowed his eyes to shift away from Neil made Beth breathe a little easier.

"They were under my command during the war, and since then they've worked for me in various, uh, jobs for the government— something that I'll thank you not to tell your sister." Nick addressed this aside, along with a monitory look, to Beth, "who has an unfortunate tendency to worry." He directed his attention back to Hugh. "They're totally trustworthy."

"There is a man named Fitz Clapham," Neil said in a negligent tone, as if the discussion was purely academic and the outcome didn't matter to him at all. "He, too, is a government-sanctioned killer, and unfortunately he knows what I look like."

Beth gave him a quelling look. The last thing they needed was him throwing rubs in their way.

"Does he?" Hugh's frown deepened.

"But only as the Angel of Death. He has no knowledge that I am in truth the Marquis of Durham."

"You will never encounter him. He will never see you," Beth interjected. "The two of you will henceforth exist in different worlds."

"That's a problem," Hugh said to Nick, as if she hadn't spoken.

"A negligible one," Nick replied. "As Beth said, it is highly unlikely their paths will ever cross."

"Everyone is deserving of a second chance, Hugh." Beth begged him with her eyes.

"Do you wish for a second chance, then?" Nick asked Neil directly.

Beth held her breath as she redirected that beseeching look to Neil. He met her gaze, and his mouth tightened.

"Who would not? Certainly I do."

She let out her breath on a little sigh.

"Hell and the devil confound it—saving your presence, of course, Beth." Hugh looked, and sounded, immensely put out. He looked at Nick. "So what's to be done, then? Accept him into the family?"

Neil stirred at the savage tone of that, but before he could add more to the conversation, as Beth was quite sure he meant to do, and probably to his own detriment, because Hugh's words had clearly put up his back, Nick forestalled him.

"I think the thing to do would be to follow their original plan of repairing to London and letting him shelter at Richmond House until the dust settles. Meanwhile, the body must be buried with a great many witnesses, and word sent to the proper authority that the Angel of Death is no longer among us—which, if he comports himself as we must hope he will do, will be perfectly true."

"And what about this havey-cavey marriage?"

"A problem for another time." Nick lowered his pistol. As Hugh, with a hard look at Neil, slowly followed suit, Beth flew across the room to hug them both.

Chapter Twenty-nine

THE JOURNEY TO LONDON was accomplished in a speedy three days. Because it was agreed that they should be seen as little as possible, Neil and Beth were closeted together in a hired closed carriage that jolted and rocked and pitched sickeningly from side to side, although Neil would have much preferred to ride. His every move was watched with suspicion by the men who accompanied the carriage, namely Richmond and DeVane riding beside, and two others on the box, which irked Neil to no end. Fearing that so many outriders would attract the very attention they most wished to avoid, the rest had been deputed to stay behind and accord the body a proper burial, then make their way to London separately, and at a more leisurely pace. Two nights were passed upon the road, in small, unfashionable inns where they were less likely to encounter their fellow travelers. Though it was clear that it stuck in the craws of her disapproving relations, Neil slept both nights with his wife, and took some small degree of satisfaction from the look on Richmond's face when they retired to a single chamber together. It was, however, the only satisfaction he got. They passed no more than seven hours in each inn, Beth was exhausted from the day's jolting, with the surety of another day just like it before them, and he was far too canny in the ways of women to do more than sleep at her side. Besides, he was tired, too, and maddeningly aware of the thinness of the wall separating them from the others. It did not require superior judgment to conclude that those brief rest stops were no place to tutor Beth in the true joys of lovemaking. And after his recent assault on her—because, in the cold light of another day, that was the only way he could,

shamefacedly, think of what he had done—
he had a great deal to make up for in that
regard. He was fortunate that she seemed
prepared to give him another chance.

He had never actually wooed a woman,
but he meant to woo Beth, with as much
gentle care as he could command. On their
wedding night, when she had ordered him
to just go ahead and bed her, he had seen
the fear that had prompted her speech and
realized that, although his intention had
been to take his time and seduce her until
she was mindless and melting with passion, the actual best course of action was
to get her damned virginity out of the way
and have done. Afterward, his thinking had
gone, he would have all the time in the
world to make things right. Having most
unexpectedly found her, he was not about
to let her go again. She had married him
to save his life and keep him from killing
Richmond. He had married her because
he wanted her, because having found the
lovely bright warmth of her, he was loath to
lose it again and plunge back into the darkness his existence had been before she
came into it, because—oh, for any number
of excellent reasons that he had no desire

to sort through just at present. Having wed
her, he had then made sure of her by bed-
ding her. With that done, there had been,
he judged, no need to rush his fences.
Then the Butcher had attacked, scaring the
life out of him for Beth's sake rather than
his own, and he had lost control along with
his temper and his judgment and made a
complete debacle of his plan to gently woo
her. As a result, her initiation into the plea-
sures of sex had been, he feared, shamefully devoid of pleasure, which he meant to
do his best to remedy as soon as he had
the time and privacy to do so. So far, that
had not yet been accorded them, but once
London was reached he had every hope
that the situation would be speedily reme-
died.

"Explain to me," Beth said, fixing him
with a sapient look as they were once
again being jarred to pieces in the ill-
sprung carriage, "why you and Hugh must
be constantly at each other's throats?"

That was after the brief nuncheon break
on the second day, when Hugh had inquired for what must have been the doz-
enth time of Beth, as she was mounting
again into the carriage, if she was sure she

would not like either him or Nick to ride inside with the pair of them. Beth replied, as she had each time before, that she was perfectly fine with being left alone with Neil. Neil, already inside the carriage, as his breaks were of necessity of much shorter duration than Beth's, with a view to keeping him concealed whenever possible, held out his hand to her to assist her over the threshold, smiled at Hugh over her head, and assured him that he had no thought of harming his new bride yet.

In Neil's estimation, Hugh's fuming expression was almost worth the glare Beth shot him.

"He doesn't like to see me with you," Neil answered. He was seated across from her, in the backward-facing seat because he was too inured to discomfort to be bothered particularly by it and because he had no wish to add to her misery by crowding her on the other seat. Honesty compelled him to add, "I don't blame him. Were I in his shoes and he in mine, I wouldn't like it either."

"But you were friends once."

"At Eton." He had already told her, when she had asked how he knew Hugh, that they had been at school together, with the older boy, Hugh, sometimes stepping in to protect the more belligerent, younger one, Neil, from the consequences of his hasty tongue and ready fists. "He stopped a few fights, interceded with a few prefects on my behalf. I was usually grateful—once my temper cooled, that is. But after I left—all right, ran away from—Eton, I didn't see him again until we encountered each other in our professional capacities during the course of the war. As each of us was operating under an assumed identity at the time, our renewed relationship did not flourish. In fact, he probably felt as uneasy about my existence as I felt about his. Either of us could have exposed the other for who he really was at any time. Neither of us ever did, though, and I suppose, since his continued silence has made it possible for me to hope to be able to pick up the threads of my old life, I owe him one. I expect I will tell him so, one of these days, when he is a little less ready to believe I mean to ill-treat you."

"He regards me as his sister, you know," Beth said excusingly. "He has done so much for us. Indeed, I tremble to think what would have happened to Claire had she not met him. We all—Gabby and I, and Claire most of all—love him devotedly."

Neil made a face at her. "I don't doubt it. Richmond was always most heroic. The last time I saw him, on the field at Waterloo, he was leading a charge into an almost overwhelming sea of Frogs, pluck to the backbone all the way. I should say, the last time I saw him before yesterday."

"You were at Waterloo?"

He nodded. "Every military man who could get there must have fought on that day. I served under Wellington's command. I have no great opinion of him, but by God he turned Boney back! It was a near run thing, I can tell you, with the very future of England at stake."

"But that makes you a hero, too!"

The pride in her eyes both surprised and touched him, but he gave a derisive laugh and shook his head. "Not I, my girl. I leave the heroics to those of Richmond's stamp."

She smiled at him, clearly unconvinced, and he found the smile disturbing enough on many levels to cause him to change the subject.

It was not until the following day that she came back to it. By this time the novelty of being confined for long hours in a stuffy, poorly sprung carriage, existing on bad food and little sleep, had completely waned. Not even the riders were in a good humor, and they at least had the felicity of being out in the open air. Beth had been lying back against the seat for an hour or more with her eyes closed, having complained of a headache after quarreling with him again over what she termed his obstinate refusal to be conciliating with Richmond. The landscape outside the window—he had parted the curtains a little, despite having been straightly charged not to do so—was dull, and so he occupied himself with looking at her.

He studied the resplendent waves of her hair, which had been twisted up in the most ladylike of fashions when they had begun their journey that dawn, only to have devolved into a precarious knot that let many delightful tendrils escape to curl against her creamy skin as the day wore on. His eyes traced the slim black brows that had, when she had last looked at him, signaled her displeasure at him by slanting to almost meet above her nose. The dark fans of her lashes lay still against her cheeks, making him think she truly was asleep and not just avoiding conversation. He took in the slender length of her nose, the square lines of her jaw and high cheekbones, the lush curve of her lips.

Beautiful was the first thought that came into his head. His second, close on its heels, was a fierce *Mine*.

"What I don't understand," she said, opening her eyes to catch him staring, causing him to flush a little, as though she could somehow divine the tenor of his thoughts, "is how you came to be at Eton in the first place."

"My father sent me there." He recovered from his surprise with aplomb.

"But I thought your mother took you with her to France." He had already told her that his parents had separated when he was very young, with his aristocratic French mother fleeing with Isobel and himself to her native country.

"She did. We lived with her widowed mother, most happily, until at the height of the Terror a servant appeared and whisked me away. Stole me away, rather, leaving a message for my mother to tell her that His Grace the Duke of Wychester did not care for his heir to be exposed to the danger that was France and would henceforth care for him in England."

"That must have been terrible. How old were you?"

"Not quite eight."

"Poor little boy!"

"Indeed, I thought so. I hated my father for taking me. He was a cold, cruel man in any case, not one to endear himself to children. My mother came once to try to beseech him into letting her have me again, but he threw her out on her ear. My emotions when I was forcefully detached from her on this occasion were violent enough to persuade him to send me away to school. I threatened to kill him, I believe."

"Anyone might have done so!"

He smiled at her. "You are determined to see me in the best possible light, aren't you?"

"*You* are determined to see yourself in the worst!" She shook her head at him. "But continue. You were sent to school. Did you not then have any more contact with your mama until—" There she broke off delicately.

"She wrote to me at school. She and Isobel were most faithful correspondents. When I ran away from Eton—I was on the verge of being kicked out for fighting, and had no wish to be sent back to my father's tender care, which was what they were threatening to do—it was with the intention of making my way to them in France. I ended up working for Mr. Creed at the White Swan in an attempt to raise the ready. The rest you know."

"Yes." She looked thoughtful. "But what I don't know is how you wound up becoming an assassin. It doesn't seem like the kind of thing one could just fall into."

He laughed, and as he did so he realized that he had never in his life thought that he could laugh about such a topic. But she was so ridiculously matter-of-fact about something that should by rights have had her shuddering with revulsion that he couldn't help it.

"What's funny?" She regarded him so suspiciously that he laughed again.

"You, Madame Roux." When she gave him her quick frown he was conscious of a strong urge to shift to the seat beside her, wrap her in his arms, and kiss her breathless, but given the exigencies of the situation he most nobly refrained. Instead, he chose to answer her question. "After my mother and sister were killed, I went, I admit it, a little mad for a while. I thirsted for vengeance, and I took it as best I could. My tribute to them was to kill everyone I could get to who I felt was responsible for their deaths, from the prison guards who took my bribes but did nothing to help them, to the farmer in Dijon who sold the whereabouts of their hiding place to the soldiers who sought them. In the course of this bloody rampage, I encountered someone else who was bent more or less on the same job, except he was being paid by the British government to do it. He recognized in me a like-minded soul who he judged suitable to be trained as an assassin, and passed the word up the chain. I was approached, accepted, trained, and sent out. As Richmond told you, I became the best at what I do. I was even proud of how good I was at it."

She looked at him with trouble in her eyes. Then, to his great surprise, she slipped from her seat to his, put her arms around his neck, and pressed her warm, soft lips to his cheek.

"It's over," she said softly. "You don't need to ever think about it again."

After that, he couldn't help it. There was simply nothing else to do. He kissed her. The sweetness of her lips made him dizzy, and the soft warmth of her invited his hands. He pulled her onto his lap, leaned her back over his arm, and kissed her until he ached with wanting her; she was sighing and yielding and kissing him back with an abandon that set his blood to boiling and made him think that a closed carriage might not, after all, be such a bad place to continue his bride's education. In fact, had it not been for a most inopportune banging on the roof—the coachman's way of announcing an impending stop—he might have lost his head to the point of taking her right there in the carriage.

But the coachman did bang, and she pulled her mouth away from his, sitting up on his lap and blinking at him for a moment in the most adorable confusion. Leaning back against the squabs, grabbing hold of his willpower with both hands against the effort it cost to let her go, he managed a lazy smile for her and had the pleasure of seeing her cheeks turn crimson.

Then the carriage started to slow, and she scrambled up off his lap and back to her seat, hastily trying to put her hair and dress to rights as she went.

Again he counseled himself to patience. Shortly they would have all the time in the world.

Along with dinner, which was carried to him in the coach while she went in to dine at the inn, which was busier than any they had stopped at so far, came the intelligence that they could shortly expect to reach London.

"Hugh sent a message on ahead, so Claire and Gabby will be expecting us," Beth told him when the carriage was under way again. She was excited, happy at the prospect of being reunited with her sisters and being once more at home, while he was conscious of a most unfamiliar sensation. It took him a while to work it out, but finally he did: he was, he realized to his own disgust, increasingly nervous about what was to come. Meeting her sisters, reentering society, becoming part of the world again—the prospect made his gut tighten in a way it hadn't done since he was a boy.

It was past nine o'clock and dark except for the occasional flaring street light that flashed past the crack in the curtains by the time the carriage wheels clattered onto London's cobblestone streets. On the opposite seat, Beth peeped out the window, remarked on the sights they passed, and chattered blithely on about her sisters while he listened with half an ear. Absolutely fearless in the face of physical danger, so hardened to the prospect of pain or deprivation that he barely noticed either, he found he could not face this change in his circumstances with anything other than the most profound misgiving.

He was a creature of the dark, not the light.

"At least, I had not thought—I'm not entirely sure how it works, but Hugh has been kind enough to provide me with a considerable portion, and perhaps . . ."

That slightly disjointed statement, tacked onto some comment about how pleasant he would find it to live in Richmond House, caught his attention.

"We won't need to rely on any funds from Richmond," he said crisply, pulling himself together to focus on what she was saying to him. "Or to live in his house, either. I inherited a great deal of money from my mother, and I am Wychester's heir as well."

"Are you saying you're rich?" Beth regarded him with open delight.

He had to laugh. "Are you glad of it?"

"Extremely. I've been poor, you know, and I don't care for it a bit."

He laughed again, and felt the better for it. Moments later, the carriage rocked to a stop. With Richmond and DeVane following as grimly as a pair of damned guards, they were ushered into the magnificence that was Richmond House, not through the front door but through the mews, and the back garden, and along a narrow corridor, up a set of back stairs, and into a grand hall until finally a stately butler—Graham, Beth called him as he welcomed her home—flung open the doors to a warmly lit saloon.

"They are here, Your Grace."

Chapter Thirty

"BETH!"

As the new arrivals entered, two slender young women rose from chairs by the fire to fly toward Beth, who embraced both with a laughing fervor that left Neil in no doubt that he beheld her much-talked-about sisters. The raving beauty he had no trouble in identifying as Claire, who of course belonged to Richmond. The older sister, who possessed her own quiet loveliness, was Gabby, and belonged to DeVane. Two much older women, one a tall, mannish-looking battle-ax with a crown of iron gray braids who was undoubtedly a lady by birth, the other also tall but spare, with silvery hair confined primly at her nape and the look of an upper servant about her, were then hugged by Beth in turn. The resultant jumble of conversation amongst the women proved impossible to keep up with, and he did not try. Instead, he watched Beth and her sisters with idle appreciation for a trio of beauteous females while the chatter rose in volume until, as abruptly as the clap of a pair of hands, it stopped. Every female eye in the room then fastened on him as one.

Neil barely managed not to blanch.

"Beth, pray tell me I cannot have heard you correctly," the battle-ax said in an unpleasantly piercing voice that matched the look she was giving him. "Even you cannot have done anything so shocking as to contract a Gretna Green marriage!"

"Well, I did," Beth said, unrepentant, and came forward to slide a hand around his arm and draw him—most unwillingly, though he hoped he had more bottom than to let it show—into what he could only regard as the arena. With, of course, the quartet of more or less obviously appalled ladies cast as lions. "This is Neil

Severin. The—the Marquis of Durham. Neil, this is my sister Claire, Duchess of Richmond, my sister Gabby, Mrs. DeVane, my aunt Augusta, Lady Salcombe, and our own dear Miss Twindlesham, who has taken care of Claire and me since our birth."

It had been many years since he'd had cause to engage in the ordinary social conventions of his class, but as he found himself thus put on the spot, the way of it instantly came back to him. He stepped forward and, with a most insincere murmur of pleasure on his lips, shook hands all around.

"We owe you a great deal of thanks for your kindness to Beth," Gabby said, and smiled at him, which made him realize that she had a deal more beauty than he had at first supposed.

"Oh, and for rescuing her," Claire added, with a warmth in her eyes that put him in mind of Beth's engaging twinkle. Neil thought that, save for Beth, he had never seen a more ravishing female. He would have shot a purely male congratulatory glance at the husband standing so protectively behind her, had the man been any other than Richmond, who was observing his discomfiture with a sardonic expression that awoke in Neil the quite unworthy desire to plant him a facer. DeVane, having embraced his wife, had retreated to stand near the fireplace, making it clear from his expression and posture that whatever occurred, his intention was to stay well out of it.

The battle-ax—Lady Salcombe—still glared at him. "Marquis or no—and from all I ever heard, Wychester's heir has been dead these many years—a Gretna Green marriage will not do!" She transferred that glare to Beth. "Your credit won't stand any more scandal, as you certainly should know. And as for you"—that blistering look once more fell on Neil—"you should have known better than to have helped her to it! A fine bumble-bath this is! When word of this gets out, every door will be closed to you, Miss Sauce-mouth, and the pity of it is however well deserved such a catastrophe may be, we shall all be tainted by it!"

"The fault is entirely mine, Lady Salcombe." Neil stepped gamely into the breach in an attempt to draw the lady's fire from Beth.

"Of course it wasn't." Beth was having none of that. "It was my idea, and I had to talk him into it. Anyway, you have been after me to marry this age, Aunt Augusta."

"Not at Gretna Green!"

"There is no sense repining over what can't be helped." Her voice as soothing as cool water on a burn, Gabby smiled at him. "We are just so thankful to have Beth restored to us that a scandal seems a small price to pay."

"To you, maybe," Aunt Augusta said in the bitterest of accents. "I have borne much from you gels, but this—" She broke off, an arrested expression on her face. "Well. I have just now hit on the most famous notion, and now know how we may all come about. You are not breeding, are you?"

Even Neil blinked at this piece of plain speaking, which was addressed to Beth.

"I'm surprised at you, Aunt, for asking such an improper question!" Beth answered with a pert wrinkle of her nose, then as her aunt frowned direly tacked on a quick "No, certainly not."

"Then this is what we will do. We will say nothing to anyone about any marriage.

You must know, miss, that your sisters have given it out that you have taken to your bed with the influenza, from which you have supposedly been suffering most dreadfully. Rumors have certainly been flying to the contrary, but when you arise from your sickbed to rejoin the world, I am confident that we can put them to rest. Durham—if that is indeed who you are, sir!—must pretend to be an old friend of Richmond's, newly returned from foreign parts, who has just arrived to stay with him for a while. As far as the outside world is concerned, you two will meet, fall in love under the eyes of the ton, and be married by special license at the end of the Season. No word of Gretna Green need ever get out at all."

Lady Salcombe looked triumphantly around.

"How romantic everyone will think it!" Claire was the first to speak, though her eyes slid with some worry in them to Beth.

"It will serve, I think." Gabby's response was slower as she, too, looked at Beth. "Unless you dislike the scheme, of course, Beth."

"I must say, I think Lady Salcombe has

hit on the very thing, Miss Beth," Miss Twindlesham said with more enthusiasm. "'Tis better than owning to a Gretna Green marriage, I'll be bound."

"Why, I think so, too." Beth gave her aunt an approving nod. "I must say, I wasn't looking forward to the scandal, but I saw no way around it. How very knacky you are, Aunt Augusta!" As the old lady permitted herself a small smile, Beth's gaze shifted to Neil. "You don't object to the scheme, do you?"

"I know nothing of the matter," he said. "You must do as you see fit."

With those unwary words, his life was turned upside down.

By everyone save Richmond and, to a lesser extent, DeVane, both of whom clearly remained suspicious of him and seemed to take turns following him around, he was from that moment on treated as a friend of Richmond's and a house guest in town for what remained of the Season. He had his own apartment in Richmond House as far from Beth's as it was possible to get (he suspected that was deliberate), and was most bluntly told by Lady Salcombe that she had no wish to have the whole scheme undermined by servants' gossip or a pregnancy, and so he would oblige her by staying out of her niece's bedroom until the official wedding, which would, after all, take place in just a few weeks, so it was to be hoped he could contain himself. As Beth, having also been taken roundly to task by her aunt, agreed to the stricture, and he had no real objection to waiting since the ultimate outcome could not be in doubt, he was content to use that time to get his affairs in order and do his possible to fit into Beth's world.

Although he had been raised in accordance with his rank, he had never lived the life of a gentleman of the ton. It was, he discovered as he was introduced to it under the somewhat jaundiced wings of Richmond and DeVane, who seemed to be helpless to resist their wives' directives even though they were clearly unenthusiastic about the chore they had been set to perform, an exhausting and complicated business, and he could discover in himself no great liking for it. But, since it was, in fact, better than being hunted, as he recently had been, or even dead, he persevered, and shortly found himself in

possession of such an extensive wardrobe that he was embarrassed to own it, a
number of horses, including a perfectly
matched pair of sweet-goers designed to
draw his new curricle, and a valet. His
man of business—he had one of those,
too—was looking for a town house, with
every expectation (so he said) of achiev-
ing a happy result within a short period of
time, as well as a butler and other servants, possibly a dozen in all, to staff it.
Three maids—Mary, Peg, and Alyce, to
be precise, and mighty gleeful they were
about it, too—already had been personally engaged by Beth. Having discovered
on the morning after his and Beth's arrival at Richmond House that the gaggle
of gooseberries had been given houseroom
in the servants' quarters until such time as
other provision could be made for them,
Beth had been in her element, securing a
position in a most superior milliner's shop
for Dolly, finding work in an apothecary for
Nan, and dispatching Jane to be the companion of a dear old lady who lived near
Gabby's country home of Morningtide.
Mary still called him "yer worship"—though
with more respect in her voice now that

she had learned he was a genuine marquis and would be her employer—whenever she encountered him, but as neither she nor the others knew anything of his past beyond his rescue of them from Trelawney Castle, about which they had all agreed most fervently to say nothing, and because Beth desired it, he raised no objection to what Beth described to him happily as just the thing for them, and resigned himself to having them as a more or less permanent fixture in this new chapter of his existence.

A second chance: that was what DeVane had called it, but at some point in the process of resurrecting the almost forgotten Marquis of Durham, Neil realized that it was far more than that. He was embarking on a whole new life. Besides Claire and Gabby, to whom Beth had promptly confided the whole story—"Get accustomed to it; they tell each other everything" was Richmond's caustic advice when Neil expressed some dismay upon learning that Beth's sisters were in possession of the truth—no one outside himself, Beth, Richmond, and DeVane knew who and what he had been. The ruse had worked, according to Richmond; there seemed to be no suspicion in any of the circles Richmond had his ear to that the Angel of Death was not dead.

"Thank you," Neil felt compelled to say to him, when Richmond revealed this bit of news in the very library where he had first met Beth. He was fully though less than happily conscious of the fact that he owed both Richmond and DeVane a great deal.

"Believe me, 'twas done for Beth, not you."

"What of Clapham? He is the only one who could recognize me by sight, and I'd as soon keep track of his whereabouts for a while." The knowledge that Clapham could identify him made him only slightly uneasy. Although it had been made clear that Clapham bore a personal animosity toward him and would kill him with alacrity and with no need for government orders at all if given the chance, he had no real expectation of ever encountering him again. Still, many years of having to work hard to keep himself alive had taught him to be careful, and much as he'd disliked requesting anything of Richmond, he had, in fact, asked him to locate Clapham if he could and find out what new assignment he was working on.

"There was no way of discovering precisely where he is, but I was able to ascertain that he had turned his attention to eliminating another of your ilk."

Neil would like to have known more, but since it was Richmond, he was not about to say so.

"Again, I have to thank you," he said instead.

The look Richmond gave him was hard.

"Beth is my wife's little sister, and I count her as my own sister as well." They were both standing, this private meeting having been of the shortest duration, and Richmond moved past him toward the door as he spoke. "As long as you are good to her, and she is happy with it, the situation will stand."

The warning nature of that almost prompted Neil to a pithy reply, but he kept his tongue between his teeth, and from that point on something very like a truce existed between him and his unacknowledged, reluctant brothers-in-law.

It was not to be supposed that the banks

would just open his accounts to him after so many dormant years with no questions asked, so Neil had a good many meetings to go to in the city, and a number of persons he had to satisfy as to his identity. As he was, indeed, exactly who he claimed to be, not much difficulty attached to that beyond the tedium of it. Another, and to him far more important piece of business required him to slip out of Richmond House during the dead of night shortly after his arrival to pay a much-anticipated call. The unhappy object of that visit was William, Lord Rosen, and the outcome was that, having quickly confessed that he had, indeed, arranged for Beth's kidnapping, Rosen took himself off to the continent within just a few days of Beth's return to town. The alternative being death, as Neil had explained to him, he was almost embarrassingly eager to go. Had it not been for the certainty that Beth would not have wished him to do so, and would very likely have felt that she deserved some of the guilt for it when she learned of it, Neil would have killed him without a qualm. Instead, for Beth, he let Rosen go.

He had become well acquainted with

London's dark and seamy side over the years, but the fashionable world was as new to him as the wilds of the Colonies would have been. There was White's with its bow window, Watier's with its deep play, Gentleman Jackson's boxing establishment, Tattersall's for the acquisition of horses, shooting at Manton's Galleries, and Cribb's Parlour for imbibing Blue Ruin and other libations. Neil did little more than give these establishments a look-in, and shunned completely the lesser gaming houses with which the city was rife, as well as the elegant brothels, the cockpits and the hells, and the other, even seedier establishments in which all manner of vice might be found. He drank no more than was good for him, played some at piquet, and dice, and faro, winning more than he lost, and rode his new horses with real appreciation for their quality and the freedom to do so. With the Season in full swing, there were callers and card parties, balls and soirees, musicales and picnic suppers, opera and the theater, in seemingly endless procession, and his new incarnation as a typical London swell was too important to his survival for him to not play the role to the fullest. He was, to his be-musement, quickly dubbed a prize catch in the Marriage Mart, and matchmaking mamas with their debutante daughters in tow pursued him in numbers and with a dedication unrivaled in his experience. Finding himself catapulted into the treach-erous waters of the ton, he steeled himself to its demands and did his best to adapt to them. He submitted to the fashionable haircut recommended by his new valet, togged himself out in the snug-fitting coats, tight pantaloons, and mirror-bright Hessians that were de rigueur, and in general did his best to change his stripes to suit his surroundings. He received any number of instructions in what to do when, how to talk to whom, and other matters of general etiquette from Beth, who, he could tell, was deriving considerable amusement from his transformation. Since he found that he enjoyed her enjoyment, he was coopera-tive to the extent that, one bright sunny morning after arising from the breakfast table with the expressed intent of visiting his man of business, he found himself confronted instead with a dancing master who proposed to refresh him on such dances as the reel and the quadrille, which he had been taught as a youth, and to teach him the waltz.

Taking appalled measure of the dapper little man, whose attire consisted of a green coat, striped waistcoat, the tightest of yellow pantaloons, and shoes with pointed toes and heels, Neil almost balked. But having allowed Beth to wheedle him into the vast mirrored ballroom at the back of the house, and finding Miss Twindlesham at the piano already striking up a lively air, and Beth ready to cavort around the room with him under the interested eyes of her sisters, he surrendered to force majeure and got on with it. With Beth issuing nonstop instructions even as he held her in his arms, the dancing master demonstrating the steps with Claire, and Gabby, who he understood had a weak leg and thus rarely danced, clapping out the rhythm, Neil allowed himself to be tutored in the art of the dance. The chance to hold Beth close made up for a host of other ills, he discovered, and as a result he enjoyed himself far more than he expected.

This enjoyment lasted until, at a break

in the music, heavy-handed clapping from the doorway caused Neil to glance around and discover, to his chagrin, Richmond and DeVane standing just inside the door, watching. They were clearly a good deal entertained at what they had witnessed, and if he'd been Beth, he would have no doubt reacted by turning as red as the walls. Thankfully, he was not. He sketched them an ironic bow instead, and had his revenge as their wives fell upon them and dragged them onto the floor. The three couples then twirled most elegantly around the room—although he was loweringly aware that Beth was the only female counting out the time—until Graham interrupted with a sonorous announcement that callers had arrived.

"You did wonderfully," Beth said, beaming up at him. They were at the back of the room, in front of the long windows that overlooked the terrace and the garden, and the others had already begun to head for the hall. He held both her hands, looking down at her, surprised to find that he was reluctant for the session to end. Clad in a gown of lavender silk that was caught up with purple ribbons under her truly delectable bosom in such a way as to reveal the curvaceousness of her slender shape, with another purple ribbon threaded amongst her bright curls, smelling once again of the lavender scent he recalled from their first encounter, she was so lovely she took his breath. Had they been alone, he would have kissed her. As it was, he contented himself with raising both her hands to his lips and kissing them, one at a time.

"Very pretty," she approved with a twinkle. As he smiled down at her, he felt the weight of several pairs of eyes on him, and looked up to discover that they were being observed by everyone else, who had apparently turned back instead of proceeding out the door.

The expression on his face must have been something to see, because Claire, whose eyes caught his, suddenly broke into the sweetest of smiles.

"You learn very quickly," she said to him with approval. They were the first words she had addressed directly to him since he had made her acquaintance, and he bowed slightly in response.

"We must see to our guests," Richmond

said, his hand possessive as it settled at Claire's waist. She nodded and turned away. The party broke up, with Beth tucking her hand in the crook of his arm and pulling him along to the drawing room, where several eligible maidens and their mamas were amongst those waiting for them. That the females included one of this Season's reigning beauties, Miss Rockham, an ethereal blonde who had just attained her eighteenth year, and her mother, was a matter of little interest to Neil, although he was well aware they had him in their sights. The Rockhams had come ostensibly to call on Claire, whom they called "the dear duchess" in a most ingratiating way, and their presence was a source of considerable annoyance to his hostess and her elder sister, as he learned from a whispered comment from Claire to Gabby that he was not meant to overhear. But if Beth felt displeasure at Miss Rockham's presence, she did not show it. She was her usual animated self, vividly beautiful and vibrantly alive and the life of the gathering as always, which he would have appreciated more if there had not been a number of other gentlemen present who clearly also appreciated her charms. When Mr. Charles Hayden and the Earl of Cluny, who, he had learned, had been amongst the most assiduous of her suitors until Rosen had beaten them out, arrived and started paying her such extravagant compliments that she blushed and exclaimed, he decided that it was time to take himself off.

There was no need to stay and make a cake of himself, after all. The issue could not be in doubt, because in point of fact she was already his.

On other days, he took her driving in Hyde Park at the fashionable hour of five o'clock, escorted her to all the most modish shops and to Hookham's bookstore, and walked with her along Piccadilly, enjoying her company immensely even if he was denied her bed. But, in his guise as a friend of Richmond's, he could not live in her pocket, as the saying went, and this still left plenty of time for her to enjoy other pursuits, including, as he realized to his growing annoyance, the company of other men. Riding his new bay, Talavera, in Hyde Park with DeVane at his side, as they were both returning from a fencing session at

Angelo's that sent them along the promenade at the time it was most crowded, he was floored to discover, amongst the cavalcade of riders and carriages thronging the drive, his wife bowling toward him in a high-perch phaeton driven by Cluny, laughing gaily at something the fellow was saying.

When she saw them she waved in the friendliest of fashions, and clearly desired Cluny to pull up, which he did, holding his restive horses with a firm hand. To Neil's eyes, she was looking particularly beautiful in a severely cut riding habit of moss green velvet with a darker green velvet hat perched atop her fiery curls, her blue eyes sparkling, her complexion glowing in the fresh air.

"Nick! Durham!" She greeted them with a sunny smile as they pulled up their horses in turn. "Is not Cluny's carriage the most famous thing? He has offered to teach me how to drive it!"

Neil could feel himself stiffening. His hands tightened on the reins to the point where his horse sidled, and he immediately loosened his grip. The emotion that he struggled with was both new to him and notably unpleasant. It was a fight to keep the polite smile on his lips.

"Only if you permit, of course, DeVane," Cluny said, with an easy smile. He was a slender man of perhaps thirty-five, with a narrow, attractive face and sandy hair. His white drab driving coat was all the crack, as was the curly-brimmed beaver on his head. "Or should I apply to Richmond? When you are both in town, it's devilish hard to know."

His voice held a note of gentle complaint.

"Lady Elizabeth will do as she wishes, of course," DeVane said, while Neil met Beth's eyes. She gave him a quizzing look.

"What do you think, sir? Should I accept Lord Cluny's very obliging offer?"

"You must do as you think best, ma'am," he said. And tried very hard not to sound grim.

She laughed, then turned that dazzling smile on Cluny. "We are blocking traffic, my lord, and must move on! Good-bye, gentlemen, I'll see you at home!"

This last was called over her shoulder as Cluny was obliged by the press of vehicles behind him to drive on.

Neil and DeVane rode on, too. Neither of them said anything for a moment, although that unfamiliar emotion continued to plague Neil. He also did not much like the flicker of amusement he thought he saw in DeVane's eyes.

"She's as sound a girl as ever was made, you know," DeVane said at last. Then that lurking grin broke through. "But I must say I'm glad it's you, and not me, she's married to. I prophesy she'll lead you a pretty dance!"

Neil's mood was not helped by the fact that he and DeVane arrived at Richmond House in time to see Cluny press a kiss to Beth's knuckles as he handed her down from his carriage.

"Softly," DeVane said to him as they rode their horses around to the mews, and this time there was no mistaking the amusement in his voice. "'Tis, I've discovered, the best way to get over treacherous ground."

Though he wasn't in the mood to hear it at the moment it was given, DeVane's was, Neil realized, sound advice.

"A little too free with your favors earlier, my girl," was all he said when, later, looking ravishing in a gown of sky blue satin overlaid with some frothy pale lace, Beth came downstairs to join him in the hall, and they had the briefest of moments alone. He was engaged to accompany her, and Claire, and Richmond, and a party of their friends to the theater, no very great treat as far as he was concerned. But it gave him the chance to be in Beth's company, and though he hated to admit it, that was enough to recommend it to him.

"Oh, pooh! You are not talking about Cluny?" She laughed and looked up at him with a twinkle. "There was nothing in that! I wouldn't have thought you the type to be jealous, Neil."

"I know how to guard my own."

"Indeed?" Something about that appeared to displease her, because she tossed her head. "Perhaps this would be the moment to warn you that I will not *be* owned."

"Beth . . ."

The carriage pulled up to the door just then, and the others came out of the saloon to join them, and so no more was said. But the small dispute was not forgotten. Beth seemed determined to prove the truth of her assertion, and racketed about over the next few days with so many different suitors and such determined gaiety that Neil, observing, realized that such wildness was best left to spend itself unchecked, and set himself to presenting an unmoved facade in the face of much provocation.

Claire, for one, was not fooled. Three nights later found a number of their party at Almack's, that preserve of the haute ton where only the most select could hope to gain admittance. The fact that they admitted *him,* oblivious to everything about him save his birth and title, was, to Neil, much in the way of a private joke, sort of like letting a tiger in amongst pigeons. But he was there, nobly playing his role, although he could not be said to be enjoying it very much. The rooms were crowded and hot, the refreshments abysmal, the company flat, and the main amusement, dancing, was not one that suited his taste. With the last notes of a reel still hanging in the air, Neil had just returned his dance partner, a debutante whose name he had already forgotten, to her mama. On his way to the card room, that place of refuge for reluctant dancers, his attention was caught by Beth, who was as usual the lively center of a court of admirers. With white roses in the bright flame of her hair and the pearls around her neck and in her ears no more luminescent than her skin, she was breathtaking in a white spangled gown that clung to her shapely form in a most eye-opening way. Many of the old tabbies with which the room was rife eyed her with disapproval, and several younger ladies watched her with chagrin while whispering to one another behind their hands. Unless he wished to join her court—he did not!—he could do no more than admire her beauty from a distance as she laughingly bestowed a blossom each from the posy of white roses some admirer had sent her on two swains, before taking the arm of a third and allowing him to lead her into the set that was at that moment forming.

That unpleasant emotion—jealousy, there, he'd given it its name, though admitting he was troubled by it bothered him worse than all of the bullet wounds he had suffered combined—raised its ugly head again as he watched Beth glancing coquettishly up at her partner while playfully dusting something off the lapels of his coat.

Apparently Claire was not fooled by the bland expression he had thought he was maintaining while observing this most affecting tableau. Appearing beside him as he—instead of retreating as he had intended—folded his arms over his chest and took up a position against one wall to watch the quadrille that was just being struck up, she touched his arm. When he looked down at her in surprise, not having seen her come up to him, she nodded toward Beth, who was now pirouetting prettily in a movement of the dance while she laughed up at her partner. Annoyed at himself, he realized that he had been following the blasted chit with his eyes the whole while.

"She is used to being very popular, you know. You should not regard it."

"I don't, I assure you."

Claire looked up at him rather shyly. Her beauty was undeniable, and it registered on him in that moment simply because he was a male, but having already been thoroughly dazzled by her sister, he noted it merely in passing as his gaze slid back to Beth.

Claire persevered. "Being married—she has always feared it, I think."

"So she told me. Also why, a little. Forgive me, but from the sound of it you three had a wretched childhood."

"Did she tell you about that? In the normal way of things, she will never speak of how we grew up. Only very rarely to me, or Gabby, who of course share her memories. You should consider yourself honored by her confidence."

"I do."

"Then, too, she has been enduring rather a lot at the hands of some of the high sticklers these last few weeks, you know. I have no doubt that she means to show them that she is just as 'fast' as they say. To do the very thing that she shouldn't is absolutely Beth."

Realizing that she was attempting to paint her sister's behavior in the best possible light for him, Neil smiled down at her. "Are you trying to defend her to me? There's no need. Her courage, and her defiance in the face of adversity, are two of the things I most admire about her."

Claire met his gaze and smiled, too. "Do

you know, I begin to think that you and Beth will do very well together, my lord."

"I intend that we shall, Your Grace."

"We are family. I am Claire. And I hope you won't object if I call you Neil?"

Neil laughed. "I won't, but I'd give a monkey to hear Richmond's views on the subject."

"Hugh is very protective of my sisters and me. As soon as he realizes that Beth will be happy with you, he'll come around, believe me."

Polite clapping broke out on all sides as the music stopped. With the best will in the world not to do it, Neil continued to watch Beth as she was once again swallowed up by a crowd of admirers. She was in great beauty, her eyes sparkling, her cheeks flushed, her bright head tipped a little to one side as she listened to something one of them was saying.

"How came you to let that dratted girl leave the house looking like that?" Lady Salcombe hissed. Looking very put out, she had just joined Claire, to whom that remark had been addressed. Neil hadn't even noticed her advent until he heard her fierce whisper. "Everyone is talking, and I declare I'm ready to sink with mortification. *Anyone* can tell that her petticoats are damped."

Though he caught only a hint of the movement out of the corner of his eye, Neil was ready to swear that Claire committed the considerable solecism of elbowing Lady Salcombe in the ribs.

"Hush, Aunt!"

He pushed away from the wall. Claire's gaze turned to him, faintly apprehensive. He smiled reassuringly at her.

"Excuse me, ladies," he said. "I believe I must not miss this dance."

Chapter Thirty-one

BETH DID NOT *CARE* that they were talking about her, the young ladies and their mamas and the starchy matrons and staid dowagers. She did not *care* about the sidelong looks or the whispers that seemed to follow her like a sibilant hiss wherever she went. She did not *care* that several ladies, including William's odious sister, Lady Dreyer, had given her the cut direct when she had encountered them over the three weeks since she'd been back in London, or that that old cat Mrs. Drummond-Burrell, the haughtiest of Almack's patronesses, had greeted her with a frosty stare tonight. She

did not *care* about the rumors, which her
cousins, Maud, Countess of Wickham,
and her pie-faced daughters, Desdemona
and Thisby, had been kind enough to re-
count during a morning call two weeks
before. She did not *care* that, as Cousin
Maud told her and Claire and Gabby with
the concerned air of one imparting painful
but necessary information, stories were
flying about the ton to the effect that her
bout with influenza was nothing but a
hum, and that what had really happened
was an elopement that had been thwarted,
or, alternatively, that she had run away to
a love nest with a most unsuitable man and
been forcibly brought back, or even disappeared briefly to bear a love-child, now
given away.

She did not *care* that she now found
herself watched, and judged, and disap-
proved of everywhere she went. She did
not *care* that the highest sticklers were
saying of her that she was not quite the
thing. She did not *care* that the latest on-
dit had it that her shocking behavior was
why Rosen had not in the end come up to
scratch, as well as being the reason why,
despite the numbers of her suitors, she

was, at the end of her third Season, on the verge of being left on the shelf.

She did not *care* that behind her back she was being called an outrageous flirt, a shameless baggage, and shockingly fast.

And most of all, she did not care that Neil, far from needing her help and guidance to find his place in the ton as she had thought he might, by now seemed at home to a peg in his new surroundings, and was causing quite a stir amongst the ladies to boot. In fact, Richmond House was quite overrun with females hoping to attach him. Cousin Thisby, with a malicious little smile, had been only the first of the ladies of Beth's acquaintance who had taken care to warn her that people were saying that it would be a sad thing if she, at her age, with her reputation, were to set her cap at Durham, taking advantage of his presence in her household to try to compete with all the fresh young debutantes from whom the dashing marquis might choose a bride.

In fact, she cared so little for all of this that she was making devilish sure to be just as outrageous and fast as they thought her, and to encourage her admirers to the point where no one could suspect her of having lost her heart to Neil, as she was very much afraid she had done. Most of all, she wanted to keep her guilty secret from Neil. Her pride was too great for her to be able to endure the thought that he should know that she had somehow or other accidentally tumbled into love with him, unless and until she could be sure he loved her back. And he had given no indication of that.

Which is why, knowing herself to be the cynosure of a great many eyes, including Neil's, she permitted Mr. Hayden to brush his fingers over her shoulders, which were laid bare by the small dropped sleeves of her prodigiously elegant gown, under the pretext that he had clumsily dropped cake crumbs on them. Which is why she laughingly straightened the rosebud she had bestowed on the Earl of Cluny, which he had chosen to wear as a boutonniere. Which was why she agreed to dance the waltz that was just striking up with Lord Vincent Davenport, one of the ton's most notorious rakes, who had been pursuing her in his desultory fashion for years.

Which is why she responded with a

brilliant smile and a gay "You are too late, my lord" to Neil when he showed up scant seconds later to say in the most peremptory fashion, "My dance, I think."

"Not at all," he replied with aplomb, detaching her from Lord Vincent by the simple expedient of removing her hand from that affronted gentleman's arm and swinging her onto the dance floor and into his arms.

"That was very ill done of you." She gave him her quick frown even as he whirled her away. The feel of his strong hand clasping hers and his hard arm around her waist was so familiar that she could not help but relax a little, even though she was perfectly aware that their progress was being followed by a good portion of the people in the room. With her hand on his wide shoulder and his honed body only inches away, she felt strangely comforted. Strangely, because she had not known until that moment that comforting was what she needed.

"On the contrary, it was very well done," he replied with a laugh. "I only hope your gentleman friend will not see fit to later call me out."

"I doubt there is any fear of that." Her grudging tone was leavened by reluctant admiration. The severe black coat and knee breeches that were the only accepted attire for gentlemen to wear at Almack's suited his tall, broad-shouldered form to perfection. They certainly showed off his muscular frame, which was imposing enough to make it unlikely that Lord Vincent, many inches shorter and many pounds heavier, or, indeed, anyone else, would relish incurring his displeasure. For the rest, the arrangement of his cravat was elegant, and his shirt points, although moderate in height, were nicely starched. His swarthy skin contrasted most attractively with the snowiness of his linen. With his now modishly cut black hair waving back from his hard, handsome face, he should have looked every inch the gentleman, and he did. But there was something in his expression, and bearing, that made him appear at the same time different from all the other gentlemen in the room. He looked too untamed for his surroundings, that was it, like a man who would be, to quote something recently said about Lord Byron, mad, bad, and dangerous to know.

But he was Neil, after all, and while un-like Byron he might actually *be* danger-ous, he could never seem so to her. She enjoyed his company, and his conversa-tion, and yes, blast it, his lovemaking. His advent into her life had changed it, and her, forever. As she had most reluctantly come to realize over the course of the last few weeks, in his arms was now the only place where she truly felt at home.

Not that she meant to reveal it to him or anyone by look, word, or deed.

"All the unmarried young ladies in this room are giving me dagger looks, you know, and wishing me at Jericho," she added care-lessly. "You are looking very handsome, by the by."

"Thank you. Allow me to return the com-pliment: you look spectacular. Did you, by the way, damp your petticoats?"

Her eyes flashed. "From which of the old cats did you hear that?"

He swung her around in the movement of the dance so that her skirt belled out around her legs and she had to cling to him to keep her balance.

"Suffice it to say that a rumor of it reached my ears. Is it true?"

Her chin came up. "Yes, indeed."

"Very fetching."

"Is that all you have to say?"

His brows went up. "What else would I have to say?"

"You are not shocked?"

"Dazzled, rather."

"Oh, you." Her smile was quick, and a little tremulous. "They are saying I am on the catch for you, you know."

"Are they indeed?" He smiled. "Take comfort in the knowledge that in just a short time now they will be saying you have caught me."

"Perhaps I don't wish to have caught you."

His hand tightened on hers.

"Too late for that, my girl," he said, and twirled her with a surprising degree of dexterity around two other couples.

"I am beginning to think I will miss all this—the flirting, the attention—when it becomes known I am an old married lady."

"I have every confidence that you will adapt."

"And what if I don't wish to adapt?"

"I sincerely hope we neither of us have to find out."

"Oh, ho! Are you threatening me, sir?"

"Certainly not. You know I would never threaten you. If the situation should ever arise, I would merely make certain that you were far too busy—or tired—to have the least interest in other men. I would chain you to my bed, in fact."

"And that is not a threat?"

"I would call it, rather, a delightful promise."

Beth could feel heat stinging her cheeks at the images this conjured up. Over his shoulder, she encountered the censorious gaze of a young lady who was also dancing: Miss Emily Granville, a pretty debutante who with her mama had made several calls to Richmond House in pursuit of Neil. Beth smiled mockingly at her.

"You are putting me to the blush," she said to Neil as he swung her out of Miss Granville's orbit. "Everyone must guess that you are saying the most shocking things to me."

"I feel that they will rather put your delightful rosiness down to the exertions of the dance. Only you and I can know that I am saying shocking things to you." He smiled at her. "And they are only shocking because you have not yet got used to the idea that we are married."

"Have you?"

"I am growing accustomed."

"You cannot wish to be married," she said, a tad pettishly.

"Whether I wish it or not, or you wish it or not, makes no difference. The deed has been done, and can't now be undone."

"We are stuck with each other, in fact." Her voice was flat.

"Something of the sort." The music ended, and Beth stepped quickly out of his arms when he would have held her longer. He frowned at her. His voice was low. "Beth . . ."

But whatever he had been going to say was lost as Cluny appeared out of the crowd and gave a curt nod to Neil.

"Servant, Durham," he said, then smiled at Beth, offering his arm. "Mine is the next dance, I think."

"It is indeed," she agreed gaily, and placing her hand on his arm, she allowed him to lead her away without a backward look.

For the rest of the evening, she was at her sparkling best. She laughed and chatted, flirted and danced, and in general seemed to be having a marvelous time. What she didn't do was dance again with Neil, who in any case seemed to have disappeared, or respond with more than a toss of her head and a smile to Claire's whispered demand to be told what in heaven's name was the matter with her, or attend to Aunt Augusta's quelling glares and grimaces with more than a hunched shoulder and a deliberate glance away.

The knowledge that Neil was prepared to make the best of their marriage stung worse than anything she could have imagined. It bruised her heart, and flicked her pride, and made her wild.

Eventually, so much vivacity took its toll. She developed a headache. Escaping to the ladies' withdrawing room, she washed her hands, then, shooing away the attendant, bathed her temples in cool water, which helped. Finally emerging into the dim hallway that led back into the ballroom, she discovered Cluny waiting for her.

"I saw you go in," he said by way of explaining his presence. "I thought you looked pale, and stayed in case you should wish me to fetch your sister to you."

"I missed our dance, didn't I?" She rec-
ollected that it was to him she had promised the boulanger, the last notes of which
she could hear just fading away. Holding
out her hand to him, she gave him her bright
smile. "I do beg your pardon. I seem to
have most stupidly developed a headache."

"Shall I go for your sister?"

She shook her head. "I'm better now,
thank you."

He took her hand and pulled it through
the crook of his arm, but instead of escort-
ing her back to the ballroom, he stayed
where he was, putting his hand under her
chin and turning her face up to his. His gentle blue eyes swept over her face. Then,
before she knew what he meant to do, he
pressed his mouth to hers. His lips were
warm and firm, and a little dry.

She was so surprised that in that first instant she remained unmoving. A gasp from
somewhere close at hand made her start,
and recoil. Cluny's lips no longer touched
hers; indeed, like she, he had already
stepped back and was looking around toward the source of the sound.

Claire stood there, just inside the hallway,

looking stricken, with her bronze silk cloak tied over her sumptuous amber gown, doing her best with her slender person to block the view of those behind her. But Aunt Augusta, who was also wearing her cloak, was too tall to have her vision blocked, and her puce face and bulging eyes told Beth that she had seen all. Taller still was Neil. He stood in the doorway behind Aunt Augusta, as still as if he had been carved from stone. His jaw was set, and his mouth had an ugly twist to it that she had not seen there before. The look in his eyes sent a shiver racing down her spine.

"I brought you your cloak—you looked as though you weren't feeling well—I thought you were probably ready to go home." Poor Claire was the first to break the silence, and Beth saw that her blue cloak with its swansdown trimming indeed lay over her sister's arm.

"It was my fault." Cluny's voice was jerky. "I beg your pardon most earnestly, Lady Elizabeth. Your Grace, please inform your husband that I will call on him tomorrow, with the object of asking permission to pay my addresses to your sister."

"Oh, no," Beth said. Tearing her eyes away from Neil's was difficult, but she did it and managed a rallying smile for Cluny, who was looking rather pale himself. "You must not offer for me, because we would not suit, as you must know very well. You've no need to look so guilty! It was only a very little kiss, after all. I would prefer to forget it, if you please."

Cluny's lips compressed, and then he bowed. "If that is what you wish."

"Oh, for heaven's sake, let us get out of this hallway before someone else comes this way." Aunt Augusta sounded as if she labored under a severe strain. "Claire, hand Beth her cloak. My nerves can take no more. We *shall* go home."

More than ready to fall in with Aunt Augusta's wishes, Beth moved, heading for the doorway. Claire, falling in beside her, draped the cloak around Beth's shoulders and tucked her hand in her arm. This silent gesture of support was accompanied by a quick, apprehensive look at Neil's face, after which Claire hurried into speech.

"Richmond is playing cards, so we will leave him, I believe. Durham, if you would be so kind as to tell him we have gone home, I would appreciate it. You two can take a hackney, perhaps, or a chair. Or—"

"I'll take the message to Richmond, and we will both manage to get home." Neil broke in on this nervous speech as he stepped back into the ballroom to let them pass, Beth and Claire first, with Aunt Augusta and Cluny bringing up the rear. "Don't trouble yourself about it, Your Grace, or anything else."

Beth, giving him a quick look as she walked past him, saw that his face was utterly expressionless now, and she was maddeningly conscious of feeling a little nervous herself. Then she straightened her shoulders and stiffened her spine and gave him a defiant stare. If Neil didn't like what he had witnessed, then all she could say was he must look away. She would not study to please him, no matter how grim he looked.

He left them then, she supposed, to carry Claire's message to Hugh. Cluny melted away into the crowd, and she, Claire, and Aunt Augusta were left to climb into the barouche, which had already been brought round to the door.

Once inside, Beth threw herself into a

corner, resting her head back against the sumptuously upholstered squab and closing her eyes. This did not prevent her from having a peal rung over her, as she had known must happen. No sooner did the carriage lurch into motion than Aunt Augusta launched into speech.

"Well. You have certainly gone your length tonight, miss. I declare I was positively in an agony of embarrassment over your conduct! To appear—at Almack's of all places—in that shocking gown! To damp your petticoats—and don't you tell me you did not! To positively invite the attentions of every gentleman in the place! To behave with such an utter lack of decorum, such a disregard for your own reputation—which can't bear much more, as well you know!—such a want of concern for my feelings, or your sister's, or, indeed, those of anyone who wishes you well! You might as well have tied your garter in public as behave as you did tonight! Then to let Cluny kiss you! And Durham to see! Well. 'Twill serve you right if you come by your just deserts at last, and that is all I have to say!"

But it wasn't, of course. Beth kept her

eyes shut and maintained her silence as a scant moment later another wave of recriminations broke over her.

"Never would I have believed it if someone had told me this was how we would end up. Ashamed as I am to admit it, I can no longer avoid facing the fact that you are, just as everyone is saying, an incorrigible flirt. And if anyone knew the truth! You are married, Beth, married! For a married woman to behave so with a man who is not her husband is *not done*. It would ruin you if word of it ever got out! And Durham—did you see his face? I would not play fast and loose with such a man were I you, missy. And I imagine he will have a few words to say to you presently himself. Did you—"

"Pray stop, Aunt Augusta," Claire intervened wearily. "You have said quite enough. If Cluny overstepped the line tonight, it was not Beth's fault."

"I make every allowance for your natural partiality for your sister, Claire, but . . ."

Beth opened her eyes. Gentle-natured Claire would defend her to her last breath, she knew, but the battle was hers. "It's all right, Claire. I am sorry if I embarrassed you, Aunt Augusta, and I will endeavor to behave better in the future. There, how is that?"

Aunt Augusta snorted. "If you think to turn me up sweet with that paltry excuse for an apology—"

The carriage jolted to a halt. Aunt Augusta broke off in surprise. The journey to Richmond House usually took twice as long.

"This is your house, Aunt Augusta. I instructed John Coachman to set you down first," Claire said as the door was opened and the steps were let down.

"Well." Aunt Augusta stood up. "You are fortunate in your sisters, is all I can say, Elizabeth." And with that parting shot, she took the hand the footman held up to her and descended majestically into Berkeley Square.

"I must say, that was very clever of you, Claire," Beth said when the door was closed and they were once again on their way.

"Oh, I knew she would scold."

The inside of the carriage was dark save for flashes of light as they passed the street lamps that illuminated many of the corners and squares, but she could see that Claire was regarding her with worry in her eyes.

Beth sighed. "I behaved very badly to-night, didn't I?"

"Not so very badly."

Beth gave her sister a wry smile. "Yes, I did, and I know it. Indeed, I meant to!"

"Oh, Beth, why? I knew there was some-thing wrong. I've known it for a while. Is it that you are married? If you are regretting it, you can tell me so, and perhaps—perhaps something can be done."

"Nothing can be done—and I am not regretting it. Precisely. Oh, don't worry about me! I will come about."

"Is it Neil? I like him, you know, and I was beginning to feel that you would suit most wonderfully. But it is easy to forget his past, and what he was. If you are afraid of him, Bethie, pray tell me."

Beth gave a little laugh. "I am not in the least afraid of him."

Claire looked at her earnestly. "He did not like to see Cluny kissing you. I am afraid— Oh, Beth, shall I have Hugh send him away? I fear he means to confront you about it, and . . . and . . ." Her voice trailed off, but it was clear that visions of beatings and worse danced in her head. Once again Beth was reminded of Claire's terrible first marriage, and she felt a wave of protectiveness toward her sister.

"He will not ill use me, Claire, I give you my word, however angry he may be. Despite his past, he is very much the gentleman, I promise you."

Claire frowned. "Then why on earth are you behaving as you have been? Aunt Augusta was a deal too harsh, but she was somewhat in the right of it, you know. You have been positively encouraging Cluny as well as a great number of other gentlemen to dangle after you. I don't quite understand, since you are wed to Neil and say you don't wish to undo it—"

"He doesn't love me," Beth broke in quietly, the pain in her heart spilling over under her sister's compassionate eyes. "He is all that is kind to me, and says he is perfectly content to be married to me, but—Oh, Claire, I want him to love me! The way Hugh loves you. The way Nick loves Gabby. I want to be the most important thing in his life. I want him to think the sun rises and sets in me. I want—I want him to love me madly! And the sad truth is, he does not."

"Beth . . ." Whatever Claire was going to say was lost as the carriage clattered to a stop in front of Richmond House. Following her sister down the steps and into the house, Beth, already sorry she had said so much, handed her cloak to Graham, who had already taken Claire's, and made desultory conversation for the benefit of the servants as she and Claire went together up the grand staircase.

"If he does not love you, he will." As they reached Beth's bedchamber, Claire stopped and took Beth's hand. Her quiet voice was fierce. "No one who knows you could not love you, so you need have no fear of that."

"You are the best of sisters, Claire." Beth squeezed Claire's hand affectionately and let it drop.

Claire still looked troubled. "Shall I come in with you?"

"No. I don't need you. Besides, Twindle is waiting for you, and if you come in with me, you will undoubtedly bring her down on us both. That I don't think I could face tonight." She smiled at Claire and turned to open her own door, saying over her shoulder, "Go on to bed, goose."

Claire appeared to see the force of Beth's argument, because she made no further protest, instead heading for her own chamber as Beth went into her room, which, she saw at a glance, was in the process of being prepared for the night. The bed-clothes on the big mahogany bed were turned down, the fire crackled, and a can of water waited on the hearth near it, un-doubtedly to keep warm until such time as she arrived. Her nightgown and wrapper had been flung over the back of one of the pair of big wing chairs that stood before the hearth; doubtless the intent had been to lay them out in the dressing room where they belonged, but that intent had not yet been carried out. Mary, whom she was training to be her own personal maid against the day when, as Marchioness of Durham, she would move into her own es-tablishment and leave Claire's servants behind, was most improperly seated in the other chair, her eyes closed, her head drooping against the wing, her arms hang-ing limply over the sides. Beth got just a quick look, because as soon as the door closed behind her Mary's eyes popped open. Seeing Beth, she sprang at once to her feet, giving a twitch to her black silk skirts and straightening the fine lace cap on her head even as she greeted her mistress.

"Be ye 'ome, then, miss? Did ye 'ave a grand time? Eh, ye look a right treat." Not having yet quite gotten over her delight at discovering Beth was a real lady, the daughter of an earl, the sister of a duke, Mary was quick and devoted, but still getting the hang of her newly elevated station.

"Thank you, Mary." As tired and dispirited as she was, Beth managed a smile for Mary as she headed for her dressing room. "If you could just help me out of this gown, we can both be off to bed."

"Looks like ye'd be wantin' me to brush yer 'air out for ye, and rub lotion into yer 'ands, and mebbe ring down for some hot milk to help ye to sleep. I'll 'ave ye know that that's the sort o' thing a proper lady's maid should do, so I been told." Coming up to stand behind her as Beth stopped in front of the tall pier glass at the end of the dressing room and kicked off her delicate dancing slippers, Mary shot a reproving look at her through the mirror.

"All I want is to be out of this gown so I may go to bed."

"Tired, are ye? No surprise in that, the way ye've been gaddin' about to all hours lately." Mary unfastened Beth's pearl necklet for her as she spoke. Removing the earbobs from her ears and handing them over to be stowed away with the necklet in the jewelry chest in the corner, Beth stifled a sigh. As fond as she was of Mary, she had a tendency to speak her mind that Beth sometimes felt was a most regrettable trait.

"Just unfasten my dress, Mary, would you please?"

Mary returned to get started on the dozens of tiny pearl buttons that did her gown up in the back. "Did ye get aught of supper, then? They was sayin' belowstairs that ye didn't eat so much as a bite afore ye went out."

"I had plenty to eat. Mary . . ."

But what she was going to say was lost as they both heard, at the same time, the unmistakable sound of her bedroom door being opened and then closed again.

Before they could do more than exchange surprised glances through the mirror, a firm tread could be heard crossing the bedroom floor. Clapping a hand to her bosom to hold the now partly unfastened dress in place, Beth turned to face the doorway just as Neil appeared in it. His mouth was hard, and his eyes were the gleaming black jet that she had learned meant trouble.

Chapter Thirty-two

WHY BETH WAS SURPRISED by his visit, she didn't know. Clearly, she saw in retrospect, she should have expected him.

His gaze raked her, but neither of them had a chance to say anything because Mary was before them both, hurrying toward him, making imperious little shooing motions with her hands.

"I dunno what ye think yer doing in 'ere, but ye've no business in Miss Beth's bedchamber, and that ye know as well as I do, yer worship. And there's no manner of sense in ye giving me the evil eye, either, acause I know what's right and what's expected as well as the next person." Having nearly reached him, Mary stopped, put her fists to her hips, and glared, because it became obvious that he was not going to be shooed away.

"I need to have private speech with Miss Beth, Mary." He stepped out of the doorway and into the dressing room, leaving the way clear for her to depart. "You may go on to bed now."

"Hah! No chance o' that! If you think I be goin' to abandon—"

"It's all right, Mary. Please leave us," Beth said. Neil's eyes met hers again, and she held that hard glance without a flinch.

"But, miss, your gown be 'alf undone, and—" Mary said in a scandalized undertone.

"Go, Mary," Beth said.

Mary looked from her to Neil and back, and her expression turned aggrieved. "If ye say so, miss, I'll go, but ye know as well as I do that this ain't a bit respectable. And as for ye, yer worship, I'd take shame on forcing myself into a lady's bedroom." As Beth did not relent, but instead gestured at her to be gone, Mary moved with obvious reluctance out of the dressing room, expostulating all the way. Neil followed her, and for a moment Beth stood as if rooted, listening to Mary's fading protests. "This be the 'ome of a real, 'onest-to-goodness *duke,* ye ken, not some 'urly-burly establishment where anything might 'appen. 'Tis all very well for ye to behave so free with miss when we was all trapped in a cave, but—"

The sound of the bedroom door opening and then closing again cut Mary off in mid-spiel. The click of the lock shooting home startled Beth out of her stillness, and she turned to face the mirror, still holding her loosened gown up with one hand pressed to her bosom. A glance at her reflection told her that she was wide-eyed and pale, nervous-looking, even, so she lifted her head and firmed her lips and was in the process of using her free hand to disengage the rose from the bright waves of her hair when Neil came back into the room.

"I take it you've come to rake me down?" Beth asked coolly as Neil came up behind her, looking very tall and dark and formidable as she viewed him through the mirror. The rose came free, and she set it aside on the small table that was within reach of her left hand.

He laughed, and his hands closed over her bare shoulders. They were warm, with the suggestion of calluses on the palms and pads of his fingers, and she was acutely conscious of their size and strength. Their eyes met through the mirror.

"You're very brave, Madame Roux, I'll give you that."

"You don't frighten me, if that's what you mean."

"You've made that very clear."

His hands left her shoulders. She shivered involuntarily as she felt a warm finger trail down her back.

"What the blazes do you think you're doing?" she asked sharply, unable to see.

"Unbuttoning your gown. That's what Mary was doing, wasn't she?"

She drew in a quick breath as he took hold of the sides of her bodice and gave them a less-than-gentle tug to bring the edges together sufficiently for him to free the first button. Her heart, she discovered, was beating way too fast. Her knees felt unaccountably weak. She could feel his hands moving down her spine, and the tiny buttons falling prey to them at an alarming pace.

"And what if I were to tell you to stop, and go away?"

"You could try it, and then we'd see."

"I tell you to your head, I have no intention of explaining my conduct to you."

"Have I asked for an explanation? Let go of your gown."

With the last button undone, the fragile garment sagged. Only her hand pressed to her bosom kept it from dropping at her feet.

"Let go of your gown, Beth," he said again, very softly, his hands sliding inside the opening he had made to rest on either side of her slim waist. She could feel them clear through the layers of her shift and stays.

Their eyes met in the mirror. At what she saw in the glinting black depths, her breath caught. Her heart fluttered. Holding his gaze defiantly, she nevertheless allowed the gown to drop and stepped out of its gleaming folds.

"That's my girl." As he shoved the garment aside with his foot, Beth was left to look at herself in the mirror. The creamy globes of her breasts spilled over the gossamer top of her chemise, and beneath them her stays closely hugged her rib cage and nipped her in at the waist until the circumference was so impossibly small that the big, dark hands that rested so possessively there could probably have spanned it. Below her stays, the single petticoat she had most scandalously dampened hours earlier, though dry now, still clung tenaciously to her legs so that their outline and slender shape might be clearly seen.

He said, "I see a damped petticoat works best when you're wearing only one."

He was looking at her through the mirror, too, she saw, and felt her cheeks begin to heat as his eyes lingered on her legs. His hands tightened on her waist, and her heart pounded, and her mouth went dry. Then his gaze moved to something behind her back, and his hands moved, too, and she felt him untying the knots that held her stays.

"If you have something to say to me, I wish you would say it and have done." Her tone was cross as she felt the knot come free and her stays loosened.

"What would I have to say to you?"

Her stays fell into his hands. Dropping

them on the floor, he reached for the tapes of her single petticoat.

"It's perfectly clear that you are angry about . . . what you saw."

The petticoat dropped next, to be stepped out of and shoved aside. She was left to face the mirror in nothing but the filmy chemise that ended at the tops of her thighs and the white silk stockings that were tied up with blue garters above her knees. To her mingled shock and dismay, she felt her nipples tighten and saw that they now jutted wantonly through the thin fabric. Watching his eyes slide over her, she felt the beginnings of the hot, sweet quickening he had ignited in her before, and fought the urge to wet her lips. That he meant to undress her down to the skin now seemed perfectly clear. At the thought, her breathing grew erratic and her fingers curled into impotent fists. She didn't know whether to stop this right now or not. She didn't know if she wanted to stop it. She didn't know if she could.

"Let us be precise, if you please. Cluny kissing you is what you're referring to."

Crouching behind her, he slid a stocking down her leg, garter and all. Through the mirror, Beth looked at his dark, bent head, and the breadth of his shoulders, and the powerful lines of his arms and legs, and felt her pulse go haywire.

"Step out," he told her in an aside as the stocking reached her ankle, and she did.

"Very well, then, it's perfectly clear that you're angry about Cluny kissing me." She kept her head high and her voice strong as he did the same to her second stocking. The feel of his warm fingers sliding so intimately down her bare leg sent swarms of electricity coursing over her skin.

"You will at least own that I have every right to be angry."

He straightened as he spoke, and their eyes met again in the mirror. He moved closer to her until she could feel his big body against her back. His hands slid slowly down her arms and back up again.

With his gaze on her, she barely repressed a shiver.

"I do not own that at all," she said, her voice a cold counterpoint to the waves of heat that now undulated inside her.

"Then your notion of how a wife—particularly my wife—is expected to conduct herself as regards other men needs some adjusting." His hands closed without warning on the hem of her chemise, and he pulled it up and over her head. "But then, we haven't been married very long, have we? I've no doubt you'll soon get in the way of it."

"I don't . . ."

As she caught the first shocking look at herself in the mirror sans chemise, what she had been going to say was lost. Her immediate impulse was to jerk free of the black-clad arm that was now curved firmly around her waist and find something, anything, with which to cover herself.

"No, don't pull away from me." There was a sudden husky undertone to his voice that caused her loins to clench and release in a hot, convulsive rhythm. The arm circling her waist tightened, but there was no need. After that first abortive attempt, she didn't try to get away from him again. "Look in the mirror."

She looked, heart pounding, at herself standing there naked in front of him, facing the mirror and held in place by his hard arm circling her waist. Then she looked past herself to his tall form, still fully clad in the evening clothes he'd worn to Almack's, so much larger and stronger than she was that the idea of any physical contest between them was laughable, and met his eyes.

"Is this how you mean to use your wife, then?" Rallying her forces, she had indignation in her voice.

"Unless you object to it. Do you?" Warm and hard, his hand covered her breast, caressed it.

Dizzy with the sudden sharp wanting he had wakened, remembering against her will the dark, unbelievably arousing way he had used her before, Beth bit down on her lower lip, unable to deny the hot, molten longing that seemed poised to make her as wax in his hands.

"No, damn you."

"Don't swear."

As he continued to caress her breasts, playing with her nipples, stroking and cupping and rubbing the creamy, strawberry-tipped globes, she watched through the mirror with widening eyes and parting lips. She couldn't speak. She could scarcely breathe. By the time his other hand slid down between her legs to fondle her there, she was leaning bonelessly back against him, her head resting against his broad shoulder, her eyes slightly glazed as she watched him pleasuring her, a flush in her cheeks, her lips clamped resolutely together against the soft little moans that crowded against them, which she refused to demean herself by letting him hear.

Observing and at the same time participating as he awakened the most unbelievable sensations inside her was more erotic than anything she had ever imagined existed in this life.

"You were made for loving, Beth. We could deal extremely, you and I." His voice was thick. His tongue traced deliciously along the shell-like curve of one ear and delved inside. Then he pressed a line of tiny burning kisses down the sensitive cord at the side of her neck. Her legs had turned to jelly, and she was now moving in helpless, burning response to the ministrations of his knowing hands. At some point he'd shrugged out of his coat and waistcoat, and she saw with a slightly fuzzy glance back at him that he'd removed his cravat as well. She could feel the hard swelling of him pressing close against her bottom. He was big with desire. His eyes glittered with it. His hands were unsteady with it.

"I won't be ruled by you." As a warning, she realized it lost something because her voice was made breathless and husky by passion. She felt dizzy, and burning hot, and on the verge of that elusive something he seemed to rouse so easily in her. Just the thought of finally reaching it made her shiver with anticipation. She wanted, wanted . . . him.

His eyes sliding over her face, he first stilled his hands for the briefest of moments, then removed them altogether, completely distracting her. As one of those shameful little moans escaped her after all in protest, he turned her to face him.

"You can rule me, then. How does that suit? I find I've no objection whatsoever to the thought of living under the cat's paw, as long as the cat is you."

"Liar," she said. Pinning his eyes with hers, she wrapped her arms around his neck and melted against him.

He laughed and found her mouth, and then passion exploded so fiercely between them that conversation was at an end. He bore her down to the expensive Aubusson carpet that covered the dressing room floor and kissed her in places she had never imagined she would ever be kissed and put that huge, hot part of himself inside her and made love to her until she had forgotten everything but him, until she was so mindless with need that she moaned and clung and cried out his name with abandon, until finally he showed her what that something was she had felt herself on the verge of for so long. He loved her until she learned firsthand what ecstasy was all about, until the hot, burning quaking inside her finally broke and she was borne away by the fierceness of her own response, until a fiery whirlwind caught her up in its toils and swept her away.

When it was over at last, when he rolled off her and pulled her against his side and she had regained her senses and breath enough to realize what exactly it was they had done on her dressing room floor, she smiled and opened her eyes and ran a questing hand over his bare chest. It was warm and faintly damp and taut with muscle, and she loved it. Actually, she decided, bestowing a sweeping glance over his sprawled body, she loved everything about him. Then she looked the truth in the face: the fact was, she loved him.

"You're looking very pleased with yourself," he observed. Beth glanced up to meet his eyes. Lying flat on his back, he'd tucked an arm beneath his head.

"I've decided being married may not be so very bad after all," she said. Then, with the air of one making a handsome confession, she added, "I should probably tell you that Cluny forgot himself and surprised me with the quickest of kisses. There was no more to what you saw than that."

He smiled. "Had I not realized that almost from the outset, my girl, my reaction to seeing Cluny's mouth on yours would have been far less mild than it was, I assure you."

Beth stared at him. Her brows snapped together.

"You knew there was nothing to it?" She propped herself up on an elbow, the better to see him.

"After I had a moment to think? Absolutely."

"You couldn't have known. I have been flirting with Cluny—indeed, with a good many gentlemen—quite desperately. You had no way of knowing if I was or was not kissing them."

"Ah, but you see, I know you, Madame Roux. Until that moment with Cluny, I never even entertained the possibility that you would kiss anyone but me." He gave a gentle tug to a curling lock of hair that dangled near his hand. A lurking grin touched his mouth. "To tell you the truth, I thought you were probably doing all that flirting to get a reaction out of me."

Beth glared at him. After a moment, honesty compelled her to say, "I was."

"Would you care to tell me why?"

"The devil take it!" She hesitated, and to her annoyance felt a blush heat her cheeks. "If you really want to know, it was because I discovered that I love you. Quite madly. There, I've said it. Make of it what you will."

"Why, Beth." Surprise flared in his eyes, quickly followed by an emotion she couldn't quite name. Then, even as she searched his face for something—some answer to the question her announcement tacitly posed—he rolled over with her and kissed her with a fierce hunger that drove everything else out of her head, then got to his feet, picked her up, and carried her to bed.

By the time he left her, dawn was just lighting the sky. Beth knew that, because she opened her eyes to the sound of her bedroom door being quietly closed, registered that she was alone in her bed and in the room, and saw gray fingers of light creeping around the edges of the curtains all at the same time. Of course, he needed to get back to his own room before the servants began stirring, which would be soon now.

She stretched, smiling, luxuriating in the soft warmth of the covers, knowing she needed to get up and put on her night rail but postponing the moment for as long as she could, as delicious memories of the night they had just passed unspooled through her mind. He had introduced her to a whole new world of sensual experiences that she had never even dreamed of, in the process making of her a willing pupil who was eagerly looking forward to learning more. As Claire had assured her countless times, marriage was indeed a wonderful institution, if entered into with the right man. And for her, Neil was the right man.

Then realization hit her like a thunder-clap. She had told him she loved him. But never, not even in the hottest throes of desire, had he replied in kind.

Beth's eyes snapped all the way open. She sat up in bed. Once more she reviewed her confession, and the events that came after. He had made love to her until their passion steamed up the night, but no word of love had ever passed his lips.

A horrible, crushing thought occurred: perhaps he hadn't told her he loved her because he did not.

Beth knew with a certainty as solid as bedrock that she wasn't going to be able to live with that. A moment later she knew that she couldn't even bear the uncertainty of not knowing.

She had confessed her love, and she wanted—no, needed—to hear him do the same.

And if he did not love her . . . ?

Well, she needed to know that, too.

Now.

Swinging her legs over the side of the bed, she got up, pulled on her night rail and wrapper, tying the pretty ruffled garment at her waist, and headed for Neil's apartments at the back of the house. The hallways were dark and deserted, and she hadn't thought to bring a candle, so she had only the faint fingers of dawn stealing in through the occasional window that opened onto one or another of the halls to light her way, but it was enough. Twisting her unconfined hair into a long, loose rope over one shoulder, padding silently in bare feet, she saw not another soul. When she reached Neil's door, she didn't even hesitate. Turning the knob, she pushed it open and went in.

The sight that met her eyes stunned her. She stopped with her hand still on the knob, gawking for the briefest of moments in disbelief. Clad only in breeches and a shirt, Neil lay prone on the carpet of the firelit room, limbs sprawled, eyes closed, to all appearances unconscious, she thought with a thrill of horror. Leaning over him, a burly man in a frieze coat and buckskins seemed about to loop something—a garrote?—around his neck. Two more men stood nearby, both aiming pistols at Neil.

Startled, the intruders looked around at her as she entered. Beth recovered her wits, instantly backpedaled, and screamed like a steam whistle. A pistol snapped in her direction and fired. The explosion of sound hit her with the force of a mule's kick, throwing her back into the hall. As she hit the floor she felt nothing, no pain at all, but somewhere in the back of her mind rose the shocked realization: *I've been shot.*

Chapter Thirty-three

BETH.

Sheer terror for her pulled Neil from semiconsciousness. Her scream slicing the air caused the hair on the back of his neck to stand on end and sent adrenaline surging through his system. Forcing his scattered senses to function, he realized, in his first instant of restored awareness, what had happened: Clapham, Parks, and Richards had been waiting for him in his room. Preoccupied by thoughts of Beth, lulled by the safety he'd thought his new life afforded him, he'd had no notion of being on his guard and walked right into the ambush. One of the three had clouted him over the head as soon as he'd stepped inside the chamber. He had no doubt that in a few moments more, he would have been dead and his assailants would have vanished into London's mean streets.

Beth had followed him to his room. That was the thought that overrode all else. Propelled by deadly fear for her into frenzied action, he caught just a glimpse of her bright hair and pale wrapper in the doorway as he rendered Clapham impotent and perhaps dead by chopping him savagely in the knee, then in the neck as he fell. Even before Clapham hit the ground, Neil dove for Parks, but it was already too late: the slimy little bastard had fired his pistol. And not at him. At Beth.

Christ in heaven, please let her not be dead.

He hadn't prayed in more than a decade, not since, he remembered, the terrible day he'd watched his mother and sister die. God hadn't granted his prayer then.

Please, please, God, grant it now.

Even as he felled Parks with a single savage blow and watched Richards, knowing himself far overmatched, flee like the coward he was through the door, his thoughts, his prayers, every ounce of his will were focused exclusively on Beth.

She was no longer in the doorway. She was no longer screaming.

If she's dead, I can't live.

Bolting for the hall, for Beth, with that thought ricocheting through his brain, he wondered if it was his fate to always lose the people he loved.

I love her.

He hadn't been able to face the truth of that until this moment, and now it brought agony with it. Love equals pain and loss; he'd known it, deep inside his soul, and that was why he'd turned away from admitting how he felt about her even to himself. His love for her was like a guilty secret his subconscious had kept locked away. Until now.

Please don't let it be too late.

She was lying in the gloom of the hall, on the dark hardwood floor, crumpled on her side with the hem of her wrapper fanned out around her bare feet like the frill of a pale flower. Her eyes were closed. She didn't move. She didn't seem to breathe.

Cold dread seized him even as he dropped to his knees beside her.

"Beth." His voice was a hoarse croak as he touched her neck, checking for a pulse, afraid of what he would find.

Please God please God please. . . .

She had a pulse.

"What the hell . . . ?" It was Richmond, clad in a barely secured dressing gown with a pistol in his hand, who first came pounding toward him. More members of the household poured onto the scene from every direction. Neil, preoccupied with ascertaining how badly Beth was hurt, barely heard any of the shouts or questions and didn't look up.

"She's been shot," he said in answer to Richmond as the other man reached him, spewing questions, leaning over Beth. "Two men"—he gave a jerk of his head toward his room—"in there. Another fled through the house. Be careful, they're killers. They came for me."

Richmond barked sharp orders at his household. Neil neither listened nor cared. A dark stain spreading over the front of Beth's wrapper caused Neil to wrench it open. What he saw made his gut clench. His head reeled. His heart filled.

Had he been that much younger version of himself, the one who had fought so desperately to reach his family before the guillotine fell that day, he would have dropped his head and cried.

Because this prayer had been answered.

The ball had hit her high in the shoulder. He was no sawbones, but bullet wounds he knew.

"Beth!" Claire reached the scene just as Neil, gathering Beth up in his arms, stood up.

"Beth!" Gabby was not far behind her. Clad in wrappers, hair spilling over their shoulders, panic in their faces, rife with exclamations and questions that he couldn't make enough sense of to even try to answer, they both crowded around him as, almost light-headed with relief, he carried Beth toward her bedroom.

"She's going to be all right," he told them, and sent a grateful prayer winging skyward that it was so. "She's been shot, but she's going to be all right."

"Fetch hot water and bandages," Gabby ordered someone he couldn't see.

"A doctor's been sent for." DeVane spoke behind him just as Neil reached Beth's room.

"What happened?" There was terror in Claire's voice.

"They came to assassinate me. Beth surprised them in the act. They shot her."

"Oh my God!"

"How do you know that's why they came?" DeVane's voice was sharp with tension.

"I know them. Fitz Clapham and his associates. They've tried to kill me before."

"Damn it, everyone who knew you before thinks you dead. And Richmond and I have been working on securing a pardon for you, just on the off chance that someone might recognize you in the future. It was granted late yesterday. There is no longer a kill order for the man who was known as the Angel of Death. This should not have happened."

Neil heard DeVane's talk of a pardon being granted, and knew he owed his brothers-in-law a great debt because of it, but he didn't reply, because just then Beth started to moan and stir in his arms. Pale and big-eyed, Claire opened the door to

Beth's chamber for him, and he carried Beth toward the bed.

"Neil." Beth's eyes fluttered open. Her voice wasn't much louder than a sigh.

"Don't talk. You've had an accident."

Alarm sharpened her gaze. She stirred in obvious agitation, then winced in pain. "Those men! Your room . . . I thought they would kill you."

"It's all over. I'm fine." He laid her gently on the bed. "You're going to be fine, too. Don't try to talk anymore."

"I remember. They shot me." She sounded faintly disbelieving that such a thing could have occurred.

"Yes."

When he would have straightened away to let the women, who were hovering with towels and who knew what else, take over, she caught at his shirt.

"You didn't say it," she said. "I was coming to ask you."

"Say what?"

"I love you. I told you, but you didn't tell me." Her eyes had clouded with what he was sorely afraid was pain, but still they clung to his. Neil felt his gut clench. The knowledge that she was suffering wrung his heart.

"I do," he answered in a low voice, conscious of listening ears but unable to deny her. That admission was a weak, sad thing and he knew it, knew that Beth deserved better, deserved more, even if the entire household was listening in. Looking into her eyes, he tried again. "I love you, Beth. More than my own life. So much that if you died, I wouldn't want to live. I love you with all my heart and soul."

For a moment the pain that had so worried him receded, and the faintest hint of a twinkle came into her eyes.

"Very pretty," she said, and smiled at him.

Then her sisters practically pushed him out of the way, going to work to stanch the bleeding and make Beth as comfortable as possible until the doctor arrived.

Epilogue

"DON'T LOOK SO NERVOUS. 'Twill all be over soon." That was DeVane, speaking humorously rather than soothingly in Neil's ear.

"Unless Beth decides to leave him standing at the altar. You know the odds are running twenty to one in the clubs that she will," Richmond said with some relish, though, like DeVane, he was careful to keep his voice low enough so that his words wouldn't reach beyond the three of them.

"She can't bolt. They're already wed," DeVane objected. "That's why I put a monkey down on her going through with it.

Otherwise, I wouldn't have wagered so much as a groat on the chance."

"When it comes to weddings, I put nothing past Beth. Claire was telling me only last night that little sister was so nervous about today that she couldn't eat. This big Society do wasn't her idea, and she don't like the thought of it."

"Probably shouldn't tell *him* so." DeVane's tone was faintly reproving. Neil realized that he was the "him" DeVane referred to. "Don't want him taking it to heart and ripping up at Beth."

"Oh, he knows if he doesn't treat Beth right, there'll be the devil to pay. Isn't that right, Durham?"

Neil set his teeth without replying. Though it had nothing to do with any threat of Richmond's, he was practically quaking in his boots. Neil acknowledged the sorry truth of that even as he willed himself not to reveal it by so much as a twitch of a finger. He, who had survived so many attempts to kill him that he'd lost count, who'd faced down without feeling so much as a stomach flutter the most vicious men of his time armed with every imaginable deadly weapon, who for more than a decade had rarely known from one day to the next whether he would be alive to greet the next dawn, felt his throat tighten and his mouth dry and his skin grow cold with nerves as his gaze ran over the assembled crowd, all of whom seemed to be looking directly at him as they whispered to their neighbors.

Waiting. Just like he was waiting, with something akin to bated breath, for Beth to appear.

Or not.

It was his wedding day. Or, rather, his officially recognized wedding day. He was standing at the altar of St. James Church in Piccadilly, Richmond and DeVane at his side supposedly for support, though with their jocular comments they'd so far provided precious little of that, waiting for his wife to arrive from Richmond House, walk up the long, flower-strewn aisle, and remarry him. Unless, of course, she succumbed to an attack of wedding-day jitters and at the last minute decided not to go through with it. Which he wouldn't precisely blame her for, although it would leave him looking every kind of a fool in the eyes of the ton. Of course, to almost everyone present—and the large and fashionable church was packed—what they were preparing to witness was a wedding, period. It had, in fact, been dubbed the Wedding of the Season, the much-talked-about union between one of Society's most scandalous beauties and a prized catch on the Marriage Mart. Nobody, as it had turned out, wanted to miss that.

Which was why this was shaping up to be a debacle of major proportions. Being in a church in and of itself made him uncomfortable. He couldn't help feeling he needed to beware of stray lightning bolts. Finding himself the cynosure of all eyes didn't help. And knowing that his beloved was as skittish about wedding days as an unbroke yearling was of a rider—that was the icing on the cake.

He figured that his chances of being left at the altar on this bright sunny June morning were about even.

Richmond cleared his throat. "It's five minutes past the hour. I've got James"—Richmond's longtime valet—"on the lookout, and he just gave me the signal: no sign of the bride's carriage yet."

As the wedding was supposed to commence at precisely eleven o'clock—five minutes ago—this bit of needling by Richmond was designed to make him sweat, Neil knew. But, conscious of several hundred pairs of eyes on him belonging to several hundred people who knew Beth's record with weddings and were waiting most avidly to see if history would repeat itself, he sweated anyway.

"By God, if she doesn't show, won't we roast her forever?" DeVane was sounding amused again. "By the by, Hugh, if she does stand him up, you get the happy task of announcing to this circus that the ceremony's off."

"You're the elder. And you've been in the family longer," Richmond objected.

"Don't matter. You're the duke," DeVane parried.

Neil stopped listening to them. "Circus" was, he thought, exactly the right word to describe the glittering extravaganza this supposed family-only wedding-for-show had turned into. For that, he knew precisely who to blame: Beth's aunt Augusta. After the storm of gossip that had followed Beth's second weeklong confinement to bed in the course of little more than a month—the story was that she'd suffered a recurrence of the influenza, because of course admitting that she'd been shot was impossible—the old battle-ax had gotten a bee in her bonnet and the bit between her teeth and taken control of the wedding.

After that, special licenses and private ceremonies were out the window. The only thing that would satisfy her, and, she insisted, go some way toward restoring Beth's reputation, was the kind of huge, fashionable Society wedding expected of the sister of a duke who had become betrothed to a wealthy and handsome Marquis.

Beth had been busy recovering from the gunshot wound. He had been busy dancing attendance on her, accepting a job from the War Office (who better to assist in rounding up the other renegade assassins than one such as he, after all?), and extracting from Clapham, who had survived, the details of how he'd found him. (Like so many things, it was a matter of pure chance: Clapham had spotted him on a London street, recognized him immediately, and been convinced that the Angel of Death had bamboozled them all by faking his own death. This he had immediately set out to rectify.) Claire had been distracted by the happy news (so Beth told him) that she was increasing at last, and by her concern for her sister. Gabby had been consumed by a desire to take care of them all. Richmond and DeVane, of course, were worse than useless: though uninterested in the details, they were amused enough at the whole to throw no rub in the old cat's way.

And so the wedding had just kind of snowballed without him or Beth really realizing what was afoot until it was too damned late to do anything about it.

"The carriage must be here," DeVane said suddenly. "Look, Hugh, there's James over there nodding like his neck's broke."

"Doesn't mean Beth's in it," said Richmond the tormentor. "Could just be sending round a message saying the whole thing's too much for her."

From the outside, somebody was already pulling open the huge oak doors that opened into the church. Neil recognized the grizzled little man: a favored servant of Gabby's, by the name of Jem, he thought. Beyond him, he could see Gabby in her lilac silk bridesmaid's gown, clutching a silver filigree holder with some kind of purple flowers in it, already ascending the church steps on Barnet's arm. A glimpse of another lilac skirt just stepping down from the carriage convinced him that Claire was not far behind. And with them, he hoped—no, he was sure now—would be Beth.

Beth the brave would not leave him to face this arena full of gossip-hungry lions alone. He should have known it from the outset.

"They be here," Jem called from the back of the church, where he'd closed the doors to the chapel, which meant Neil could no longer observe the wedding party's approach.

Immediately the music, which had been playing softly, swelled. The archbishop— no ordinary cleric would do for Lady Salcombe—shook out his robes. Richmond and DeVane fanned out into proper position on either side of him. The congregation rose.

Then the doors opened again, and with a slow and stately gait Gabby began to walk toward them. She smiled at DeVane, whose heart was suddenly there in his eyes, plain for all to read. Some distance behind her came Claire, so beautiful that she drew every eye and caused Richmond, beside him, to swell with love and pride. Watching them come up the aisle as he waited for Beth to enter, looking over the faces of the assembled company, Neil realized something: in the months since that failed assassination attempt had driven him from France, he had acquired not just a wife but a whole extended family that he was learning, slowly but inexorably, to care about. Two sisters, of course, in the persons of Claire and Gabby. Brothers (a little less caring about here) in Richmond and DeVane. A masterful, managing battle-ax of an aunt. A pair of sweet-faced nieces and one noisy and mischievous nephew, whose ranks were apparently soon to increase by one more. A ghastly array of cousins he intended to avoid whenever possible. Loyal retainers by the dozens. Six women—Mary, Peg, Alyce, Dolly, Nan, and Jane—whose lives he had saved and who had, in the process, changed him forever. A raft of friends and acquaintances.

All tied to him by Beth, and all here in this church to celebrate his and Beth's official wedding day.

The door to the chapel opened one more time. The congregation let out a collective breath—of relief, disappointment, or excitement, depending on their individual natures—as Beth entered. Aunt Augusta, claiming the honor as Beth's late father's representative, was beside her, beaming in triumph as she prepared to escort her niece up the aisle. But after one glance, Neil had eyes for no one but Beth.

Mine. That was the thought that crowded out all others.

He'd never seen a woman look more beautiful in his life. Vaguely he was aware of her dress, some confection of satin and lace that she and her sisters had spent countless hours fussing over, the delicate veil that floated behind her, the pearls around her neck, the flowers in her hands. But what he mainly saw was Beth: her glorious hair as vivid as a flame amidst all that white, her lovely face faintly flushed with, he thought, happiness, her eyes bright and smiling as they met his.

He smiled back at her.

Then, as she drew near, he moved forward to meet her. She gave him her hand. Instead of being cold, as he might have expected, it was soft and warm and alive. Lifting it to his lips, he kissed it briefly, then tucked it in his arm as they turned to face the archbishop. The old man started saying some words over them, but Neil wasn't really listening. Instead, he was preoccupied by the sudden realization that he'd just been granted his own private miracle.

All these years, he'd thought heaven was past praying for. Now he knew he'd been wrong. He'd found heaven right here, in this red-haired snip of a girl he meant to cherish for the rest of his life.